The Secrets of Blythswood Square

Also by Sara Sheridan

The Fair Botanists

Sara Sheridan

THE SECRETS OF BLYTHSWOOD SQUARE

First published in Great Britain in 2024 by Hodder & Stoughton
An Hachette UK company

1

Copyright © Sara Sheridan 2024

A CIP catalogue record for this title is available from the British Library

Hardback ISBN 978 1 399 70157 0
Trade Paperback ISBN 978 1 399 70158 7
eBook ISBN 978 1 399 70160 0

Typeset in Adobe Garamond by Hewer Text UK Ltd, Edinburgh
Printed and bound in Great Britain by Clays Ltd, Elcograf S.p.A.

Hodder & Stoughton policy is to use papers that are natural, renewable and recyclable
products and made from wood grown in sustainable forests. The logging and manufacturing
processes are expected to conform to the environmental regulations of the country of origin.

Hodder & Stoughton Ltd
Carmelite House
50 Victoria Embankment
London EC4Y 0DZ

www.hodder.co.uk

This book is dedicated to my husband, Alan,
who has the tough job of being the rock to my roll.

'As I never saw my father or my mother, and never saw any likeness of either of them (for their days were long before the days of photographs), my first fancies regarding what they were like were unreasonably derived from their tombstones.'

Pip, in *Great Expectations* by Charles Dickens

Chapter One

Calton Hill, Edinburgh. 20 March 1846

It is a sunny spring day and in the small garden to the south of Rock House two women, one older with dark hair fixed in a severe bun and one younger, with flaming orange tresses to her shoulders, arrange furniture on the lawn. The harling on the walls is the colour of marmalade in contrast to the green mound of Calton Hill behind. The bright colours make the scene look like a child's drawing: a rustic fantasy. Strands of ivy trail across the facade and wind up a wooden trellis. To one side, a bundle of mismatched scarves spills onto the grass beside a screen open like an accordion. In front of this, with gloved hands, the women meticulously position a mahogany balloon-backed chair, upholstered in dark leather. Beyond the house, over the rough stone wall, two ragged boys have climbed into a horse-chestnut tree. The children whisper and point as the women check the shadows cast by the tableau.

'They'll be almost finished with the tea,' Jessie, the dark-haired one, says to her cousin. 'I'll see, shall I?'

Ellory waits. Once Jessie is gone, she motions to the boys, who swing over the low wall. Efficiently, she takes two toffees from her apron pocket and hands them over. 'Sit down,' she instructs. 'You can have the sweets after.'

1

The boys obediently fall cross-legged onto the grass, toffees softening in their palms, their knees smudged with mud. Ellory, checking over her shoulder, swiftly inserts a photographic plate into the camera with a competence that demonstrates this is not her first calotype. She has taken more than a dozen of her own compositions now; on the sly like this. All for her own portfolio. A cluster of girls with dolls made of clothes pegs. A tabby cat sleeping in the sun. A shifty-looking chimney sweep. A photograph of Edinburgh Castle with a scatter of crows along the ramparts, perched like geriatric old men outfitted in black.

'Stay still,' she orders as she removes the lens cap and counts silently, her gloved hand in the air holding the children in place as if she is a conductor at the symphony.

From round the corner, a gentleman appears: on his way, no doubt, to Miss Short's observatory on the summit of Calton Hill. He peers over the wall. Ellory's heart pounds.

'Good lord,' he says. 'You're taking a photograph.'

'Yes, sir,' she replies briskly.

'This is Mr Hill's studio, is it not?'

'I'm that gentleman's assistant,' Ellory elucidates more confidently than she feels. Another minute will do it, but this gentleman must not commandeer her attention and the boys have to be out of the way by the time Mr Hill, Mr McPhee and McPhee's niece emerge from Rock House. She has a few minutes still. Two or three, if she's lucky.

'I thought Mr Hill's assistant was called ...' the gentleman searches his memory for the name. 'Adams,' he decides.

'Mr Adamson is Mr Hill's business partner, sir,' Ellory corrects him. Nobody usually asks after Mr Adamson though he is the more pleasant of the two gentlemen – to the staff, anyway. 'He went home to Fife for the winter,' Ellory adds. 'I assist both gentlemen,' she admits, though fearing this makes her seem boastful, she adds, 'I'm one of the assistants anyway.'

'Extraordinary,' the man says. 'A woman.'

'Yes, sir.'

The gentleman clears his throat and motions loosely towards the camera. 'That plate will need to be treated with silver nitrate so a negative can be produced,' he explains. Although this fellow has never taken a photograph, he attended a lecture last year at the Edinburgh Calotype Club. He knows how to do it. Ellory smiles patiently. Gentlemen are often disquieted by her proficiency. 'The word "calotype" comes from the Greek. It means beautiful impression,' the gentleman adds as an invisible clock ticks inside Ellory's head.

'I see you know a good deal about photography, sir,' she replies calmly. Five seconds more. Four. Three. Two. One. She replaces the cap. The boys spring back over the wall unwrapping their toffees as they disappear in the direction of Waterloo Place. Ellory, meanwhile, stows the exposed paper in the lined wooden box ready for her attention later. As she does so, her imaginary clock switches to a new countdown. Once the paper is exposed, the quality of the image depends on delivering it timeously to the print room.

The gentleman lingers as if he is present in a supervisory capacity. He does not notice Ellory stiffen at the sound of footsteps on the flagstones. 'They're coming,' Jessie announces, stepping onto the path.

'This is my cousin, Miss Jessie Mann, who also assists the gentlemen.' Ellory makes the introduction as he peers at this new arrival.

'I'm Mr Hill's primary assistant,' Jessie says firmly. 'Can I help you, sir?'

The gentleman bows and notes that Miss Jessie Mann neither resembles her pretty cousin nor sounds like her. The difference between the women is almost elemental. Jessie is a hard winter's night, dressed in black with a thin line of white at her collar and eyes like cold lumps of coal in contrast to Ellory's tawny colouring and softer brogue. Whereas the younger woman is like a colourful painting of a country lass, her cousin is an austere black-and-white print. He wonders briefly if the older woman is in mourning, but if

Mr Hill's assistants are cousins, it is unlikely one would be bereaved and not the other.

'I was passing and noticed the camera obscura,' he says.

'Mr Hill is about to start, sir. If you don't mind,' Jessie cuts in, 'it's better for the sitters if there are no spectators.'

The gentleman takes a moment to absorb this firm but polite telling-off. Then he touches his top hat by way of valediction. 'Fascinating. Women assistants,' he mutters to himself and turns back up the hill.

*

As soon as he is out of sight, Jessie rounds on her cousin. 'I hope you weren't gossiping about Mr Hill,' she hisses.

'The fellow stopped of his own accord. You know what they're like. He wanted to talk about the equipment and that,' Ellory explains.

Jessie snorts. 'And that,' she mimics. 'Speak English properly, for heaven's sake.'

Ellory never defends the way she speaks, and Jessie does not push her criticism further for Ellory's lack of grammar means Mr Hill will never let her talk to clients on his behalf, as she is allowed to. 'You need to be more careful,' she says as if Ellory somehow encouraged the fellow.

Ellory knows there is no point in retorting that there was nothing she could have done. Jessie makes it clear on a daily basis that she regrets recommending her cousin for the job at Rock House. 'You're lucky to be here,' she says, holding back from adding that Ellory is as bad as her sister and one day will come to the same tragic end. Since she can remember, Ellory's side of the family has been a source of disappointment to the more respectable Manns. That's why she sleeps at the studio in a small room off the kitchen: a second-class citizen to her own relations, while Jessie goes home at night to Alexander's house; her brother, the solicitor, that is.

The women wait another minute in silence. It is especially tense today. The last time that Mr McPhee sat to the camera, he gave Jessie a shilling. 'For you and the other girl,' he said. Jessie added a pork chop to her cousin's housekeeping basket which cost an extra thruppence, but kept the money for herself, even though Ellory helped ready the gentlemen for the image and processed it too. They have not talked about it, but Jessie is hoping for another shilling and Ellory is hoping she might get a share of it in cash this time. They are both cross: Jessie guilty but not willing to give way; and Ellory annoyed that she has done more work than her cousin for less reward, which isn't fair.

Edinburgh's most respected photographer, the artist David Octavius Hill, emerges, spruce, through the open door. Then Mr McPhee and his niece after him. The girl is wearing a wildly patterned gown and has such a tiny waist that her shadow looks split in two. McPhee is sombre, wearing a black frock coat that contrasts his white hair. His skin is pink and plump, with no wrinkles. 'There is grand warmth in the sun this afternoon,' Hill says enthusiastically, motioning the others across the threshold. 'It's often chilly when I make calotypes in the garden at this time of year. We are lucky today. But you are always lucky, Mr McPhee.'

McPhee smiles. 'You'll do a wonderful job, as ever, Mr Hill.' He gives his vote of confidence. 'The image you made of my nephew is remarkable. Now it's Winifred's turn.' He hands the lady forward.

Behind them, Jessie steps back through the door, as if subsumed into the house. She will appear again later, no doubt, when Mr McPhee is leaving. Ellory, meanwhile, tarries to watch the picture being captured. The lady smooths her skirt as she sits, propping herself uncomfortably on the wooden chair. The bodice must sting in movement.

'Lovely,' Mr Hill murmurs.

The woman smiles. 'It's new,' she replies referring to her frock. 'Uncle bought the fabric.' She smiles at the old man who, it seems, is generous with everybody.

A crease furrows Ellory's freckled forehead. 'It will not photograph,' she mumbles and then straightens up, shocked that she has said this out loud. Mr McPhee catches her eye, suddenly attentive, though it is his niece who speaks. 'Sorry?' the girl says loudly and peers past Mr Hill as if everything behind the photographer has been relinquished to some kind of netherworld.

'The paper, Ellory,' Hill snaps, holding out his hand to receive it.

'What did she say?' the young lady insists.

McPhee's gaze lingers as if he is seeing Ellory for the first time. She is always keen to make the best picture. There is an art to overseeing Mr Hill's work but not seeming to. When Mr McPhee came with his nephew, the lad allowed her to darken his brows with burnt clove. Mr Hill disapproves of such artifice, treating Ellory's occasional ministrations as if they are a lie. The resulting image of Mr McPhee's nephew, however, is a lot better than it would have been. Now she has broken the bounds again. Hill is clearly disquieted. Still, she judges it would be rude not to answer Miss McPhee's question. 'The fabric will not photograph, miss. The contrast is marked by colour not by tone. The camera will only capture the latter,' she says. It is a problem they have come across often with tartan woven with vivid colours that appear indistinct in sepia.

Mr Hill's jaw tightens. There will be a black mood to contend with later.

'Is that correct?' Winifred asks Hill.

'The camera will not capture the pattern as it appears to the eye,' he admits.

The lady looks disappointed. 'But it would provide such interest,' she says, as if she might convince the camera to see her differently. She turns to her uncle as if he ought to be able to fix it.

Hill walks past the trellis to the property baskets laid on the grass and withdraws a small guitar. 'Here,' he hands it to her. 'This will help the composition.'

Ellory thinks one of the pale shawls would be better as she removes the salted paper from its box and gives it to Mr Hill. She can see the lady is discomfited and she wants to relieve her of the guitar and reassure her that her skin is radiant and that the camera will capture that. When sitters are confident, the images are always better. But she has already gone too far. 'Stand straight,' Hill directs Mr McPhee. 'Straighter,' he adds, and the old man stiffens in an unnatural position like a puppet hung on a peg while his niece holds the guitar awkwardly. Ellory sighs inwardly. Mr Hill sometimes has this effect on his sitters. Ellory is certain that the camera is best used to capture images of people doing ordinary things; unposed, or at least seeming to be so. Mr Hill took an impromptu picture recently at Edinburgh Castle of some soldiers of the 92nd Highland Regiment. The image transfixed Ellory when she processed it, as if she were standing among the soldiers with their bearskin hats and dress kilts, eavesdropping upon the conversation. She realised then that while the best paintings are visions or perhaps dreams, a photograph feels like a memory, whether or not you are there when it is made. Mr Hill will not entertain such a notion. He endeavours to photograph people as he paints them.

'Stay absolutely still,' he directs, and all life disappears from the McPhees' eyes as he opens the camera lens to the light. The world holds its breath. Ellory counts silently. Hill leaves the image a good three seconds longer than she would have done before he pronounces, 'I'm done,' and returns the plate to her keeping now the hard work is set to begin. 'Go on, Ellory,' he says, shooing her in the direction of the print room where she will fix the image, make a negative and return to the sunlight of the garden to print copies.

As she disappears into the hallway, she hears him talking about his plans for the summer exhibition and recounting a conversation he has had with another, more famous painter he met at his brother's gallery. She knows she should not have intervened. Inside, she passes Jessie in the kitchen, taking stock of the tea caddy: the closest there is to a mistress at Rock House and mindful of every ha'penny. The accounts book is open on the table and the smoky scent of Lapsang pervades the kitchen like a creeping shadow. 'Will it be all right?' Jessie checks. She is concerned about the shilling tip.

'The lady hoped her dress would come out,' Ellory says.

Jessie casts her eyes upwards as if Winifred McPhee is some kind of hysteric.

Ellory continues to the print room, which is little more than a scullery lined with dark bottles on a low pine shelf. The tiny room cocoons her from her cousin's disapproval and Mr Hill's disdain alike. At work in the darkness she might be a master, not an assistant.

She lights a tiny candle in the amber lamp and settles into the acrid, chemical atmosphere. Among the bottles on the shelf there is a jar of jam made from last year's raspberries. She brings it down, opening the top with her thick gloved fingers and melting a teaspoonful on her tongue while in her mind's eye she sees another calotype, one where Mr McPhee and his niece are in conversation; where they are smiling and their friends might easily recognise them. She turns her attention to the exposed papers. People think the only time that matters is how long the cap is off the lens, but it is here, in the pale amber light, that being fast and accurate really counts. She smiles as she starts on her own image of the boys in the sunshine. As she immerses the paper, their shadowy figures shimmer into being like ghosts and she is immediately transported by the picture's magic. The way it stops time. And in the background the rest of the world moving so fast that the camera cannot catch it. It may be science, but it never feels that way. It always, always delights her.

Chapter Two

Glasgow

Murray Urquhart sips a cup of coffee and ties his cravat at the bedroom mirror. Today he has chosen a sky-blue that contrasts the embroidery on his silk waistcoat; a trellis covered in finely stitched ivy. It is his habit to give people something to look at, other than the crest of his shoulder, hunched from birth. As a boy the attention Glasgow society paid to his twisted spine had pushed him to minor infractions, and between the ages of 11 and 14, much to the distress of his father, he constantly got into trouble for climbing trees in the gardens and pochling apples from Mr Harley's orchard at Garnethill. He knows now that it is a hopeless quest, that a well-tailored frock coat will work no better than petty thieving. His back is the first thing polite society will always mention after his name, but he does not give up trying to distract people. When he came home from London, his father swore that he had become a dandy, which made him chortle. Old Mr Urquhart, Glasgow's finest and most conservative solicitor, has worn more or less the same style of suit in dark navy and a matching thick silk, cream cravat for as long as his son can remember. When the old man's clothes wear or tear, he has them remade the same, with only small concessions to the passing of time. He is certainly not qualified to comment on whether Murray's colourful attire is fashionable.

It is not yet half after eight when there is a frantic knocking at the front door. Old Mr Urquhart left early for his offices, slightly down the hill on the other side of Bath Street. He disapproves of Murray's leisurely morning routine which means he does not get to the office until quarter to ten. Murray does not see it that way. 'We're a good combination,' he tells his father. And it's true. The older clients stick with Urquhart Senior, but the younger generation find the old man's considered manner frustrating, and the sons and indeed daughters of Glasgow's many millionaires have started to contract their business through Murray, who has learned enough of his father's wily ways to offer excellent advice while also taking the trouble to be engaging.

Murray opens his bedroom door and peers over the banister. A young footman, barely 17 at a guess, is below on the doorstep, babbling that Mr Urquhart must come at once. Glendinning, the Urquharts' butler, a dull, brown sparrow, tries to explain that Mr Urquhart has already left for the day. Murray comes down smartly. The footman steps past Glendinning, discounting him now Murray has appeared. The matter is too important to be bound by the hierarchy of the house. 'It's Mr Nicholl, sir. The maid found him dead in his study.'

'My god,' Murray lets out. Nicholl is a near-legend. A natural leader in business as much as in the Kirk. In a city where gossip renders everybody sensational upon occasion, he is famous for keeping a level head.

Murray recalls the older man taking the time not only to speak to him when he was a child, but also to listen. 'What do you think, boy?' he asked on more than one occasion when, Murray understands now, his view was probably not as interesting or important as he thought it was. It feels as if someone has told him that Glasgow cathedral has tumbled.

He turns to Glendinning. 'Send this news to my father. Tell him I've gone up to the Nicholls'.'

Glendinning nods.

'How is Miss Nicholl taking the shock?' Murray asks the footman.

'We put her in the dining room with a cup of tea while Mr Boots and the other lads lifted Mr Nicholl up to his room. The young lady could not bear to see him.'

Murray cannot blame her. When his mother died, he was made to kiss her marble-cold cheek and had nightmares for a long time after about her body being cut into the damp, freezing soil of the Necropolis, colder even than her corpse. She has been gone more than a decade, one of the first to be buried in the new graveyard.

'Your master died at his desk then?' Murray wants to understand what he will be walking into.

'Yes, sir.'

This was characteristic as the young lawyer judges it. James Nicholl was his father's almost-lifelong client and was ever about his business. The Urquharts moved to Bath Street at the same time as James Nicholl built his grand mansion up the hill on Blythswood Square. 'Too grand for only two people to live in,' Mr Urquhart pronounced, out of James Nicholl's hearing naturally. Though he added that though the Nicholls were only two people, they had nine staff to serve them. It is not lost on Murray that his father moved his house and office to Bath Street only once he knew where James was going. The Urquharts were not the only family to follow in Nicholl's wake.

Outside it is a fine morning. The footman continues rattling out the details of Nicholl's death. 'The maid dropped her bucket when she saw him,' he says. 'The silly lass scattered ashes across the carpet.'

Murray puts his finger to his lips. 'Not on the street,' he says firmly. Glasgow fires on gossip. He has known men overhear a tip at the races and invest half their fortune on the back of it. Foolish men, but still. He tips his hat at one of the neighbours as they pass on the pavement. The man does not notice the footman's distress but then many people do not regard servants. Murray generally finds those in service more interesting than their masters. He can tell a good deal about a household from its staff – or, more accurately, how they are treated. As a child it fascinated him when their old housekeeper retired and moved to a picturesque cottage with a kailyard, beyond the manufactory at Blantyre Mills. A life of her own.

At the Nicholl mansion they enter without ringing the bell. Inside, the high, wood-panelled hall smells of cigar smoke. James had a visitor last night, Murray surmises. He knows there have been more callers than usual over the last months; distressed gentlemen, who bought shares in railway companies, soliciting Nicholl's advice as their stock tumbled. He was generous that way and dispatched people kindly, fortified by tobacco and peaty, island whisky, to salvage their family finances. Last year, when Murray arrived on business with his father, they passed a fellow on the doorstep, his face wet with tears as he climbed into his carriage. Inside, Mr Nicholl was incredulous at the carelessness with which the man had staked his family's fortune. 'He mortgaged his house to raise funds to buy a defunct holding about which he knew nothing. Such people do not conceive that circumstances might not go their way.' His tone was disbelieving.

'You were wise to sell your railway stock,' old Mr Urquhart pronounced. 'You made a great deal of money, James.' He did not add that he had followed his old friend's lead and sold his as well. James Nicholl was ever a guiding star when it came to taking a profit.

At the dining-room door, Murray pauses. James Nicholl's estate has what his father would call 'complications'. He must not betray the trust placed in the firm, especially by someone so important. He nods when he's ready and the footman opens the door. Inside, Charlotte Nicholl, only a year younger than Murray at 24, sits at the table with an untouched cup of tea cooling before her. She always looks like an artist has drawn her frame; a simple pencil sketch devoid of detail. Her mouse-brown locks are held in a simple bun, fixed with a tortoiseshell comb. She leaves her hair straight instead of curling it in papers and favours plain fabrics for her dresses, with none of the extreme features dictated by fashion. Today she is wearing a pale blue worsted bodice and matching skirt fixed with covered buttons.

She veers clear of the sprigs of flowers currently in vogue 'as if girls wore wallpaper,' she said once drily when she bumped into Murray outside the haberdashery at the bottom of Douglas Street.

'Good morning.' Murray bows. 'I'm sorry for your loss.'

Charlotte has known Murray Urquhart all her life. 'A naughty boy but a kind one,' her neighbour Mrs Grieg declared when he was sent to London to sow his wild oats. 'Boys need to get it out,' she added, without stating exactly what it was of which boys were required to divest themselves. Murray had left Glasgow a sandy-haired youngster and come back only two years ago, a proper young man with a degree and experience at the bar. Charlotte knows that the gaggle of eligible young Glasgow ladies about town considers his ill-formed back before anything else. 'I'm glad it's you,' she says, getting to her feet.

'My father was not at home,' Murray adds. 'I hope it's not presumptuous to come instead, Charlotte. I'll do my best to take your instructions.'

Charlotte sits back down with a dull thump. She cannot conceive of having instructions to give. Her father always saw to everything. She might have been able to manage Mr Urquhart with his grey hair and gruff manner with some dignity, but knowing Murray better, her face twists. 'He's gone, Murray. I'm alone. I can't believe it.' Her shoulders shake and she begins to cry. Murray hands her his hand-kerchief. 'We were to be photographed this morning.' Charlotte sniffs earnestly as if by explaining what happened, she might bring her father back. For his death, surely, is impossible. 'Dr Grieg had images of buildings, the other night at dinner, you see. And Father said we must see for ourselves how it was done.'

'I understand that the staff have removed Mr Nicholl's body to his room,' Murray says. It is gentler than saying, 'He's dead, Charlotte. You must accept it.'

Charlotte nods, closing her eyes. 'I could not watch them.' She has never seen a dead body, for she was an infant when her mother died. Next door, the Howarths laid out old Mrs Howarth in the drawing room when she passed, but they are Episcopalians which, as Mrs Grieg never fails to point out, is High Church. Charlotte was a good deal younger then and not required to pay her respects. 'There is no point in sending for the doctor,' she says. It is a kind of acceptance. What she does not add is that she cannot face sending for the priest. That feels too final.

The young solicitor crouches next to her. She has always been self-contained, and Murray admires that. Charlotte is a stark contrast to her father, who was always bluff, always available. He knows she does not want a comforting hand on her arm. She is not that kind of young lady.

'Your father is at peace,' Murray says, with admirable practicality. 'I'll help in any way that I can. When you're ready, the first thing we must do is write to let folk know. Say the word and I shall manage it for you.'

Chapter Three

Edinburgh. Monday, 23 March 1846

It is sunny today and this afternoon it feels as if the light has returned at last after the long, dark winter, as Ellory walks along Waterloo Place and onto Princes Street to deliver Mr McPhee's prints. The old man did not tip in the end but she does not hold that against him. She enjoys the sun as she passes the doorway to Mr Howie's photographic studio, high on the rooftop, where he famously enjoins his sitters to stay 'still as death'. Outside Kennington & Jenner, she ignores the shop boys carrying brown paper parcels and stops to admire the monument to Sir Walter Scott that has taken so long to complete, folk can scarce believe it is finally finished. Then she picks up her pace, past the gallery at number 67 run by Mr Hill's brother, Alexander, who is Printseller and Publisher to the Queen and the Royal Scottish Academy. The Hills' other brother, Thomas, also works there. Ellory has made prints of both gentlemen, neither of whom, she is sure, would remember her name. At Frederick Street, she turns up the hill.

Ellory dresses carefully on days she undertakes Mr Hill's deliveries. Her bottle-green woollen coat is of good quality. Her hat is brown silk over wire; second-hand, though nobody would know. There are often lady tourists in Edinburgh these days, each clutching a cheap guidebook. Catching a glimpse of her reflection in a shop window, Ellory wonders if she might be taken for one of them, making a trip to the capital.

Over the crest of George Street, a brass plaque brought to a high shine announces Mr McPhee's residence. The sound of horses' hooves on the setts beats a tattoo as Ellory slips down the basement stairs. When Mr Hill delivers a photograph, he enters from the street and the drawing room welcomes him. Here, the service door is opened at her knock to reveal a moon-faced butler attired entirely in black. The man is terribly thin and reminds Ellory of a branch struck by lightning that she found once at Bruntsfield after a storm. The bones of him, she thinks, maybe they're black too.

'Can I help you, miss?'

'My name is Ellory Mann. I have a delivery for Mr McPhee from Mr David Octavius Hill.' She offers him the brown paper parcel. 'It must be kept both dry and straight. It's delicate.'

The butler does not take the package. Instead, he ushers her inside. 'Follow me,' he says.

'But—' Ellory protests. She does not like it when matters do not progress in the normal way.

'Mr McPhee left instructions, Miss Mann,' the butler says over his shoulder. 'He wants to see you.'

He leads her along a buff corridor and up a set of service stairs into the upstairs hallway, the floor of which is tiled, the walls painted a cheerful mustard and hung with pastoral oil paintings in gilded frames. At the rear, the man knocks smartly on a door. Inside, Mr McPhee sits behind a wide leather-topped desk with a tall oak clock behind, showing just past five of the afternoon. 'Ah, Miss Mann.' He gets momentarily to his feet.

Ellory places the parcel on the desk. She wonders nervously what the old man wants.

'Sit down, please.' Mr McPhee smiles.

She flexes her fingers. Beneath her long brown gloves, her skin is discoloured from working in the dark room. Both she and Jessie have worn gloves for years to hide the ugly marks. The nitrate is toxic and recently Ellory's skin has become even more indelibly stained from experimenting with the mercury required to develop daguerreotypes, though the gentlemen have now rejected this new process. The daguerreotypes are more vivid but allow only one print per exposure which must be set onto silver. 'Far too expensive,' Hill commented to Adamson. 'We'd need to charge eight shillings a plate. I can't see people being prepared to pay that.'

McPhee sees nothing of her racing thoughts. Ellory reminds him of a skittish fawn with her wide amber eyes and tidily pinned hair. The girl looks like she wants to bolt. 'Please Miss Mann,' he repeats.

Ellory sits like an automaton and folds her hands in her lap. McPhee pours two glasses of amber liquid from a drinks tray and sets one in front of her. 'They say you're talented, Miss Mann.' Ellory is not sure what to reply. 'Do you believe in chance? In Fate?' He seems keen, his eyes drilling into her.

'Sir . . .' She shifts uncomfortably. Gentlemen should not speak to members of staff this way, not theirs or anybody else's.

'It's a civil question,' McPhee encourages her. 'I'm not trying to trap you, Miss Mann. Please. Take the sherry.'

Ellory picks up the glass and sips. The liquid tastes of raisins, sweet as frumenty. She decides to answer. 'I'm not religious, Mr McPhee, if that is what you mean. But I'm not a free thinker either.'

The smile that opens on McPhee's visage is warm as a toffee sunset. 'I'm not soliciting you,' he says, suddenly understanding her panic.

Ellory puts down the glass. When she breathes it feels like she is stealing the air. Gentlemen who say they are not soliciting lasses might still be soliciting them all the same. 'What can I do for you, sir?'

McPhee sighs. 'I'm childless,' he says as if this is some kind of confession. 'You've met my niece and nephew. They're fine young people, but I decided some years ago that while they will receive the bulk of my fortune when I die, as a gambling man I like to set a wild card on the table now and then. Every year at the spring equinox, which is today, in fact, I become some soul's benefactor.'

This sounds dangerous. Ellory cocks her head to one side and wonders how long it would take her to get to the door.

'Life deals many hands,' McPhee continues. 'Some suffer, some benefit, but most will stay more or less where they are. That's the nature of people and I do not like it, Miss Mann. So each year I share a little of my luck to make something happen that would not otherwise happen, do you see?' He smiles, realising that she still does not understand. 'I give away money,' he elucidates. 'I wish to give some money to you.'

Ellory's eyes seek the floor. 'Sir, it would not be seemly—'

'You're afraid, of course, of what I might expect for my investment. I'm an old man and I'm flattered by that. So let me say outright that I do not expect anything of you. Nothing at all.'

She pauses. It seems promising. Too much so. 'But why would you give me money, sir?'

McPhee perks up. 'Both times I've visited Mr Hill's studio, I thought you interesting. You have a quiet rebellion about you.' He raises a hand to stop her denying it. 'So I have a question. What would you do with a windfall, Miss Mann? Can you imagine such a thing?'

Ellory swallows. This sounds like madness. Nothing comes to people like her that they do not graft and scrimp and save for.

'Go on,' McPhee encourages her.

'I want to go to Glasgow,' she admits, the words escaping almost involuntarily.

'Glasgow?' McPhee repeats, guffawing. 'I wasn't expecting that. What would you like to do there?'

'I would pursue my business, sir.' The words come in a rush. 'Mr Hill and Mr Adamson are in Edinburgh so I always thought I ought to move somewhere else, if I were to have a . . .' She cannot bring herself to say the final words.

'A what, Miss Mann?'

18

Ellory pauses. 'A studio of my own,' she gets out. It sounds ridiculous, there in the open.

McPhee grins. 'A lady photographer, eh? That will disrupt things nicely. Have you seen the image of Prince Albert, taken in London?'

'It is a daguerreotype,' she affirms. 'Printed onto silvered copper by Mr Constable.'

'Can you make such images?'

'I can, sir. Though at Mr Hill's studio we employ the calotype process, as you know. It's cheaper and some say the images have more character.'

McPhee's eyes fall to the parcel on his desk, the one she came to deliver. He picks up a silver letter knife and slits the string, propping the picture against his cigar box. He laughs as he considers the image of himself next to his niece, guitar in hand. 'Poor Winnie,' he says. 'She's not the least musical. My brother insisted she learn the piano. I thought yesterday that Hill would have been better to create his contrast with a piece of fabric. A shawl perhaps.' He regards the photograph. 'I prefer the one of my nephew, but this will pass muster. She's an awkward little thing.'

Ellory's gaze slips towards the threshold. Jessie's voice in her head keeps saying over and over, 'This is not right. You must shift, girl.'

'Well, Miss Mann, do you consent to my offer?' McPhee asks. Then, anticipating her refusal, 'Don't say a word.' He opens a drawer and removes a leather purse. 'Not before you have the money in front of you. Twenty guineas. I do not stake so much every year. I gave the boot boy at the Royal Society 12 sovereigns once. He has a print shop now on the Canongate. Smart lad. Will you realise your dream, Miss Mann, and go to Glasgow and take photographs? Do you have the bravery to take a chance?' He pushes the purse towards her.

Ellory can hardly breathe now. 'I have a little money of my own, sir,' she gets out. She has been saving since she got to Rock House.

'Enough to buy a camera obscura?' McPhee enquires.

She shakes her head.

19

'How much are you holding?'

Ellory clutches her reticule though her savings are stowed in a tin behind the skirting in the darkroom. 'Three pounds,' she says, not adding the extra pennies for, as she judges it, counting pennies will make her seem smaller to him, even though she has counted both pennies and ha'pennies all her life.

McPhee looks straitened. Three pounds sterling is nowhere near enough for what she wants to do, but he does not say so. 'Well, Miss Mann, the opportunity to realise your dream now lies before you. It comes with no obligation. You might squander it if you wish, though I find in general women do better with unexpected capital than men. I handed a young man this amount two years ago and it barely lasted him a fortnight. You have talent, I think. But the taking of the opportunity is up to you.'

'I would have to find a studio, sir.'

'You'll need a solicitor then.' He lifts his pen and scribbles a name onto a sheet of paper. 'I've done business in the past with this firm. Urquhart & Son. I shall wire an introduction. When will you embark?'

He is calling her bluff. Ellory regards the purse, wondering if this is some kind of devil's pact. McPhee stares. She seems, he thinks, quite young.

'Perhaps you would like to consult your mother? For advice, I mean.'

'She's dead, sir. I was brought up on the Cowgate, before my parents died. It's difficult to trust this, you see. It's so much,' she admits.

McPhee's gaze softens. The Cowgate is a rats' nest of poverty. The girl had a worse start in life than he expected. 'What age were you when you were orphaned?'

'Seven years.'

'You were an only child?'

'I had a sister a year younger. Nora.'

'She's dead too?' he surmises.

20

Ellory nods. She does not add any more detail about what happened to her sister. McPhee does not pry. Many die in the poor parts of Edinburgh. There is much to die from.

'Well, you've done well already,' he says. 'You have a responsible job. A vocation.'

'The Reverend Reid took us in. Nora and I helped in the kitchens at the rectory in Sciennes. He taught us to read and allowed us the run of his library,' Ellory explains.

McPhee searches the girl's face for an indication of what Reverend Reid expected of such young girls in return for these kindnesses, but he can find nothing amiss. 'One day I read Mrs Fulhame's book on the chemical process of photoreduction,' Ellory adds, gaining confidence. 'I walked round Hope Park several times, considering her calculations.'

'How old were you then?'

'Fourteen,' she replies stoutly.

'And your sister? Was she a budding chemist too?'

Ellory shakes her head. 'Reverend Reid discussed the book with me a little. He was acquainted with Mrs Fulhame's husband and had bought her book as a kindness, I think, rather than out of interest.'

'He hadn't read it?'

'I cut the pages myself.'

'And what happened once you had finished reading this illustrious tome?'

Ellory considers. She has started now. She might as well tell him. 'Some months later, I heard of Mr Adamson through my cousin.'

'Your cousin came to visit at Sciennes?' McPhee asks, winkling it out.

Ellory gives a little shrug. 'My cousin was in correspondence with Reverend Reid. About our welfare: my sister's and mine.'

McPhee does not ask why Ellory's cousin was not in correspondence with her. Or indeed, why Ellory and her sister were not raised by their relations. Families, he knows, can be complicated.

'I was old enough to be placed,' Ellory continues. 'Reverend Reid was looking for a suitable opening. When my cousin said that his sister Jessie was assisting Mr Adamson and Mr Hill and that the studio was busy, I walked to Calton Hill to offer my services. I wanted to learn.'

'Had you met Jessie before?'

Ellory shakes her head. 'Not that I remember,' she says. 'That side of the family is from Fife.'

'And Mr Hill and Mr Adamson took you in?'

'The reverend vouched for me.'

McPhee searches the young woman's face once more, this time for an indication that Mr Hill or Mr Adamson's motives were less than pure, but again, he finds none. Miss Mann, he concludes has been lucky. The girl is pretty enough, though her freckles are unfashionable and her mouth a little too wide. Perhaps her sense of purpose put the gentlemen off. McPhee notes he is yet to see Miss Mann smile, let alone laugh, and yet he cares about her, enough to spend his time drawing this story from her like a poultice laid on a wound. 'And your cousin who works with you? She is from the Fife side?'

'Yes. Her brother, Alexander, is a solicitor.'

'I do not know him,' McPhee says flatly.

Ellory squirms, for talk of Alexander and Jessie reminds her that she is the black sheep. Her father wed for love and he loved beneath him. The Mann family lore is that he died for it and good riddance. And then there is Nora.

McPhee accepts her story is ended. 'This money then shall be the latest stroke of luck in your adventure,' he says. 'You'll take the train to Glasgow, I assume? You should go tomorrow on the afternoon locomotive. The service is up to three carriages, I believe. I shall wire Mr Urquhart on your behalf. He will help you find a studio. The fee note for that service will come to me. After that you're on your own.'

'An engine,' Ellory says. Her mother was from Glasgow. She walked from the other side of the country when she came to Edinburgh. It took three days. She slept in a hedgerow near Falkirk. 'How much will it cost?'

McPhee smiles, his blue eyes clear as the sea at Portobello in June. He clinks the coins in the purse cheekily. 'You can afford a few shillings now, Miss Mann. Mr Urquhart will be able to advise you, but fashionable Glasgow is moving west and north as I understand it. Just as Edinburgh moved north over the loch some decades ago. You might think to seek your studio there.'

'I'd like to be near the river,' Ellory says. 'The light will be better.'

McPhee shrugs. 'The Clyde is brown as sludge. But you'll make up your own mind.'

A smile escapes her. Yes, it comes to her, I will. But what she says is, 'Thank you, sir.' And again, 'Thank you,' as she takes the money.

The butler releases her through the main door and Ellory makes off down the street, her hand in her pocket on the purse full of coins, as if she stole it. Behind her, the sun sets. The moon is a half-round of cheese. The air smells of early gorse flowers. Close to Rock House, the ironmonger at Calton Place locks the door of his shop with a padlock the size of a bull's heart and turns up the vennel. Ellory has daydreamed of her eventual progression from Mr Hill's studio almost since she arrived, and with the addition of this 20 guineas she can effect her plan, more or less.

That night she sits up late with the window open. High above, the Sickle of Leo is clear as a bell. She catches a whiff of hops from the brewery, Tennant and MacDonald on the Canongate, near the print-works the boot boy from the Royal Society set up. Twenty guineas, three pounds, four shillings and thruppence sits in the tin. She has counted it three times and on top has placed her father's gold watch, dented but still working; all she has of him. The money will be enough, though she needs to be careful. She has decided already that she will not seek ministers and other worthies to photograph. She wants to do something different, but as yet it is difficult to say what that might be and how it will make money. She is feeling her way like an infant learning to walk. She puts the thought from her mind.

At two of the clock, she lights a lamp and fetches a worn carpet-bag from the cupboard to pack her possessions: three books on the subject of photo reduction, her notebooks and pencils, a few items of clothing and a cardboard portfolio containing her own negatives and prints. She stows the money in her plain leather reticule and lies fully dressed on the creaky mattress in the little room off the kitchen, waiting for dawn. She does not expect to sleep, so it is a surprise when, as she counts her blessings, unconsciousness overtakes her. Thousands upon thousands of pennies clinking together like bells in a chorus. Better for bringing on slumber than a field full of sheep.

Chapter Four

Glasgow

When Charlotte is ready, Murray sends for Mrs Grieg. The Griegs live in a stucco-fronted townhouse just off the square. Dr Grieg looks after many of Glasgow's well-to-do and has attended Charlotte since she was born. Social calls, however, always take an extra half hour with the Griegs, James Nicholl used to say, between the doctor's habit of using three words when one might do and Mrs Grieg's 'grand oration' to credit the Church for everything. As if there was no God before the Free Kirk came into being. As if Mrs Grieg had forgotten where they all used to pray on Sunday not four years before. 'They're good people though,' Charlotte's father always said once he had finished criticising them.

Mrs Grieg hurries across the square. The stocky old woman is overbearing, but she has supported the Nicholls one way or another since Charlotte was a child. After Charlotte's mother died, it was she who insisted Cook make cinnamon bread and lemon posset to bring James Nicholl back to the world when he would not leave his room for a week after his wife's funeral. 'Make the house reek of it,' she instructed. 'He needs sweetness to draw him out.' She had been right. 'Leave this to me,' she instructs Murray as she settles next to Charlotte on the sofa. 'I'm sure you've business to see to. His will and so on,' she adds with a hawkish glance.

Within an hour of Murray's departure, the old woman has instructed Mr Boots, the Nicholls' valet-cum-butler, to wash and dress James Nicholl's body. When it is done Mrs Grieg pronounces, 'You must pay your respects, lass.' She sounds, Charlotte thinks, as if she is handing down the words like a court judgment, but nonetheless she steels herself to enter her father's bedroom. Mrs Grieg squeezes the girl's arm. 'The Lord will comfort you,' she adds ominously.

Charlotte pulls back. The old lady seems too keen somehow. 'I'm all right,' she counters bravely and they enter together.

It is not as bad as Charlotte expected. Papa looks asleep. She finds she cannot speak, or at least she has nothing to say. Mrs Grieg, efficient as ever, clips three locks of the dead man's hair. 'One of the Jews will set this for you,' she says, handing over the greying curls. 'They're Jesus's own people,' she adds, before directing Boots to dress the pillow behind Nicholl's head with tightly closed blossom from the shared garden in the centre of Blythswood Square. 'How sad your father died when the world was about to spring into life,' she adds as she leads Charlotte downstairs again. 'Only lilies and ivy in the rest of the residence,' she instructs Mrs Cullen, the housekeeper. Mrs Cullen rarely says anything. James Nicholl always claimed this was an excellent reason to employ her. 'And cover the mirrors,' Mrs Grieg adds.

Charlotte is glad the doctor's wife is here. She does not feel equal to seeing to these details. The smell of simmering lemon posset fills the hallway; a sign that Mrs Grieg's methods have not altered over the years. Perhaps it's for the best, the girl thinks. *I should just let her get on with it.*

After noon, Reverend Patterson, the stern-faced minister, arrives. 'Miss Nicholl,' he addresses her, 'you must change into black. This –' he gestures towards her blue ensemble – 'is unsuitable.'

'Father never liked me in black,' Charlotte replies.

'You must go into full mourning, dear,' Mrs Grieg echoes the minister.

'But I have none,' Charlotte objects and bursts into tears. These silly traditions seem pointless. The fact her father is gone is sinking in slowly. She cannot bear to look at the chair he used to occupy. To think of him lying lifeless now, along the hallway. Worse still is the idea that he will be removed in a day or two, so his body can be buried. It feels as if part of her will be buried too. As if she might not be able to breathe. 'I'm alone,' she gasps, the words catching in her throat. She cannot imagine how she will spend her time. Papa decided everything. Where they would go. Who they would meet. Tickets for the opera. Shopping trips. Promenading in the garden.

'Now now,' the reverend hushes her and, turning to Mrs Grieg, adds, 'we should fetch the doctor.'

But Mrs Grieg's husband has been called to his weekly duties at the Lock Hospital at Townhead, where 27 evil women are incarcerated to stop them taking to the streets to sell themselves. Pink-faced and wry, Dr Grieg is diligent in his duties. He always takes his time at the Lock and, after, spends an hour or two at the Magdalene for good measure. So dedicated is he to the benefit of Glasgow's fallen women that he will certainly be gone all day. As a result, Reverend Patterson and Mrs Grieg send Miss Nicholl upstairs to lie down. Too exhausted to argue, she lies on the counterpane and stares at the egg-and-dart cornice that fringes her room as the news of her father's death seeps through Glasgow's streets, lapping from fine business premises into ornate drawing rooms, where the city's wives, mothers and daughters discuss James Nicholl's life.

'That poor girl,' they say. 'Alone in the huge house her father built at the top of the hill.' Charlotte feels she might drown in their pity, as if the streets were canals and her gondola insubstantial.

At four o'clock Mrs Grieg insists Charlotte sups a cup of beef tea in bed. Outside the window, a message boy disappears below to deliver a parcel at the kitchen door. A minute later, Mrs Cullen brings it up. Charlotte opens the paper. An invoice from the dress-maker lies on top. Confused, she pulls out a mourning dress with jet beads sewn in a pattern at the neckline and an inky cashmere stole. 'You said you didn't have any mourning, dear,' Mrs Grieg says.

Charlotte remains silent. It seems so calculating. The dressmaker could never have made such fine work so quickly, which means she was prepared, only tailoring the dress to Charlotte's measurements when word was sent. This dress has stood ready for any grieving woman in the city, whichever order came first. Why couldn't somebody else's father have died?

Mrs Cullen takes the garment. 'Miss?' she says. Papa would have hated the damn thing but Charlotte relents and lets the housekeeper help her change.

Afterwards, Murray returns from his offices and Mrs Cullen shows him upstairs. 'Miss Charlotte is in her room,' she says.

'You had best announce me,' Murray tells her, before checking that Mrs Grieg is still there.

He has been in camera for two hours with his father discussing the ins and outs of James Nicholl's will, which they will administer together for the sake of continuity. Old Mr Urquhart's retirement plan is that his clients will die one by one and Murray will take over on behalf of their children. The wily old solicitor peered over the top of his spectacles. 'Charlotte Nicholl is a well-behaved lass. You could do worse, Murray. She wouldn't distract you from business, and the house is grand.'

Murray raises his eyes in exasperation. His father, so clever in the matter of legal strategy, has no idea about the nature of love, or the kind of love Murray hopes for, anyway. A woman who ignites him and yet someone with whom he can found a different kind of family than the one he grew up in, one where people sit together of an evening for the pleasure of it, playing cards and music and talking and reading aloud. Murray wants to desire his wife for the rest of his days. He recalls too well the sadness that his father never noticed in his mother. The coldness between them. Charlotte is pleasant but she is like a sister. It would never do. 'I prefer to listen to the music,' she told him once at a dance where she refused all invitations to waltz, so he sat next to her and they listened together, him accepting her, the same way she always accepted him – as friends but nothing more. Old Mr Urquhart, Murray thinks, does not value passion. He judges marriage like a manifest of goods. The old solicitor has been pushing his son on the matter since the boy got home from Lincoln's Inn. 'I want to meet my grandchildren,' he tried one day.

'I don't need to marry for that,' Murray quipped.

Ever the lawyer, Mr Urquhart amended his request a couple of days later to, 'I would like to know the next generation of my legitimate heirs.' This had no more efficacious an effect. Murray is not minded to take his father's advice. When Murray's mother died, the truth is that Mr Urquhart senior was contentedly bereaved. His parents bored each other and that, on his father's part, is saying something. Once when Mrs Urquhart became sick, she asked her husband to read to her and he chose the Slavery Abolition Act of 1833, in which, he pointed out, many folk were interested at the time. Murray cannot once remember seeing his parents touch each other. Not even to hold hands.

It is not that he is determined to frustrate his father's wishes. Not at all. But at 64 years of age, the old man has the air of somebody who will last, if not a century, then close enough. There is no rush, and Murray wants to find the right woman, for London gave him a taste for something beyond the daughters of his father's clients, however well turned out and beautifully housed they may be. He wants a partner, not someone to manage his housekeeper and breed his children. 'Charlotte is not for me, Pa,' he said. 'Nor I for her.' Mr Urquhart looked more sceptical than usual but waved him away.

'Is there anybody you would like me to contact? A relation perhaps?' Murray offers, taking in the sight of Charlotte sitting up in bed. She is, he thinks, like a message by telegraph, not a poem.

Charlotte lays the china cup of bone broth on the side table with a clink. 'We have no relations,' she says. 'Neither Papa nor Mama had a brother or sister. Papa used to say it was a family tradition.' She manages a slim smile.

Mrs Grieg sighs. 'That is another matter we must remedy. A single lady living by herself . . . it isn't right.'

At five Mrs Grieg suggests she should stay the night. 'For your father's sake,' she adds. 'A young lady like you needs company surely. We can sort through dear James's things, if you would like.' Charlotte shudders and there is an unseemly pause during which Mrs Grieg restrains herself from mentioning how, when the posset and bread encouraged Charlotte's father to open his door, she talked him the last of the way back to life: 'You have your daughter, James. She's what's left of Maggie now.' Charlotte has nobody to pull herself together for. 'It's no bother. I'll send a maid to fetch my things,' Mrs Grieg offers, fussing like a fat old hen scratching round the coop.

Charlotte considers the spaces that have been left by her father. The empty study. The diary on his desk. She knows if she does not step into these voids, Mrs Grieg will come to fill them. She is not a child any longer and she must stake her claim. 'I shall stay by myself,' she announces. 'I must get used to it, after all.' Mrs Grieg looks crestfallen and Charlotte takes pity on her. 'You've been such a help today,' she adds kindly.

Murray waits a moment. The old woman's attentions quickly become overbearing, he thinks. Before Mrs Grieg can regroup, however, Mrs Cullen appears with a card announcing Mrs Howarth from next door. It is late for somebody to arrive. The Howarths must have just heard the news. 'Show her into the drawing room,' Charlotte instructs.

Mrs Grieg looks as if she has been punched, rather than sent homewards for the evening. 'The Howarths are Episcopalians,' she points out testily as Charlotte fixes her hair and smooths her skirt.

Her father never stood for such divisions. 'Glasgow has near two thousand pews available to worship the Lord, it is as well they are filled, each to their own denomination,' he once said when Reverend Patterson tried to encourage him to buy empty plots of land to stop the Church of Scotland building on them. Or worse, the Catholics.

'Thank you, Mrs Grieg,' Charlotte says firmly. 'I hope you'll call again tomorrow.'

Mrs Grieg hovers in a quandary for she does not want to see the Howarths nor does she want to be sent away.

'Murray is here. The doctor will be expecting you for dinner. You'll have to change,' Charlotte reassures her.

If Mrs Grieg ever changes, I'll eat my hat, Murray thinks, restraining himself from whispering this to his friend. Still, as he judges it, Charlotte asserting herself as she has is a positive sign. The two young people watch the plump old woman disappear down the hallway, in the direction of the front door.

'She means well,' Charlotte says.

'Shall I?' Murray asks, tipping his head towards the drawing room. This will be the first of many such calls. Like an actress waiting in the wings, Charlotte indicates she's ready and Murray opens the door. Inside it is not only Mrs Howarth arrayed on the blue sofas but all three of her daughters. The Howarths are blonde and ringleted and remind Charlotte of a sandy-coloured spaniel one of their cousins brought on a visit a few springs before.

'My dear Charlotte.' Mrs Howarth rises. The girls, sheepish, remain seated. Charlotte knows they have been made to come: they find her as odd as she finds them. They have always been the kinds of girls who played croquet and happily shared an array of dolls in tiny perambulators. Now they are older, they share ribbons and lace collars and gossip about the latest ball at the Assembly. They giggle as they pass on the pavement. They whisper. Mrs Howarth kisses Charlotte's cheek and takes her arm. Charlotte draws it back and sits down. 'We came straight away. We only just heard. I'm so sorry,' Mrs Howarth says.

'Thank you,' Charlotte manages.

'Such a shock,' Mrs Howarth continues. 'Your father was a strident man. That's what I said when I heard, wasn't it, girls?'

Mary, the eldest, says, 'Yes, Mama.'

'If there's anything you need, Charlotte, you need only ask,' Mrs Howarth offers. 'Where is your father now?'

31

'In his room. His valet laid him out on the bed.'

'He died in his sleep then?'

Charlotte's lips purse. Murray steps in. 'Mr Nicholl passed away last night. He was reading in his study. It must have been sudden.'

'That's what he would have preferred. To go at the helm,' Mrs Howarth says, and Charlotte restrains herself from saying that she is certain her father would have preferred not to have gone at all. She offers tea but Mrs Howarth says she would not put the staff to it.

'You must walk with us one day,' Mary says, her blue eyes expressionless.

'How kind of you,' Charlotte replies with brown eyes equally as still, for both young women know that they will not promenade. If they did not do so before Papa died, Charlotte reasons, why would they start now? Mrs Howarth launches into a soliloquy about Papa's kindness over the years. 'Your father was a lovely man,' she finishes.

'He was . . . a rock,' Charlotte manages and realises that was true. The thing she most valued about him was his steady companionship. Now she is mistress of the house and master too. This thought though terrifying also opens an unexpected avenue of possibility. She has sent Mrs Grieg away. She can spend the evening at her own will. She might order any dinner she chooses. She might read whatever she would like.

The Howarths rise and say they will see her at the funeral. As she rounds the head of the stairs Mary catches her sister's hand and their eyes meet, glad the visit is over.

Once the door has closed, Charlotte says, 'I'm not certain I can do this again and again, Murray. There will be more callers.'

'I'm sure,' Murray confirms.

'It is not in me,' Charlotte adds. 'Small talk.'

'You've never been one for society,' he admits, and she searches his face but finds no criticism, only a statement of fact. 'Perhaps you should let Mrs Grieg host for you,' he suggests, a twinkle in his eye.

'Mrs Grieg,' Charlotte repeats dismissively. 'She will supervise my meals and tell me what to wear if I let her. She means it kindly, but I'm a grown woman.'

'She doesn't want people talking. You here. Alone. A gentleman might call,' he teases her. 'Would you like me to find you another companion? Somebody younger perhaps?'

'For propriety's sake?' Charlotte shakes her head. 'I don't like people. Not you, of course,' she adds. 'I don't need a chaperone in my own home. A stranger.'

'The Church is not keen on unsupervised single ladies.'

'Widows live alone,' Charlotte objects.

'You're not a widow,' he points out and offers to read her father's will, which is his next duty.

Charlotte shakes her head once more. 'After the funeral. It will make no difference to wait, will it?'

'Things will be set in a couple of days, I imagine,' he says. 'I'll leave you alone.' He knows that is what she wants. What she needs perhaps. Charlotte will always be separate, he thinks. There is something awkward about her. Even today, shocked and vulnerable, she has dug her heels in. She will never join the dancing.

When he's gone, she calls for Mrs Cullen and asks for cheese and bread to be left in her father's study. A fleeting look of panic crosses the housekeeper's face as if Charlotte is laying out an offering for the dead. 'That's what I'll have for dinner,' she explains, smirking at the fact that everyone seems to expect her to career off like a mad horse. Downstairs she enters the silence of her father's sanctum, lined with walnut bookshelves, the fire laid, the carpet cleaned where the maid dropped the ashes in fright. She feels close to him here, as if he has only popped out to speak to Mr Howarth or across the square to visit Dr Grieg.

Charlotte has borrowed books from her father's library since she was old enough to read. Papa curated the shelves: plays bound in ox-blood leather, philosophy in pale yellow calfskin, scientific tomes in workaday tan and poetry encased in pigskin so dark it is almost black. She swears that she can tell his books' contents from the smell of the leather. When she came into her allowance, at 17, she started a collection of novels and had her books bound in Moroccan red with gold tooling. She declared that Papa was now welcome to borrow from *her* library. That made the old man chortle. 'Mary Brunton, I suppose,' he said. 'She was a rare woman. There was a fuss, you know, about her stories being immoral, but I doubt it. When I met her in Edinburgh she was the soul of the world. I was younger then, of course. Only a boy.' This intriguing notion sent Charlotte to the bookshop on Argyle Street in a flurry of excitement, to see for herself. She was quelled at first by the fact Mrs Brunton's most famous novel was titled *Discipline*, but bought it nonetheless and consumed the story in two days. She deemed the tale not immoral exactly but certainly more descriptive than Miss Austen, whose protagonists were often more the victim than Charlotte would have liked. Why did they prostrate themselves? Miss Brunton would have had none of that.

And so it is that within the hour, the grey city outside the window engulfed in darkness, she eats bubbling, fire-blistered rarebit beside the bookshelves, ignoring the bottle of laudanum that Dr Grieg sent over when he returned from the wicked women of Townhead. Outside, the Howarth girls run giggling into a carriage as it begins to rain. Droplets pool on fallen leaves and patter onto paving stones. But it is a figure dressed in a dark cape turning off the main road past the building works that catches her attention. As the fellow approaches the front door, Charlotte sits back from the window and takes in his face; an older man than Papa, and ugly, with a wide nose that has been broken and thick lips like a gargoyle on an old English church. His skin is rough as a half-finished statue.

She draws back as the doorbell rings. It is late and Mrs Cullen appears in the study's threshold for instruction. 'Shall I answer the bell, miss?'

Charlotte nods. 'See what he wants.' She feels strangely disquieted by this unexpected visitor.

The housekeeper disappears for only a moment. 'It's a gentleman. Calls himself Lennox,' she announces. 'A papist, I should think,' she adds, giving no reason for this remark.

Charlotte shudders. Whatever her father's views on brotherly acceptance, at base she has been brought up to distrust the Church of Rome. Every ragged, muscle-bound Highlander and slow-eyed Irishman building the railway line might be a papist. The Jews are God's own people, but Catholics belong to the devil. They reside too far from what Mrs Grieg calls 'our own dear Free Kirk'. Suddenly Mr Lennox's presence feels a heavy omen.

'Have you seen him before?' Charlotte asks, trying to remain rational. Mrs Cullen shakes her head. 'Ask him what he wants.'

The old housekeeper disappears, returning a moment later. 'He says he's a friend of your father's, come on business.'

Charlotte glances sideways through the uneven pane. The Howarths were tiresome but this caller feels like a threat. 'It's too late for me to receive,' she says. 'My father is dead. You told him that, didn't you?' Mrs Cullen nods. 'Send him away.'

The housekeeper closes the study door and Charlotte watches as she delivers the news on the doorstep. The man hesitates, then crosses the road to the railings that surround the park. She wonders nervously if he might loiter, like a spectre in the gaslight flame, until morning, but only a few moments after Mrs Cullen closes the door, he strides off, his trousers flapping at his ankles. Charlotte feels a flood of relief and returns to picking half-heartedly at what is left of the bread. The silence of the house is her only ballast. She scans the desk but the papers held in place by her father's Venetian glass paperweight do not bear the name of Lennox. Perhaps, she thinks, she ought to have allowed Mrs Grieg to stay with her after all.

Grief is a strange state of affairs: like a ladder, up and down. One person is missing from the world. Only one. Yet he was the bridge between her and everybody else and now she must find her way across the void alone, like a figure from some kind of fable. 'I have nobody,' she announces to the empty room. 'I'm entirely by myself.' She pulls up her courage out of nowhere, for she feels like a child in a forest, searching for the right path home.

Chapter Five

Edinburgh

Ellory starts from her slumber at the slam of the kitchen door. She glances at her packed bag. The Manns' duties do not extend to housework, so Mr Hill engaged Jane Ramsay, or 'Plain Jane' as the women call her between themselves, as a half-day girl for the cleaning. Jane arrives daily before six to set the stove and clean the lamps. She is a skinny scrap who has looked no more than 15 years of age since the day she was taken on.

'Good morning, Miss Ellory,' Jane says without looking up from brushing ashes into a bucket as Ellory comes into the kitchen.

'I'm leaving,' Ellory announces as if saying the words out loud will make it more real.

'Breakfast before you go, miss?' Jane gets to her feet. 'Where are you off to today?'

'I'm leaving,' Ellory repeats.

Jane turns, understanding. Her brow wrinkles in disbelief. 'But, miss, it's a good position.'

Ellory pours two clay cups of milk and sets them on the scrubbed, pine table. 'It is,' she says. 'I've learned a great deal.'

'What did Miss Mann say?' Jane asks, forsaking the stove.

'I'll tell her when she gets here,' Ellory replies. It seems suddenly odd that she has not lain awake thinking of what to say to her cousin.

Ellory always shares her breakfast; one egg for her and one for Jane with bread and dripping, butter being a luxury reserved for the gentlemen when they take lunch in the studio. Jessie has no idea that Ellory never eats both the eggs which have been allocated to her, counted carefully into the basket each week. Nor the full pint of milk she is accorded each day. Nor the dozen oysters delivered on Fridays, with a slice of haddock. If she ever found out Ellory's generosity, she'd consider it a failing and calculate the housekeeping rations downwards. Jane sets the eggs to boil, watching Ellory carefully as if she is checking over a piece of needlework for stray threads.

'You can't have thought I'd stay at Rock House forever,' Ellory says, but Jane does not reply.

After breakfast, Ellory washes in the bathroom sink, using the scented soap reserved for guests. She writes a note and seals a coin into it, calling one of the boys from further along the row and giving him a penny to make the delivery. 'To the wifie in the cottage down Broughton Loan. You went before, remember?' The boy pockets his penny and takes off like a billiard ball hit at an angle. Then Ellory sits in the parlour. For once, Jessie is late. Only ten minutes, but still. Ellory listens as her cousin removes her coat and hat in the hallway and comes into the sitting room.

'What's this?' she asks, taking in the scene: Ellory in the chair with her coat buttoned and her bonnet tied, the carpet-bag at her feet and a vague smell of roses. Ellory rises, butterflies in her stomach fluttering like the red cardinals on the gorse in the Queen's Park.

'I'm giving notice. I'm moving on.' She hesitates to divulge the tin of money for fear Jessie will laugh at her ambition.

Jessie freezes a few seconds before her temper flares. 'How dare you? After everything we've done for you!'

'I'll leave at once,' Ellory continues steadily.

'That is not handing in your notice,' Jessie snaps. 'That is no notice at all. Whatever has got into you?' She glances out of the window. 'It's a man, isn't it? You've got yourself into trouble.'

Ellory shakes her head. She does not want to explain her plans, but she must say something. 'I'm going to Glasgow. To set up a studio,' she gets out.

Jessie's lips purse.

'It will be my studio. I'll be the photographer,' Ellory says, surprised at how calm she feels.

There is another moment of silence that widens the space between the women as if they are looking at each other through a long lens. Then a cruel laugh emanates from Jessie's lips. 'How could *you* have a photographic studio? Where in Glasgow?'

Ellory knows it sounds ridiculous. 'I'll find a place,' she says and picks up her bag, a strand of her hair the colour of fire slipping from under her hat.

Jessie casts round, flustered as if calling upon the very fabric of Rock House to restore the order of things. 'You cannot go,' she snaps.

Ellory pauses. The Manns have always held sway. Suddenly Ellory realises her cousin only has power if she chooses to give it to her. 'Thanks for everything,' she says. 'I've learned a lot.' That is true. It has been an education and not only in Mr Adamson's process. Jessie is good at organising things. Mr Hill never runs out of paper or chemicals because of her watchful eye.

Jessie, however, is not giving up on the argument. 'Mr Hill will be furious,' she continues. 'He has enough on his plate with the child to look after.' She is swept up in it now. 'I can't imagine how he manages the hours at George Watson's College and his clients at the studio on top. He's a widower,' she adds, as if Ellory does not know. Then she stares at her cousin, realising her monologue has not had the effect she hoped for. 'Nobody will want you to take their photograph,' she spits. 'Mr Hill is a celebrated painter. Mr Adamson developed his process over many years. You're just ...' Jessie, panicked, searches for the word.

'I'm a drudge,' Ellory admits, tipping her chin. 'That's how you see me. But I've had my eyes open. And I've decided to take my chance.'

'You're just like your sister,' Jessie spits in a final attempt to douse her cousin's fire.

Ellory sighs. Nora is long dead but, she realises, it is her face Jessie sees when she casts her eyes in Ellory's direction. She wonders if there is anywhere that people do not carry their past on their back like some kind of saddle.

'I forbid you to leave,' Jessie pronounces, her eyes alight. 'I shall send a note to Alexander. As the head of the family he will have something to say.'

Ellory weighs this for a moment. Alexander Mann is unlikely to support her. 'I don't care what your brother thinks,' she gets out, observing as she says it that it is true. 'I'll write when I'm settled,' she promises and walks out. There's no point in arguing. It is better just to go.

Down the hill, she looks back but the door to Rock House remains resolutely closed. At the other end of the row, two of the carpenter's many children are playing hopscotch. One of them raises her hand and Ellory waves back. She is almost at the end of the street when she hears steps clitter-clattering after her. She stops and turns, surprised that it's Plain Jane who wheels into her, a tattered, greying wrap tucked into her skirt.

'Miss.' Jane catches her breath, a faint flush on her cheek. 'Take me with you.'

Ellory glances back at Rock House but Jessie has not appeared. 'What? You?' She sounds shocked.

'I've a brother in service in Glasgow. He says it's a place that makes its own luck. I'd like to work for you, miss. In your new studio.'

'You're young to leave your family, Jane.'

The girl grins. 'I'm 19 years of age. Not that much younger than you, miss. My mother won't mind. She has more of us at home.'

Ellory peers at the maid who might have said she was five years younger and caused not the least surprise.

'You know I'm a hard worker,' Jane continues. 'You'll need somebody. I've learned a good deal at Rock House. Like you said to the other Miss Mann.'

'What have you learned?'

Jane's face lights up. 'Not to be afraid of the shade for there is no light without it. The properties of some of the chemicals in the darkroom, and that a woman should always wear gloves there. That it's as well to question the apothecary's bill. And though Mr Hill disregards it, the sitters like to look their best.'

Ellory laughs. If only she had had this wisdom when she arrived, the skin from her fingers to her forearms would still be smooth and pale and the tips she received might have been more generous.

'It's a risk, Jane.' She wants to be clear. 'I've nothing arranged, and though I have money I'm not sure it's enough.'

'I'll help,' Jane insists, appreciating Ellory's frankness. 'When it's done it'll be better than here, won't it?'

Ellory considers this. The work in Glasgow will be hard and there is much to do.

'We'll have to live in the studio to start with. You shall have bed and board and four shillings a month. I can't pay more.'

'And a half-day every week,' Jane bargains.

'It'll be difficult at first.'

The girl grins. She reaches for Ellory's free hand and shakes it enthusiastically. 'Och, I know that.'

'Shall we fetch your things?' Ellory asks. She has never seen Jane wear any clothes other than her worn woollen skirt, blouse and wrap. Her boots, though always well-polished, have seen better days. The laces have been repaired rather than replaced and the soles are loose.

'I've nothing to bring,' Jane admits without regret. 'We should get on,' she glances towards Rock House. 'Before your cousin notices I'm gone.'

*

Murray Urquhart meets them off the train that afternoon and in Glasgow it is raining. The sky is so overcast it's difficult to imagine blue behind the soot-smeared clouds. Plain Jane took the carpet-bag in third class and now walks reverently behind Ellory through the billowing steam on the platform, like a soot-smudged, tatty brides-maid. The station is only half built; the roof, though incomplete, intensifies the sound of navvies hammering. Ellory's heart beats as fast as a piston. What if Mr McPhee has played a trick? What if the solicitor here sends for Alexander Mann? What if she and Jane are sent back to Rock House, marched home like naughty schoolgirls?

'Miss Mann?' Murray hails them from the end of the concourse, removing his top hat and smoothing an errant lock of hair before it falls across his eyes. 'I'm Murray Urquhart. Your solicitor.'

Ellory stops, Jane halting behind her. She takes the man in. He is a queer fellow. His body looks strong, like a fruit tree with twisted branches, she thinks. He is bountifully dressed in a bright waistcoat with golden fleur-de-lys and a verdant velvet coat the colour of moss in summertime, a tone not far from her own woollen coat and yet he is far better dressed than she is, or more expensively anyway. He gives a slight bow. She puts out her hand to shake, and looking up, notes that his eyes are brown and he smells warm, like a sunny day on the grass. The hammering suddenly no longer troubles her.

'Mr McPhee sent a wire to meet the afternoon train,' he says. 'How can I help?'

'Mr Urquhart,' she announces, 'I'm in need of a photographic studio. Somewhere with light.'

Murray's smile widens into a delighted grin. 'It's true then,' he says. 'You're a lady photographer. Are you familiar with Glasgow?'

'Not at all,' she admits.

He regards her. She's a hale-looking lass with intelligent eyes. Her pinned-back hair is an extraordinary ripe colour. He wonders her connection to an elderly gentleman like McPhee. 'I've made enquir-ies. Mr McPhee wrote that you hoped to be by the river?' he says.

Ellory nods.

'There's one place I heard was available near the Clyde, if that's your desire.' He motions Jane forward and hails a cab, ushering the women out of the rain. Outside, his voice is only a little lower than it was in the station, for the pitter-patter is loud on the cab's roof. 'We should go directly. It's available straight away. Of course, you may prefer somewhere further west. This is in an older part of town, but a respectable address. Your nearest neighbours will be the College of Physicians and the Church.'

From the unaccustomed vantage point of the hackney, Ellory looks over George Square Gardens. On the grass, a boy of no more than seven years of age is dodging the ministrations of a nanny wearing a pink uniform with a complicated white apron that appears to have entrapped her. She remembers somebody long ago saying that they slaughtered horses on George Square, but it looks as if things have changed since her mother's day. Edinburgh folk talk of Glasgow as if it is beyond the pale, yet behind the park there are houses easily as fine as those along Princes Street. She begins to worry about money, wondering what she will be able to afford. Murray Urquhart chats on unaware, politely pointing out landmarks: a monument to Sir Walter Scott smaller than the one in Edinburgh, and a statue of Lord Wellington near the new British Linen Bank. 'Is your equipment following? Sent by canal?' he asks.

'I shall have to buy everything,' she replies, turning her attention back into the carriage. 'Until now I've only been an assistant.' She wonders if she ought to admit it.

Mr Urquhart thinks she is the pluckiest lass he ever met. 'Good heavens,' he says. 'A new venture then. And Mr McPhee is—?'

'A client of my old master,' she says. 'He has backed me.'

Murray's gaze softens. 'I only met him once. He seemed a kind old gentleman. Well, I can commend you to Wylie & Lochhead on the Trongate for furnishings,' he says generously. 'They'll be able to accommodate your general needs, and Mr Allen is an excellent apothecary. You'll require chemicals, will you not?'

43

'I will,' she says, but it is hard to focus on such details when the street distracts her. The houses are so much grander than she expected. 'Is this Glasgow's New Town?'

'Mostly that lies across the river,' Murray says. 'There are several imposing streets.'

'Where do you live, Mr Urquhart?'

'Further west,' he admits. 'In my family's home. They are building all the time. Fashionable new stucco houses, like London.'

It is strange, Ellory notes. Edinburgh's New Town is separated from the Old by the chasm of the drained Nor Loch. The private gardens planted on the old riverbed form a gully between the monied and the poor. Working people live on the lanes behind the mansions, but there are no slums in Edinburgh's New Town. Here, however, down the side of a huge edifice she catches a glimpse of a rookery. There is a familiar stench on the air; faint in the carriage, but a warning that abject poverty is not far off. They pass a vacant lot, piled high with huge coils of rope and a mountain of barrels. Then, as they turn onto the Trongate, a bevy of hawkers shout their wares, new season's potatoes and a creel of crabs. Dusty carts drawn by weary horses deliver goods. The buildings, she thinks, are magnificent. This city was made for sepia.

'What inspired you come to Glasgow, Miss Mann?' Murray enquires. Jane, who has been staring out of the window, turns to hear the answer to this question, as if she too has wondered about her mistress's choice.

Ellory remembers her mother's face. It seems ludicrously sentimental to admit it is that and perhaps the fact that she cannot stay in Edinburgh for Mr Hill and Mr Adamson would not thole her opening a studio so close by. She should be vague, she decides. This man seems kindly, but he is a stranger. 'A family connection, sir. Long past,' she gets out.

'You have visited before then?'

Ellory shakes her head. She recalls Reverend Reid calling Glasgow a place of opportunity. A port, like Leith, but onto the Atlantic. 'We should not judge them,' the reverend had added inexplicably, his Adam's apple bobbing as he spoke, more like a cherry, as she saw it.

'I lived in London for four years. I apprenticed at the bar,' Murray offers.

'But you returned?'

'I was drawn back.' He is surprised to hear himself admitting this to a young woman who, after all, he has only just met.

Ellory turns towards the window again. The streets seem haphazard, unlike the capital's carefully orchestrated architecture. 'They call it the Dear Green Place, do they not?' she says.

Edinburgh is nothing if not green. Even in the Old Town the vertiginous backs on the north side run down to the old waterline, peppered with goats and a variety of ancient trees. In the New Town almost every street has a green pocket in which residents may promenade.

'Certainly this part of the city does not live up to its moniker.' Murray is enjoying playing the tour guide. 'Glasgow Green lies to the east however. And new parks are being laid out . . .'

'In the west?' she chimes, teasing him.

The carriage draws up at a small square with a church cutting into it. The clock on the stone facade declares it is quarter past three. A scatter of thin bushes and two dripping sycamore trees shelter half a dozen sheep on the other side of the grass. Down a thin street past the livestock Ellory catches sight of moving water. 'Is that the Clyde?'

'We're not used to sightseers,' he says. 'But yes, that's the river.'

Ellory notes that McPhee's observation was pessimistic. The Clyde isn't sapphire but it's not mud-brown either. 'It lies to the south?' she gestures, getting her bearings.

Murray nods. Ellory can place Glasgow on a map. As a child at Reverend Reid's she pored over the atlas of Scotland, taking in the details of her mother's hometown. She knows there is a seminary for Free Kirk ministers beyond the river at Rutherglen. And further still a grand estate called Castlemilk that makes her think of milk and honey. There are weavers and colliers at Cambuslang and fishermen hauling salmon out of the river to sell on the Saltmarket. Now she gasps as a ship sails across her sightline, a glimpse sudden as a gunshot. She has never seen a ship in movement, only images in paintings or the upturned rowboats Mr Hill likes fisherfolk from Musselburgh to pose in front of. This image will be difficult to catch, elegant between the dark buildings. But she will try. She can hardly believe she's made it this far.

Murray helps her dismount. Jane jumps down behind and makes straight for a gnarled tree on the far side of the square, dressed with ornaments hung on old shoelaces and ragged pieces of string: buttons and whittled wood and oyster shells with a hole punched in them. Two tin spoons clattering together make the sound of an ungainly bell.

'What's that?' Ellory asks.

'I heard it's to be felled,' Murray replies. 'Women hang offerings there to St Enoch to keep them safe in childbirth.'

Ellory squints. Worn slivers of cloth are crammed into the bark: secret wishes. 'It's beautiful,' she says.

'A right binding spell,' Jane agrees.

Murray's eyes widen as he watches at the women. If they are interested in the tatty old tree, he is happy to accommodate them though it makes no sense. 'St Enoch's body was buried in the grounds of the church that stood here before this one,' he says. 'Enoch was the mother of St Mungo who is Glasgow's patron saint. She survived a great deal to bear her son. However, the building on the east side of the square is the College of Physicians and Surgeons. It is those gentlemen who will keep Glasgow's mothers safe.'

Ellory appears hypnotised. 'I'll make my first Glasgow calotype of this tree,' she decides.

Murray Urquhart gazes quizzically at his new client. 'Who'd want a picture of an old tree?'

Ellory rounds on him. 'Any woman bearing a child, sir,' she replies.

'The women who tie their buttons there do not have money to buy a calotype,' Murray retorts with a half-laugh.

'You think only poor women fear what will happen when they give birth?' Ellory regards him with a critical eye. 'You've perhaps never known a woman of your own class to perish in the act of motherhood?' Her jaw sets.

Murray is taken aback by her forthright reaction. 'I have, Miss Mann,' he admits. 'Still, I stand that it's the doctors who are best placed to help them.'

Mr Hill would dismiss the tree for the same reason, Ellory thinks. And he'd be wrong too. 'The belief that somebody is on your side is powerful. Men going into war carry totems,' she persists. 'This is the same.'

The solicitor stares at her. He realises he should not have sneered. Did he not have a lucky penny in his pocket when he passed the bar? It is refreshing to be pulled up. Not many women have the nerve. 'I stand corrected,' he concedes with a little bow. 'I apologise.'

Ellory's eyes widen. The excitement has made her bold. Murray tries not to stare at the sheer green of her gaze. He's glad McPhee referred this woman. He can see why he wanted to help her. She is extraordinary. 'Shall we?' he gestures towards a doorway almost directly opposite the college.

Ellory and Jane fall in behind as he rings for the caretaker. Together they climb five storeys through the wally close, towards the light of the cupola. At the top, the caretaker, heaving for breath, turns the lock. Inside, the attic stretches the length of the building.

'It's huge,' Ellory says and does not add that the attic is grander than she expected. It's workmanlike too. The glass panels in the ceiling could have been custom fitted for her purpose. She never dreamed of anything so perfect.

'It faces north,' Murray adds. 'Painter's light.'

Ellory walks in, taking in the details. There are two iron stoves for warmth placed at either end and three small rooms in the gable: an office, a bedroom and a print room, as she immediately names them. She chooses the largest of three for the printing: its tiny window faces south so once she has processed a negative with the shutters closed, she can open them and use the sun to make pictures on the sill. The clock face of the church peers in as if a giant is spying on them.

'It was a manufactory,' Murray says.

A sweatshop, Ellory thinks, but does not say so. 'How much?' she asks.

'Five pounds a year,' the caretaker says reverently. 'There's a water closet on the floor below and a tap on the stair.'

Ellory summons the spirit of her cousin. Jessie might be a prude but she cuts a decent deal. She must make her money stretch. 'I'll pay three pounds and ten shillings cash,' she says firmly and holds out a gloved hand, which the caretaker eyes with suspicion.

'They'd take that, I'd say. Three months up front and monthly thereafter,' he adds brusquely.

Murray Urquhart smiles. Few men among his clients are so decisive, let alone the ladies. 'My goodness, Miss Mann, you're quite the businesswoman. I'll see to your lease, shall I?'

'Yes, please.'

They both linger a moment, neither wanting the exchange to finish. Jane shifts, putting down the carpet-bag on the long wide boards. The caretaker lays the key on a ledge by the door.

'Right then,' he says and disappears into the stairwell.

'I must take my leave too,' Murray announces at length.

Ellory realises she is going to feel forlorn without his reassuring presence. Usually when she speaks her mind she feels guilty afterwards but not with this gentleman. 'I'm sorry I snapped at you,' she says. 'About the tree.'

'You were right, Miss Mann.'

'Do you know where might I find out more about it?' she asks, stretching the conversation. She doesn't usually do that either.

'I'm sure St Winifred wrote about Enoch. There's a subscription library on Buchanan Street,' he offers.

It feels like a sign. It was the photograph of Winifred McPhee that set things off, after all.

'Are there other photographers nearby?'

'One or two. I'll have a Glasgow directory sent up.'

'They produce daguerreotypes, I imagine.'

'I think so.'

'All gentlemen?'

Murray nods.

'We shall be a novelty then. And cheaper,' Ellory says firmly.

Again, he likes her spirit. 'I'll call on you soon with the leasehold papers and to attend to anything else you may need. I'd like to help in any way I can.'

'Thank you, Mr Urquhart.' She holds out her hand and he shakes it. Miss Mann is a breath of fresh air, he thinks. He is already looking forward to seeing what she brings about in this wide empty attic.

As he closes the door, Jane rolls up her sleeves. The mistress has done well, she thinks. She is like her cousin when she has to be. About the money, that is. 'Those stairs will not make us popular with delivery boys.'

Ellory stares at the glass ceiling and the endless grey clouds. 'But the light,' she says.

Jane grins. 'It's perfect, miss.'

Ellory turns her attention to the tasks in hand, which are legion. 'I'll set the camera here. We have space to build two sets, perhaps three. I wonder how people will know we have opened.'

'You must fit a glass box at the front door,' Jane reasons, steadily. 'With pictures showing what's for sale. And the prices. People prefer to know the price. I always thought Mr Hill was too cagey about that.'

Ellory smiles. Jane has a practical streak. 'And perhaps a sign that can be seen from a way off,' she adds. 'We must buy everything. Good-quality paper – Whatman Turkey Mill if we can get it – and chemicals. A camera obscura, of course. And you must have a uniform, Jane.'

Jane laughs.

'You're my assistant now as well as my maid. We must have you turned out,' Ellory insists. 'When sitters come I want them to feel

49

they're in good hands. No foolish frills,' she adds, thinking of the maid in George Square fighting her apron.

Jane's head is not turned by the prospect of a new outfit. She inspects the contents of the cupboard, lifts the bucket and disappears outside to the tap. 'I've flitted before,' she says. 'You have to start clean.'

Alone for only a moment, Ellory feels the silence descend. If they are to sleep here tonight, she must buy mattresses and order something to eat. Then they must set to trade quickly. She will spend her capital fast and will need the return to live on. Looking round she hopes it is possible. After the rent is paid, she will have McPhee's 20 guineas left for the rest. She must stretch it.

I'm here, she thinks, scarce able to believe her luck. She draws herself up as Jane clatters back. 'I'll start with the necessaries,' Ellory says with determination. 'I'll be as quick as I can.'

Chapter Six

The day of the funeral is set for Wednesday. Charlotte paces the drawing room in the morning, peering intermittently onto the deserted green square. Papa's body has gone, his coffin moved into an ornate hearse festooned in black feathers and drawn by three Friesian horses, their coats slicked with oil. Ahead, a single magpie bobs on a branch. 'For sorrow,' Charlotte notes, under her breath. At noon, the Griegs arrive. Dr Grieg takes Charlotte's pulse, uninvited, his fingers cold as dead fish. With a tone verging on disappointment, he pronounces her uncommonly well. 'Don't worry, my dear,' he says, casting a queer look at his wife which indicates the exact opposite.

For a while they sit in the drawing room, until the doctor says the time has come and Charlotte ties on the ruched black silk bonnet that, unbidden, Mrs Grieg procured from the milliner at the bottom of West Regent Street. In the hallway, the mirrors are covered but Charlotte can see in the silver candlesticks that she looks dun and dark. Papa would have hated this. 'The Lord gave us a colourful world,' he said when Reverend Patterson chided him once about the frivolity of his purple frock coat. The minister did not reply but his stare made it clear that, in his view, if the Lord created many colours he did so to test his people. Still, it was difficult to argue with James Nicholl. Especially as he single-handedly procured over 1,000 guineas for the Free Kirk when it split from the Church of Scotland.

'Explain to me why we are better to be free,' Charlotte had asked.

'I believe a congregation should appoint its own minister instead of a lord endowing one. It's a kind of democracy,' her father replied.

Charlotte bowed to his greater knowledge in this as in all things and joined him on Sundays at the Free Kirk where, she noted, with a modicum of surprise, the services and indeed, the minister, were exactly the same as they had always been.

When they reach the Necropolis, foggy skeins wrap round the tree trunks beyond the old cathedral. The rain is so fine it's like silk. Charlotte processes up the path behind the coffin, held aloft by six strangers, a curl of horror gesturing its finger like a nightmarish ghoul as they approach the Nicholls' family plot. With determination Charlotte ignores the hole dug into the clay. It is too final. Ahead, a crowd has gathered. Politely she acknowledges the Bruce family and the McAllisters. Mrs Howarth, flanked by her, husband and daughters, gives a supportive nod. Murray Urquhart manages a smile. 'He was well-loved,' Mrs Grieg whispers, and Charlotte looks beyond the familiar faces to a cluster of older gentlemen in glossy top hats with whom she is not acquainted, some younger men who look like shopkeepers and two soldiers in uniform who bring up the rear. How did Papa come to elicit loyalty from all these strangers?

She's glad they won't hold the service inside. Churches always smell the same: a musty scent of varnished wood and something sweet, which, as a child, she assumed was God. Unaccompanied, in the way of the Free Kirk, those assembled sing the hymns Mrs Greig laboured over choosing, harmonising extempore. The singing is Charlotte's favourite thing about church. The sound is like lace hanging in the air, a fancy she can disappear into. Once the singing is done, Reverend Patterson speaks in glowing terms of a life well lived, ignoring the many doctrinal disagreements he had with James Nicholl. Then Charlotte lays an ivy wreath on the coffin after which it's lowered into the ground. She tries not to cry though her features twist a little. Afterwards, people linger, shaking her hand and offering condolences. She feels 1,000 miles away as Mrs Grieg invites the mourners back to Blythswood Square where refreshment will be served.

One by one they turn down the hill, back to their carriages. Charlotte, however, loiters, unable to leave. It feels as if she is abandoning her father to the thick cold sod. She called him a rock when Mrs Howarth visited, but he was more than that. He was the ground beneath her feet. The person who made the world certain. Papa always knew what to do. The last mourner, she stands alone as the noise reaches her from below of horses' brasses clinking and wooden wheels turning on the setts. Two gravediggers, smoking their pipes under the meagre shelter of a spindly tree, turn away to afford her some privacy. Now only the dead will see her tears, she thinks. But no sooner has she started to cry than a hand curls over her shoulder. It is adorned with a gold signet ring worn over a leather glove. She recoils in horror, swinging round to find the ugly old gentleman she sent away the first night she was alone.

'Don't touch me,' she snaps.

The man bows. 'I apologise. I didn't mean to scare you, Miss Nicholl.'

'You called the evening after my father died.' Her tone is an accusation.

'That was wrong of me,' the old man admits. 'I was shocked when I heard. I knew your father . . . and your mother too,' he adds with an incongruous smile as he hands Charlotte a well-laundered handkerchief. His voice is kind, she notes. His eyes, now that she is close enough to see them, a clouded tawny green. The handkerchief smells faintly of rosemary, for remembrance. 'James Nicholl was a great man who understood the world,' the gentleman continues. 'Your mother was a beauty. She had grit too. In her final days she refused to stay in bed. She had a walking stick with a blade concealed within it. Of course, Glasgow was more dangerous then,' he pronounces. 'Please accept my condolences, Miss Nicholl. Many will be at sea without James's steady guidance.'

Charlotte feels both intrigued and strangely comforted. However, she remains suspicious of this odd old fellow. She did not notice him among the mourners. Was he watching the burial from further up the hill? And if so, why has he approached her now? 'We have not been introduced,' she says, pointing out he has no right to speak to her.

'I'm Lennox. I was an associate of your father's for many years, as well as a friend,' he takes the liberty. 'I'm sorry I called the other evening. It got us off on the wrong foot. I had just arrived in Glasgow, you see, to execute some business I had with your father. I'll raise the matter with his solicitor now. Today I came to pay my respects. God be with you,' he says and inclines his head.

A strange chill snakes through Charlotte's veins, a kind of panic. 'Are you a papist, sir?' she blurts.

Lennox's ugly lips pull into a wide smile. 'I have no faith,' he admits frankly. 'None at all.'

Charlotte blushes. 'You said "God be with you".'

'I hope your god is, Miss Nicholl.' He gives a curt bow. 'Each to their own. Your father believed that. He did not dictate to people.'

This is true, Charlotte thinks, though James Nicholl oftentimes judged. 'I wonder that I have never met you before,' she says.

'Our dealings were in business. Your father chose not to introduce you for that reason, I imagine. I'll raise a glass to him later. *In memoriam*,' Lennox adds. He lets this stand in the air. 'Might I accompany you to your carriage, Miss Nicholl?'

Charlotte hesitates. She knows it is rude not to invite him to Blythswood Square. Besides she is curious. Lennox said he knew her mother.

'Will you come to the house?' she ventures. 'We can raise a glass together.'

At home, Mrs Cullen has organised everything. Tea is served and tiny square cakes glazed with sweet orange jelly. Crystal balloons of brandy are passed on silver trays and the drawing room is awash in black silk so that Charlotte's guests look like silhouettes against the crisp china-blue walls. It is, she realises, the smartest party ever thrown in the house. Her father's gatherings consisted of small groups to play cards after dinner, with Charlotte sent to bed after only a few hands so the men could discuss business. Occasionally James Nicholl had hosted a gathering before the Clyde Regatta or the opera; short and sweet, he always said, with something to go on to. Now he, or rather his death, is the main event. She watches as Mrs Grieg fusses round the room. The old woman pulls Mrs Cullen aside and instructs her. 'Yes ma'am,' Mrs Cullen takes her orders, though Charlotte is glad when the housekeeper is quietly testy with the Griegs' footman, sending him down to fetch more cake. A small act of resistance.

Mrs Grieg, unaware, moves on to Mr Lennox, honing in on the one person in the room she does not have the measure of. 'I've not had the pleasure of meeting you, sir,' she announces, adding with a hint of pride (a sin, Charlotte notes), 'my husband, Dr Grieg is known to you perhaps?'

Mr Lennox shakes his head. 'I don't think so, madam. I'm always in excellent health,' he says drily.

Charlotte's lips widen. Had she been asked to wager when her first smile would break, she would have placed it several months away. There's that, at least, she thinks, though in truth the well-wishers feel too much of a crowd at once, as if she is being pulled down against her will by too strong an undercurrent.

Murray Urquhart is loitering by the windows, puddling the brandy round his glass. 'Don't leave me alone,' Charlotte whispers as she passes, and takes her place in front of the empty chair in which her father always sat, as if in attendance upon his ghost. She has said, 'Thank you for coming,' so many times that the words have ceased to have meaning, and she wonders if that renders them no longer a lie.

'Your congregation is here to help, Charlotte,' Reverend Patterson assures her, placing a hand on her shoulder. He eyes the Howarths as if they are encroaching on his territory. 'We must talk about your future,' he adds ominously.

Charlotte forces a smile. 'Thank you for coming,' she says and he moves on.

At length, the reverend and old Mr Urquhart leave together. Mr Lennox disappears next, after a perfectly paced political round of the room. Then slowly, one after the other, the rest. After an hour, most people have gone, except the Griegs, of course, and Murray by the window, as he promised.

'That went well, my dear,' Dr Grieg declares. Then he promptly sits in the chair James Nicholl used to occupy. Charlotte feels the skin on her neck prickle and has to hold herself back from shouting, 'Get up! That chair is his!'

'Why thank you, dear,' Mrs Grieg says, assuming the mantle of mistress of the house as she plonks herself opposite. Charlotte wonders that the old woman does not unlace her boots.

'Now that's over,' the doctor says, 'we must think of your future, Charlotte.'

'Reverend Patterson is worried,' Mrs Grieg adds. 'People are talking about you living here alone. It's unsuitable for a young lady not to have a guardian.' She casts her eyes towards Murray.

Charlotte's jaw sets, though she does not wish to be rude to the Griegs, however tiresome they may be. Still, it feels irksome that these self-appointed worthies have clearly been discussing her with no thought to her own wishes. 'Yes, Patterson mentioned the same,' she says and is about to add something about being tired when, sensing her irritation, Murray comes to her rescue. 'Miss Nicholl has a great deal to see to,' he says. 'We've not yet read her father's will. She'll have little time to spend on gossip over the coming weeks, Mrs Grieg, and I'm sure you agree, her actions should not be fired by tittle-tattle anyway. The minister would not want that, surely.'

Charlotte manages a smile. 'We ought to get on,' she says, and sensing an out, she adds, 'You may read the will to me now, Murray.'

'Now? Are you sure?' Murray asks.

'Please.'

The young lawyer acquiesces. 'I have the document,' he says. 'I brought it in case. Shall we sit by the window?'

Both turn to stare at the Griegs who, it seems, have no sense of boundaries. There is a moment's awkward silence, but when no invitation to stay is forthcoming, the doctor and his wife rise, Mrs Grieg fussing as she drives out the footman and one of the maids ahead of her. 'I'll be back tomorrow,' she says, 'to help.'

Murray and Charlotte listen to them going down the stairs and out of the front door. Charlotte checks at the window as Mrs Grieg leads her husband the long way round the square, the old woman's short black cape bouncing in a jaunty fashion quite at odds with the solemnity of the afternoon. Her husband trundles behind, swinging his ebony cane as if he has no notion of the shortcut through the gardens where, above the lawn, stark budded twigs move in the wind, as if conducting an orchestra.

'You don't need to read the will today,' Murray says.

'I want to,' Charlotte replies.

He fetches his leather briefcase and they sit down.

'I'll summarise,' the lawyer starts. James Nicholl's will is far from standard and Murray has been considering over the last few days how he might best present this to his friend. He does not want to distress her. 'The bulk of the estate bar three bequests goes to you, unencumbered,' he says. The good news first of all.

'Me?' Charlotte's mouth feels dry. She had some notion that Mr Urquhart would manage her father's estate as a trustee. That she would be given an allowance. Since turning 18, she has received 240 guineas a year, though she rarely manages to spend all of it.

Murray reads from the parchment. 'To my daughter, Charlotte Margaret Nicholl. There. To you.'

'There's no entail?' she checks, seeking a limit. The kind of trusteeship everyone expects.

'None. You are of age and have legal competence,' Murray announces.

Charlotte's cheeks flame. Murray lays the will on the table. 'Are you all right, Charlotte?'

'Father did not prepare me is all. What if I make a mistake? I might lose everything.' Her heart is racing at the responsibility.

'You'd have to do tremendously badly,' Murray says gently, making light as usual. 'As your father's solicitor, my father ought to run you through the investments. There are a couple of things you'll need to deal with. He'll explain. It might not be entirely as you expect.'

Charlotte bites her lip. Old Mr Urquhart is always stony-eyed. 'I'd rather it was you who told me,' she says. 'What are the bequests?'

Murray's eyes fall to the parchment. 'The Church, of course: 100 sterling. And some money to be divided among the servants. He provided 24 guineas for his valet, Mr Boots, and 12 for Mrs Cullen. And a gift to Mrs Grieg of the ormolu clock she always admired in the day room.'

'I see,' Charlotte says, battling a flash of anger, for this bequest legitimises the Griegs' overbearing interest in her.

'He knew the Griegs would want to look after you, I suppose,' Murray continues. 'You see, you're not an orphan, Charlotte. You're an heiress. We shall sort it all out, you'll see.'

Charlotte does not ask what sorting it out will entail. Instead, she begins to cry. She had not expected this. Unfazed by her emotional outburst, Murray calmly hands her a white cotton handkerchief and she wonders if she will ever stop bursting into tears? Will it always be like this? Feeling at sea?

'Perhaps some laudanum?' Murray offers but she shakes her head. She will bear it without medicine. 'Your father was something of a financial genius,' he continues. 'I've been reading his papers. It's extraordinary. He never put a step wrong. Every stock. Every parcel of land. For years. It's as if he knew what was going to make money. But two years ago, he sold almost everything.' He sounds puzzled.

Charlotte takes a gulp of air. 'The railway stock, you mean?'

Murray nods. There is something amiss. She can see it in his eyes. 'Perhaps we should fetch my father. He administered your father's portfolio. He's best placed to answer your questions.'

Charlotte pauses. ' "We'll sort it out",' he'd said.

'All right,' she replies. 'Walk round and get him, would you?'

'I can send someone.'

'I'd like a minute to take it in.' It surprises her how accustomed she is becoming to taking charge.

'Of course.' Murray bows in that queer way of his.

Alone, Charlotte gets up and stands by the fireplace. Her gaze flits over the walls, resting on a portrait her father commissioned of her, standing by a rosebush when she was 15. Flat white blooms of Rosa arvensis. She had become a debutante not long after the portrait was made. Charlotte shudders at the memory. Other girls were always excited when they talked about parties, balls, suitors and weddings, but being out in society did not suit Charlotte and after only a few weeks, her father let her make her own schedule, as long as it fell in with his plans. 'You'll marry when you're ready,' he said. She had been unable to explain to him that the problem was not her age, it was that marriage did not interest her. She cannot bear the little touches that others find normal. The proximity of people and their endless expectations. The messy business of childbirth is beyond her imagination, not to mention the hold that a man has over his wife. And all to be mistress of a home. Yet today, she realises she has achieved that milestone and as a result has even less need of society than ever. Is this perhaps why Papa bequeathed her everything? So she could look after herself? He knew her better than she realised. Still, she cannot imagine a life where she will be completely alone.

Idly, she moves to the satinwood table and picks up the will. A red legal ribbon is attached with a thick blob of wax. The parchment is thick and the clerk's script tidy. The words are mostly Latin but that poses little problem to Charlotte. She leafs through the pages stopping at the codex, translating as she goes. 'Nobody other than those concerned (not to include my daughter, Charlotte Margaret Nicholl) is to be informed, but the other half of my estate, including Helensburgh House and its contents, is to be endowed upon the occupant residing at the property.'

Charlotte puts down the manuscript abruptly. Then, heart racing, she picks it up again and rereads the words, making sure she has translated correctly. She has never heard of Helensburgh House. *The other half of my estate.* Charlotte's hands feel clammy and her stomach shifts. She turns over the will to see if there is anything to illuminate this final, inexplicable sentence that has, by her father's command, been withheld from her, but finds nothing. She tries to reason with her racing thoughts. Papa after all might leave whatever he had to whomever he liked. She supposes he could pick a name out of a hat. *The occupant of Helensburgh House.* Her mind turns to Murray. How can he have kept this secret from her? His face showed no sign as he read from the paper. Is this what he meant by matters being complicated?

Mrs Cullen interrupts, appearing on the threshold. 'Miss Charlotte,' she says, 'there remains one guest. Downstairs.'

'A guest?'

'In the study, miss.'

Charlotte rises. Already alarmed, this feels like another intrusion. Why can't people simply leave her alone? Who on earth feels they have the right to simply wander about her house? Charlotte's temper lit, she descends the stairs, swinging into her father's sanctum to challenge the trespasser. She draws herself up as the man raises his eyes.

'What on earth are you doing?' she snaps. It is Mr Lennox. Of course it is. He is seated at the mahogany desk, quite at home. Is this why he spoke to her after the funeral, insinuating an invitation? Has he duped her? 'Well?' she presses her point.

Lennox looks faintly annoyed at being disturbed. 'I did not wish to bother you,' he says. 'Business.' He gestures vaguely. 'I've always liked this room.' He sits back in the chair.

'You've been here before?' She does not recall any such visit.

'Many times, though too late at night for a young lady to be up,' Lennox replies. 'It's a man's room, isn't it?'

She shifts in annoyance at being dismissed in this way. Things have been moved. The jar of spills on the mantel and some books that were on the side table propped now on the shelf. Lennox has been searching for something.

'I'm my father's heir,' she says defiantly. 'This is my room now, sir. If there's something you want, you may ask me.'

Mr Lennox smiles. 'It doesn't surprise me that he left his estate to you. He was never a conventional man. I admired that about him.'

'And yet you have rifled his things.' She feels herself expanding as she says the words.

Lennox looks as if he is about to admit something, but the bell sounds at the front door, followed by an energetic rap that echoes in the hallway, and instead of talking, Lennox gets to his feet.

'I should go,' he says.

'Yes,' she agrees. 'And I'd prefer if you did not return. I don't appreciate you searching my father's things. You might raise any business matter outstanding with my solicitor.'

Lennox pauses, then bows formally as Mrs Cullen glides across the hallway to answer the bell. 'Good day, Miss Nicholl,' he says as if she had not just berated him. 'My apologies and my sympathy for your loss.'

As he pushes past the Urquharts and smartly down the steps, Charlotte's mind races. She rifles the papers that are laid out, to ascertain what Lennox was looking for but there is nothing unusual. Mr Urquhart contracted all her father's business, and neither he nor Murray showed any sign today of having met Mr Lennox before. But then Murray smoothly concealed the clause about the occupant of Helensburgh House earlier. Perhaps the Urquharts do know Lennox and have concealed that too. She is wary of asking. If Lennox was searching the study, it must mean there is evidence of her father's business there. Something she might find herself if she looks for it. *Helensburgh House.*

She is interrupted in her thoughts by Murray appearing at the study door. 'Charlotte,' he says, 'would you prefer to talk here?'

Charlotte shakes her head. Her heart feels as if it is not beating to her own rhythm any more. She thought he was her friend. 'We should go up,' she says.

'Are you all right?'

'I feel closer to him in the study,' she adds, for it is clear she must play her cards close. She should not have read the will, but it is too late for regrets.

Murray ushers in his father, who kisses her hand and says, 'My dear Miss Nicholl, are you sure you are ready to have these conversations?'

Charlotte takes a moment to compose herself. If Murray shows no sign, she will not do so either. 'I must see to my own business, Mr Urquhart,' she says. And as she settles on the blue velvet sofa upstairs to hear the details of what she now knows is only half of her father's fortune, she suddenly realises that sweet smell in the church isn't God at all. It's the smell of honey that is tainted.

Chapter Seven

Saturday, 28 March 1846

When Murray delivers the lease to Miss Ellory Mann at St Enoch's Square, he is impressed by the changes she has made. At the front door a glass box displays a print of Edinburgh Castle on sale for four shillings and another of two urchins sitting on a muddy lawn marked at only four. He regards the image carefully. It is quite charming. And below it a sign: *Miss Ellory Mann, Photographer. Lately assistant to Mr David Octavius Hill. Enquire top floor. Commissions welcome.*

Murray takes the stairs at a bound and arrives in the studio to find Jane, the maid, almost unrecognisable. She is attired in a thick leather apron over a practical green day dress and long brown pigskin gloves. She curtsies, silently takes his hat and hands him a cup of beer as he catches his breath.

'Mr Urquhart.' Ellory greets him with a smile, emerging from the office. She too has changed. There is something matter-of-fact about her well-made brown gown and the demure low bun of flaming hair fixed at the nape of her neck. A pencil acts as a barrette, holding it in place. He feels suddenly proud of the transformation all around him and has to remind himself that he has played little part in it. 'What do you think of the studio?' Ellory asks, her nose crinkling. He will come to realise that this tiny movement denotes Miss Mann's nervousness when she awaits confirmation of something she has done. He does not know it, but her nose also crinkles the moment before a picture emerges on the paper.

Murray looks round. It's as bright as the first day he brought the women here, but the place has been scrubbed so clean that a speck of dust would stand out. Three sets are assembled under the long windows: a dark velvet curtain, a formal backdrop painted to look like a garden, and a fancy screen. In the middle of the room a pine table and chairs are set with a workmanlike box of powders and salves, a mirror propped to one side and a portfolio case. At the far end an old oak wardrobe, which took three men more than an hour to heave up the stairs, lies open, revealing a shawl and two hats. Beyond, the three small rooms show signs of similar transformation. In the office a small desk and chair now sit in front of the safe, papers piled neatly. The room next to it has been painted dark brown.

'What have you done, Miss Mann?' Murray asks, pointing at the wall.

'Am I not permitted?' Ellory replies, nervous she has done something wrong.

Murray smiles. 'It's allowed – as soon as you've signed, that is. I wonder the purpose is all.'

Ellory looks shy. 'I thought to darken it. That's the print room. I'm not sure what the effect will be, but light spoils the negatives when they are being made.'

'How clever. I think you have made the place quite splendid,' Murray declares, and he feels a curl of excitement.

Ellory lifts the contract and begins to read. At length she says, 'I'll sign,' and removes to the office for a quill and ink.

'Let me witness it.' Murray follows her.

'Then the place will be mine?'

'For a year, Miss Mann. Renewable at your request. Is there anything more I can do?'

Ellory looks across the desk as if she is going to say something, but she halts.

64

'Go on,' Murray encourages her.

'I don't yet have a camera,' she admits with a small laugh at the ridiculousness of this state of affairs.

'But the prints at the door?'

'I made those in Edinburgh. I've sold two of the castle already. It's a promising sign. But I need a camera as a matter of urgency. It seems one must order from London. It takes weeks and the cost . . .' Ellory raises her eyes to the coombed ceiling at which she sat staring for some hours the night before. Setting up the studio has been costlier than she guessed and now she cannot afford a camera: not a new one anyway. Some photographer I am, she sneered, and tried not to picture Jessie's face. 'I thought to find a camera second-hand,' she says diplomatically. 'I heard there's a possibility at Glasgow Observatory.'

'But you're nervous to go alone?' Murray guesses, for the observatory is open at night.

A peach blush lights Ellory's freckled cheek. 'Yes,' she admits, though it is not only that. The camera is priced in guineas. She has never bought anything in guineas before. It feels like a Rubicon and she has only just enough in her purse to cover it. She would like somebody she can trust to go with her. Someone more accustomed to such transactions.

'I'll come for you this evening,' Murray reassures her. 'I'd like to help. You'll have your camera, Miss Mann. It will be my pleasure,' he adds and wonders if he is too forward.

*

That night the moon is a mouse's tail. Only a sliver. Murray's carriage waits on the square, the horses braying as their breath clouds the spring air. Ellory pulls on her coat and hat in the studio while he waits. 'Is it far to the observatory?' she asks.

'Horselet Hill? Not half an hour,' he assures her. He remembers as a child the huge telescope leaving Garnethill when the city's sky became too tainted by gaslight for it to function any longer. The cart that carried it had a gentleman on each corner all the way to Dowhill, to hold the thing steady. Now the university has moved its facilities again for the same reason. Murray has not visited the new site. Ellory fetches her reticule. There is not as much money left as she would like, though the sale of the castle prints has restocked some of her spent shillings.

The route up Buchanan Street and along Sauchiehall Street affords her first sight of Glasgow's famed westwards development. As if they are tourists, Murray points out the stucco houses on Bath Street and the sandstone double-fronted Georgian mansions of Garnethill. 'Edinburgh makes much of its hills, the Athens of the North, but Glasgow has its fair share,' he says. The buildings become less frequent at Woodside, though there are pretty crescents to the left through the trees.

'I can see why people find it pleasant to live here,' Ellory says, taking it in. This city can change in a block, she thinks. One thing to another. She likes that Murray is proud of the place.

Eventually there are no more gas lamps on the street and the carriage rumbles on through darkness, climbing the unlit pebble-strewn path to the observatory at the top of Horselet Hill. 'It belongs to the university,' Murray informs her as they pass the gates. 'They are laying out a botanic garden nearby to replace the old one on Sauchiehall Street. I believe there are to be extensive hothouses. It's taking a long time for there is a good deal of work in it. They've said it'll be open to all during the Glasgow Fair. You might like to take pictures, I suppose.'

'Of the plants?'

'Why not? Ladies are accustomed to making botanical sketches.'

She considers a moment. She had not thought of this as an outlet for her work. 'Thank you. I'll look into it,' she says.

The coachman pulls up and Murray hands Ellory down. Her tan boots are brought to such a high shine that little stars bounce from them reflected from the gaslit lamp outside. The building is low and wide, larger than Miss Short's observatory in Edinburgh but the same shape. A burst of laughter emerges from within, gentlemen gathered.

Murray opens the door and a whiff of tobacco and warm air escapes. Ellory's palms are sweating now and her fingers feel weak. If she does not buy the camera tonight, she will not be taking pictures of botanical specimens or anything else. But if she secures it, it will be the most money she has ever spent on anything.

Inside, a footman takes their things. 'I sent a note,' Murray says and gives his name.

The man bids them wait and disappears. Through a wide glass pane in the door, Ellory peers at the main room. It is not unlike a library though fitted with more brass equipment. Three gentlemen, two in evening dress, sit round a mahogany table while the other lounges in a leather observing chair with his eye to a huge telescope that pokes through the roof. To one side an assistant is decanting a bottle of port, taking care not to let slip any sediment from the sieve. He ferries the decanter to the table where the gentlemen pour for themselves, still smoking. The footman whispers in a man's ear.

'Murray Urquhart,' the fellow says and gets to his feet. 'Bring him in.'

The gentlemen rise at the sight of Ellory. One of them slaps Murray on the hunch of his shoulder in greeting, like a long-lost friend. 'Urquhart,' he says. 'Good to see you. You've come about the camera obscura? And who is this?'

Murray presents the gentleman. 'Miss Ellory Mann, this is Mr Gordon Thompson,' he says, and she feels her heart race. To introduce a man to a woman, rather than the other way round, marks her as a lady.

'How do you do,' she manages.

'Good heavens,' Mr Thompson bows, his silk evening scarf slipping down his jacket as if even his clothes are surprised. 'Am I right? Is the camera for you, Miss Mann?'

Ellory nods. She wants to live up to Murray's confidence in her. She lets out a shy smile.

Thompson laughs. 'Capital. I can teach you how to use it.'

'That won't be necessary, Gordie,' Murray cuts in, clearly enjoying his friend's surprise. 'Miss Mann was trained by David Octavius Hill, you see.'

There is a moment's absolute silence. 'I know Hill,' the gentleman who is not wearing evening dress ventures. He is a self-contained fellow with tidy clothes, plain mulberry and navy. His shoes, Ellory notes, are well cared for. 'He's an excellent fellow. He wants to photograph the view from Edinburgh Castle, though the photographic process cannot catch it yet,' the gentleman adds.

'Miss Mann?' Murray passes the comment to her as if it were a question.

'In fact,' she says, 'there are methods for capturing such images; grand views, I mean. But you are correct, sir, they're not perfected. It will be great progress being able to represent the world as it is, not waiting for an artist but using lenses. Mr Hill and Mr Adamson are adamant that photography is an art not a science, but I'm not so sure. In my experience, it's all in the processing.'

Mr Thompson's face is a picture. Murray feels inordinately proud that Miss Mann is so unusually spirited. He lets the silence hang another second before asking. 'Might we see the camera for sale?'

They are taken to another room, where the camera is laid out on a leather-topped desk. Ellory makes an examination, her gloved fingers nimble. She opens the back and checks the lens. It is German, she surmises. Perhaps four or five years old. The stand is broken but can be mended. New, a decent camera would cost 20 guineas at least. This one is priced a modest 13, which will nonetheless leave her with so little that if she does not sell a print tomorrow, she and Jane will not eat.

'The box is only pine,' Mr Thompson admits. 'The lens belonged to the observatory at Garnethill and was reset. It's not British-made. There's another in the box, smaller. It was a masterpiece, I suppose. We can throw that in as a curiosity, if you like.'

Ellory raises her eyes. Her nose crinkles. The Germans produce excellent lenses and she does not care what wood the box is fashioned from. She can fix the stand. However, she does not say any of this, affecting to be deep in thought instead. It is what Jessie does when she wants a particularly large discount and is, in Ellory's experience, an excellent negotiating tactic. She has to buy the camera for less if she can. 'I wonder, Mr Thompson, if the observatory might accept ten guineas and ten shillings?' she says at length. 'It's closer to what I have, you see.'

Thompson shifts in embarrassment. He has never in his life been short of money. The camera has been languishing for several weeks. The pine box put off one or two buyers who preferred mahogany and it will always be clear that the stand was broken, even if it is repaired. Miss Mann is interesting, he thinks, and 13 was perhaps a tad ambitious. 'Of course,' he says. 'Ten guineas and ten shillings will do fine.'

Ellory feels herself flush, part embarrassment, part relief. She shakes his hand. 'Thank you,' she says warmly. 'I appreciate it, Mr Thompson. Truly I do.'

'Well, that's set then,' Murray says.

Thompson takes her coin and gives it to one of the assistants to put in the purser's office. Then they return to the main room where they are offered a glass of port, which they refuse. These gentlemen, Ellory realises, are rarely in bed before sunrise. Alight with energy, they discuss the craters of the moon and Mr Naysmith's ambition to photograph them. She finds herself smiling at their enthusiasm. 'Do you consider it possible to photograph the moon, Miss Mann?' Mr Thompson asks.

She feels a rush of energy at him asking her opinion. 'Everything is possible, sir. It is only a matter of innovation and of time.'

He offers to let her look through the telescope and, flattered, she sits in the chair as Murray chats amiably with the fellow who is not dressed for dinner. She is glad he came with her. His introduction has made everything easy. He has been a protector of sorts.

'You have the hang of that too, I see,' Mr Thompson says as she puts the telescope to her eye.

'Mr Hill's studio is close to Miss Short's observatory on Calton Hill,' she admits. 'I've viewed the sky through the telescope there.' She does not add that the assistant, Lewis, was her friend and sneaked her in on quiet evenings, for Miss Short herself would not have admitted a woman of her class. In return for her showing him the darkroom, Lewis also taught her to use a sextant. 'This is how to find your way,' he said. And now, unexpectedly, she has.

'Well,' says Murray at length. 'Shall I accompany you back to town, Miss Mann?'

They are donning their coats in the hallway when a small gentleman in a top hat as long as his forearm appears at the door. 'Rutherford,' Thompson greets him, not as enthusiastically as he greeted Murray. 'Miss Mann, this is Mr Rutherford,' he adds. 'He's a photographer too.'

Rutherford cradles his hat in the crook of his arm as an awkward father might hold a baby. 'Miss Mann? Miss Ellory Mann?' he says as if her name is an accusation.

'Good evening, sir.'

'You've opened a studio on St Enoch's Square?'

'Yes, sir.'

The man makes a sound that indicates he does not approve. 'You're taking the art out of photography, madam, with your female subject matter and your four-shilling prints. I make daguerreotypes,' he spits. 'None of your scaffy calotypes in my portfolio.'

'I see,' Ellory says, her cheeks colouring. She had almost forgotten she doesn't belong here. She must remain polite, she thinks. 'Where's your studio, sir?'

'Buchanan Street,' Rutherford replies testily, clearly thinking she ought to know.

'We're neighbours then,' she tries. She dare not look at Murray or at Mr Thompson. Jessie would pillory her for less criticism than this from a gentleman. She would not be allowed to deal with a customer for a week.

Rutherford looks down his nose. 'You demean our expertise, madam,' he says, 'by charging so little.'

And with that he stalks into the observatory. Neither Thompson nor Murray says anything. Ellory feels sick. Then Murray laughs. 'Mr Michael Rutherford,' he mimics. 'Artist photographer.' And he gives an elaborate and ridiculous bow. 'It's Miss Mann who's the artist, Thompson,' he adds. 'She'll be taking Glasgow's best photographs from now on. I'm not surprised Rutherford's disquieted. Miss Mann is extremely talented.'

Ellory's heart feels as if it has only just started beating, the relief of an unfurling flower. Nobody has ever stood up for her like that, against a gentleman too.

'Och, the man's a terrible gowk.' Thompson says dismissively.

Glancing at Murray, Ellory offers Thompson her hand. 'Thank you,' she says.

'The world is full of fascinations, Miss Mann. We can only seek to master them,' Thompson says, cheerfully.

Outside, they bundle into the coach and Murray wedges the camera in beside him. Ellory nestles opposite contentedly. 'You did well at 10 guineas and 10,' he says. 'You drive a fine bargain, Miss Mann. First the rental and now this.'

'I'm close to an empty purse,' she admits. 'But I have everything I need now and enough left to provision us a few days. Thanks for your help, Mr Urquhart.'

Murray takes this in. Does she mean she has only enough to buy food? He cannot conceive of it. Miss Mann is brave to hazard so much of her capital. The gentlemen inside the observatory are dabblers by contrast. He feels a sting of respect. 'Call me Murray, please,' he offers. 'I'll suggest to some of my friends they have a portrait taken, shall I?'

Ellory's face lights in a smile he has not seen before. 'That's kind of you.' She can hardly wait. 'Now I can make as many pictures as I want to,' she says.

Chapter Eight

It is not quite a week since the funeral, and as Charlotte wakes, the distant sound of hammering from the building sites beyond Sauchiehall Street drowns out the pigeons. The air smells faintly of Purbeck stone, the dust's sweet odour distinctive. Her maid has lit the fire but not yet opened the curtains, and in the half-light Charlotte gets up barefoot. Papa is gone. He will always be gone. How many times will it sink in, only for her to forget?

She has business to see to. But the first thing is to get dressed. Then to eat. Mrs Cullen has changed breakfast. Papa preferred fish in the morning. Lobster and shucked oysters; a habit he got used to over many years doing deals on boats at the slipway. Now the oyster plate no longer lies on the sideboard, replaced by buttered eggs and warm bannock. Instead of tea, Mrs Cullen has drinking chocolate set out, a treat that was erstwhile served only on Sundays in the Nicholl household. 'To fortify us through Reverend Patterson's sermon,' her father always said, a twinkle in his eye. The house-keeper is mollycoddling her mistress, opening the door, fetching parcels rather than the maids doing it. It is her way of caring, and Charlotte lets her.

Every day since the burial, Charlotte has dedicated herself to understanding her situation. When he arrived with Murray to explain matters, old Mr Urquhart brought a sheaf of papers.

'The thing is, my dear, I cannot see what your father has done with the rest of his money,' he admitted, his forehead wrinkling gently, the closest she has ever seen to him looking worried.

'What do you mean?'

Urquhart swung round a small ledger: her father's account book with his firm.

'He sold his railway shares and a large swathe of property two years ago next month,' Urquhart said, reading the column upside down. 'He made almost 20,000 guineas.' The old lawyer raised an eyebrow. 'A handsome profit. But he didn't reinvest. He sent no instructions. Is there a safe in the house?'

'There's no safe here. Do you mean he had all this in cash?'

'He must have. I enquired at his bank, but he held no deposit box there, though his account is in credit, of course.' Nimbly Mr Urquhart swung the book back like some kind of magician. 'Less the sum of Mr Nicholl's cash bequests, it amounts to 507 sovereigns, 18 shillings and 9 pence. That sum is yours now. The bank will allow you to draw on it. And you have the house and contents, of course.'

Charlotte felt suddenly unsteady. Five hundred and seven sovereigns, eighteen shillings and ninepence was not enough to live on indefinitely in a five-bedroomed house on Blythswood Square, with nine staff and running a two-horse carriage. She has a little of her own: almost 90 guineas, saved from the excess in her allowance. But still.

'What did he do with the rest?' she asked faintly.

Mr Urquhart leaned in as if sharing a confidence. 'I hoped you might know, Miss Nicholl.'

Charlotte thought she might be sick. She must have gone pale because Murray poured a balloon of sherry and handed it to her. She took a sip and set it on the table. 'Good heavens,' she managed. 'What a lot to disappear. It does . . . not seem like him.'

She restrained herself from asking about Helensburgh House, though, she reasoned, Urquhart would not have told her about the money at all if it was in the possession of the property's mysterious occupant, who according to the terms of the will, must be allocated a similar 500-sovereign sum.

'I must consider what to do,' she said, though the truth was she had no clue and could scarcely grasp that her father had left her in this situation. Surely, she thought, he would have resolved the matter, if he had lived.

'Well, for a start, Mr Boots can go,' Murray suggested. 'You don't need a butler as well as a housekeeper. With your father no longer with us, there are no valeting duties.'

This would save a few pounds, and Boots had his bequest to see him right. But it would take more than that. Charlotte's mind raced. 'Perhaps I'll invest the capital,' she said.

Old Mr Urquhart's eyes were like mine shafts down which the whole world might disappear. 'What would you like to invest in, my dear?'

Charlotte's fingers fluttered. She clasped her hands in her lap. This was Papa's territory and he had not left any kind of map. 'I don't know,' she admitted. Briefly she imagined selling the house and moving to something smaller. She knows it may come to that, but her skin prickles at what Glasgow will say.

'You need to agree a good marriage, my girl,' Mr Urquhart said, eyeing her intently. 'A lad with some business sense from a family you can trust.'

Murray set a sideways glance at his father that would freeze a summer puddle. 'You need not do anything hasty, Charlotte,' he countered firmly.

By nine o'clock, every morning since this meeting, she has been in the study behind Papa's desk. She feels close to him in his old lair, which smells of whisky and woodsmoke and a little of pine; the soap he preferred for bathing. The pine is fading now. She started to search the room immediately after the Urquharts left, looking for whatever Mr Lennox had sought there and reading her father's papers: dull correspondence, illegible notes and calculations. She has found a few shares in an ochre pit in the Mendips, quarter of a small

75

distillery run by the Haig family and a 12-per-cent share in a seed merchant near Kew. It is all most welcome and will provide a further 380 sovereigns in capital but, as Murray said, she will need to cut her cloth.

Mr Boots leaves, having packed her father's clothes using a boxful of cedarwood slabs to keep off the moths. She instructs the coachman to sell the old carriage and one of the bays and find her a second-hand one-horse conveyance, which might, after all, be considered smarter. It will take more than these small changes, but beyond them she is lost. She never minded being solitary before, but now she feels lonely. Papa's absence has opened a vast chasm. She must look after herself: a revolutionary notion.

At first, she expected Sunday to be the worst, but Reverend Patterson did not mention James Nicholl from the pulpit, and as most of the congregation was at the burial, their respects were already paid. Charlotte was simply greeted with a 'How are you, Miss Nicholl?' Afterwards, it was drizzling, and nobody dallied outside the Kirk's new chapel on St Vincent's Lane but strode purposefully into waiting carriages as they commented on the weather. 'At least there's no wind. Last month in that terrible storm, my Hanway turned inside out,' a lady confided and pressed Charlotte's arm. He is gone, she thought, and nobody but me cares any longer.

After, she tarried on the pavement in the rain. Papa always had a plan, but what might it be? Every day she has dodged Mrs Grieg's increasingly pointed enquiries about her future and has managed to avoid Reverend Patterson's afternoon visits by hiding in her room and instructing Mrs Cullen to say she is out visiting one young lady or another. She does not want to directly address the contention that her living alone is unsuitable. That anybody might call on her. That she is vulnerable. She knows she is vulnerable, of course. Just not in the way the reverend assumes. She is financially vulnerable. That is the rub.

Above the arch of the church's door, Charlotte watched three blackbirds perched on the edge of the roof, glossy in their mourning garb. Then her eyes fell to Reverend Patterson in the doorway, his expression as dark as a biblical curse. Smartly, she mounted the carriage and ordered the coachman to take her home. Catching sight of herself in the mirror in the hall, her coat as black as the wee birds, Charlotte wished she could fly away, across the blank grey sky, over the Campsie Hills and the icy Irish Sea. Beside Papa's chair in the study, his walking sticks remained. She always trusted that she was the most important thing to her father, but Helensburgh House has put paid to that. Another kind of lady might fill this emerging void with social calls or ignore the ledgers on the desk. Not Charlotte Nicholl.

After lunch, it has become that she and Mrs Grieg promenade in the garden amid the daffodils. Charlotte readies herself in advance now, wearing the inky silk bonnet and a black coat that covers what the doctor's wife no doubt considers unsuitable attire; blue taffeta skirts with purple woollen bodices. People have such superficial expectations. Charlotte had not understood how much her father's presence shielded her from society. How much he truly provided: her friend amid a world of acquaintances. How could he leave her unprovided for? And what on earth did he do with the money from the railway shares?

On the afternoon when everything changes, it is damp but not raining. Mrs Grieg cups Charlotte's elbow to steer her along the path. 'The doctor and I are concerned,' she says.

'Father left me well enough provided for,' Charlotte replies defensively. She does not want to face Mrs Grieg's undoubted panic at the changes she will have to make. Getting rid of Boots did not need to be explained but what is coming will be more comprehensive – at least four more of the staff, and money to be raised from selling the house and moving somewhere smaller.

Mrs Grieg purses her lips. 'It's only that you are living alone, Charlotte. That is the thing,' she says. She has never felt that Charlotte accepted her as a kind of aunt, which is the role she had hoped to step into when Maggie Nicholl died. Now

James's death has provided another opportunity to fill what she sees as a vacancy.

'It has not been a week,' Charlotte sighs and then proffers, 'Perhaps I will engage a companion. Would that make you more comfortable?' The truth is, she has no intention of welcoming a stranger into her home, but saying so will buy time. A slim smile flickers on her lips, like a guttering candle, for it is not as if she is having to fend off admirers. People sense her natural separation and do not intrude.

'I can enquire,' Mrs Grieg offers.

'No, thank you,' Charlotte replies firmly. 'I shall choose for myself. I'm still grieving,' she adds.

'People are talking,' Mrs Grieg says.

Charlotte is well aware of this. The neighbours, the congregation and the servants too – she heard the coachman gossiping with one of the maids in the backyard about the change of carriage. It is not that people are unkind, but more that an unmarried woman living alone is a peculiarity, and Charlotte is an heiress to boot, though not as rich an heiress as everybody assumes. She has made the calculations during her time at her father's desk. The money might last two or three years in her current circumstances, but not much longer. She has no way to earn more. Daily she resolves to take charge of her situation, but doing so will make a huge public statement, and it has crossed her mind that it might be easier to simply allow matters to peter out, selling her father's things one by one, letting one maid go and then another. It would give her four years that way. Perhaps even five. She has never had to think like this before. The feeling is as uncomfortable as an ill-fitting corset. It's too soon, she tells herself, to make such decisions.

'With your father gone, I imagine you're thinking of marriage,' Mrs Grieg says wistfully. 'A girl of your age.'

Charlotte momentarily cannot speak. 'I must be out of black first,' she manages.

'I always thought you and Murray Urquhart were a good match,' the old woman continues blithely. 'You seem easy in each other's company. I mind the pair of you at the summer ball the year before he left for London. He's a lawyer now, like his father,' she adds as if it is a biblical lesson. 'You'd make a good pair.'

She means we're both odd, Charlotte thinks. Murray with his hunchback and she, awkward in company, not like other young ladies. She cannot imagine marrying anybody, not least Murray, whom she considers a friend.

'Day to day it's a comfort to have a man at your table. And in your bed,' Mrs Grieg adds, trying to draw the girl out with this confidence.

Charlotte shudders. Watching other girls dancing, a man's hand on their waist, induces a cold kind of panic. She breaks free of the old woman's grip as they round the corner. 'Murray is seeing to my business. That's all,' she says.

'You could do worse, you know, than become Mrs Urquhart,' Mrs Grieg insists. 'There are no nuns in the Free Kirk, Charlotte. It's a lady's duty to have a family.'

Charlotte holds back. It would be unkind of her to point out that Mrs Grieg has not had any children. Still, the doctor's wife is not giving up. 'Mary Howarth was seen arm and arm with a young gentleman last week. Some fellow from Northumberland. He's Right Honourable, I believe. The Howarths will be making an announcement soon, no doubt. Several girls of your age are already bouncing babies on their knee.'

'I'm in mourning,' Charlotte repeats, her fingers weak at the thought as she flexes them. Her chest tightening. 'Papa has only just died,' she adds. Mourning or not, she will never consider it. No matter what happens. She tries to hold her features in check as they take another turn of the park, but she cannot help glancing at the windows on all sides, wondering how many people are watching. Will she be forced into marriage due to penury? If the money simply runs out, what will she do? At the gate she breaks away, managing to restrain herself from running. 'I've a great deal to see to,' she says. 'You must excuse me.'

Back in the study, she as good as falls into the chair at Papa's desk, her fingers flying across its surface. She straightens his box of cigars, the letter knife, blotter and inkwell. She must resolve the mystery of the missing money. She will set herself to it. She is sure Papa must have had a plan. The frustration of not knowing what it was stings. She wishes he had confided in her about his financial intentions. He knew how awkward she was in company, that any suggestion of romance horrified her. Surely he did not expect her to marry her way out of this problem. Or did he? She has no idea about anything any longer. Except that she was a child only a few days before, entertained easily by her father's attentions, content shopping in town, and riding in the carriage, going to recitals in well-appointed drawing rooms, playing a hand of canasta and occasionally being taken to a ball where she enjoyed the music. Why did Papa not share his interests if he intended her to inherit them? Is the occupant of Helensburgh House in the same position? What on earth is she supposed to do?

Determined to find a different perspective she moves to the far corner of the room. She has searched every inch of the study now, taking each book from its shelf, opening every drawer, even checking behind the velvet cushions on the leather chairs, but the room remains a puzzle she is yet to crack, though there is one place that remains unexplored: the drinks tray set on a small lacquer table. Now she approaches it. There is nothing unexpected: a crystal decanter of whisky and another of brandy, each with its own silver label, several glasses and a bucket for ice, which Papa never used even in high summer. 'Beware a fellow who likes his spirits cold,' he said, though the ice bucket was placed there in case such a fellow might ever be a guest.

She checks behind the table and sighs. Nothing. She is about to take a seat in Papa's old reading chair, when she notices it. Only a small thing. The rear leg of the drinks table is worn. She blinks. How strange, she thinks, for being one of the back legs it would not be got to by anybody pouring a measure. The lacquer is almost rubbed through.

She runs her fingers up and down and sure enough, on the rear side there is a boss with a carved thistle. She pauses momentarily and presses. Nothing. Then she pulls. There is a decided click. A tiny compartment opens; inside: a key. Charlotte looks round. There are no locked drawers or cupboards in the room. She casts her eyes over the bookcases. The roundels between the sections are decorated. Napoleonic bees. Sheafs of barley. Thistles. She goes straight to the thistles and runs her fingers over them until one of the roundels moves to reveal a keyhole. As she turns the key inside it, the bookcase shifts like an old maid giving an involuntary shudder. Charlotte gasps, reaching out to open what she now realises is a door.

What is revealed is a deep cupboard. The houses on Blythswood Square are redolent with cupboarding, but this is different. Charlotte's hands shake as she peers inside. The cupboard must cut into the Howarths' house next door. It is no more than six feet in width but as long as the room at least. Quickly, Charlotte locks the door to the hallway to stop anyone from coming in and, candle in hand, peers into the dark void. Could Papa have stored his lost money in here? *Light is a splendour*, she tells herself as she ducks inside – the familiar words of a hymn.

The first thing she sees is a pale body looming out of the darkness. She lets out a squeal and almost drops the candlestick. Her heart is pounding. But it's only a painting, a large one in a fine gilded frame, propped against the interior wall. Charlotte cocks her head, taking it in, the flame flickering as her fingers shake. The figure is a female nude lounging on a bank of orange flowers with golden plates of fruit around. A smile plays on the woman's lips as she reaches towards the viewer. Charlotte studies her face but she does not recognise the painting's subject, though, she reasons, she must be a classical goddess. Athena, perhaps? Or Aphrodite, given the fruit. Behind, another picture is propped. This time a bare-chested Boudicca brandishing a sword. And behind, another painting: a Madonna and then a woman who is half goat with long curled horns, pert breasts and a disarming stare: the devil's daughter. At the back Charlotte tips a framed oil of a young couple on a bed, engaged in . . . but before she can think of the word, she loses her grip and the frames clatter against the wall. She feels her cheeks flame. She takes a single step backwards and glances at the open door, but steels herself to continue.

Further in, shelves are stacked with books and leather portfolio cases. Charlotte places the candlestick on the highest surface. It isn't dusty, which means somebody has cleaned here. He did it, she knows suddenly. Her father. A man who never attended a domestic duty in his life. He must have, or else how could it be clean? She lifts down the first book: a volume by Robert Burns, not his familiar poetry but instead ditties and letters of quite a different nature. *I have given her a guinea, and I have fucked her till she rejoiced with joy unspeakable* . . . Charlotte stares at her trembling fingers as if they are traitors as she closes the book with a thump. She replaces it, unable for a moment to peel her eyes away. *Joy unspeakable.* She swallows and regards the top portfolio with determination before she unlaces it. Inside lie several charcoal drawings of naked women. Not classical figures, just women. Women bending over. Women on their knees. Women touching their parts. One with a man looming over her. Then a bundle of lithographs, the same but signed in French: *Eugène et Achilles.* The papers are uneven along one side as if cut from book bindings.

As she closes the portfolio, Charlotte feels flustered: a mixture of fright and horror. This is forbidden. A waltz is too intimate. She can hardly bear anyone even to touch her arm. She makes herself pull another book off the shelf. The flyleaf declares it poetry by John Wilmot, Earl of Rochester. Worse than Burns, she reads as much as she can of a ditty titled 'A Ramble in St James's Park'. Replacing the tome, she nervously pulls out an ode by Alexander Pope, just as horrifying. Then love sonnets which, frankly, are a relief. She closes the book and lays her hand to a mahogany box with a brass key. Stomach churning, she opens it and discovers ivory figures; two women and a man who comprise a kind of jigsaw. Not of a map, the sort that she used in the schoolroom as a child, but three-dimensional and graphic. A jigsaw that can be put together several ways. She picks up one of the small ivory women and looks at it from all sides like a medical examination. Then she lays it back in the box and snaps the lid shut. Her palms are sweating. Beside the shelves more paintings are propped against the wall. Three naked women reclining on a day bed and an Egyptian goddess with an intricate ornament in her hair but wearing nothing else. 'Oh god,' Charlotte breathes. She grapples up the shelves to retrieve the candlestick before turning her back on the far end of the cupboard, which is peopled by a crowd of naked statues in front of yet more paintings.

Panting, she hurtles back into the study as if the cupboard is haunted. She locks the door and flings herself into her father's chair, staring at the bookshelf in horror. Oxblood. The drama section. Is this what Mr Lennox was looking for? She searches for words to describe what she's found, her mind racing through 'degenerate', 'disgusting', 'obscene', 'inverted' . . . and, she realises, 'illuminating'. For here he is, she thinks, her cheeks burning. The secret part of him. Is this what he did with the money from the railway stock? Does this have a bearing on Helensburgh House? She feels as if she has been personally assaulted. It is as if she has written a final line and it has changed the whole story.

After she cannot tell how long, Mrs Cullen appears beside her chair. 'Dr Grieg,' she says.

Charlotte surfaces as if she has been underwater. 'Pardon?'

'Dr Grieg.' Mrs Cullen motions towards the study door. 'You locked it. We knocked, miss, but you made no reply. We sent for the doctor. The coachman broke the hinges. Did you not hear?'

Still in shock, Charlotte splutters, 'A lady is entitled to privacy, Mrs Cullen.' The key remains in her hand. She squeezes it tightly and slips it into her pocket.

The doctor hovers on the threshold. 'Charlotte, dear,' he says hopefully, 'are you hysterical?'

Charlotte laughs before she can stop herself. 'I'm in grief, doctor, is all,' she says flatly, for how else can she explain the shock? She has been hoodwinked by her own father into believing herself a respectable young lady when she might as well have been brought up in a whorehouse. She has no idea who she is any more.

'The Lord allows us grief,' Dr Grieg pronounces, 'but it can be overwhelming. The laudanum I left . . .'

Charlotte rises. She wants to get rid of him and suddenly she realises how. 'Do you know,' she says, 'I have an appetite. My first in a week. I have a fancy for a plate of meat and roasted potatoes. Are there bottled pears with that whipped cream Cook laces with brandy? And soft cheese from Mr Drew's dairy at Carmyle?'

'That's good, Charlotte,' Dr Grieg pronounces enthusiastically.

'You've been such a comfort,' Charlotte lies, guiding him out of the study. 'Will you join me at the dining table?'

Dr Grieg glances at the front door. He is, she knows, the kind of man who would only stay if she put up resistance to him doing so. She finds the strength to pretend he's welcome. A lady must be clever about her business. A lone lady more so. 'I'd love your company,' she says.

The doctor takes a moment, 'Thank you, but my wife is expecting me.'

Charlotte breathes out. 'Tell Mrs Grieg I'm much improved,' she calls after him. As the door clicks she rounds on Mrs Cullen. 'You're my housekeeper, not Dr Grieg's. Do I make myself plain?' she hisses. 'I'll be playing the pianoforte upstairs. I've a sudden fancy for Mr Liszt's hymns.'

Mrs Cullen looks contrite. 'And your dinner, miss?'

'Don't be silly,' Charlotte snaps. 'I was only getting rid of him.'

Upstairs she sinks onto the blue sofa and stares at the portrait of herself in younger, more innocent days. Her father has turned out a liar and a fraud. One thing is clear however, she must direct her own affairs to get out of this mess. She will not be the innocent girl in this picture ever again. Her choice now is to rally or to sink. She places her fingers on the piano keys, starting on script. As the music soothes her, she considers sending Murray Urquhart a note that she wishes to sell the house on Blythswood Square and damn what society will think. Perhaps she will move to one of the astylar terraces at Newton Place. Such a residence might be run with three staff at a push. But, it comes to her: how can she move house with naked women fornicating behind the walls of her father's study? The secret cupboard is a rotten carcass in the belly of her home. She must cut it out.

Seeing that she must be fortified, she rings the bell and Mrs Cullen appears. 'Have the study door mended. Tonight,' Charlotte instructs. 'And I will have dinner after all, in an hour.'

Mrs Cullen disappears, and Charlotte considers the enormity of what she has to do. She recalls momentarily what Lennox said about Maggie Nicholl in her last days, not staying abed but abroad in the city with her stick, a blade concealed within it. A woman about her business. She wishes Mr Lennox was a person she could trust. He is in a position to answer some of her questions. She would like to understand how her mother took charge. Margaret Nicholl seems to have been a lady capable of sorting matters out. Now Charlotte must follow her lead without knowing the details.

Downstairs, Charlotte slips into the study and replaces the key. She pours a whisky and calls for ice. Why not? Sipping it at the desk, she stares at her father's library noting the Machiavelli in translation and volumes of military strategy. Then her eyes settle on the drama section, or as she now thinks of it, 'the door'. She feels both ashamed and resolved at once, surrounded by people she cannot trust in a world that makes little sense.

'I must change entirely,' she mutters, accepting that now she will become a different kind of lady. Slowly she pulls out a piece of paper and pens a note to Murray. *I wish to have my photograph taken*, she scribbles. *Do you know where it can be done?*

Chapter Nine

The first day of April dawns and Charlotte has scarcely slept. She paced her room in the early hours frantically searching her recollections for someone she might trust, but she has come up short. She feels unprepared for the tasks that lie ahead. Not the lack of money any more, for that is a matter of mere arithmetic. But the rest of it. As the sun rose, she determined that a woman should know her father and decided that she will change in order to do so. She has changed already.

'You seem different,' Murray observes in the carriage later that morning as they rattle down the steep hill through Grahamstown. The black silk mourning rosettes have been removed from the interior of the cab and tiny narcissi pinned in their place with three daffodils in a slim glass vase attached to the window frame. Charlotte is arrayed in a side-skirted crêpe lavender frock.

'Grief has changed me,' she says drily.

'Doctor Grieg remarked it when I bumped into him this morning. A new confidence, he called it. I think it suits you,' Murray declares.

'There has to be more than one way to grieve, though the Griegs are keen on a single way to do everything,' she says. The thought of them finding out her father's true nature makes Charlotte's blood run cold. She is surprised that she feels at once protective of James Nicholl's good name and horrified by his legacy.

Murray leans forward. The edge of his forest-green waistcoat appears at the lapel of his burgundy greatcoat, like a flash of inspiration. 'There's something candid about you, Charlotte. I'm guessing, forgive me, do you intend to do business as your father did?'

Charlotte tries not to blanche. 'Not exactly,' she replies. 'But there is nobody to take responsibility but me.' She momentarily ponders admitting what has changed her swift as a gas lamp alters the dark, but she cannot bring herself to it. Seeing the pictures is one thing. Reading the words, saying them out loud, is quite another. Then there is the fact that Murray has not shared his secret. She has made tentative enquiries but she still has no clue about Helensburgh House.

'This dress suits you well,' he says. 'I have no strong views in the matter of mourning clothes, but I can see why you would not want to be photographed wearing them.'

'This dress was one of Papa's favourites,' she replies, cursing that she feels so distrustful of her father now she cannot say definitely if he liked the dress at all. And yet, when she refers to him, she is cast back to happier times, promenading along the West Sands at St Andrews the summer before when she last wore this outfit. Was that a lie too?

'Have you had your portrait taken?' Charlotte asks, attempting conversation to shake off all thought of her father's lies.

'Who would want a portrait of me?' Murray replies wryly. A lock of his hair loosens itself as the carriage goes over a pothole. Charlotte regards him. Mrs Grieg shook her with the suggestion that they might make a couple. Though he will make a good husband, she thinks, for another lady. Secrets aside, he is always in good humour. She can easily picture him taking an interest in his children. The idea makes her smile. It seems ludicrous that most people consider his twisted spine before anything else. 'He's a strange creature,' she heard one girl comment at the regatta last summer, as if Murray were a blond bear or a dog with three legs. Charlotte does not gossip, nor does she take issue with gossip, though on that occasion she had to bite her tongue.

Now she watches the crowds on the pavement as the carriage wheels eastwards and draws to a halt on Argyle Street outside a shop with a huge sign mounted on the roof that says 'Bonanza' in showy white script. 'Here?' she asks.

'On the square.' Murray points out of the other side of the carriage. 'Where those women are standing.'

Charlotte peers at the group: three respectable-looking women, not ladies, loiter at the foot of the chambers. Two are examining a mounted glass case while the other checks her purse. High above, a sign hoisted from the guttering proclaims 'Photographs taken' with a drawing of a camera obscura balanced on spindly legs and 'Top floor' in smaller script beneath. Charlotte is pleasantly surprised.

'It's a lady photographer,' Murray announces with satisfaction.

Charlotte grins. 'A lady?'

'I've been dying to tell you. The talented Miss Mann arrived more than a week ago and set the place up from scratch. She trained in Edinburgh at the studio of David Octavius Hill. Perhaps she will inspire you in your new life as a lady in charge of her own affairs.'

Murray hands Charlotte down and accompanies her across the square. The women part to let them through. The glass case, Murray notes, no longer contains the image of the boys but one of the tree in the corner, marked at four shillings, like the castle. He is surprised by the picture's clarity, the edges of the oyster shells and grubby old spoons bright against the dark bark. It's almost beautiful. He smiles that she has proved him wrong now in practice. Inside, at the top of the stairs, a small open window lets in a breeze and the slow peal of ten bells from St Enoch's. Murray raps on the door and a slip of a girl opens up. 'Mr Urquhart,' the girl greets Murray with a bob and then adds 'miss' in Charlotte's direction.

The studio feels busy though there is nobody else there. 'Where's your mistress, Jane?' Murray enquires as they cross the threshold.

'Working in the print room, sir,' Jane says. 'I'd say another four minutes.'

The girl has been occupied at a guillotine beside the wardrobe, trimming the edges of prints commissioned by one of the doctors on the other side of the square. The images are gruesome: a surgical collection that includes unborn Siamese twins and a canker the size of a melon encased in a glass jar of soupy fluid. The calotypes of these curiosities have been the very devil to get right, but it is done now and all that is left is to pack the prints in tissue and carry them to the surgeon's offices in exchange for payment.

Approaching the doctors was one of Ellory's middle-of-the-night ideas. At first she was concerned that the College of Surgeons looked too grand, but behind the facade it quickly became clear there was little pomp; the college was an office building like any other, with ochre walls and dusty mantels. Her foray into the interior has kept the two women busy this week. Mr Hill always resisted such commissions. He considered himself a painter foremost and refused to photograph any subject he would hesitate to capture in oils. Ellory has no such qualms. She needs the money and is learning as she goes, as is Jane who assisted in Ellory's use of mirrors in photographing the cankers. 'That's clever, miss,' the girl noted. Mr Hill moved items into their best position wherever the light fell, but Ellory has started manipulating the light itself. So far, she has sold work to the value of one sovereign and three shillings, keeping up with the outlays for paper and chemicals, feeding them both and buying coal for the stove. The surgeon will add ten shillings when he pays. It will keep them going several more days, what with all their expenses.

'May I fetch you something while you wait?' Jane offers.

'That isn't necessary,' Charlotte says. 'My, what a place!'

'Would you like to see Miss Mann's portfolio?'

Charlotte nods and Jane lays the case on the table. Charlotte pulls the string to reveal a calotype of the tree on the other side of the square, identical to the print at the door.

'I've heard of this,' she says. 'It's a totem, isn't it?'

'Yes, miss. It's popular with the ladies,' Jane replies as if the studio has been open a year, they are financially secure and know exactly what they are doing.

Charlotte continues to leaf through, Murray peering over her shoulder. There are only a dozen prints but Miss Mann has not been in Glasgow long and, as Murray knows, has only had her own camera since Saturday. He smiles, impressed by her industry. 'You see,' he tells Charlotte, 'you're in good hands.' A minute later, the door to the print room opens and the air becomes sharp with iodine.

Murray introduces the women. 'Miss Nicholl, this is Miss Mann, Glasgow's only female photographer. Miss Nicholl hoped to have her portrait taken, Miss Mann, as I said in my note.'

Ellory bobs a curtsy. Charlotte immediately likes her. Ellory's hair is colourful and her demeanour warm. She feels suddenly safe.

'Good morning,' Ellory says. Above, a seagull swoops in the direction of the Clyde, narrowly missing the skylight. 'It's a fine day. We're lucky with the light.' She studies Miss Nicholl with an artist's eye. Charlotte's outline is the clearest she has ever seen. She likes the simplicity of the lady's style, devoid of the high fashion of sleeves with complicated ruching or ribbons and ringleted hair set in an intricate bun. Miss Nicholl is elegant. Beyond fashion.

Charlotte points at the picture of the boys. 'However did you induce these children to sit, Miss Mann?'

Ellory smiles. 'Toffees,' she confides.

Charlotte judges her the kind of woman who can manage anything. She seems to have a curiously sunny demeanour, though perhaps that is her colouring.

'How would you like your image to appear, Miss Nicholl?' Ellory asks, businesslike.

Charlotte hesitates. She had not thought there would be a choice. 'Like myself,' she says, although she realises that she isn't sure what that might look like.

'What is the purpose of the portrait?' Ellory pushes her, squinting as she assesses her new subject.

Charlotte considers. 'My father had a painting made of me some years ago. He died recently.'

'I'm sorry.' A pause. 'Tell me about the painting.'

'I was younger. It was ten years ago. My father chose a garden setting. I stood like this,' Charlotte stands as the painter posed her, her back straight and one hand raised. 'There was wisteria behind me,' she adds. 'Though the artist changed it to roses.'

Ellory's eyes flit to the backdrop. 'We might have you in the garden again, if you like. Perhaps with a bough of flowers in your arms? We have silk flowers.' She motions to Jane who disappears into the wardrobe and emerges with a haphazard bunch of roses and silk blossom.

'I don't think such a bouquet is likely,' Charlotte says with a smile. 'The roses won't be out till June and the blossom will be done by then.'

Jane immediately begins separating the blooms into two bunches.

'Do you prefer spring or summer, Miss Nicholl?' Ellory asks.

Miss Mann is admirably pragmatic, Charlotte thinks. 'I'd like something different from what I've had before,' she says. 'How would you pose, Miss Mann?'

Nobody has ever asked this question. It surprises Ellory that Miss Nicholl is interested. 'I never have,' she says as it comes to her. 'Though there's definitely an art to looking like oneself,' she adds. Once, when Jessie put on a summer bonnet for Mr Hill, Ellory tried to get her cousin to change into something more congruent with her outfit, not to say her personality. 'The image will work better if you dress for it,' she argued, but Jessie stuck to her frock in dark brocade, oddly plain below the fancy hat with its festive pale silk roses. The resulting picture was entirely out of step with Jessie's character. It made Ellory realise that the notion of a photograph capturing what is there might sell short the complex nature of reality. It convinced her that sitters needed to be presented to the camera, though perhaps not posed as was Mr Hill's habit, placing each hand, moving each finger. Something with more understanding perhaps.

Charlotte takes a breath. 'Can you make me look like an independent lady, Miss Mann? Since my father died, I'm in charge of my own affairs,' she confesses, 'That's what I want to reveal. That I'm going to make a success of it.'

Murray looks up, as though about to reassure her, but Charlotte lifts her hand. She does not want to be interrupted. Ellory smiles. 'Yes,' she says vaguely as if she can see something now that wasn't immediately apparent.

'I'm curious about the photographic process,' Charlotte adds.

This is something Ellory can speak to. 'You'll need to stay still for some time. Taking a calotype is not the work of an instant. It can be uncomfortable. But, as I said, we're fortunate in the light today. Some studios require their subjects to pose outdoors.'

'Really?'

'There's seldom enough light inside. Mr Hill and Mr Adamson make portraits in the garden, but we're blessed with so much glass here and being north-facing means the light is clear. I can make photographs even on rainy days.' She casts a grateful glance at Murray, before adding, 'In my view, the dress you're wearing is of a tone too close to your skin. It's a lovely colour, but we don't think of ourselves in shades of sepia and that's what the camera captures.'

Murray smirks. 'You ought to have worn black after all,' he declares with satisfaction. 'Old Ma Grieg was right.'

Charlotte ignores him. 'You have sets here so you must have . . . what do they call them in the theatre? Properties?'

Ellory grins. 'Oh yes.'

'Might you dress me, Miss Mann? Might you take the photograph now?'

It takes 20 minutes. Murray helps Jane move the chair in front of the velvet curtain, while Ellory organises Charlotte to change into an old-fashioned spencer the colour of dark purple pansies. The tone matches her eyes. Then Ellory fetches a small pot of coloured salve. Charlotte flinches. The artifice of painting a face brands a woman a harlot, as Mrs Grieg has been known to rant, though her father once confided that as a girl coming out, the doctor's wife wore patches and white lead so her skin would glow in the candlelight. 'That's how she captured the doctor's heart,' he said. Charlotte curses once more at her father's memory intruding.

'It's all right,' Ellory promises as she scoops pink cream onto her finger. 'Nobody will see. It's made of Grenache grapes; mere shading. Will you allow me?' Charlotte's gaze flicks towards Murray who is standing on an upturned wooden crate, enjoying the studio's outlook towards the Campsie Hills. She nods quickly. Ellory applies the salve and poses Charlotte beneath the skylight.

'You must remain absolutely still,' Ellory warns, retreating behind the apparatus, which Jane has readied.

It is difficult. After only a minute Charlotte's back is stiff. After almost two minutes, her eyelids feel unaccountably itchy and her hands and feet are freezing. Murray withdraws a pipe from his pocket and lights it while he inspects the outfits hanging in the wardrobe. Then he sits down to watch, impressed by Miss Mann's concentration as she stands, absolutely focused beside the camera, as still as her subject. She is quite as efficient as he would have expected. It is pleasant, he thinks, to watch it.

'Only a second or two longer, Miss Nicholl,' Ellory says and then, finally, just as Charlotte is almost at the point of deciding it would be worth the relief of scratching her eyelid even if they have to start again, Ellory deems the image captured. She quickly removes the salted paper into the darkroom. 'I'll be some time,' she says, closing the door.

Charlotte stands and peers stiffly in the direction of the Campsies. 'More difficult than you expected?' Murray asks.

'Ladies deride artists' models but it's not easy simply to stand.' She bats away an image of lounging naked whores.

Murray bows. 'You did well, Charlotte. A gentleman of my acquaintance, who sat to Mr Hill, had to have a brace. Your deportment is excellent, of course.'

'I feel I have earned a toffee,' she jests.

He moves towards the table. It feels relaxed here. It's not exactly an office nor a retail premises but somewhere different; creative. In the corner Jane works quietly at the guillotine. They are, to all intents and purposes, alone. 'Have you heard there's a plan to dredge the Clyde?' he asks.

'No.'

Murray's eyes shine. 'It'll be a feat of engineering. Would you like to see the plans? The scheme will transform the city.' He laughs at the look on Charlotte's face. 'I see that was a terrible idea. I apologise.'

Charlotte regards him. 'I have an admission,' she ventures, her heart skipping a beat. She cannot say it all, but perhaps she can get at least some help from him. 'My father didn't prepare me to run my own affairs,' she starts carefully, 'but if I'm to do so, I must educate myself. The world is wide. I need to know more about it.' It is the most she can say. 'Though perhaps not in the way of engineering plans,' she adds. 'Can you help me, Murray, to understand how things work?'

'Of course.' Murray shows no inkling of what she is really seeking information about – the paintings, that is. 'You wish a wider experience?' he says.

'Yes,' Charlotte replies warmly. 'That's it.'

He nods curtly. 'In that case, I have another idea. A talk which might interest you, though Reverend Patterson wouldn't approve of your attendance, or mine.'

Charlotte turns. This is more promising. 'You'll be taking me to a den of vice next.'

Murray ignores this slur. 'It's a lecture tour. The testament of a freed slave who's no friend to our church.' He pauses to see how Charlotte responds. 'Your father I'm sure would have shown an interest though I don't expect he would have taken you. A different viewpoint is always an education, is it not? The talk is tonight.'

A grin spreads across Charlotte's face like a sunrise at Murray's response. He is prepared to admit she has been protected. And the prospect of going to such a lecture is intriguing. 'Papa supported the freeing of the slaves,' she says.

Murray continues enthusiastically like a child telling a story. 'That's the nub of it. There's doubt, you see, if those enslaved truly have been freed. I'm sure your father would have sought information. He always did.'

Charlotte considers. 'I'd like to go.'

'I'll collect you at seven.' Above, three sparrows flutter carefree at the window. Momentarily Charlotte wishes she could join them. 'I changed, you know, when my mother died,' Murray confides. 'I was angry. It shifts the whole world, doesn't it?'

She wonders if he knows what she knows. 'I hope I haven't been bad-tempered,' she says.

'Perhaps a little unconventional.'

'Like my father,' Charlotte counters, her lips pursed. She is testing him.

Murray does not answer directly. 'Your father was kind and well-loved. You'll find a way,' he says, not giving her what she is looking for – an indication of James Nicholl's true nature.

She turns away, catching a glimpse of herself in the mirror. The spencer she is wearing recalls her mother and she feels a sting of excitement seeing it. The wardrobes at home still contain Maggie Nicholl's things: satin reticules, a pretty French silver dressing-table set, a leather portmanteau and several dresses, some of which have been altered over the years to become Charlotte's; taken in at the waist, the bodices remade from their old-fashioned Empire line to something more modern. 'Does your father ever talk of my mother? I'm curious about her,' she tries.

Murray smiles. 'We could ask him. For myself, I can't bear it when he talks of my mama. My parents didn't get along. I know only a scant amount about your mother,' he admits. 'Maggie was her name, wasn't it?'

'Yes,' Charlotte sounds eager. 'I don't mind, even if it's only tittle-tattle.'

'I believe it was a love match,' Murray continues. 'But the union had other advantages. Your father was educated but had little money. It was your mother's capital that fired his career. She saw his talent.'

'The ability to see the future,' Charlotte says, wondering what future her father had in mind when he stowed a brace of whores in his cupboard and did not leave her enough money to live upon.

Unaware, Murray's smile widens. 'The future is not set. But your father had the ability to think laterally, to choose his friends wisely and keep his options open. He was somebody who knew how to wait. You can see that from his investments. I've learned a lot from reading his papers.'

Charlotte is on the point of admitting she has learned things too. It strikes her that this is the first real conversation she has ever had with Murray. But as Ellory returns to the studio, she's glad to be stopped. If Murray would only hint at the other beneficiary of her father's will, she would admit what she knows, but until then, she cannot trust him.

'Shall I print you a copy, Miss Nicholl?' Ellory asks as she emerges from the darkroom.

'I'll buy two, please.' Charlotte is decisive. 'I want to bury one in my father's grave.'

'Calotypes are expensive to put in the ground,' Murray cuts in.

Charlotte considers it kind of him, knowing how much money she has inherited, to try to save a few shillings of it. She knows what she wants though and is not penniless yet. 'Nevertheless,' she says, thinking it will be satisfying to show this image of herself to the dead man who betrayed her. If it turns out as she hopes; a lady in charge.

It's eccentric but Ellory likes this new client. Besides, only a fool would argue with someone about what they want to do with their own property. 'I'll deliver two prints as soon as I can. If you'd like the one for your father's grave to last in the earth, I suggest placing it between two pieces of glass and wrapping it in oilskin. We have an excellent glazier in Margaret Walker on Jamaica Street. She'll be able to supply a frame too should you want one for the other print.'

'Another woman?' Charlotte lets out in surprise, but then why not? Women organise their own affairs it seems, if they are given the opportunity.

'Shall I help you dress, miss?' Jane asks, motioning towards the office and Charlotte follows her.

Once they are gone, Murray turns to Ellory. 'It's been fascinating to see you work,' he says, smiling.

'Thank you for bringing Miss Nicholl,' Ellory replies. 'She's a good subject.'

Murray relights his pipe. 'I've recommended you to another two of my clients. I hope they come as well.' He wonders what she would look like with her flaming hair about her shoulders. There is something poetic about the way she works so efficiently to create her images. He has met a few artists over the years but they were all more showy. Miss Mann's containment, her modesty, intrigues him. In the running of her business she seems focused almost entirely on her subjects, which is, of itself, admirable.

Five minutes later, as they leave the studio, Charlotte shakes Ellory's hand. 'This is what gentlemen do,' she says with a smile. Ellory feels her cheeks flare. Were she a man she would not be a gentleman. She wonders if Miss Nicholl is teasing her but she seems in earnest. 'I'll deliver your prints myself,' she promises.

'I'll look forward to it.'

As Murray and Charlotte trip smartly down the stairs Ellory lingers in the doorway. She wants to hold onto this moment. This is her first proper portrait. The first time she has been able to charge a normal sitter's fee with no extra negotiation because she is a woman. She is determined to make a good job of it.

Chapter Ten

Jane is frustrated that her brother, Cormac, who holds the position of second footman in a grand house on Ingram Street, only has one half-day a month. The night after Charlotte Nicholl's image is taken, Ellory sends her to Rab Ha's to fetch chops and two tankards of stout and Jane decides to go the long way, past the servants' door so she might talk with Cormac a few minutes. Glasgow is proving as exciting as she had anticipated. She loves its glossy gaslit streets. Down the rookeries at night there is only the dim glow of tallow lamps, for the poor cannot pay for the luxury of gaslight which casts yellow squares from the long windows of the fancier residences, and pools on the paving slabs around the street lamps in wee golden puddles after dark. The nest of streets at the foot of Calton Hill where Jane lived the last three years is almost black by contrast. The kitchen maid fetches Cormac but he can only spend a couple of minutes talking before he has to go back inside. Jane misses having friends. At home she knows everyone about the doors.

Later, after she and Ellory have eaten the chops and drunk the stout, she takes back the empty tankards and on her way home tarries by the black void of the river, lit only by ships' lamps and the reflection of lights on the bridge over the Clyde and the distant glimmer of Carlton Place on the south bank.

She likes the thick smell of the river mingled with the sharp scent of damp horses and leather harness on the sodden night air. Like the smell of wooden crates and rope and canvas, it is wholesome. Glasgow has its own glamour, she thinks, especially at night. She is becoming accustomed to it. During the day the town centre buzzes with industry from the shoeshine boys on Buchanan Street and the costermongers who cry their wares along the Trongate. But at night that changes, and the city is at play. She is glad she came. The night before she walked as far as the dark expanse of Glasgow Green where men gather to wager on pitch and toss by moonlight. She is never afraid, for her appearance does not attract attention. Along the river, she has noticed showy women selling their wares, or, to put it more bluntly, themselves. She ignores them in the doorways. Sixpence for an upright, so she's heard. And nearby, sailors scrapping over the price of a pint and gentlemen shoved into dead ends for nefarious purposes which Jane would, for the most part, be hard pressed to name. But there is dancing on the pavements and laughing on the stairs, women gabbing out of windows across the close and men racing to row the black snake of the Clyde. The smell of meat roasting and perl being brewed and the tang of the stinking night-soil men. It's like a circus, she thinks. She wants to explore it. Surely she'll make friends here, in time.

Tonight, she tries something new. She cuts up from the river and loiters at the far end of Dunlop Street, listening to the banter of couples on their way to the night's performance at the Tuppeny Theatre. Little sound emanates from inside, though now and then she catches a snatch of an organ being played: not in the manner of church music but something more cheerful. This is one stage of two in the town, since the Queen Street Theatre patronised by Mrs Siddons burnt down. Glasgow changes so much it's thrilling. Edinburgh has had its castle for hundreds of years and the spill of the Old Town down to Holyrood. Though the Georgian streets north of the old loch were built in Jane's grandmother's day, the cityscape of the capital feels unchanging. By contrast, Glasgow is perpetually in motion.

It strikes Jane that to Ellory the city is something to freeze in sepia, but she prefers it as it feels now – alive and slipping through her fingers. If she could, she'd spend every evening watching the glint of the gaslight and catching snippets of conversation.

The theatre is busiest at intervals and it's during one such break that Jane notices a tall man of her own age in a yellow waistcoat and bright blue cravat emerging from the stage door into the cool night air. He heaves a sigh, pushes his dark hair back from his face and draws an egg from his pocket which he taps on the door frame and chucks raw down his gullet with a smack of the lips, tossing the shell into the gutter. After this impromptu supper, he withdraws a cigar from behind his ear and pulls a long matchstick down the rough stone: a burst of brightness as sudden as a firework. That is when he notices her. He peers into the gloom of the doorway in which she is standing: a plumber's office with a mottled brass post box.

'Are you all right, lass?' he asks, his accent unexpectedly redolent of high cliffs and low crofts and generations of men who pulled their food from the sea in nets their wives had repaired repeatedly.

'Aye.'

'Do you want to go in?' He motions elegantly towards the stage door.

'I've no money. I like to watch the people passing,' she admits. 'Some of those going inside are very fine.'

The man's dark eyes soften. 'I can let you backstage,' he offers. 'Just ten minutes, but you can keek through the curtain.'

Jane measures her response. 'Mebbe,' she replies, her tone betraying her doubt.

His face lights in a grin. 'I don't want anything from you,' he reassures her. 'Where do you hail from?'

'Edinburgh.'

'Ah,' he replies as if this explains something. He puts out his hand. 'I'm Jeremiah.'

'Jane.' She shakes it. His grip is firm, and he does not move closer, as some men might.

'Where are you from then?' she asks.

'Not here anyway,' he says. 'Up north. I belong to Banff.'

'Were you cleared, aye?'

He nods. Most Highlanders tell the same story: brutal rent collectors, heartless landlords and a long walk south on an empty belly.

'You do not look like a Highlander.'

'And what, pray tell, does a Highlander look like? Do we all have tartan hearts and bushy beards, like savages?'

Jane considers this. All the Highlanders she has met look poor. The laundrywomen on the Cowgate have raw red hands and eyes like dead women. On some closes their mournful singing marks the place as a slum, no further investigation required. Here, in Glasgow, close to St Enoch's Square, so many unemployed porters congregate out of the rain under the lip of the roofline at Argyle Street that it is becoming known as the Hielanman's Hanway. The lucky ones are paid a pittance to haul sandstone out of the new quarry at Bishopbriggs.

'I don't know,' she says. 'I've never seen someone from the north so colourful as you. Tartan or no.'

Jeremiah takes a deep draw of his cigar. 'That's one way to put it.' He smiles, the smoke clouding. 'I must go. Come in if you're coming.'

She follows him. Backstage looks much like below stairs, she thinks, slipping past the limed walls and chipped doors in plain buff. Jeremiah is businesslike as he breezes along the corridor but to Jane the place feels extraordinary. The air is tinged with lilac, which she later finds comes from the dancers' talcum. They pass a woman dressed in a scanty crimson frock, with her face painted like a whore. In the wings there is laughter as a man in a strangely shiny black coat and top hat and shoes of glossy patent leather amuses a cluster of girls arrayed in pink ostrich feathers and silver chintz, who are sharing a draught of small beer.

Jeremiah halts at a half-open door. 'This is my room,' he says.

'Are you a singer?' Jane asks, though this does not seem the kind of place that mournful Highland ballads would delight a crowd.

'Not at all,' he says. Inside, lit by candle lamp, he is younger than she thought; perhaps only her own age. She realises he is wearing kohl round his eyes.

'What is your act?'

'I don't have an act, mo ghràdh,' he says, the Gaelic tripping off his tongue easily as English. 'I am myself. Finally,' he adds dramatically, stubbing out his cigar on a broken saucer balanced on the rim of a mirror. 'I create them,' he adds. 'The outfits. If there's anywhere that clothes make the man, or the woman, then it's here. I'm a seamstress of sorts. A seam-master.'

Jane stares at the rows of dresses and brocade-festooned bodices hanging on rails and pegs. Several startling blonde wigs on wooden stands the shape of large inverted eggs run along a shelf. Beside them sits a green flacon of whisky and four small pottery cups stacked in a crooked pile ready for a party.

'May I?' she asks, indicating the frocks.

'Please.' He sits down, watching as her fingers seek out the pintucks and fringing. 'You're a seamstress too, perhaps?'

Jane turns. 'I'm a photographer's assistant,' she says. 'My mistress is Glasgow's first female photographer.'

'No,' says Jeremiah as if it is quite a different kind of word. Nobody Jane has ever met says 'no' the same. He brings down the whisky and tips the bottle towards her by way of invitation.

'I've never tried it,' Jane admits. 'My mother says it's a ruination.'

Jeremiah laughs. 'Aye. My mother blames it too. But won't anything ruin you if you take too much? There's a fellow from the Great Glen who died of an excess of cheese. Would you give a single dram a go?' She smiles. He pours. 'To the things we have in common,' he toasts. 'I knew you were an interesting lassie. I knew it.'

Jane pauses. Nobody has ever noticed her before, let alone considered she might be interesting. She clinks her cup and sips. She coughs.

'Careful,' he says. 'Not too much at once. My pal works at the distillery on Kirk Street. They sell this swill to the gentry for two shillings a bottle. That's a sovereign and three shillings a case. More than a guinea.' Jeremiah's tone makes it clear that he's no fool; he gets the whisky for less.

Jane tries again and this time the liquid opens on her tongue like a sunny day in the green of the country, shadows beneath the trees and a low fire burning.

'You can taste the peat, can't you?' Jeremiah sounds satisfied. 'It's the only thing I miss: the smell of burning peat. They use coal in the city. It has the tang of death.'

Jane removes a green dress with a wide skirt from its place.

'You've good taste,' Jeremiah proclaims. 'That's for Grace Sutherland. She's the star of the show. They say there's not a dry eye left in the house after she has sung "The Rose of Kelvin". That includes the boy who works the curtain and he's heard Grace's repertoire a hundred times.'

'Sutherland?' Jane enquires, wide-eyed.

'She's from the wrong side of the bedsheet, but a noble bed. It's her mother was a Sutherland.'

Jane thinks it is a grand name and wonders how directly Miss Sutherland is related to the duke. 'This is beautiful,' she says, stroking the skirt. 'Did you make it?'

Jeremiah lifts his whisky by way of admission. 'As you're hanging around the stage door, do you have ambitions, yourself, Jane?'

'No,' she says shyly. 'I can't see me performing.'

Jeremiah spends a moment taking this in. 'But you have ambitions some other way?'

Jane regards him plainly and decides to speak her mind. 'I took my chance when I followed my mistress from Edinburgh. To find something better,' she says. 'I don't know what, but I don't look such a skivvy any more. Though I scrub the place half the day all the same. I like wearing the gloves,' she admits, lifting her arm to show him. The pigskin ones are Miss Mann's cast-offs.

'Very elegant,' Jeremiah agrees.

'And I'm learning,' Jane adds. 'Miss Mann is teaching me the darkroom. You have to wear gloves because of the chemicals. That's why she gave them to me. I like it here. Glasgow, I mean.'

Outside in the hallway a scuffle distracts them. Two large moustached Irishmen huckle a smaller gentleman in a satin opera cape down the corridor. 'Now, now, Mr Ferguson,' one of them says, his voice sharp with the tang of Tyrone. 'Miss Sutherland is busy. You must come back after the show.'

'I have to see her,' the gentleman exclaims, but the men simply lift him towards the exit.

'What was that?' Jane asks. There has been, she knows instinctively, something glamorous about the exchange.

'Men go mad for Grace. She's . . .' Jeremiah pauses, not sure how to put it, 'well-loved. The tokens she gets, you wouldn't believe. Suitors at the stage door. Some days there's a queue. Especially when it's the variety.'

'Popular then,' Jane says.

'She is, aye.'

She pauses as an idea forms. 'I expect they'd pay for a likeness of the lady?'

Jeremiah's eyes become suddenly sharp as if Jane has only just come into focus.

'Oh aye,' he says. His instinct, as ever, has been good. 'I see what you mean. I could say to her. Assuming there might be . . . a consideration.'

'You must visit us at the studio and meet my mistress, Miss Mann. Tomorrow perhaps?'

He smiles. Jane leans against the dressing table. 'There's a skill to dressing for a photograph,' she adds.

'I'm sure.'

'Will you come to St Enoch's Square? In the morning?'

Jeremiah generally does not get out of his bed (or any other) until past noon. After the music hall closes and the wardrobe is returned to his care, he used to go home to his mother, but she threw him out of the family's two-room tenement flat off the High Street more than a year ago, after she found a snake tattooed round his upper arm when he was washing in the back yard. 'The devil had Adam and Eve expelled from Eden on account o' that,' she hissed. 'Why won't you just play shinty with the other lads?'

'Och, Ma,' was the most Jeremiah could summon in reply. He had no wish to start a fight. His mother, as far as he knew, was blissfully unaware of his night-time activities; but she told him not to come back again anyway on account of the snake, and so far he hasn't. Generally, he calls into the Old College Bar or the Saracen's Head after work and falls into conversation with gentlemen who frequent the premises in the hope of falling into conversation with the likes of him. It matters little to Jeremiah whether they are students at the university on the High Street, or ministers of the Kirk, or married men with a brood of children. It is always their first time. Every man he has kissed down an alleyway has claimed the same surprise. Not Jeremiah. Sometimes he sleeps in feather beds so soft that he wakes hardly able to feel his own bones. Other times he comes into consciousness here in the dressing room, on the splinter-flecked floorboards.

'The morning?' he repeats as if it is a strange notion. 'Thank you for the invitation. I'd like to see the studio. I could come around two of the clock?'

As Jane slips back into the street, she feels she has somehow made progress. At St Enoch's Square, the ash-bound fire shifts in the stove as she quietly hangs up her coat. Ellory has gone to bed but Jane is not ready for sleep. Her mother always called her a night owl, but the truth is the girl doesn't need much rest and is just as much a morning lark. Now she perches at the window and watches fine carriages trundle past. She will tell her mistress in the morning that she has made her first friend in Glasgow and that between them they have had an idea.

Chapter Eleven

The same evening

Murray eats a sandwich instead of dinner, brought to him on a tray as he changes. Staring at himself in the mirror as he buttons his waistcoat, he cannot help wonder how Ellory Mann would style him. He has found himself thinking often of Miss Mann this afternoon. He does not meet many people he admires, certainly not many women. He has often derided gentlemen of his acquaintance for focusing on the way women look, drawn by a pretty countenance over anything else. Miss Mann, he knows, is far more than a pretty face though he keeps coming back to the striking green of her eyes and the sweep of her flaming hair.

He is disturbed in this guilty pleasure by his father who, passing in the hallway, pokes his head through Murray's door. 'You're out tonight?' he says.

'A lecture,' Murray replies stoutly. 'I'm taking Charlotte Nicholl.'

Old Mr Urquhart looks almost sprightly. 'You're spending a lot of time with Miss Nicholl,' he says hopefully.

Murray turns. 'There's nothing going on, Father,' he pronounces. 'Although for my sake, you might make my spending time with her more comfortable if you were to let me tell her about

Helensburgh House. God knows, she has a right to know. It does not sit well with me to keep this kind of secret.'

Glasgow's most trustworthy solicitor shakes a finger back and forth. 'We're trusted by our clients because we keep their secrets, beyond the grave if need be,' he says in what Murray considers his father's 'harbinger' voice. 'We're protecting the lass, just as her father sought to. This fashion for sharing information . . .' he shudders momentarily, 'no good will come of it.'

Murray pins his cravat. 'If you say so, Father,' he says though he feels uncomfortable. He is Charlotte's friend, after all, as much as her legal representative.

*

In the dark past seven of the clock, Murray and Charlotte take the carriage through town. Beyond George Square, the streets are hardly lit for the residents there have no money for gas lamps. 'You're sure you want to come?' Murray checks.

'It'll vex the Griegs,' Charlotte says cheerfully. 'Tell me why Reverend Patterson wouldn't approve of this freed slave.'

Murray sits back. 'Mr Douglass is questioning money that was donated to the Free Kirk given by the owners of American plantations. It's in the sum of three thousand pounds sterling. He's of the view that the funds were the ill-gotten profits of slavery and the Kirk should hand it back.'

'And should we?'

Murray considers. 'Probably,' he says. 'I doubt we will.'

'What would my father have said?' she asks, realising that all she knows about the case against slavery has been gleaned from James Nicholl's comments over the years.

'I don't know.' Murray shrugs. 'Perhaps we'll understand better once we've heard Mr Douglass's case. Your father considered fairness important certainly. He raised money for the Kirk after the Disruption. But it was not this money. I daresay he showed good judgement, as he always did.'

Charlotte regards her friend across the dim light of the carriage.

She spent the afternoon counting the misdemeanours in her father's secret cupboard and has a catalogue now of over 500 sins. It hurts to hear James Nicholl praised but she cannot reasonably complain.

Mr Douglass is to speak at North Portland Street at the Quaker Meeting House. The rooms lie further east than polite ladies generally venture, near the university and north of Glasgow Green. It is said a gentleman might procure many things in the ragged tenements: a woman, a drink, a plate of passable stew and, if he isn't careful, a dose of the clap and a sound beating. By contrast there is nothing for a lady amid the dingy alleyways scattered with whorehouses. As they pull up, the horses stamp, for the building is set on such a hill the carriage drags them down. 'Can you imagine going up an incline this steep on a Sunday in winter?' Charlotte says as she envisages a tumble of ladies, grasping each other as they slide precariously up the icy slope.

'Quakers are determined,' Murray says, before adding mischievously, 'Dull too, mind.'

He instructs the coachman to park on the level, round the corner. Then he hands Charlotte down. There is a crowd at the door, men with handwritten placards that say 'Down with Douglass'. Two ministers, one very thin and one very fat, argue loudly on the pavement, shouting into each other's faces like raging pugilists. A gentleman and a lady sing 'A Mighty Fortress is our God' behind them. Charlotte recognises some of the protesters from Reverend Patterson's congregation as they peer into the dark to see who is walking down from the carriage. She has never seen anything like this. It feels like mayhem. Murray glances over and she nods, confirming she wants to continue.

'Don't go in there, Urquhart,' one man spits as they cross the road. 'You betray us all, Judas.'

'Men are free to speak and to listen,' Murray snaps back as he pushes through the crowd, shielding Charlotte.

'Your father will turn in his grave, Charlotte Nicholl,' the man sneers as she bundles through.

Over the threshold, they pause. The shouting on the pavement sounds further off than it is. Another carriage stops and the horse lets out a wild neigh.

'This man merely wants some money returned?' Charlotte whispers.

Murray regards her. 'Returning it admits the Kirk is wrong,' he says under his breath by way of explanation. Feelings are running higher than he had expected. 'Perhaps I should not have brought you.'

'I want to be here,' she insists. The truth is, after a lifetime spent in polite drawing rooms, the passion of this outing is a glimpse into something Charlotte recognises as forbidden, but also fascinating. An experience of the world as she has never seen it before.

They decide not to remove their coats as the hall is barely heated, only a brazier to one side. It is strangely silent, the audience waiting patiently and the commotion outside subdued by the thick walls. Across the auditorium two Quaker ladies in black dresses with white collars smile a genteel welcome as Charlotte and Murray sit. Behind, there is a row of three men who look like porters. And, Charlotte notices, two Chinese fellows by the door. Three women of mixed race. Some gentlemen Murray recognises. As each person emerges into the hall, it is as if they have been baptised in the fires of hate. The minister who was screaming at his opponent in the street, regains his dignity as he stalks inside to take a final vacant chair at the front. The hall is full now.

'This is the strangest collection of people,' Charlotte whispers.

Murray casts a knowing look. He is about to say something about how protected she has been, but the noise outside escalates as a man screams at the top of his voice, 'Damn you to hell, you devil!' An egg shatters against the window. Charlotte peers at the smeared glass.

'Mr Douglass is arriving,' Murray explains, low.

'Down with Douglass,' the crowd in the street chants in unison, and inside three or four gentlemen go to help as the rest of the audience shifts. A man coughs but it does not break the tension. There is palpable relief when Mr Douglass comes in, flanked by a lady on one side and two men on the other. A polite ripple of applause moves like a wave across the chamber as he takes his place at the pulpit. Charlotte regards him. She has never seen a Black man before, or at least not one dressed like a gentleman in a midnight-blue frock coat and black cravat. He looks tremendously serious, but then, she thinks, no wonder.

'I'm not afraid,' he says. 'They're angry because they are wrong. They're angry because my case has veracity. I thank you all for coming tonight.'

As he starts to speak, the audience focuses solely on his voice, though the shouting outside continues. Charlotte's eyes shine. 'Look at them,' she says under her breath, as the audience fixes upon him.

Douglass is not much older than either Charlotte or Murray, nearer 30 years of age perhaps. He is dapper, distinguished and talks eloquently for half an hour. His accent is soothing with its soft, American vowels as he talks about equality, freedom and regret, for he is not free himself. In America, he admits, he remains enslaved. He ponders the evil of that and goes on to discuss retribution. The meaning of money. The fact that white men often expect Black men to be grateful that slavery is nominally over, whereas Black men continue to pay a high price in indentured labour and the charges of their manumission. Charlotte finds she can hardly breathe. Douglass is talking in a way she has never heard before, articulate yet direct.

When Douglass is finished he invites questions. An earnest old man asks his view on whether reparations are due to freed slaves. A younger fellow asks about forgiveness. Then Charlotte freezes in her seat, rigid a moment as she raises her hand, surprised at herself. She feels her cheeks colour, a whole new world. He has talked of his own situation, of course, but, she thinks, hers is related.

'Madam?' He motions towards her. She rises.

'Mr Douglass,' Charlotte says, 'your words resonate most of all with women, I should think. For, like you, women are not free no matter the colour of their skin. We understand what it is to be contained.'

A prickly discomfort passes along the rows, for there is no question that the trials Mr Douglass has endured are greater than the trials of Charlotte Nicholl or indeed any upper-class lady. Yet Mr Douglass remains calm. 'White women are not enslaved, madam, but you are correct, neither are you free. Although here in Scotland, as I understand it, women are freer in law than their English cousins. I'm a married man but I don't wish to own my wife in the way the law prescribes. It's unconscionable that any person should own another. Even by marriage. Times are changing. When white people see Black folks truly free, it follows men must see women the same. The two struggles are not disconnected, you are correct. Making one case makes the other. Freeing one frees all.'

Charlotte breathes out. Murray gives a silent smile. As the meeting breaks up the two Quaker ladies come to talk to them about the importance of female education. Mr Douglass plans to give ladies-only lectures, they say. 'He hit a chord with you, Miss Nicholl,' they enthuse. 'You must come along. As Mr Douglass has said, women will never be taken by their brothers and lifted to a position freely. What we desire, we must fight for. And education is a start, don't you think?' Charlotte is interested in being free, of course, but attendance at university lectures is not the form of emancipation she would choose.

'Excuse me,' she says, brushing off the chatter about lectures in Holland and the ins and outs of graduation at French colleges. She joins the small crowd forming round Mr Douglass who is holding forth about his manumission, which he hopes will be completed soon.

Charlotte curtsies. 'It was a most interesting talk, sir,' she says. 'I'll think upon what you said about one change making another.'

Douglass stares as if he is measuring her soul. 'They deride division, miss, but there can be no change without it. The picket does not bother you?'

She leans in. 'It's thrilling,' she admits as if it is a confidence.

Douglass laughs. 'It's not a game.'

Murray introduces Charlotte and it suddenly strikes her as odd she did not simply say her own name. Behind them members of the audience begin to leave, steeling themselves against the wrathful cordon outside.

'Sir, we must go,' a gentleman says to Douglass.

But before he does so, Mr Douglass leans in. 'All political rights which it is expedient for man to exercise, it is equally so for women,' he confides.

Charlotte nods. 'Thank you.'

Ahead through the door she watches the waiting crowd surge as Douglass pushes into his carriage, girded by three gentlemen. The carriage pulls away.

Outside, the number of protesters has lessened, though there are the same amount of placards, three or four propped against the railings as if the people who held them could not bear their voices silenced. A man wearing a clerical collar, his nose an alarming shade of pink in the freezing air, shouts, 'The Lord will damn you!' as Charlotte and Murray emerge. He is holding two placards, one in each hand.

'Jesus turned over the moneylenders' stalls,' Charlotte hisses. 'And you, sir, must send back the money.'

'Send back the money!' the Quaker ladies take up the chant behind. 'Send back the money!'

They jostle up the hill to the carriage. Safe inside, Charlotte smiles. Murray had said he considered the Quakers boring, but she cannot agree. The emerging attendees together outnumber the protesters now. Behind them the vertiginous pavement disappears into the dark night below as if they are floating. It feels like a dream and yet here is proof she is alive and making her own choices. Murray settles opposite. 'Mr Douglass is to meet the Kirk elders,' he says. 'That's what has provoked the protests. A sniff of money will bring out the worst in people. I understand the Kirk intends to defend its actions in the name of God and the Bible. The more I think on it, I can't defend doing so, for it places us in fellowship with traffickers in human flesh.'

'Our Kirk lacks principle,' Charlotte says, realisation dawning. The sky feels wider than when they walked into the lecture hall and as a result she feels overwhelmingly hopeful. For a start, why would she ever marry when to do so is to consent to being owned? This, she thinks, is a choice that no Black slave was ever accorded. She sits up, feeling powerful suddenly and grateful too that her father has accorded her more freedom than most.

'The Kirk's stance against Mr Douglass is unconscionable,' Murray says.

Charlotte looks at him straight. 'If it is unconscionable, are you going to leave?' she asks. 'If the money is not returned?'

'I don't know. Will you?'

She looks at her right hand, the one Mr Douglass shook. His answer to her question, unlike Reverend Patterson's sermons on Sundays, has inspired her to consider her place in the world. 'Last week I winkled a story out of Mrs Grieg about my mother. She raced my father, you know, and she won. A stretch along the river and up Partick Hill. It seems she was a skilled horsewoman. The more I hear of her, the more I realise she was someone who believed in herself. That's a kind of freedom, isn't it? I knew Papa had that, but I did not know a woman might have it too. I hope I can acquire the same liberty. These last days I have tried to see what it would be like. To be free, I mean. For I must make my own decisions now. I can't thank you enough for bringing me tonight, Murray,' she adds. 'Truly. It took me out of myself.'

'And the demonstration hasn't shaken you?'

Charlotte shrugs. 'It's a Free Kirk,' she replies. 'That's why we left the Church of Scotland, so we might make up our own minds.'

Murray sees a storm is brewing. Maybe it will shake something clear.

Chapter Twelve

The hour of three in the afternoon is clearly displayed on the clock face beneath St Enoch's steeple as Jeremiah Catto crosses the square the next day, past the scatter of grazing sheep beneath the trees. As he reaches the doorway, the bells start to toll. The bell-ringers are sober types, not too enthusiastic. St Enoch's is a dissenters' church and Jeremiah smiles as his mother's words chime in his head. 'Well might they peel the bells with restraint, for they should be ashamed of themselves.' He stops momentarily to examine the calotype of the wishing tree in the glass case and notes the price written in ink below. He wonders how well the images sell and how much profit is in them, as he bounds up the stairs and raps on the door. As Jane opens up, his curiosity is piqued by the scene inside. The studio is bright. It is cold today so both stoves are alight and the attic smells of woodsmoke. The patter of raindrops sounds a gentle tattoo on the glass. Below, the sets are like open doors into a series of curious worlds: a grand sitting room, a garden and some kind of boudoir. It feels familiar, not entirely unlike the theatre, only brighter and more open in its artifice.

Jane's sleeves are rolled up. She has been cleaning. 'Hello,' she says cheerily.

'Am I late?' Jeremiah asks.

'Not at all,' she replies though she expected him a full hour ago. It makes little matter. She has been up since five and will continue till near midnight. Jane has risen at five every morning since she was a child and has come to realise lately that it is as if her life until now has been haunted by the ghost of a great clock, the time of which has been set by other people. Time to bring up the wood for the fire, time to run to the shop for her mother, time to get to Rock House, just enough time, sometimes, when she returned to read her younger sister a story. She has always had a kind of internal tick-tock. She admires Jeremiah's ability to be a whole hour late and not appear to realise, whereas she counts the minutes and seconds required for preparing the salted papers as though each tiny fragment of time were vital as her heartbeat. No mechanical piece could be more accurate and, indeed, there is no clock on display in the studio bar the hungry eye of St Enoch's at the window, which of course has no second hand.

'Miss Mann is in the print room,' she says as Jeremiah strides towards the table as if he owns the place.

'Busy, then?' he checks.

'She is printing two portraits of a lady.'

'And the picture of the tree downstairs?'

'People believe it lucky.'

'It sells well?'

Jane decides discretion in this matter will serve her best. The prints sell well enough, but money remains tight. Yesterday, for example, the women could only afford a pot of brose for their dinner. 'As if I'd be telling the likes of you who buys our wares,' she brushes him off. 'We'll get there,' she adds, as much to herself as to him.

Jeremiah takes a seat, so dapper and colourful that he might be a German porcelain figurine brought to life. Jane smiles. At Mr Hill's the visitors never called for her, and besides, they were dowdy in the main. There is something about Jeremiah that would make him colourful even dressed in dun tweed.

'I'm glad you came,' she says and offers him a slice of pork pie from a wooden board on the table. He picks it up and draws a tin hip flask from his pocket.

'Is that the camera obscura?' he asks, motioning towards the pine box. The dovetail joints at the edges are like clasped fingers.

'Yes. Miss Mann got it second-hand from a gentleman at the observatory.'

He offers her a swig of whisky. Jane shakes her head. 'Did you have a chance to speak to Miss Sutherland?' she asks.

Jeremiah puts his whisky on the table as if he's staking his ground. 'She's interested. It just depends on the money.'

Jane sits, poised for this, the nub of the business. 'How much would she want?'

Jeremiah's mouth twists. 'As much as she can make of it. Miss Sutherland's dressing room is a regular banking hall. She has several admirers who send gifts.'

Jane settles in a chair to consider this. 'Gifts?' she declares in wonder. It seems impossibly glamorous simply to be given nice things.

Jeremiah does not lay out the reasons gentlemen might send presents to Miss Sutherland. Instead he paints the picture Jane wants to see. 'There are satin dresses, sometimes,' he confides. 'I remake them. She had an amethyst necklace once. Miss Sutherland is a costly habit. There was a brooch in the shape of a heart. And gold bracelets. Emerald rings. Flowers. Sometimes so many that the chorus girls sneeze. Oh, and velvet cushions that arrive in boxes wadded with cotton. Eau de parfum from Paris. Boxes of chocolates and candied fruit. Brandy too. And French champagne.'

Jane gasps. Jeremiah lets a laugh escape. This girl is both knowing and joyfully naive.

'One of the gentlemen offered her rooms on the other side of the river, but she told him she could not accept it for it would curtail her freedom. He gave her money instead.'

'Money?' Jane becomes suddenly more attentive.

'Miss Sutherland pays her own bills. But she dines with that gentleman at least once a week.'

His eyes fall to what is left of the pork pie as if to comment that the meals Miss Grace Sutherland consumes are much more sophisticated. Jane recalls the fancy cakes on display in the bakery on Broughton Loan, the stiff icing formed into daisies. Jeremiah leans in. 'They eat ices,' he says, low. 'Gooseberry and vanilla.'

Jane looks as if she might faint and he wonders if a decent meal might be the height of the girl's ambition. When he left the north, it would have been the full extent of his. On the croft everything was cooked over the fire in a single pan. Meals were either broth or brose, or sometimes a fried egg from the griddle. Coming to town, he was bowled over by what he could buy at all hours. Public houses with menus. So many places with ovens that he might choose. Street vendors shucking oysters and selling shrimp potted in butter. Hot sausages. The first year he lived entirely off baked goods: hogget pie and mutton in short pastry. Apple puffs. Eels in a foldover, the crust thick with dripping. Anything from an oven felt the height of luxury. It is not as exciting to him now, but still. Jane picks at the pork pie and he realises she is not the same. This is a woman who has always lived in town and picked up food from street stalls. She has had a choice all her life, if only she could pay for it.

'Do you miss Edinburgh?' he asks.

Jane looks surprised. Coming to Glasgow has been her greatest adventure. 'No,' she says. 'In Edinburgh I was the maid of all works and I didnae live in. Now, though I'm employed to clean the place, Miss Mann lets me work on the negatives.'

Jeremiah can see there is skill involved in the making of images. Since the night before, he has been considering the scheme and he genuinely cannot conceive why he did not decide upon it before. After Jane left, he thought of drawing Grace Sutherland reclining on her dressing-room chaise, but such a portrait even if made into some kind of engraving would never command the price a photograph might achieve. He has pondered at length why this might be, and what he has come to is that a calotype is an image of something real, so the man who owns such an artefact will come the closest he ever can to possessing his angel. For Grace's admirers, he knows, this notion will be tantalising, for they are like addicts. He can see, in this space, that the women are vital to pulling off what he has in mind. From the moment he stepped over the threshold he sensed it was a goldmine.

'As I see it,' he says, leaning in, 'Grace will make her own deal but we shall do well out of it. We must make a picture which might be . . . shall we say, *auctioned*?'

Jane cocks her head in a mechanical movement, as if she is a clockwork toy. 'Auctioned?'

Jeremiah's eyebrow arches. 'To the highest bidder. And those bids,' he adds as if it is a grand announcement, 'will be made in guineas, I'm sure. The picture would be of Miss Sutherland as no member of the audience has seen her. That's where the money is,' he pronounces. 'We must get what we can for making it.'

He pulls a cheroot from his pocket and lights it. Jane is about to ask a question about what this might entail exactly, when the door to the print room opens and Ellory comes in. Jane springs to her feet as if she has been caught at something illicit. Years of cleaning for Jessie Mann has left her jumpy. 'Miss Mann,' she says. 'This is Mr Catto. I told you about him.'

Ellory reaches out her hand. 'Ah yes. From the theatre on Dunlop Street.'

'You're from Edinburgh too, Miss Mann,' Jeremiah says. He balances his cheroot still smoking on the edge of the table and shakes.

'Yes. Edinburgh,' Ellory replies, judging Jeremiah's appearance eccentric. He is thin, taut and well dressed, yet clearly no gentleman. Her immediate sense is that she can trust him as long as what she is trusting him with is in his own interest.

Jane clears her throat. 'Mr Catto has an idea for a portrait of Miss Grace Sutherland.'

'Miss Sutherland the actress?'

'Yes,' Jeremiah says.

'I think what Mr Catto has in mind is something . . . intimate,' Jane ventures. 'Miss Sutherland has wealthy admirers who will be interested in the print.'

'Ought we not discuss this with the lady herself?' Ellory asks.

'She's in rehearsal but is curious about how the venture might work,' Jeremiah says.

Ellory hesitates. She needs more commissions but there is a lot to be considered here. Mr Hill would not dream of photographing an actress, for such women can be bought. This never made sense to her. He photographed ladies in the guise of classical characters, which surely is the same thing actresses do. He paid his Newhaven fishwives for their time. They would hardly have tarried otherwise. These two things coming together might be successful, though she understands immediately that if she wants to retain respectable sitters, discretion will be of the utmost importance.

Jane has no such qualms. She rises from her chair to explain to Jeremiah what they need to do.

'We would set up here, under the skylight,' she says enthusiastically. 'We must take the image during the day.' She emphasises the word with a meaningful glance, for Jeremiah, it is clear, does not keep sunlight hours. 'We can choose how to make it; a drawing room or a garden, like a stage set, though unlike a stage set it will look real.'

Jeremiah eyes the long dressing mirror next to the wardrobe. He indicates it with his finger. 'I like that,' he says.

'I'm interested in using the glass more in my work,' Ellory admits. 'It catches the light. So far I haven't included the mirror as a prop, only reflected light from it onto objects from the doctors' collections on the other side of the square.'

This is not why Jeremiah is interested but he lets it pass. 'So an image of Miss Sutherland, say . . . dressing,' he says, letting the idea drop like a drip of fresh whisky from a still. 'I mean as I dress her,' he says. 'For the stage. A peek into the private world forbidden to her audience.'

Jane moves the chair behind the screen and hauls the mirror into its place. Then she stands before the glass and gazes backwards over her shoulder as if checking her apron strings are tied. The hem of her skirt flicks over her boot, revealing a surprisingly elegant ankle. Ellory is about to stop her. The pose should look ridiculous, Plain Jane with her sleeves rolled up and her apron dusty from cleaning the stove, hardly the stand-in for someone like Miss Sutherland who is all strawberry-blonde curls and corsetry. Yet the image is sculptural. It immediately tells the story of a maid in her mistress's chamber, stealing a moment for herself. There is something charming about seeing the girl in the round.

Jeremiah sits up. This is not what he had in mind. Grace has an array of fancy undergarments, but, like Ellory, he recognises something diverting in the tableau.

'Is the shape all right?' Jane asks.

As Ellory reaches for her camera, Jeremiah makes a split-second decision, stepping in and moving Jane's hair over her shoulder. 'Perfect,' he says.

'Yes,' Ellory agrees. The girl has seen so many sitters being posed that she has a natural sense of what will work. Ellory lays the camera on the table's edge and rushes to the print room to fetch one of the salted sheets Jane prepared first thing. She fits it and opens the aperture. Jane freezes but still manages somehow to look perfectly relaxed. Ellory counts 110 heartbeats and closes the lens. They all breathe out. Jane kicks her hem to the floor and tidies her apron.

'Will you print it now?' Jeremiah asks.

'It takes a while,' Ellory explains. She can fix the image and make the negative immediately, but it will take an hour to lay the processed sheet next to a blank paper and make a print, perhaps more as it is cloudy outside. She has rigged up a way to do this on the window-sill; a glass box like a fernery drilled into the stone. The prints can only be made one at a time.

Jane returns to the table. Unposed she looks dowdy again, the drama that gathered around her entirely disappeared. As Ellory heads for the print room, Jane clears the board of the last crumbs of pie and hands Jeremiah his cheroot.

'For Miss Sutherland we could add a feather boa over the mirror?' she suggests.

'And a fringed velvet chair?' Jeremiah posits as he lights his smoke. They can both imagine the image now though neither one has said that it will work best if Miss Sutherland is dishabille. The more dishabille the better.

'White brings light to a picture,' Jane says, the closest she will get to making a plan to have at least some of Miss Sutherland's under-wear in the composition.

Jeremiah settles in his seat. He is here with high hopes to make money, but he likes the studio too. There is a kind of magic that happens in such places: fitting rooms and properties stores. He likes illusions, especially ones that move people, like when Grace sings a song about being in love, or here, where Ellory has made the print of the tree that gives childless women hope. He is drawn to people who have an effect. He likes being part of it.

As they wait for the print, Jane falls back to her tasks. Jeremiah smokes lazily and inspects the dresses in the wardrobe, pinning a silk flounce round the neckline of a black bodice so that it looks worth twice the price. When the door to the print room opens, Ellory returns with a paper bearing Jane's image. Her eyes are alight as she lays it on the table. Jane starts to laugh, and moves her head shyly to one side. Jeremiah's face looks like some kind of sunrise. 'That's a wonder,' he says.

A hundred people at least stood before the camera at Mr Hill's and not one of them with the magnetism Jane displays. The print is crisp. Though not as vivid as a daguerreotype, it is as close as a calotype might come and with more character. For, as Ellory judges it, that is the difference between the two forms. Daguerreotypes turn out so formal. 'In the mistress's mirror,' she announces by way of a title.

Jane is giggling openly now. It is ridiculous but the picture draws the eye in the most extraordinary way.

'It's you,' Jeremiah pronounces. 'Something in the way you stand.'

'I thought hard about how I wanted someone to see me,' the girl admits.

'Well, you did a good job. It's gey bonnie. I wish it were smaller,' Jeremiah says. 'It's the kind of thing a gentleman might keep in his pocketbook.'

Ellory considers this. A smaller print would be cheaper to make. Having Jeremiah in the studio is most stimulating. 'Let's try another,' she suggests.

This time Jane poses in bare feet, curled in the chair, her uniform unbuttoned and her hair half down with the mirror beside her, like an imp in a lady's bedchamber. There is something lascivious in the pale curve of her elegant neck. Something forbidden. Jeremiah pins the hem of her skirt to show her ankles. Jane doesn't feel shy, for he is clearly accustomed to the company of women in various states of undress. 'That's perfect,' he says. 'Just like that.'

Ellory pauses before opening the aperture. Facially, the girl's expression is so bland the viewer can impose their own belief upon it, she realises. Jane looks as if she is dreaming, but what she is dreaming of is in the eye of the beholder.

'Good,' Ellory murmurs. She feels as if she is balancing on the cusp of excitement and fear, for this is something new and forbidden. She is unsure how she ought to feel about it. It is different from photographing objects or taking portraits of people who expect to look like themselves. Jane, despite the artifice employed, looks as if she is caught in a private moment. She is soft somehow, open to having an image imposed upon her and yet simultaneously in charge of it. When ladies pose for Mr Hill it is as if they are pretending to be statues. Jane, by contrast, is alive. Real, almost. Women do not show their skin this way, she thinks. Jane's ankles. Her toes. But that is exactly why this image tells a story. As she opens the aperture she wonders if anyone has ever made a calotype like this before. They wait in silence. Tick-tock. Ellory covers the camera's eye, removes the paper and disappears to fix the image with her mind racing at the possibilities of a picture telling a story that is not true. Jane tidies her clothing. She reties her boots and pins up her hair. Then she gets back to work as if nothing has happened.

While the first picture is cheeky, saucy even, the second one that Ellory lays on the table an hour later is disarming. The three of them stand in a line with the rectangular papers fanned out like a winning hand at rummy.

'I can take them to sell, if you like,' Jeremiah offers.

Ellory pauses. She cannot post these pictures in the box at the bottom of the stairs. They are not appropriate in view of the respectable doctors she wants as clients nor the hoi polloi of Glasgow society over the river. The pictures are entirely original, but she instinctively knows that to stamp the back of the paper with the rubber and ink bearing her name and the studio address would be an error. This is not the same as her other work. 'How much will you get for them?' she asks.

Jeremiah doesn't hesitate. 'As much as I can,' he says. 'You charge four or five shillings for the pictures in the box but I see these being worth seven shillings easy.'

'Each?' Ellory's tone betrays her shock. It is a lot of money.

'I might try for eight. I've never seen anything quite like them. Have you?'

Ellory shakes her head and gets down to business. 'We'll take three-quarters,' she says. 'Jane must be paid a shilling per print of that and the rest to me at the studio.'

Jane's face widens into a grin. 'Thank you, miss,' she says.

'It's a collaboration,' Ellory pronounces. 'As our agent, you will be discreet, Mr Catto.'

Jeremiah stacks the photographs. 'I will,' he says as if it is a solemn vow. 'Have you paper to cover them?'

Ellory disappears into the office and returns with two Mulreadies.

'Will you come to the theatre with me, Jane?' Jeremiah asks as he fits the sheathed images into the lining of his jacket.

Jane glances at Ellory to elicit her permission. 'You can finish your work when you get back,' Ellory tells her.

'Yes, miss,' Jane says and pulls on her coat.

As the pair troop out, Ellory listens to their footsteps fading on the stair. She reaches into the cupboard and pulls out a jar of raspberry jam made at an inn in the village of Cathcart and sold in the grocery on the Saltmarket at a premium. 'Yon jeelie's gustie,' the grocer said when he brought it from the shelf. 'The sugar came in at Stockwell Place,' he added as if this alone merited the hefty price tag of thruppence ha'penny a jar. Ellory is glad she paid it. The jam is thick and delicious and studded with seeds like some kind of culinary punctuation. She takes half a teaspoonful and lets it melt on her tongue as she wonders how on earth Jane managed to show so much of herself while in fact disappearing. It is a rare skill. Ellory has never seen such a thing despite all the models who have passed through Rock House. It is different from what an actress does on stage. It is quieter. She feels as if she has achieved something and, though it is earlier than she usually would do so, she decides to close the darkroom. Jeremiah is a most stimulating young man, and he has given her an idea. Smaller prints. Reaching for her coat, she locks the door and leaves the key under the mat for Jane on her return. Then she sets off in the direction of the carpenter on Fox Street.

Chapter Thirteen

At four on Friday afternoon, Charlotte notices Ellory Mann in front of the house on Blythswood Square, swithering between ringing the doorbell like an acquaintance or taking the steps down to the kitchen, where deliveries are received. She taps on the window and gestures Ellory to the front door, which she answers herself, glancing into the street in case anyone might notice her unusual visitor. The pavement is thankfully deserted.

Yesterday Charlotte spent some time examining the exterior of her residence and realised there has to be a matching secret room hidden next door at the Howarths'. As far as she can tell, it is located off Mrs Howarth's day room at the rear. Mr Howarth and Papa must have arranged it when the houses were built. Christopher Howarth is a practical gentleman who owns a foundry that makes rivets near the slipway at Govan. Her father declared his success surprising. 'A rivet is not much more than a nail,' he mused. 'And the Howarths so wealthy on the back of just that.' In any case, Charlotte thinks, neither Mrs Howarth nor her ringleted, gossipy daughters can be aware of the secret. She recalls a discussion once about the design of a fancy chimney pot. Mrs Howarth called it 'an ungodly notion' and professed to preferring 'things being as they seem to be'. The secret room, Charlotte guesses, must be Mr Howarth's alone though she could not say what he keeps in it. Once you know the space is there, it is obvious, though cleverly done. Like her father's study, Mrs Howarth's day room looks perfectly proportioned.

'Will you stop, Miss Mann? I can ring for tea,' Charlotte offers.

Ellory smiles. She likes Charlotte Nicholl. There is something intriguing about her, more than any other lady she has met. Making deliveries along Heriot Row and George Street she has never been offered tea. But she wasn't the artist then, only a lackey. When she took photographs at Rock House it was if she lived in a dark lacuna like a dusty statue, unseen until Mr McPhee raised his eyes. 'Thank you,' she says. 'That's kind of you.'

Charlotte leads her to the study and presses the bell as Ellory lays the brown cardboard box on the desk and removes her coat. Charlotte instructs Mrs Cullen to send up a tray. Then she pauses, unexpectedly nervous. 'Go on, Miss Nicholl,' Ellory says. 'It turned out well.'

Inside, nestling in packing paper so sheer it's almost a cobweb, the prints are pristine. Charlotte gasps. Her father never encouraged her to consider her appearance. The main thing was always to be tidy. As she lifts the images from the box the woman immortalised in the calotypes has a confident expression as she gazes into the lens. Her hair is glossy, her skin clear and the old-fashioned spencer has somehow transformed into a more elegant item of clothing: something classic. If she were describing this woman, she would use the word 'magnificent'. She can see now why Ellory advised her to change her outfit.

'Thank you,' she breathes. 'You're a magician, Miss Mann. You've captured a part of me that has been kept in the shadows.'

Ellory flushes. 'You think it's magic because you can't see the workings,' she says. 'When an artist draws his subject, the sitter sees how it's done, but a photograph feels like a trick because it emerges complete.' This belies the hours she spent conjuring the prints out of sunlight. She raises her hands as she saw a player do once at a street fair at Haymarket. 'I'm pleased with it too,' she admits.

Charlotte lifts the invoice at the bottom of the box, written carefully in Ellory's best copperplate. 'Ten shillings is not enough,' she says and reaches immediately into the cash box in her top drawer.

This feels too easy, Ellory thinks as she takes the coins. There is a natural generosity to Miss Nicholl, unlike some of her other clients. The surgeon's payment has still not come in and last night she could not sleep on account of her empty purse. They need more nitrate or she cannot run the darkroom. Mr Hill complained about money endlessly, she recalls, and she is beginning to understand why. The studio is expensive to run. 'Shall I receipt it?' she offers.

'There's no need. Please, sit down.'

Mrs Cullen delivers the tea things and the footman follows her with a packet.

'Thank you,' Charlotte says and gestures the man to put the parcel on the desk. 'Maps,' she explains.

'Are you going somewhere?'

Charlotte pours the tea. 'I thought to take a trip to the coast. There's a pretty harbour in Dunoon.' A lie glibly delivered. Her initial enquiries about Helensburgh House have come to nothing and she has decided to take further action. She needs to find out where the house is and then, who lives there. It should be an easy task in a city like Glasgow, close enough to the Atlantic to be amply supplied with surveyors and mapmakers. Joseph Swan was not able to provide her with anything useful, but McArthur, Fleming and Smith furnished a map of Helensburgh with adequate detail, although she has not, as yet, been able find Helensburgh House upon it. Now she has ordered a map of the environs, but she does not want to discuss that. 'Mr Hill must have been delighted with you as his apprentice.' Charlotte turns her attention back to the prints.

Ellory's mind races. She was not exactly apprenticed at Rock House and during her time there Mr Hill was seldom delighted with anything, so she can admit neither of these things. 'He spent a season photographing fishwives,' she says. 'He calls them his Newhaven Madonnas. Mr Hill is principally a painter and his prints look like paintings. He poses his sitters against clamps and uprights, though all trace is removed in the final pieces. I wanted to create something

more relaxed. Something that is a new form in itself, do you see?'
She hopes she is not being indiscreet.

Charlotte indicates the image of herself. 'You have a rare talent,
Miss Mann. You've captured my spirit.' She cannot help thinking
that if she had had her photograph taken with Papa, as originally
planned, she would not have looked like this. She has changed and
the photograph is proof of it.

'They say the camera does not lie.' Ellory picks up her cup of tea.
'But it can be guided, like a line of argument, to see a subject in a
particular way.'

'And you can alter the image? Taking out these uprights you
mentioned?'

Ellory nods. She bites thoughtfully on a piece of shortbread.
'Perhaps a painting is how the painter sees his subject, entirely in his
control, but a photograph is how the subject wishes to reveal themselves.' It is strange, she realises, only to consider what things look
like rather than how they really are. A painter represents everything.
In a photograph the revelation is always on the sitter's side. 'This is a
lovely library,' she adds, looking round.

'The books were my father's. I have a collection of my own upstairs
though I might bring them down, I suppose.'

'Have you read them all?'

Charlotte shakes her head. 'Some,' she says with only the merest
thought of Mr Burns's *other* poetry. 'Tell me, what else do you plan
to photograph?'

Ellory puts down her cup. She likes Miss Nicholl. There has been
a natural frankness between them from the moment the lady stepped
into the studio. She pauses, however, for she is not accustomed to
confiding her ambitions. Not to Mr Hill or Mr Adamson. Nor Jessie
either. But Miss Nicholl seems the sort of person who gets to the
nub. 'I want to make smaller photographs,' she announces, 'to be
kept in a pocketbook. I had the idea from a friend.'

Charlotte is intrigued by the notion. 'Good heavens,' she says.
She has seen old-fashioned miniatures in velvet cases and reasons if

Miss Mann can manage her plan, it will be like keeping a secret world in your pocket. 'Is it possible?' she asks.

Young ladies do not usually discuss scientific matters. Charlotte's entire education was predicated on her one day running a grand house.

'It's a matter of mathematics,' Ellory admits. 'I've made the calculations. I was given a small lens and I'm having a box made for it. The dimensions must be absolutely accurate. If it works, the prints will be three inches by four.' She cannot breathe. She waits for Miss Nicholl to laugh at her.

Instead Charlotte bursts out, 'How wonderful!' and offers the photographer another biscuit. 'You're creating something entirely new. I admire your ambition, Miss Mann.'

Ellory smiles. The ten shillings she has just received will provide nitrate and pay half the cost of the wooden box for the new camera. Now she is only short the same again. She takes a shortbread and snaps it decisively so that the powdered sugar falls like a brief snowstorm, onto her skirt.

'I don't know if it'll work,' she admits, feeling foolish. Not least because she has wagered money she can ill afford on this endeavour. She has already put down a shilling and sixpence to have oysters delivered for the next few days, in case the cash runs out. She and Jane cannot work with nothing in their bellies. It is not practicable. However, she cannot confide that to this fine lady. It would feel like begging. Jane said she'd starve a day or two if she had to and immediately began to calculate how much they might ask for the smaller prints. 'We'll sell more over all, miss. I'm sure of it,' she avowed. Miss Nicholl however, like Ellory, is excited by the notion of trying something new. Creating something that has not existed before.

Charlotte is about to ask when the first small print might be made when the doorbell rings. Ellory puts down the biscuit guiltily, as if she has stolen it. 'Oh no. Please,' Charlotte insists. She does not want her companion to be displaced by a New Town worthy come over the Clyde to pay their respects, though she notes from the low spring sun that it is on the late side for a social call. Mrs Cullen opens the study door and Charlotte's heart sinks as Mrs Grieg sweeps through, buttoned, quite unnecessarily, into full mourning clothes – as good as an accusation.

'Charlotte Nicholl,' she says loftily and peers at Ellory. She pulls out a small gold pocket watch decorated with blue enamel and examines it to make clear it is unthinkable that any visitor other than herself might be in Miss Nicholl's company so late of an afternoon. She clearly assumed she would catch the lady alone at this time of day.

Charlotte tries not to exercise herself. 'Good afternoon, Mrs Grieg,' she says. 'Shall I ring for another cup?' Mrs Grieg shakes her head and Charlotte continues smoothly. 'Miss Mann, this is a family friend, Mrs Grieg. I must admit I am surprised to see you, Mrs Grieg. Miss Mann and I were discussing mathematical calculations.'

Mrs Grieg's stare makes plain her disapproval. 'There might be no man in the house, but you do not have to fill that place yourself,' she snarls. 'I've come on important business, Charlotte. We must speak privately.'

'I apologise.' Ellory snaps to her feet but Charlotte stops her.

'I'm already engaged, Mrs Grieg,' she replies firmly. 'Perhaps we might meet tomorrow.'

'Your father wouldn't want me to wait,' Mrs Grieg says, her face like a thundercloud.

'I feel I ought to go,' Ellory repeats.

The old woman's stare would rot a gutted fish. 'Thank you, Miss Mann, for your consideration,' she says.

Charlotte looks forlornly at her new friend. The study has suddenly become a battlefield and she does not want to back down. 'Please stay. Mrs Grieg can say whatever she wishes in front of you. You have my trust.'

This is a step too far. 'This wanton piece?' Mrs Grieg's voice rises. 'I don't understand you entertaining tradespeople to tea, Charlotte. We brought you up better.'

Charlotte gasps. As far as she's concerned, Mrs Grieg did not bring her up at all. 'I'll thank you not to sneer at my friends,' she says.

'A friend?' Mrs Grieg continues cruelly. 'Eating shortbread in gloves? Quite the connection.'

Ellory's cheeks flame. Though her heart is racing, she freezes stock still as if she is a statue about to be daubed with graffiti.

Charlotte swallows her rising fury. 'Why are you being so rude?'

'Rude?' Mrs Grieg exclaims. 'Your father would be as rude I assure you. If I'm the same, it's on his behalf.' The old lady's face is flushing pinker by the second. 'Two nights ago, you and Murray Urquhart supported Mr Frederick Douglass no less. The monster determined to ruin our kirk. There's nothing about your actions which is acceptable, Charlotte. Being unchaperoned with a gentleman is one thing – Murray is your legal representative, I suppose – but going to such a place is quite another. When I think of the effort your father invested in you . . . All of us. How could you?' Mrs Grieg's eyes are blazing in fury. 'And now I find you here with this shabby wee quine. Your reputation will be worth nothing, you stupid girl. I said to Dr Grieg this morning, Charlotte Nicholl needs a good man. I tell you plain, it is either the madhouse or the girl must marry. There's nobody in charge of her any more.'

Charlotte's stomach turns over. 'Marry?' she repeats incredulously. 'The madhouse? What are you talking about?'

Mrs Grieg does not back down. She has always been a busybody, Charlotte thinks. That propensity, and the fact the old woman clearly feels responsible for her now James Nicholl is no longer here, has led to her stepping way over the mark.

'Reverend Patterson will attest to it,' Mrs Grieg continues, wringing her hands. 'Everyone is talking about you living here, in this big house on your own.'

'A moment ago, the problem was that I went to a lecture with Murray to educate myself in a matter of interest.' Charlotte's tone is becoming testier.

That is a good point, Ellory thinks, still frozen and watching the exchange as if it is some kind of performance. The older woman is making little sense, though Ellory knows Miss Nicholl is the kind of lady a gentleman like Mr Urquhart ought to pay attention to. Her stomach twists at the thought, which surprises her. *He's my solicitor*, she thinks. *It is only that I have come to rely on him.*

'The lad is spending a good deal of time, isn't he?' Mrs Grieg does not let up. 'If Murray Urquhart wants to marry you, Charlotte, he should get on with it. But perhaps he's no fool. The boy's a cripple and you've still put him off, despite all your money and this grand house! You're making a mockery of yourself. You have to behave, girl. Then if you're lucky, perhaps he'll have you. I begin to think he's your only hope.'

Charlotte lets out a frustrated sigh. The idea of becoming Mrs Urquhart, alongside the fact that Mrs Grieg does not know her true financial circumstances, strains her newfound confidence. In a moment of confusion, she wonders if Mrs Grieg can somehow make her acquiesce. Can she force Murray too? It seems insulting to them both. She feels urged to hammer the rug on the hearth with the brass poker hanging by the fire. To pound some sense into the world.

'I'm sure your father would have agreed to such a match,' Mrs Grieg continues with a smirk that clears the fog of Charlotte's emotion. 'I can talk to Murray's father. He might still take you if we move sharp.'

Charlotte feels as if she has just woken from an extremely odd dream. On the other side of her desk Ellory's face betrays her shock. They were having such a pleasant call, Charlotte thinks. 'I'm not a hand of cards to be won,' she says. She will not relinquish her newly endowed freedom. It comes to her that if Miss Mann runs her own affairs, so can she.

Mrs Grieg leans in as if explaining something of great complexity. 'It's not fitting, Charlotte,' she says.

'And your resolve is that I must marry?'

'It's a lady's duty to have children,' Mrs Grieg spits. 'Just because your mother died after giving birth, doesn't mean you are bound to do the same. There have been many advances. What's the chap's name in Edinburgh? Dr Young Simpson? I'm sure Dr Grieg shall engage him when you're with child. I hear he's a marvel.'

'That,' says Charlotte, 'is enough.' Her hands are quivering. She is sure her face must be pink for her belly has become a furnace.

But Mrs Grieg is not minded to stop. 'Your father wanted me to look after you,' she insists. 'He gave me the clock in the day room to mark it. Not that you have handed it over.' The old woman's gaze becomes suddenly hard.

'My father is dead,' Charlotte says. 'He left me his money because he trusted me.' This, she realises as she says it, is true. 'He left you an old clock. That is not the keeping of me. You're not my mother and you may take the clock whenever you like.'

Mrs Grieg looks as if she has been slapped in the face. 'After everything I've done,' she says. 'Reverend Patterson shall hear of this, you ungrateful child.'

Charlotte's eyes are cold now. 'My father disagreed with Reverend Patterson on a regular basis. It's a family tradition I expect I'll be keeping up, for the Kirk is wrong, Mrs Grieg, in the matter of Mr Douglass's campaign. The money should be returned. While we're at it, I don't hold with your insistence on mourning attire. I don't require a black frock to remind me that my father is dead. I'm not a child any longer. And I have no intention of getting married.'

Ellory feels like cheering her friend, though she holds herself back.

'Dear James would not have left you this inheritance if he knew you'd be so foolish,' Mrs Grieg retorts.

Charlotte gets up. 'Regardless, I'm mistress of this house. I want you to leave and not come back.'

'You can't do that!' the old lady exclaims.

'Can I not?'

Mrs Grieg looks confused that the exchange has not gone the way she envisaged. Charlotte has not given an inch. Not in the matter of her household circumstances or the match with Murray Urquhart or anyone else. And neither has she wavered in her support for that disgusting man and his attack on the Kirk.

'You will apologise this instant, Charlotte Nicholl,' she demands, but instead Charlotte marches to the study door and opens it. The old woman pauses before she realises no apology is going to be forthcoming. 'You'll regret this,' she warns and stalks into the hall, where the housekeeper is standing in readiness. 'Mrs Cullen,' the old woman instructs, 'fetch me the ormolu clock from the day-room mantelpiece.' Mrs Cullen's expression does not flicker.

'Go on, Mrs Cullen,' Charlotte instructs. They wait in silence for the housekeeper's return. Charlotte's heart pounds but she shows no sign. Then Mrs Grieg tucks the little clock under her arm and with a tiny harrumphing sound disappears out the front door without saying goodbye. Charlotte peers after her. Ellory notices her friend's breathing is more easy now. A determined smile slides across Charlotte's lips; recognition of her triumph. She briefly wonders where this steely feeling has come from. Until now she has largely let other people decide what she will do, by which she means her father. Something has changed.

Turning back into the study, Ellory looks paler than when she arrived. The women's eyes lock for a moment in understanding. 'Miss Mann,' Charlotte says, 'I hope you are all right?'

Ellory thinks it is extraordinary that Miss Nicholl has turned her attention to her guest's well-being when she is the person who was just under attack. 'That was shocking,' she manages. Jessie spent her years at Rock House deriding her cousin on a daily basis, but what Ellory has just witnessed is quite different – worse, she thinks. 'That old quine is a bully,' she says.

'I cannot thank you enough,' Charlotte says.

'For what? I only witnessed it.'

Charlotte insists. 'You simply being here was a help. A witness, as you said. Another woman who has made her own path, do you see?'

136

Ellory pauses. 'In Edinburgh I lived at the foot of Calton Hill, near the gaol, Miss Nicholl.'

'Call me Charlotte. Please.'

'The prisoners are not watched as closely.'

The light blinks on and off in Charlotte's eyes. Then she opens up. 'People notice everything,' she says. 'It's why I do not take the laudanum. I need my wits. They're trying to look after me, but I've realised I must find my own way. As you have, Miss Mann.'

'Ellory.'

'I admire your making your own decisions. Murray – that is to say Mr Urquhart – told me your story. For a woman such as yourself to forge a career. To find your passion and follow it. To make such brave and curious innovations . . .'

'I think what you did was brave,' Ellory cuts in, feeling proud that Murray Urquhart mentioned her. She waivers a moment, then adds, 'You must miss your father.'

Charlotte likes Miss Mann but she cannot admit that she does not miss James Nicholl. Given what she has learned of her father's true nature, she could not go back to life as it was, even if it were possible to do so. 'I must find a way forward,' she says as if it is an announcement. 'Visiting your studio helped. Afterwards, Mr Urquhart accompanied me to a lecture in the evening. The one to which Mrs Grieg objected.'

'What was it about?'.

'The speaker was an escaped slave, Mr Douglass, visiting from America. He has taken exception to the foundation of the Free Kirk. His talk was about liberation, which I'm coming to realise is relevant to all of us. Mrs Grieg feels she has the right to speak to me in the way she did because in her eyes I shouldn't be free to make my own decisions.'

'But why is Mr Douglass opposed to the Free Kirk?' Ellory asks. She is well acquainted with the Kirk's luminaries, who comprised the bulk of Mr Hill's sitters. They were glum gentlemen in the main who seldom bought their prints, though Mr Hill was always hopeful they might. He had started a grand painting of them all together two years ago. It wasn't finished by the time she left.

'Because plantation owners gave money to fund the Kirk. It's blood money from the profits of enslavement and wrong to keep it. Mr Douglass wants the Kirk to send the whole sum back.'

'And Mr Urquhart agrees with you that they should?'

'Yes,' Charlotte admits as if she is testing the effect of such a robust statement. A man agreeing with her rather than the other way round. 'Mrs Grieg and Reverend Patterson will argue no doubt that the funds are best put to use in the service of God. However, I think the Kirk must do the right thing whether it's convenient or not.'

'The ends and means of life must match,' Ellory states plainly. That was what Reverend Reid always said. He was right, now she considers it.

'Will you join me in the drawing room?' Charlotte asks. She is enjoying this refreshing conversation. Most women are like the Howarth girls and only talk about fripperies. 'Shall we have a proper visit?'

Ellory looks down at her gloved hands, still peppered with powdered sugar. Miss Nicholl is being kind, but the truth is she does not belong in this world of teacups and fancy cornicing. She will never be a lady.

'Ah,' Charlotte reads her. 'You didn't remove your gloves to eat the biscuit.' She realises that such niceties present a minefield to someone who is not educated to it. 'Please, I don't give a fig about that. Mrs Grieg is a rude old woman. She should not have said what she did.'

Ellory stutters her reply. 'I can't remove the gloves. In company, I mean.'

Charlotte smiles. 'Don't be silly. Of course you can. I'll show you. It's considered quite elegant, in fact. A lady lays her gloves in her lap when she's eating.' But Ellory draws away as Charlotte reaches for her arm. 'What's the matter?'

Ellory shifts. She feels suddenly as if she is about to be exposed. 'I'm ugly,' she gets out.

'Ugly?' Charlotte perches on the edge of the desk. The fire crackles behind her. 'I cannot conceive of you being ugly.'

Ellory considers a moment. Friends ought to share confidences but it has been a long time since she had a true friend. Probably not since her sister died. She fiddles with the edge of the leather glove. She has spent much of the week photographing medical anomalies: cankers and tumours and strange bodily contortions. If she had shown the doctor her skin, perhaps he would have asked her to photograph that too. 'All right,' she decides. Charlotte has been brave and she should be so too. 'I hope it doesn't offend you.' She unrolls the glove slowly and Charlotte gasps. At first, it looks as if ink has been spattered over Ellory's skin but on closer inspection it is not only that. The marks are puckered; a sharp contrast to Ellory's rosy freckled features and her lively green eyes. The tips of her fingers are black as a curse. Charlotte's face betrays her shock. 'I'm sorry,' Ellory says and scrambles to pull the leather back up.

'I'm the one who must apologise,' Charlotte insists, unable to take her eyes from her new friend's skin which is now rapidly disappearing.

'My cousin is the same,' Ellory admits. 'She says being a spinster is the price of our profession. At first nobody realised the damage the chemicals inflict. Nor that it was permanent. Mr Adamson was a pioneer, you see.'

Charlotte draws herself up. 'And Mr Adamson's skin?'

'His fingertips are marked.'

'Only the tips?'

'He instructs others in his experiments,' Ellory explains. 'I know it's ugly. You're the only person I've ever shown, bar my cousin.'

'You've never had a suitor then?'

'I'm not interested in such matters.' Ellory waves the notion off. She thinks of her sister but does not say so. The bounds of friendship extend only so far. What happened to Nora made it impossible for Ellory to admit any man, marked skin or not. Her place at Rock House was too important. 'We use instruments now for the photographic work. The chemicals,' she continues. 'Jane, my assistant, won't suffer the same.'

'Won't your skin recover?'

Ellory gives a little shrug. 'I like the gloves,' she says lightly.

Charlotte crosses to the drinks tray. 'We need not go up,' she says. 'But perhaps a brandy?'

Charlotte pours two balloons, her eyes drawn to the thistle boss. Miss Mann has shared a confidence. Two in fact if she were to count her scheme with the little camera, but Charlotte still feels too ashamed to reveal what's on her mind. As she turns, she takes a breath and with it some courage.

'I lied before,' she admits.

'Lied?' Ellory repeats as if she cannot conceive of such a thing.

'The map,' Charlotte gestures. She has spent hours peering across the sprawl of Argyll and Inverclyde as if she is a general planning a campaign. It's difficult to get the words out. She has not voiced these suspicions before. 'I've been searching for a particular house. I suspect my father kept a mistress. I'd like to talk to her. Since he died, I've discovered I didn't know Papa in life as well as I thought.'

'Do you know the woman's name?' Ellory asks.

Charlotte is flooded with relief that her new friend shows no sign of shock, or for that matter judgement. 'I don't. She lives at Helensburgh House, which it turns out isn't in Helensburgh, as far as I can see.'

Ellory pauses. 'I should think the post office might be able to help. As you know the name of the place.'

Charlotte's face lights. A laugh escapes her lips and flies up to the ceiling like a bird released from a cage. The world has seemed impenetrable but Ellory Mann has had a more practical education. Charlotte suddenly realises that perhaps she does not have to do everything herself, poring over maps when she might simply ask a question. 'Thank you.' She casts her eyes upwards. 'I should have thought of that.'

'How does it feel?' Ellory says as she sips the brandy.

'To know my father dishonoured our family name?'

'To share a confidence?' They are both secretive, Ellory realises. Perhaps women have to be.

Charlotte smiles. 'I like you,' she replies. 'That's what it feels like. I've never had a friend before. So many young ladies are . . .' she searches for the right way to say it, 'immensely foolish.'

Ellory laughs. She feels the same. She has spent too long with people around her watching for faults. It would be pleasant to have a friend. Charlotte seems contained and yet that very sense of being separate means she does not judge. 'I thought Mr Urquhart was your friend.'

'I've always liked Murray,' Charlotte admits. 'Still I found out about Helensburgh House by chance. He knows and he has not told me. The truth is, I've not shared as much with him as I have with you.'

Ellory raises her glass as if a deal has been struck.

'Will you stay for dinner?'

It is almost dark outside and she has work to do. 'Another time. I must get back to my studio. Will you visit me when you have the leisure? Not to have a picture taken. Merely to call?'

'I shall,' Charlotte promises. 'Thank you. And I'll welcome you here again, I hope.'

They finish the drinks and Mrs Cullen brings Ellory's coat. In the hallway they are formal again, the conversation turning to where in the drawing room the photograph of Miss Nicholl might be mounted. Ellory takes the stairs onto the pavement just as the gas lamp is being lit outside. She glances in the direction of Bath Street but chooses to avoid passing Mr Urquhart's home and office on her way and turns down Douglas Street instead. Miss Nicholl and Mr Urquhart will make a fine couple, she thinks with a strange twinge of sadness. She puts her hand into her pocket and squeezes her purse. Almost enough for the new camera, she reminds herself, and wonders what Jane might bring back from Rab Ha's tonight, for there is enough for a good dinner while she sits at her desk and balances the books.

*

Much later, in a feather bed on the second floor of the Nicholl residence, Charlotte is wakeful, curled in a chocolate-brown button-backed chair, sipping warm milk and honey from a yellow porcelain cup that her mother used two decades before. Beyond the glass she watches the waxing, gibbous moon. As she turns, she catches a glimpse of herself in the mirror. Tonight, she is not the girl in the painting hanging in the drawing room, nor is she the haughty beauty wearing the old-fashioned spencer in Ellory's calotype. She is herself. She has not had to succumb to anybody else's will. She is as free as she can be and, she realises, if there is anything that she wishes her father's money to buy, it is that.

She moves her head so her face catches the moonlight, her skin bright suddenly. Slowly, she unties the cotton ribbon at the neck of her nightgown and considers her reflection as if it is an intimate portrait; not of the sort in Papa's secret cupboard, but personal none-theless. She titles it 'A Lady at her Rest after an Extraordinary Day'. Then she smiles for she has both lost and made a friend. It is, she decides, a change for the better. New ideas and new people are most invigorating. Ellory Mann will not judge her for moving to a smaller house or letting go some of her staff. Miss Mann does not consider Charlotte wicked for supporting Mr Douglass. And she would not threaten madhouses or marriage. 'We talked of mathematics,' she says out loud. Perhaps, she posits, this is what happens when a lady grows into her inheritance. Her world widens. Perhaps, yes, it is that.

Chapter Fourteen

The next morning, Mr Lennox dodges out of the spring drizzle into the Urquharts' stucco-fronted office on Bath Street, where he is hailed by Willie Duff, the building superintendent, who stands to attention in the Carrara-marble hallway for 12 hours of the day, directing visitors to the correct floor, receiving deliveries and keeping order in the event of cheeky urchins attempting to gain entrance. Lennox dries his boots on the mat as Duff directs him to the first floor, where through a further mahogany and bevelled-glass door he finds himself in a pleasant reception area, panelled in dark wood and warmed by an open fire. Well-padded leather chairs are placed about for clients to sit upon. In one a ginger cat is curled asleep. 'He keeps the mice at bay,' the young clerk says apologetically, shooing the animal to the floor. Mr Lennox is not required to tarry. The younger man takes the gentleman's sodden coat and damp hat and ushers him into the younger Mr Urquhart's office, where Murray is ensconced behind a wide leather-topped desk. He rises and offers his hand.

'Mr Lennox,' he says. 'We met at James Nicholl's wake.'

Lennox has waited several days before visiting the office. Among other things, he wanted to pursue enquiries about the Urquharts' business, which he has found to be solid. The Urquharts have only a couple of dozen clients but every one of them is a major Glasgow financier, taking money made in slaves, sugar and cotton by their grandfathers and funnelling it into industry along the Clyde. Murray's father, who founded the firm, is known to be discreet and exacting, qualities that Lennox knows are highly valued by the wealthy, and indeed form the foundation of his own employment. It is on account of these qualities that many of Glasgow's affluent businessmen choose to contract private matters through Urquhart & Son. Old Mr Urquhart is a man, it is said, you can trust with both your widow and your mistress. He might have made an excellent politician, Lennox thinks wryly. And the son seems to be following in his father's footsteps, though he knows from his enquiries that the lad's return from London has surprised many denizens of Glasgow society, who expected the capital to seduce him.

'What can I do for you, sir?' Murray asks, motioning Mr Lennox to take a seat.

Lennox's mouth tightens across his teeth as he appraises the lad. Murray shows more restraint in his dress than an out-and-out dandy, but he certainly picked up something during his time at chambers down south. He is sporting a chocolate-coloured waistcoat today with a flash of golden thread at the seams and an oxblood cravat.

'I understand you're friendly with Miss Nicholl, Mr Urquhart,' Lennox starts.

Murray does not smile. 'Charlotte and I have known each other all our lives,' he says. 'Our fathers were friends as well as solicitor and client. Do you have business with the lady, sir?'

'I had business with her father. How well did you know Mr Nicholl?' Lennox enquires.

'My father was his friend and his solicitor since early in both their careers, before either Charlotte or I was born.'

'Nicholl had some run.'

'His eye to investment was second to none,' Murray agrees, without adding either that what James Nicholl did with the bulk of his fortune remains a mystery or that his father made substantial additions to their own family's fortune by following James Nicholl's lead.

Lennox, meanwhile, notes Murray has not answered his question. Lifelong acquaintance does not mean the knowing of a fellow. Still, he pushes on. 'I wonder if in the estate you have discovered any investments Mr Nicholl may have made in art?'

Murray shakes his head. Mr Nicholl had excellent taste in stocks, shares and bonds, but he was not somebody who patronised the arts. 'There are a few paintings in the house on Blythswood Square,' he says.

The older man's eyes show no spark of interest. He brushes an imaginary speck of dust from his dark trousers. 'He was a connoisseur,' he says.

'Really?' Murray finds this unlikely. The decoration of Charlotte's house is restrained, almost old-fashioned compared to many well-to-do residences in the city. He thinks briefly of the crimson flock wallpaper recently installed in the drawing room of the Ainslie family mansion on Abbotsford Place. He privately wondered the last time he was there if Mr Ainslie's gout had been brought on by it. Murray certainly felt heavy in the feet by the time he left.

'I always admired Mr Nicholl's library,' he says. 'I believe some of the editions are rare. Miss Nicholl has recently added to it. A selection of writings by Miss Eliza Whigham. A lady Quaker from Edinburgh.'

Lennox sighs. 'I ought to speak to your father,' he says.

'Of course.'

Murray leaves the room, returning immediately with the old man who enters in a flurry of cedarwood as if he has been hung in a wardrobe to preserve him from the moths. 'Mr Lennox has come to enquire after a collection he believes James Nicholl owned. Art,' Murray explains.

Old Mr Urquhart slowly pours himself a whisky and offers the others a glass, which Lennox accepts and Murray declines. 'A collection?' the old man says. 'I know of no such thing. I don't think James had that kind of eye, though he had both the money and energy for such a venture.'

'Mr Lennox says so. I have read all the papers in the Nicholl portfolio and I have never seen a collection mentioned beyond what is on the walls at Blythswood Square.'

'My son will be Miss Nicholl's solicitor,' Mr Urquhart explains. 'It's time to pass the baton.'

Lennox sips. 'I see,' he says. The whisky is excellent, and his face betrays this.

'It's from the Haigs' still.' Mr Urquhart lifts his glass. 'It's one of my favourite drams.'

Lennox ignores this. 'The paintings aren't in the house,' he says, leaning forward. 'I'm afraid it's a delicate matter. James Nicholl wished to sell his collection. In fact, he had been . . .' here Lennox pauses, '*induced* to do so.'

'Induced?' old Mr Urquhart repeats as if he is spitting the word onto the Aubusson carpet beneath his feet. James Nicholl was never induced into anything in his life. It crosses Mr Lennox's mind that if the solicitor finds his vocabulary distasteful, he dreads to think what the old man will make of the nature of the artwork James Nicholl consented to sell.

'Mr Nicholl agreed a price about a week before he died. He was an excellent negotiator,' Lennox says.

The lawyers silently acquiesce. James Nicholl never made a deal that was not of the best.

Lennox continues. 'That's why I came to Glasgow,' he posits. 'I was to enact the transaction and see to the packing and shipping.'

'You do not live here?'

He shakes his head. 'I'm familiar with the city. I was brought up in Argyll. I knew James Nicholl when we were young men. That's one of the reasons my employer chose me to complete the purchase.'

'And your employer's name?' Urquhart presses. The solicitor might be elderly, but he is accustomed to getting to the crux of things.

Instead of answering, Lennox reaches into his inside pocket and passes three papers over the desk: letters written in James Nicholl's hand.

Murray picks them up and reads. His eyebrows raise as his father waits patiently to be handed the missives one by one. The lamp dims and glows, an inconsistency in the oil. Murray suddenly notices the tick of the clock on the mantle. 'This is a substantial sum,' he says, laying the final letter on the desk. 'More than 40,000 guineas. You might build a mansion for less. You might buy a brace of well-fitted ocean-going ships.'

Mr Lennox's lips part in what might almost be described as a smile. 'It's a large collection and of high quality. It's the content, you see. My employer had a specialist prepare an inventory some months ago.'

'Do you have it?'

Lennox hesitates. He misses London and this is the most direct route to a packet back to his house in St James's. He has made enquiries about the town in the city's art galleries, but the dealers are quite useless. Yesterday in John Finlay's on Buchanan Street, Lennox spotted a nice enough engraving of a Parisian scene which, though marked by Jean-Michel Moreau, was at best a mediocre copy. Finlay had started as a shipfitter on the Trongate who got ideas above his station after he framed a few prints for the club room on a steamer. Between badly educated dealers and the ill-informed buyers who rely on them, Lennox privately despairs of the state of British art.

He decides he has to trust Urquhart. After all, James Nicholl did. Up to a point. He pulls out a further sheaf of ivory paper inked with close-packed handwritten notes and lays it on the desk. Murray starts to read. His mouth opens. It closes. He looks at his father. Old Mr Urquhart reaches past his son and picks up the first page of the inventory. Experience tells, Lennox thinks, for the old man's face betrays nothing. The list is detailed and leaves as little to the imagination as the paintings themselves.

'The deal was agreed,' Lennox continues. 'Nicholl shook hands upon it. It would constitute a breach of contract were it not to go ahead, though I recognise that Mr Nicholl's demise could not be helped.'

Mr Urquhart sits back in his seat with the first page of Lennox's notes before him. His fingers arch in front of his face. This is a legal point which he is qualified to address.

'You say your employer had an expert take this inventory?'

'Yes.' Lennox does not add that the man was a teacher at the Royal Academy of Arts.

'So the man saw the collection?'

'Indeed.'

'Where?'

'I don't see what that has to do with it,' Lennox says.

Urquhart's mind closes like a steel trap. 'We have no idea where these items are, Mr Lennox. I think we can all agree that we'll not be able to find out from Miss Nicholl.'

Lennox gives a sharp nod.

'Ergo, if we're to locate the items in order to conclude the sale, knowing where the gentleman inspected them is a good first step.'

'I'll write to him,' Lennox says, cursing now that he had not thought of it.

'Good.' Mr Urquhart finishes his whisky, signalling that the exchange is over. Lennox retrieves his papers and rises. No sooner is he on his feet than the clerk appears in the doorway holding his coat and hat, dried and brushed. 'You can find me at McLaren's Hotel,' Lennox says. He bids the solicitors good day and leaves smartly.

Murray starts to babble something about finding it hard to believe that James Nicholl owned such items, but his father, older and wiser, raises a hand to quiet him and watches from the window as their visitor turns down Bath Street. Rivulets stream down the side of the paving stones and puddle into muddy pools at the junctions.

'You may speak,' he says when Lennox finally disappears down West Nile Street, towards town.

'Do you think it's true?' Murray bursts out.

Urquhart considers. 'On balance, I do,' he pronounces, his expression no more shifting in surprise than it did earlier. 'He has the paperwork. The letters are in James Nicholl's hand. What would be the point of the man coming here if it weren't true? He might win a small amount in compensation for a broken contract, but that would be hardly worth it. His shoes were well made. His hat too. He's not short of money. Let's see what we can find out about Mr Lennox, shall we?'

'Charlotte knew him. He was at the funeral and the wake.'

'Ask her then. Carefully. We don't want her catching wind of this.'

'And the money?'

'The proceeds will be added to the estate. With a finders' fee deducted, for we are brokers now. Ten per cent. Though you must not say a word to Charlotte until we've sorted it out, Murray. There's no point in raising the girl's hopes. She'll only receive half, of course. Those are the terms of the will. But that's more than ample, I should think. James was wily. He doubled the money from the railway shares in two years.'

Murray takes this in. 'Do you think James kept these paintings at Helensburgh House?' he asks.

'I think somebody would have made comment, don't you?' Mr Urquhart replies. 'It's surprising, is it not? He was not the moderate man he appeared to be.' James Nicholl had had the ability to surprise him in life, but he had not expected him to be able to do so in death. 'At least we've found the missing balance. That was troubling me. You must call tomorrow on Charlotte and see what you can turn up,' he instructs.

'About Lennox?'

'About all of it. And Murray,' he adds, 'I've noticed the time you've spent on the lass McPhee sent . . . Miss Mann.'

Murray stiffens. He has visited Ellory's studio three times now, drumming up custom on her behalf. That and the night at the observatory. He has been attentive, it's true, and it is, he knows, because he is drawn to her. His father misses nothing. Never has.

'McPhee has settled the account. Unless you are opening a new receipt, your time is best placed elsewhere,' Mr Urquhart says, certain as a prophesy. Murray knows his father wants him to direct his attention to Charlotte or at least to one of Glasgow's other young ladies. Old Mr Urquhart has no interest in a penniless lady photographer with whose parents he is not acquainted. But Murray cannot help himself. It is a chemical reaction, he realises, like an image emerging in the developing tray.

'Miss Mann is talented,' he posits.

'The account is closed, Murray,' his father repeats with finality and heads for the door that connects his own office to his son's. 'Let me know what you get out of Charlotte Nicholl,' he adds. How the boy handles the affair will be a good measure of whether he is ready to take over the business. Urquhart is always interested in the truth. It is, as Reverend Patterson says on Sundays, the Lord's way. Aye, Urquhart thinks, and the devil's too. Naturally, as a solicitor, he would charge both the same.

Chapter Fifteen

Later that evening

Down from the new Gaelic church, the cockpit on Hope Street looks like nothing from outside. There is no sign and the entry down the return is barely lit with only a single, guttering candle lamp on the damp cobblestones at the foot of the doorway. To get in, one raps on the door and a muscle-bound docker opens up and demands a tanner a head, a penny of which he keeps for himself. Inside, the building has no graces either. The brick walls have not been plastered and the floors are lined with cheap wooden planks stained with mud stomped into the grain by thousands of boots over the many years the pit has been in operation. The last time Jeremiah came here, he took a beating when he misjudged a fellow's intentions. But having considered it, he reckons his best chance of selling the pictures of Jane is among a crowd of men with their blood up, so it is either here or the bare knuckle on the Broomielaw. Or else at the races in Ayr where the prize money is 2,000 sovereigns but, on the downside, there are frequently ladies.

He dresses carefully, donning a padded vest underneath his clothes in case things come to blows. In the wardrobe he finds a sturdy blackthorn walking stick to use as a weapon. It was a prop for a new act: two boys from Stonehaven who did not last a fortnight in front of Glasgow's discerning theatregoers. Now it will prove useful. Last time Jeremiah came this way he was lucky not to crack a rib for the fellow got carried away, but all the Cattos can take a beating. His father was never shy with the belt. Still, it would be a double indignity to be robbed as well as thrashed, for he hopes to be carrying a decent amount of coin by the end of the night.

He slips the doorman a sixpenny bit and trips down the open stairs into the basement, lit by iron lamps pinned into the brick. The floor is beaten earth, the cockpit cut into it. There have already been a couple of fights and the arena is strewn with blood and feathers. Among the crowd, he notices several working men with dogs on short ropes; not Newfoundlands or Labradors as the ton possess, but dogs from the mines round the city. The dog pit at the Saltmarket would be another good place to ply his wares. But he's here now. It is ten of the clock. Scattered about are fellows in evening dress; black tie and capes amid the thick tweed-and-cap crowd, and even some uniforms – sailors off the merchant ships docked on the Clyde. All of them will be armed if they have any sense. It was a fellow in evening dress who beat him before.

The building reaches over the back plot. At the grubby rear door, a young lad is selling drink from two barrels, one of perl and the other of stout. In the summer the second barrel was filled with ale, Jeremiah recalls. On the other side of the door in the corner, the birds are stacked in cages, with their owners loitering nearby. A man would be a fool to leave a prize cock alone, for the bookmakers are not above feeding grain laced with poison if it brings an advantage.

The pit is noisy, the low hubbub of conversation running like a steam engine. Two young gentlemen smile at Jeremiah as he pushes past, and he has to think before he places them backstage at the theatre rather than his other night-time haunts. That is the difficulty he got into before. He seldom remembers men's faces, for that is not what is important to him. He might come across a dozen gentlemen in a day between the crush for Miss Sutherland and his outings to

Glasgow's dens of iniquity. He cannot remember them all. 'Gents,' he greets the men. 'You're here to wager?'

'Indeed,' one replies and takes a draught from a silver hip flask. The way he eyes Jeremiah prompts him to think that there is a second purpose to the gentleman's outing, but in that case the pictures of Jane will not be of interest, and Jeremiah is here for business tonight, not pleasure.

He strolls casually onwards towards the fighting ring as he draws a pewter watch from his pocket. 'Running late,' he comments casually, as if he is impatient.

The gentleman next to him turns. 'They draw things out to encourage the betting,' he says knowledgeably.

Jeremiah considers the man. He is no more than 40 and best described as wide rather than portly. He is well dressed and, at a guess, has come from a formal dinner. As he breathes out, Jeremiah catches the whiff of port.

'You do not bet, sir?' he asks.

'I prefer to wager on cards.'

'A discerning fellow.' Jeremiah grins. 'And you've come alone?'

The gentleman reaches inside his cape.

'Oh no, sir. I didn't mean anything,' Jeremiah calls him off. 'I also like to attend the cockfights by myself. I prefer them to the dogs or the rats.'

The man withdraws his hand from his weapon.

'Still, it's a low part of life for a gent such as yourself, if you don't mind me saying.'

'Nothing wrong with the lower classes,' the gentleman says. 'Salt of the earth.'

'I agree,' Jeremiah lies. It always surprises him that so many gentlemen mistake poverty for authenticity. Although thank god they do for it's where the main portion of his income comes from. 'The cockfight's a rare pastime,' he adds, 'if you like something individual.'

The gentleman professes that he does, and that is the opening Jeremiah has been casting round for. 'That being the case, I've something that might interest you,' he says. 'Have you ever seen a photograph?'

The man laughs. 'My brother had a daguerreotype made. He was leaving for India and my mother wanted a likeness. Downright spooky, I call it.'

'It's not a daguerreotype. And it's certainly not for your mother,' Jeremiah adds. 'I can show you if you like.'

The crowd is pressing in now for the fight will start soon. The handlers crowd round the cages at the back. Laughter breaks out as if an engine is letting off steam. The man follows Jeremiah to the side where under one of the lamps he draws a single envelope from his pocket and opens it.

The gentleman peers. 'My, my,' he says. 'The hussy. Who is she?'

'Just a girl I know,' Jeremiah replies. 'In service.'

'She's pretty. Caught in her mistress's chamber, I daresay? Upstart minx.'

Jeremiah's smile widens. He has the gentleman now, for the man is dreaming, not thinking. How could such a photograph be taken? A girl caught in her mistress's chamber would not sit still for the 110 seconds required.

As two of the cages are brought forward, the hubbub increases. The master of ceremonies has a voice that would reverberate through rock. 'A fine fighting cockerel, this Hatch has won every engagement!' he booms. 'In the other corner a White Hackel bred on the Home Farm of Scotstoun House. A vicious bird that's killed over two dozen challengers. Known as the Destroyer. Roll up now! Roll up!'

'It's yours for a sovereign,' Jeremiah says seductively, low in the man's ear.

'I'm sure I could buy the girl's attention for a good deal less than that,' the gentleman retorts. Jeremiah feels anger in his belly. Jane's attention, he knows, cannot be bought. But it is not her person he is selling, only a dream of it. The same as Grace Sutherland sells on stage six nights a week and twice on Saturdays.

He turns the photograph over. Jane is a treasure that the man will not be allowed to look upon without it costing him. 'But her attention would wane, wouldn't it?' Jeremiah points out. 'This way you can keep the lass forever. You can use her as you will.' And with that Jeremiah promptly pockets the picture.

The words snare the man as sure as a lasso. 'I'll give you a crown,' he says.

'I canna let her go for that. The calotype is unique, sir,' Jeremiah objects, despite the fact a second paper bearing Jane's likeness is languishing in his pocket. He steps away, only slightly but it is enough to make the man draw closer. 'I'd let her go for a half sovereign,' he says. 'I can see you're an afficionado.'

The man's eyes narrow. 'I'm not a bally foreigner,' he says. 'If that's what you mean.'

Jeremiah struggles not to laugh. 'No, sir. I mean an expert. A gentleman of good taste. She's yours for ten shillings. Not a wager. A certainty.'

'She's real, isn't she?'

Jeremiah winks. 'She is, sir.'

He realises that is the magic of a photograph. It's real even when it isn't.

The man pauses to consider but not for long. He reaches into his pocketbook. 'There,' he says, passing the coin under his palm. Jeremiah hands over the envelope the same way. 'Thank you,' he says, and the fellow glances at Jane and smiles to himself before pushing back through the fray.

Jeremiah's share is an easy two shillings and sixpence as he calculates it. The rest to Miss Mann and Jane herself. It's a good haul; a bit around double what Miss Mann usually charges. He feels light, as he always does when he is in funds, and is about to go back towards the stair when a hand descends firmly onto his shoulder. Automatically, he pulls up his stick, stout as a truncheon.

'Steady,' says a voice in his ear.

Jeremiah turns. The gentleman is old. His nose is the shape of a brass door knob, mottled with broken veins. His eyes seem too small though they are keen and his gait as he moves is ungainly though he is clearly strong. I'll remember this face, Jeremiah thinks.

'I'd like to talk to you, son.'

'Would you, aye?'

'What's your name?'

'Jeremiah.'

'The preaching prophet sent to reveal the sins of the people.'

'You're a priest?'

The ugly face twists into a laughing countenance. 'As much as you're a prophet. Come with me.'

Jeremiah looks round. The fight has started, and the crowd is focused on the pit where a white cock with vicious-looking spurs is gaining the advantage over a smaller bird with dull brass blades bound to its ankles. 'The birds are set to,' he says.

'That's not what you're here for. You want to make some money? Come with me.'

There is little point in argument. Jeremiah was heading for the stair anyway, and besides, he is intrigued by this fellow. In the normal run, he is difficult to take charge of. He feels as if this man has charmed him, the way they say Indian lads at the dock can mesmerise vipers.

The gentleman pushes Jeremiah upwards into the cold night air. 'That way.' He gestures down the lane as if Jeremiah is a hunting dog. 'I'll fight you if you like,' he adds. Jeremiah reasons that he has his stick should matters go awry, but he realises as he walks on with the fellow behind him that he is enjoying this. A thrill courses through his veins as he is directed along West George Street. 'Keep going,' the man says, turning onto Wellington Street, where they progress smoothly into a fancy hotel with a glazed mahogany sign hoisted on its pale stone facade. McLaren's. Jeremiah has never been inside this establishment. It is as grand as a private home with sturdy red carpet and fancy mirrors. Through double doors he glimpses the lounge, lit by a crystal chandelier.

The gentleman collects a key from a porter behind an ebony desk. He orders a bottle of good whisky sent to his room. Then they carry on up the carpeted stairs to the second floor and into a comfortable suite where the fire is set and the lamps are burning. Jeremiah is drawn to the window to look down onto the almost-deserted street. When he turns, the gentleman has removed his cloak and hat and is right behind him.

'What are you called, sir?' he breathes.

'I am Steven Lennox. Show me,' the man says and holds out his hand.

Jeremiah pulls out the other picture of Jane; the one of her sitting on the chair in front of the mirror. Mr Lennox regards it. He falls back, dropping onto one of the chairs by the fire. 'Where did you get this?' he asks.

Jeremiah is intrigued. The man seems fascinated but he senses it is not Jane that has piqued his interest, but the print itself. 'It's a photo-graph. A calotype,' he says.

'I know what it is,' Lennox snaps. 'That's not what I asked.'

'Do you like her, sir?'

Lennox snorts as if this is ridiculous. 'You sold one to the fellow with the patent galoshes?'

Jeremiah had not noticed his previous customer's footwear.

'How many more have you sold?'

He pauses a moment and the man's eyes light with a flash of impa-tience. 'Tell me,' he snaps. 'There's no point in lying.'

Jeremiah believes him. He often takes night-time risks with gentlemen but, he thinks, it will take him a while to get away from here, if he has to bolt. They are two storeys up for a start. 'I've only sold one,' he admits. 'The image was taken a day ago.'

'And it's the first time this was done?'

'Aye.'

'It's a clever composition. Do you have more?'

Jeremiah shakes his head.

'Did you make these?'

Another shake.

Lennox rises. He removes a coin from his pocketbook. A half sovereign. 'I will buy it. Tomorrow you'll introduce me to the photographer,' he says.

157

Jeremiah takes the coin without argument, and as he does so, Lennox pushes him against the chintz curtains. The money remains in Jeremiah's palm as the gentleman brushes closer with more purpose, in a way there can be no misunderstanding. Jeremiah feels himself stiffen in the best kind of way as the gentleman undoes the buttons on his inexpressibles and slips his hand inside.

'But—' Jeremiah manages to get out before the feeling overtakes him. This is not how such exchanges normally run. Lennox smiles in plain satisfaction when Jeremiah cries out. Then he goes back to his seat as if nothing has happened.

There is a smart rap on the door. Jeremiah is aware his face is flushed and his clothing in disarray, but if the bellboy who brings in a bottle on a tray notices it, he shows no sign. The boy deposits the bottle and disappears into the hallway as Jeremiah tidies himself. He is a veteran of the illicit fumble, but this whole encounter has taken him unawares. Gentlemen who prefer men are generally terrified of being caught and open to blackmail because they can no more help themselves than Jeremiah can. Not this man. Lennox looks entirely calm as he pours himself a glass of whisky and does not offer any to his guest.

'This is why you went to the cockpit?' Jeremiah asks. He does not want to leave, though as he judges it, their business is over. He fears he may be ill-equipped to deal with Mr Lennox, but he feels the urge to try. It has been a long time since he's felt out of his depth.

Lennox regards him plainly. 'How could I have known you'd be selling calotypes at the cockfight?'

'That's not what I meant.'

'I prefer the bare knuckle,' Lennox admits. 'You get the measure of the men. But it's a cold night and the cocks were closer.'

Jeremiah moves across the hearth. 'At the bare knuckle you get to see the colour of a man's blood and the colour of their shit,' he says.

Lennox sips. 'It's a matter of taste,' he observes.

'Taste,' Jeremiah repeats lasciviously and slides onto his knees where he proceeds to pleasure Mr Lennox, who does not make a sound, not even a whimper. He places his palm on Jeremiah's head, the most intimate action of the night as his face twists in pleasure.

When Jeremiah is finished, he cannot help but smirk.

'You'll stay tonight,' Lennox directs, and Jeremiah does not dissemble.

He falls back onto the rug, and hates that he is aroused again. 'I don't understand why you want the picture,' he says. There is no question that Mr Lennox is any more titillated by the image of Jane than he is.

'They're for my master,' Lennox replies. 'He likes new things. I've never seen anything like the image of your girl. The composition and the content. The photographer is talented.'

'She is,' Jeremiah agrees.

'She?'

'Aye.'

Lennox takes in this extraordinary fact. 'Marie Antoinette had a female portrait artist,' he says. 'Sometimes women have a good eye.'

'Are you in Glasgow for long?' Jeremiah asks as if casually.

His companion sighs. 'I've no idea. I thought my business would be done inside a day or two but there have been complications.'

'It's your master's business?'

'Yes.'

'And Glasgow bores you?'

'It's more lively than I remember. I haven't been home to Scotland for years. There is . . .' Lennox searches for the words, 'a kind of carpe diem to the place. I'd forgotten that in the west people live for today.'

'Where do you live?'

'London,' Lennox says. 'The carpe diem is more contained. People machinate.'

'Do you have a wife, sir?'

Lennox gives an involuntary shudder. 'Why would I keep a woman?' he says with a finality that forbids further questioning.

159

Jeremiah looks round and engages in some machinations of his own. The hotel will not have come cheap. Lennox's clothes are of the finest. He must charge as much as he can for the introduction. 'I'd like another sovereign,' he announces.

'When you take me to the lady,' Lennox says. 'I'll commission her on my master's behalf. He'd like an album perhaps.' As he judges it, he might as well salvage something from the so-far-hopeless quest for James Nicholl's lost treasures. If only a sop.

'All right,' says Jeremiah. There will be no negotiation, he knows. What Mr Lennox says seems to be a matter of fact, not a proposition. Idly he wonders about Lennox's master. What kind of person has a gentleman such as this on his staff?

Lennox cuts his thoughts short. 'Take off your clothes and go to bed,' he directs. 'I'll follow when I've finished my whisky.'

And Jeremiah, suddenly and unexpectedly, does as he is told.

Chapter Sixteen

Monday, 6 April 1846

Ellory sits at the desk in her office for a long time, perhaps a full 20 minutes. Jane is out and the studio is strangely quiet. Eventually she gets up and opens the safe which contains her copy of the lease, the tin of money, now almost empty, and her father's pocket watch. Charles Mann was an educated gentleman, but his family cut him off when he married Ellory's mother.

She tips the money onto her desk and sorts it into a neat pile. Eight shillings is not enough to collect the new camera, and the surgeon has gone on a trip to Portpatrick to visit his cousin without paying his invoice. He will be away for three weeks. Ellory picks up the watch and turns it in her hand. She cannot remember her father wearing it. He worked as a clerk from what she can recall. Mostly she remembers him telling her and Nora stories. She recalls the smell of carbolic from the soap Mother used to wash his shirts filling her up when he hugged her. His stories were fables full of strange creatures: selkies and mermaids, and faerie folk. Always with a happy ending. It felt he was some kind of magician, in charge of the whole world. But he wasn't, as it turned out, or he would not have died when she and Nora were still small.

She regards the money before her again. There is nothing for it. She has been waiting for someone to commission a print, but though they have sold another image of St Enoch's tree, there are still only eight shillings in the tin, once the bills have been paid. Blind optimism will get her nowhere. Ellory will do whatever she has to in order to succeed and the clearest path is to widen her portfolio by using the new camera. She does not want to rely solely on hope when she has other paths to pursue. The pictures of Jane might be a short-lived success, after all. Over the years of her apprenticeship she watched Mr Hill wait forlornly for business to come to him. For something to work magically as things do in stories, when it would have benefited him to be more pragmatic. She does not want to fail the same and quicker, for she does not have a gentleman's credit to rely on. She must be canny. The thought of having to return to Edinburgh if it all goes wrong is intolerable. To endure Jessie's I-told-you-sos or work in the studio of another photographer would be more humiliation than she could bear. She must make it work here, whatever way she can.

Pulling on her coat, she slips the money and the watch into her purse and takes the stairs. She thought at first that she might pawn the thing but Mr Anderson, the broker, only offered four shillings which is nowhere close to what it's worth, and besides, it might be some time before she has four shillings spare to retrieve it. Her father would not want her selling his legacy short, nor her dream either, so she heads for the jeweller's shop at the end of the Trongate. 'Take the jam today,' her mother used to say, with a sting of lavender and a whiff of crushed mint on her well-aired linen. 'Never forgo what you need, girls, for a maybe.'

The shop is dark, and the jeweller weighs the timepiece in his hand before taking it to the window to examine it with a loupe to his eye. He winds the movement and listens to it tick. Then he opens the back. 'Fine work,' he says. 'Where did you get it?'

'It was my father's.'

He looks her up and down and sucks his teeth. 'I can give you eight shillings,' he says.

'It's gold,' Ellory objects, 'and worth a good deal more than that.'

'Not to me. Though you might auction it. That would take time, of course.' He is playing with her.

Ellory takes the watch back. 'I'm sure you'd sell it,' she says, unbowed. Jessie, she realises, has endowed her with the ability to talk prices up as well as down. She's not going to settle for less than it's worth. She pops the watch into her reticule. 'Good day, sir.'

The jeweller reconsiders immediately. 'Perhaps ten shillings, then.'

Ellory turns. Her tone is that of a nanny telling off a recalcitrant child. 'It's worth more than a sovereign, sir, and you know it.'

'A sovereign!' he says as if she has told a joke and is repeating the punchline.

'We might split the difference at 15 shillings. I would shake your hand on that,' she puts out her hand, her face not betraying the pace of her heartbeat.

The jeweller considers offering twelve and sixpence but Ellory pre-empts him by putting her other hand on the doorknob. 'All right,' he says. 'Though it's daylight robbery.'

Ellory shakes on it. 'Daylight robbery on your part,' she counters with spirit and waits while he fetches the money.

The small camera obscura has been ready for two days. The lens-maker on Stockwell Street has fitted it but she could not bring herself to collect it, slow to let go of her father's timepiece. Now she sets off. She will have only a shilling and sixpence left in her purse after she has paid the lens-maker's bill. She wonders if her father is watching from somewhere beyond. At least, she thinks, he did not leave behind a mistress like Charlotte's father. She sensed the mayhem around Miss Nicholl. The way her world had been turned inside out. Why is it that secrets are always about desire, she wonders. And desire, Ellory knows, hovers startlingly close to downfall. She remembers the women on the Cowgate where she grew up, naming their wants. Kissing their husbands. Noises from the box-bed in the night. Such people were not concerned with respectability, but somewhere along the way Ellory became more like Jessie and less like them. Reverend Reid always said that he taught his charges goodness, but that wasn't the case, not really. She wonders if the truth is that he taught them shame. In any case, Miss Nicholl clearly has a good deal on her hands and Ellory has her own business. Her own secrets, if it comes to that.

On Stockwell Street, one floor up, the lens grinder hands over the camera. His workshop smells of grease and the tang of metal filings. 'You must bring it back for adjustment if it doesn't work,' he says.

'Do you think my calculations incorrect?'

The man shakes his head. 'It's not that, Miss Mann. I'm interested is all. I want it to be right.'

'You must come to the studio,' Ellory offers as she hands over her shillings. 'If you want a portrait, I'll give you a good price.'

As she turns right at the Bridgegate, her stomach turns with excitement the last few yards to the door. Upstairs she bursts into the studio, where Jane is on her knees now, feeding coal into the stove. Ellory puts the camera on the table and together the women look at it proudly as if they are inspecting a newborn. 'It's so small,' Jane says.

'It has to be to make the smaller prints. A sixth of a sheet.'

'Less paper and fewer chemicals,' Jane muses. 'How will we price the prints?'

This is exactly what Ellory has been considering. It strikes her, not for the first time, that at Rock House Mr Hill underestimated her abilities quite as much as originally she underestimated Jane's. Not any longer. She smiles as she turns her mind to the business in hand. 'A copy of the tree, large, sells for four shillings. The small will be a sixth of the size but I think we can ask more than a sixth of the price. I'd say a shilling each, perhaps a shilling and tuppence.'

Jane shrugs. A shilling is still a lot of money for most folk but far more achievable than five. 'We'll sell more,' she says as if it is a decision.

Ellory is counting on it. 'It's a good size to fit into a reticule or a pocket,' she reasons. 'If we sell more than five times than we do of the large we shall make a greater profit. Come on. We must try it.'

They prepare the papers, marvelling at the size as if the sheets are for a doll's camera. Then they head downstairs to St Enoch's tree. The sun is out. Ellory sets the new box on the large camera's stand, smiling at how ridiculous it looks. Then she calculates the timing and removes the lens cap. Jane stands to the side. At the far end of the square, she notices a gentleman in patent shoes, watching the women with a curious expression. Ellory, oblivious, closes the aperture. 'We'll need to write a note to explain the innovation,' she says. 'For the box at the door.'

'Perhaps we should advertise, miss. A small entry on the front page of the *Herald*.'

Ellory shakes her head. It's not a bad idea but today there is money for either an advertisement or for food. 'We have to see if it works first,' she says. 'Then we'll see if a note brings more women upstairs.'

She lifts the camera and Jane takes the stand. As they go back into the hall, the girl could swear the gentleman winks at her. Startled, she follows her mistress inside and closes the door.

Chapter Seventeen

The next day

Miss Grace Sutherland resides on Glassford Street where her suite of rooms extends to the whole of the first floor of a grand sandstone mansion, satisfyingly close to the new offices of the British Linen Bank, where one of the directors is an ardent admirer of her work. The rooms were lately vacated by the family of a gentleman involved in the shipbuilding industry and, as a result, the apartments came with a modern system of communication behind the walls, which works using vulcanised rubber tubes.

Grace sits up in her four-poster, emerging like a dryad from the crumpled sheets. The bed is raised on a podium, beneath a ceiling painted with a scene from the legend of Poseidon, King of the Sea. To one side there are mermaids, an image Miss Sutherland watches out of the corner of her eye as she falls asleep every night. She feels like a mermaid, a woman out of her natural environment. Neither the rush of the Clyde nor the coastal iconography around her comes close to the feeling of living beside the sea where she grew up, outside Wexford, under wide Irish skies in a shanty kind of cottage with sandy floors and an upturned boat on the dune outside. Not that anyone in Glasgow is aware she is Irish. Even before she arrived in Scotland by way of a fair in Waterford, rising through the chorus line of a travelling theatre as she worked her way north towards Dublin, her Irish accent was eradicated, and Grainne Dubhan transformed into Grace Sutherland, which sounded British enough and noble enough and still secretly thrills her when she sees it on the billboard outside the theatre. When gentlemen ask, she tells the tale of being Highland nobility from the wrong side of the bedsheet. People hate the Irish, more so since the Lumper blight brought a shameful wave of walking skeletons across the water last winter. Grace wants no part of that.

She reaches an elegant, long-fingered hand strewn with gold rings to pick up the brass handset that will alert her staff she is awake and announces down the tube, 'I'm ready for breakfast.' This morning routine was set upon so as not to embarrass the gentlemen who stay in Miss Sutherland's rooms and prefer not to come across a maid when they rise, or indeed anybody else, as they sneak into Glasgow's misty morning streets to wend their way back to the marital home.

Today however, Grace is alone and, having breakfasted upon good Indian tea and toast with two boiled eggs, she dresses in a frothy lace bodice with a sober well-cut skirt the colour of absinthe and teal leather boots. The maid closes the last buttons as Miss Sutherland regards herself in the long mirror before fixing on a large hat embellished with a single ostrich feather. Grace has been curious about the female photographer since Jeremiah mentioned the woman. She has a nose for money and can always winkle an advantage, but as much as the financial possibilities, she senses the sweet scent of immortality in this development. She calls for a carriage, for though it is not far, Miss Sutherland never walks anywhere unless it is in a garden with one of the gentlemen who invite her to their country houses at Rothesay, Millport or Ayr to entertain private parties with her singing and later, in the early hours, to even more private parties to celebrate her other accomplishments. Today she will develop a new talent as a photographic model. As she draws on her gloves, she feels excitement at the prospect.

It is ten of the clock when she arrives, though the bell-ringers at St Enoch's are otherwise employed this morning as she peers at the images in the advertising box. 'Stay at the door,' she directs Owen, her muscle-bound footman. Then she disappears through the entrance and glides up the stairs towards the studio, her steps so well-placed it is as if she rises like a bubble through champagne. When Jane opens up, Grace steps inside. 'I'll speak to your mistress,' she announces.

'Aye, miss,' Jane bobs a curtsy and steps backwards.

Taking in the studio, Grace senses greatness immediately. She has seen daguerreotypes before, for some gentlemen of her acquaintance have had images of themselves taken. One even presented her with his photograph, encased in purple velvet in a leather box with a brass catch. 'You have me now, always,' he said and Grace smiled mysteriously, for frankly she would have preferred pearls. Now she is here, it surprises her that she has not had the idea of making her own image before, although, of course, the photographer is most important for they must be both talented and discreet. It reassures her that Jeremiah has recommended Miss Mann in glowing terms. She trusts his eye.

As Ellory looks up, Grace takes the decision to offer her hand. She respects people who make things; especially things that are useful to her. Besides, Ellory is beautiful in a haunting way with her ripe red hair and freckled cheeks, like a fawn fresh from the woods.

'We expected Jeremiah to accompany you, Miss Sutherland,' Ellory says. 'He has a notion of the image he believes would sell best.'

Grace sits down at the table, though the chairs are only bare pine. 'I'm sure he does. But it's my image, Miss . . .'

'Mann,' Ellory confirms.

Grace waves away the offer of refreshment. 'I've come to see what you do here. What *you* can do, that is. To discuss the possibilities.'

Ellory offers her portfolio and Grace flicks through it. The gentlemen of her acquaintance take pictures of each other and of grand houses.

This woman, she notes, is more interesting from the off. The cat. The children. The tree. Though there is nothing here in the style Grace would prefer. 'These pictures are . . .'

'Domestic. I know.' Ellory smiles. 'They bespeak technical skill. You will require more.'

Grace closes the book. 'Your work is more atmospheric than a daguerreotype.'

'You've seen daguerreotypes then?'

'They look, to my eye, as if the person is dead. Your pictures, on the other hand, are full of life and that is the main thing. Is it the sepia, do you think? Or the paper?'

Ellory is not sure and does not want to posit that it may be her eye rather than either of these other things. 'I can see you will photograph well,' she pronounces.

'Really?' This interests Grace.

'The contrast of your skin and hair will work,' Ellory confirms, sticking to Miss Sutherland's physical attributes though she notes that there is something else about the actress beyond that. A wildness that will be difficult to catch. Ellory looks forward to trying to do so. 'Your features are well defined,' she says. 'Dark eyes work best, and you have a lovely figure. We must show it to advantage.'

Grace knows it is her figure that interests the gentlemen who are the font of her fortune; the reason the theatre manager will pay her as much for a single performance as a maid receives in a year for her drudgery. The reason gentlemen send gifts and financial inducements. Merely singing on stage did not get her where she wanted to be.

'Jeremiah felt that if we could stage something to show your ankles . . .' Ellory starts.

Grace laughs. 'Jeremiah is an exceptional tailor. Of cloth as well as of people. He showed me an image of you.' She turns towards Jane. 'You could act, you know. If you wished to.'

'Oh, miss. I could never,' Jane declares, taken aback by Miss Sutherland even noticing her.

170

Grace gives a Gallic kind of shrug and turns once more to Ellory. 'In making this arrangement, trust is paramount, Miss Mann. Anyone looking at the image will see me, not you. Therefore the print and the negative are mine. We must agree that from the start.'

'Of course,' Ellory says. Grace, she notes, is as good at driving a hard bargain as Jessie ever was. She has dived in immediately.

'There can be no jealousy over the financial arrangements,' Grace continues smoothly. 'Most of the money must go to me, for I am the subject. I'll sell the thing on and you'll have no part of that. So I'm happiest if you will charge me a fee. A generous fee. More than is paid by – ' she gestures towards the portfolio – 'your other clients. A fee puts me in charge of my own business,' Grace adds firmly.

Ellory considers this. All Mr Hill's clients are in charge when it comes down to it. A fee will do. 'All right,' she says, steeling her courage to drive her own excellent bargain. 'It will be three guineas for possession of the negative and the first image printed, and a further guinea for each additional print.' Even daguerreotypes do not cost that much in the normal run but, Ellory senses, Grace's ambitions are boundless, and the discretion required bears a price. Besides, they need the money. This feels out of control, like a child rolling down a hill. She has scrimped pennies her entire life and in the last fortnight has spent more than 20 years' savings at a stroke and made at least some of it back to boot. Grace considers the offer carefully. She wishes to make an image that will devastate some poor fellow enough to bleed substantially more than three guineas from him. She feels this woman is capable of that.

'All right. Three guineas for the first and a guinea per additional print. As long as I like what you come up with.' Ellory shakes Grace's hand and feels a thrill. It's hard to believe. Three guineas for a single print. More than Mr Hill has ever made. Perhaps everything will be all right after all.

'I'll pay Jeremiah separately,' Grace continues. 'He'll provide the clothing and see to the set.' Ellory watches as Grace walks the length of the studio, perusing the backdrops laid out. She admires Miss

171

Sutherland's confidence. 'I expect most ladies have had paintings made before they come here,' Grace says wistfully. Nobody has ever commissioned a painting of her. She thought to commission one herself last year, but was held back by an uneasy feeling that she would be putting the charge of her image in the eye of another. She is not a lady and she knows it.

'I think it's common for ladies to be painted before they are captured in print,' Ellory agrees.

Grace likes that she will, for once, not be common. 'None of these will do,' she announces, gesturing at the chair, the screen and the pots of plants.

Ellory does not demur. For three guineas, Miss Sutherland is entitled to be choosy. 'I wonder if it might work best to photograph you like a classical figure. From antiquity.'

Grace cocks her head. 'Antiquity?' she repeats, wondering if Miss Mann is somehow commenting upon her age. She was 30 years old last birthday.

'One of history's most beautiful heroines, I mean. Cleopatra? Or Athena?' Ellory suggests.

Grace perks up. 'A queen?'

'Or you might be Nell Gwynn, of course, if you'd prefer something cheekier?'

Grace considers this and comes to the conclusion that she is worth more to her gentlemen than Nell or Cleopatra or anybody else. She fully intends to make 50 guineas from this endeavour. A hundred perhaps. She must price the picture high, she realises, for the gentlemen will not value it otherwise. 'It's a nice idea but I'll be myself,' she pronounces.

Ellory is about suggest a particular pose when they are interrupted by a rap on the door. The women stop. Before Jane can get to it, Jeremiah lets himself in, followed by an older gentleman who is out of breath. 'Hello,' Jeremiah says as he pulls back a chair into which the gentleman descends before waving Jeremiah off as if he is a fusspot. When he finds himself able to speak,

Lennox points at Jane with a thick finger, 'This is our little star,' he says.

Grace's expression freezes. She glances at Jeremiah, who is smirking. Until lately, Grace was his richest and most powerful friend. That has changed since he met Lennox, and he is enjoying the idea of Jane being the star, while the great actress is present. Still, he steps in to avoid unnecessary fireworks. 'This is Mr Lennox. He wishes to commission an album of images of Jane,' he announces. 'Mr Lennox, might I introduce the famous actress, Miss Grace Sutherland. I believe she's here to have her portrait taken by this lady, Miss Ellory Mann.' Ellory drops a shallow curtsy.

Lennox, now recovered from the stairs, gets up and kisses Grace's gloved hand though he regards Ellory with more interest. Grace stiffens. She does not relish being the third most interesting woman in the room.

'You have a fine eye, Miss Mann,' Lennox says. 'I've seen many calotypes, but your work draws the attention in a particular way. More than Mr Fox Talbot's prints, even.'

'Thank you, sir.' A blush fires Ellory's cheek. She is not accustomed to gentlemen complimenting her pictures as if she is an artist.

'I'd like to commission an album, as Jeremiah has mooted,' Lennox continues. 'Something along the lines of what I've already seen. The pictures to suggest a narrative. Are you aware of the work of Mr William Hogarth?'

Ellory smiles. Of course she is. '*A Rake's Progress*?' she says.

Grace coughs as she adjusts her hat, a gesture which Lennox misunderstands.

'You too might wish to be involved, Miss Sutherland. I've heard of your talent, though sadly not seen it. I've been in Glasgow less than a fortnight and have not had time to go to the theatre. I heard you were a sensation as Ophelia. I'm sure my master wouldn't mind if you played a part in our little tale.'

Backstage, staff have been fired for less cheek. Jeremiah knows Grace will be black affrontit that this gentleman has been in town almost a fortnight and has found the cockfight and the bare knuckle more alluring than her performance. He opens his mouth, then closes it. Grace too, is finding it hard to bring forth words to object to the offence being caused. In the end, it is Ellory who speaks. The feeling in the room reminds her of the day two ministers from kirks at opposite ends of the same village arrived at Rock House to have their portraits made and Mr Hill suggested they pose together. She endeavours to maintain a serious countenance, for she must salvage the situation.

'Jeremiah will need to sew a costume for your image, Miss Sutherland. Lace, do you think? Dark against the refinement of your pale skin,' she says in an attempt to defuse the tension. 'We must capture all of your beauty, madam.'

Grace, however, will not sidestep Lennox's insult and turns her gaze towards him. 'Who is your master to mind me at all, sir?' she says. 'I'm a lady of noble lineage. Who's your master to even peruse my picture?'

Lennox does not appear intimidated by this. 'You'd be paid well, madam. If the commission doesn't interest you, it's of no matter. Dancers from the Royal Opera House have posed for the man I work for, as well as many London actresses of note, the great Fanny Robertson and the ingénue Miss Harriet Howard among them.'

Jeremiah takes in these details, but Grace continues without realising their import. All she can think is that Fanny Robertson is at least 75 years of age.

'You've interrupted my consultation with Miss Mann,' she says coldly.

Lennox rises. 'I apologise. You're quite right. Please, ladies, go ahead.'

Ellory withdraws a bottle from the cupboard which she lays on the table with two glasses. This was what smoothed over the problem with the ministers. 'We have many plans to make today,' she says lightly. 'Please, gentlemen, enjoy some refreshment while I see to Miss Sutherland. We might consult in my office, madam, for privacy.'

This consoles Grace. She sweeps into the smaller room which is furnished with an old desk, two chairs and an oil lamp that Ellory bought second-hand from a dealer on Hope Street. Beyond the window the sky is dove-grey. 'Men!' Grace lets out in exasperation as Ellory closes the door.

Ellory attempts to channel a calmness she does not entirely feel. She does not want to lose either commission. 'Where were we?' she says, sitting down.

Grace sighs and gets back to business. 'I have questions.'

'Please.'

'How long must I remain still, Miss Mann? For the photograph to be taken?'

'On a bright day, a minute at least. No more than two.'

Grace stares out of the window. 'As I see it, the trick is that the image must seem to catch a moment. That is what worked with your maid. However, the moment has to be held a good deal longer than is natural. Am I right? '

'You said daguerreotypes look like images of dead people. That's why. Subjects freeze, you see.'

'So the maid's photograph is charming because she's caught in motion. As she looks over her shoulder,' Grace observes.

'Jane has seen a thousand photographs taken. I thought her pose inspired.'

Grace's lips purse. 'I have an idea,' she says triumphantly. 'The outfit shall be dark lace as you suggest. It will be – or seem to be – in my boudoir and I shall be laughing.'

Ellory considers this. Most people, freezing a moment of time for posterity, choose to convey their gravity or their commitment to family or devotion to their work. Mr Hill's favourite model, Miss Rigby, often poses with a wreath in her hair like a Greek statue, her hands placed by Mr Hill and an expression on her face that might be deemed 'eternal'. Nobody Ellory knows has attempted laughter. 'Could you laugh now, Miss Sutherland? And hold the pose.'

Grace does not baulk at the request. She throws back her head, her eyes light up and she becomes at once a joyous, silent tableau. Ellory leans forward in fascination. Mr Hill clearly ought to have used actresses all along. Miss Rigby – and the Newhaven Madonnas for that matter – be damned. Miss Sutherland looks for all the world as if somebody has just said something amusing. She sits that way for a full minute, absolutely still.

'Thank you,' Ellory waves the actress to relax and Grace returns to animation.

'I want the set to be of the best,' she says. 'There's a mahogany chaise at the theatre Jeremiah might have picked up by cart. The whole thing must look warm. I want wallpaper; flock of the highest quality. The Ainslies have installed a red velvet design in their drawing room; something of that sort. Thinking on it, we'll require amounts of velvet. My hair will be down. And there will be feathers and perhaps a fur throw. It must be a private moment of the utmost luxury, do you understand? I have an account at McPherson's. You may charge anything that Jeremiah cannot garner from the theatre or my own rooms.'

Ellory considers. This will look different from Jane's pose; an ordinary maid in an ordinary house. This will be regal. She feels an itch of impatience to make such an exciting image. 'You require intimacy and splendour. I understand. I'll discuss the set and the costume with Jeremiah. I can see how it must look.'

'Good.' Grace rises. She puts out her hand. 'It's a pleasure doing business with you, Miss Mann.'

Back in the main room, Jeremiah has poured drinks though he alone is imbibing. Jane has been induced to the table where Lennox is explaining the narrative quality of Mr Hogarth's work. As the office door opens, Jane springs to her feet, bobbing a curtsy as Grace sweeps through. 'Good morning,' the actress bids the gentlemen crisply.

Jeremiah watches her go before pushing a full glass in the maid's direction. 'Your shot,' he says and turns towards Mr Lennox. 'Tell me,

176

did the women come from the chorus for your master's commission? You said dancers from the Royal Opera House. But it was the chorus surely, not the stars.'

'I couldn't say. My master is married,' Lennox says with finality.

'Most men are married,' Jeremiah counters.

Lennox's stare suggests that most men are not married to the same degree as his master. 'Family is important to him,' he adds. 'Besides, he prefers to look.' Here he glances at Ellory, aware that he is perhaps saying too much. 'Not to touch,' he finishes.

Jeremiah's interest is piqued. What kind of man commissions dancers from the opera and does not wish to touch them? 'He paints?' he asks.

Lennox shakes his head and makes it clear there will be no further discussion.

'If I recall correctly, Mr Hogarth told his story in 12 prints,' Ellory says as she sits down. She had seen Hogarth's images in an old broadsheet at Reverend Reid's when she was only a child. They remain both famous and popular. 'Is it 12 pictures you wish, Mr Lennox?'

Lennox shakes his head. 'Six will suffice. A small album. I'm late delivering what I was sent here for. This will make up for it.'

Jeremiah downs the last of his glass and appraises Lennox. He has been curious since he met the older man about what exactly Lennox is doing in Glasgow, but so far has failed to extract any useful information. He turns his attention to the matter in hand. 'A maid working? Trying on her mistress's clothes? Getting caught? Pleading her case?' he says.

'Exactly,' Lennox replies. 'Might I leave you to it?' He takes out his pocketbook. 'Shall we say six pictures for three sovereigns? One paid now?' He slides a coin onto the table and holds it there with his finger.

Jeremiah catches Ellory's eye. She gives a barely imperceptible nod, motioning him to continue the negotiation. 'Plus a sovereign to me for the introduction and for my work on the images,' Jeremiah adds. 'The costuming and so forth. Three sovereigns is the fee to

Miss Mann for the images themselves and Jane must be given something on top.'

'The images must not be circulated.' Lennox gestures towards the portfolio case. He turns to Jane and eyes her intently. 'You'll not pose like this again, girl.'

'No, sir,' Jane says. Mr Lennox scares her.

'That will require a further consideration. Miss . . .?' Jeremiah does not know Jane's last name.

'Ramsay,' Jane supplies, dry-mouthed, in a whisper.

'Miss Ramsay has, you'll agree, a particular talent.'

'If it becomes too costly, it's not worth the coin, Jeremiah,' Lennox warns.

'A unique gift? And you late with your master's commission; the reason you were sent here? It will be a work of art that Mr Hogarth would be proud of.' Jeremiah is enjoying holding a few of the chips.

'Ten bob to the girl then?' Lennox offers the money to stop Jeremiah talking as much as anything else. 'And three sovereigns, ten bob to Miss Mann. To include the album which must be good leather,' he adds.

'That is five sovereigns in total. Make it six and turn them to guineas and we have a deal.' Jeremiah's stare is immutable.

'Six guineas!' Lennox objects.

'Six guineas,' Jeremiah repeats steadily. 'It's a good price.'

Lennox gets to his feet. He stares at the set where the picture he has already seen was posed. 'Very well,' he says dismissively. He hands over the single sovereign and Jeremiah gives him a look, so he reaches into his pocketbook and brings out a further two guineas and a shilling. 'That's all I'm laying down,' he says. 'When will you deliver? I may have to leave at any time, whenever my business is completed.'

'We'll start immediately,' Jeremiah promises. 'I'll come to your rooms tonight to tell you how the project's coming along.'

'Very well.' Lennox gets up.

As the door closes behind him, Jane coughs. She has hardly taken a breath all this time. 'Ten bob,' she says. She has never had as much cash. She imagines holding the coins in her hand, the weight of them.

'He got us cheap,' Jeremiah says.

Ellory is smiling. 'Six guineas for six pictures in an album. That's hardly cheap, Jeremiah.' Mr Hill was never so ambitious. For prints of Jane too. It feels as if money is raining down on them, quite suddenly, in a most exhilarating way. Ellory realises she wants to share her news but she can tell neither Murray Urquhart nor Charlotte Nicholl, who would both, she is sure, be shocked at the nature of this morning's business.

Jane walks to the set. She stares at the space in front of the mirror where she posed. Ellory watches her. 'A gentleman's eye would be higher,' she says, taking in Jane's figure. 'I might make the images as if they are from his gaze. Looking down. As if he himself has caught you.' It is a new idea, one of many over the last few days. Now she has her own space to work within, she finds herself intrigued that Mr Hill did not come up with these notions before. As far as she is aware nobody has. The use of mirrors to direct the light, reducing the size of the prints, changing the viewpoint of the lens. 'Perhaps when I frame Miss Sutherland I shall do so from below,' she adds. 'Like the audience looking up at the stage.'

'In the theatre the audience is above as much as below,' Jeremiah gestures into the air. 'The circle.'

'Oh yes,' Ellory says. There is much to do. 'Jane, run down to Crichton's and fetch two dozen oysters with good bread and butter and three pints of perl,' she says, suddenly hungry. She has felt fearful of spending too much on food with so many bills to pay, but now she thinks she will sate her appetite in celebration and in readiness. 'Go on,' she encourages the girl. 'Jeremiah and I will stage the set. We must get on.'

Chapter Eighteen

That afternoon Charlotte climbs the Necropolis in her oxblood velvet cape, looking for all the world like a fairy-tale character. She takes in the view of the city's medieval cathedral behind her, more attractive from the east, she thinks; the rear side. The sound of the works to the south-west tower floats like disembodied timpani, past the blossom on the spindly trees planted by the gate. She starts to cry quietly as she trudges uphill past the gravestones, carrying her photograph, encased in thick glass and wrapped in oilskin as Ellory suggested. It is overcast and the Nicholl plot is muddy, the flowers spattered with damp earth, a pair of crows hopping between the graves. Charlotte considers it fitting her parents lie side by side rather than interred together; a pigeon pair. Her mother died when she was so young that Charlotte has no memory of her. She likewise finds it difficult to recall what her father looked like as a younger man. One way or another, she cannot picture her parents together.

She assumed there would be a digger to open the ground for a shilling but there isn't another soul in the whole graveyard. She must dig herself, she realises, so she pulls off her tan kidskin gloves and scrabbles at the damp earth above her father's coffin. Something about getting her hands cold and dirty moves her and the tears come harder. Why did you leave me unprovisioned? Why did you buy those horrible paintings? she asks silently as at length an uneven hole is dug. 'You wanted a photograph? Well, here it is,' she says out loud. Her fingers are raw pink and freezing and so filthy they would ruin her gloves if she put them back on. 'You've left me in a fine mess,' she adds.

The day before, she had visited the post office and discovered the whereabouts of Helensburgh House. The postmistress had given Charlotte directions to find a Magnus Bain. 'He drives the coach on that run,' she said. 'He might know.'

She found Magnus tending his horses by the Scotia bar. Sharp-eyed and in a makeshift uniform, he gladly accepted a shilling. 'The house is at Greenock,' he said. 'Past the point. Direction of Gourock.'

'Greenock? Then why is it called Helensburgh House?'

'Helensburgh is the view across the Clyde,' he said as if she was a fool.

'Do you know the lady who lives there? It's a lady, I assume?'

'It was.'

Charlotte worried momentarily that the lady has died. 'What do you mean?'

'They're all gone,' Magnus said cryptically. 'The house is for sale. It's closed up. The furniture is being sent to auction.'

'So the place can be bought?' The frustration stings. She feels as if she will never get to the bottom of it.

'Through a Glasgow solicitor,' Magnus confirmed.

'Urquhart & Son?'

Magnus regarded her as if she was some kind of soothsayer. 'Aye. That's it,' he said, speaking more slowly as if the shilling was running out. 'Letters forwarded to an office on Bath Street.'

Charlotte fished another coin from her reticule. It would seem 500 was not enough for her father's mistress to live on either, but the other lady in James Nicholl's life has managed more decisive action. There's still time, she told herself. 'What do you know of the woman?'

Energised by the fresh coin, Magnus said, 'I've seen her out riding the Cut to Loch Thom.'

182

Charlotte's skin prickled. Her father always insisted on Fife and Tayside for holidays, while most of their acquaintances took places down the water. This might explain why. A fortnight on Bute in July and who knows what might have transpired travelling past the door of Helensburgh House, there and back. 'Do you know anything else about the lady?'

Magnus considered. 'Her name. Miss Blanche Nicholl.'

Charlotte feels as if she has been hit in the stomach. 'Miss Nicholl?'

'Aye.'

A flame of outrage burns through her. Her father's mistress used his name. Her name. 'Do you know where she's gone?'

'That's all I got, miss.'

Charlotte curses, for it seems that she must navigate a maze that constantly directs her to its beginning. All she has discovered is the house was occupied by a lady, which she had assumed all along. A woman kicking up her heels now, selling the place and making off god knows where. The flibbertigibbet. The phoney. Miss Blanche Nicholl indeed. Out in the world flaunting herself, no doubt, while Charlotte is weighed down by her father's secrets. 'It wasn't fair of you to leave me like this,' Charlotte berates the grave as she brushes the excess soil from her palms. Her mother's stone says *Margaret Nicholl, beloved wife and mother, 1789–1822*. The stone Charlotte has ordered for her father merely says *James Nicholl, 1782–1846*, for she could not think what else to put on it. She cannot call him beloved. Not any longer. She wishes he were here to explain. Or at least to be blamed for his misdeeds.

Sitting back, she regards her handiwork. The last two nights she has had nightmares about being buried alive, A naked Jezebel laughing as she shovelled earth on top of Charlotte's coffin. Now Charlotte feels better. Burying the photograph has afforded a release as if she has found a way to berate her father directly for the mess he has left her to deal with. She is about to turn when she hears steps behind. At the funeral Mr Lennox almost made her squeal. This time she will not be so foolish. She swings round to discover the figure of Murray

Urquhart, his face split in a grin. He is wearing a dark well-tailored greatcoat today, in contrast to Charlotte's colourful appearance. 'You're a difficult woman to find. I called at the house and Mrs Cullen said you were here,' he says, and seeing her pink eyes, adds, 'Are you all right?'

Charlotte shifts clumsily for her left foot has gone numb.

'The ground must be freezing.' He indicates the muddy grave. 'The grass'll grow. Time heals both graves and hearts. I promise.'

Charlotte wishes she could trust him. Not that he appears untrustworthy, but then neither did her father. 'I'm considering what to do,' she admits. 'Selling the house, I mean. You deal with that kind of business, don't you?'

He does not realise it is a pointed question. 'I can see to it, of course, but you shouldn't rush,' he says, missing the accusation in her voice. After all, if the Urquharts can effect James Nicholl's contracted sale with Mr Lennox, Charlotte might live at Blythswood Square as long as she likes.

Charlotte stares, weighing the matters between them. Carefully she reaches into her reticule and hands him an unsigned note, delivered this morning on her breakfast tray.

To his credit, Murray ignores the dirty smudges from her fingers. The tidy copperplate belies the paper's contents.

You shame the memory of your father and disgrace our congregation, girl. The Lord will curse his enemies, you and Wicked Douglass among them. Repent or be forever damned to <u>HELL</u>.

Charlotte can scarce bring herself to watch him reading. She has gone over the note several times, her heart pounding with shame. Mrs Cullen said it was slipped under the front door and nobody knew who delivered it. While Charlotte dressed, the maid caught a glance of the words and later, over the back wall, Charlotte heard her admit to Flora Jack, the Howarths' maid (as straight up and down as one of her master's rivets) that 'the mistress can dole it out but she canna tak it'. At breakfast, Charlotte merely tore a slice of bread to pieces and let the hot chocolate cool in her cup, before calling for the carriage.

Murray thinks he understands now why she set out for the grave-yard. 'The coward didn't even sign it,' he says.

'Thanks for taking my side. I'd be lost without you.'

'I'm your solicitor, Charlotte. Of course I take your side.'

A flicker of relief appears on Charlotte's face, then disappears like a ghost. She has faced everything with as much bravery as she can but the spiteful tone of the letter has shaken her and she is glad that Murray will take her part, even if he is keeping secrets. She wipes her cheek, streaking mud across it. Then she removes her handkerchief from her reticule and blows her nose. 'When I think of what Mr Douglass has had to endure . . . Being beaten. Being sold. The hardship of forced labour. And here I am crying over a stupid letter.' It is not only that, of course.

Murray folds the paper, his black gloves making his fingers thick. He knows Mr Douglass's views are contentious to many but that is no excuse for bullying a lady. 'Leave this to me,' he says. 'I'll speak to Reverend Patterson.'

'Oh no!' Charlotte bursts out. She does not want the note passed from hand to hand. Softly, she starts to cry again. 'They're all talking about me, aren't they? Mrs Grieg came to the house and berated me for going to the lecture with you. She was horrible. Between Papa dying and not having as much money as everyone expects . . . it's just gossip to other people, isn't it?'

'I imagine that's true. Though nobody can know about the money, Charlotte. That's your business. I'd never tell a soul.'

'Did they send *you* anything?' she asks, hardly needing a reply.

'No,' he says stoutly. He knows it's unfair.

'Only me then. Because I am alone.'

'You're not alone. And it's low of whoever wrote this to try to strong-arm a lady.'

'I'm in an impossible position,' she says. She cannot tell him the half of it. 'I wonder if Mr Douglass's other lady supporters receive such letters?' Charlotte casts around for a name. 'Miss Whigham,' she suggests, choosing Scotland's most famous female advocate in Frederick Douglass's cause.

'I'm sure she does,' Murray says steadily. 'She's a Quaker, of course, and this comes from somebody in our own church. But nothing incenses people as much as others disagreeing with them. This is no way to change a person's mind.' He flicks the paper.

'The ends do not justify the means.' Charlotte repeats what Ellory said in the study.

'Exactly. They cannot,' Murray agrees and, always the gentleman, holds out his hand to help her onto the path.

'When I die, I don't want to be interred here with my family,' she says, realising it suddenly.

Murray looks surprised. 'Where do you wish to go?'

Charlotte bats off the vision of Jezebel shovelling. 'I'll think on it,' she says vaguely, realising there is nowhere else. Do families who disagree always end up with their bones intermingled? She is angry with her father but perhaps that will pass. He has afforded her a certain amount of freedom, or a certain amount of money at least. She searched his bedroom for cash the night before, cursing that she had come to such an undignified pass. She found nothing. Afterwards, Mrs Cullen asked if she wanted to move into the larger suite, but Charlotte does not, for her father is still there somehow. Perhaps she will never fit his rooms. She has been brought up, she realises, like a decoupage pasted onto the scrapbook of her father's life. This makes it difficult to fashion a life of her own. Though it has not been so long since he died, she tells herself. Perhaps she will get to it.

They start down the hill. 'You should make a will,' Murray announces, for Charlotte is clearly considering her mortality. 'As your lawyer it's my duty to point it out.'

Charlotte wonders to whom she could possibly leave her inheritance. Mrs Cullen merits a bequest but after that there is nobody. Besides, by the time she dies she will surely have run through the money. 'I could endow a scholarship at the university,' she says half-heartedly, thinking of Mary Erskine and her school in Edinburgh. The good a woman can do.

At the carriage Murray pats the single bay. 'I like your new conveyance,' he says. He's glad she's stopped crying.

'It's a stylish kind of economy,' Charlotte admits with a smile.

'And you really buried Miss Mann's image of you like the grave goods of the Egyptians?' The image of Ellory in her studio comes to him. Her face set in concentration as she watched Charlotte pose.

Charlotte gives a curt nod. She cannot tell him why, exactly. 'Why were you looking for me?' she asks.

Murray's attention is drawn back to business. He is, after all, in search of James Nicholl's mysterious collection. 'In your father's papers, I noticed a lack in one area of investment,' he starts. When he sat up the night before, trying to figure out how to question Charlotte about Lennox and his assertions, this is how he planned to put it. 'Most estates have collections. Your father had his books, of course; his library is valuable. There's some fine furniture, but it occurs to me there's one area he never ventured into.'

'What area is that?' Charlotte asks.

'He didn't invest in creativity. In beauty. It struck me this is something at which you might excel. Neither of us has your father's eye for stocks. Railways and mines, distilleries and manufactories. The truth is, I know nobody with a sense as keen as his. But maybe you more than he might understand art. In many estates the paintings are worth more than the house. Artefacts. Glass from Venice. Silver beyond the needs of the table. Mr Doherty at Anderston has a collection of clocks that are said to be a wonder. There are few paintings in your house on Blythswood Square. It struck me something of that nature might interest you?' He watches her face carefully to see if his speech has hit home.

Charlotte hesitates. Her father's paintings are with her every hour of the day. In addition to Jezebel burying her, she has dreamed of chasing Venus barefoot along the sand at St Andrews and diving into the sea. If the writer of the poison letter knew, they would have a field day. 'Perhaps,' she says.

'I ran into your father's friend Mr Lennox,' Murray continues when she does not respond more fully. 'He made me think of it. Do you know Mr Lennox at all?'

'I do.'

'I understand he came originally from Argyll?'

'He knew my mother as well as my father,' Charlotte chips in. 'He called at the house the night after Papa died and introduced himself at the funeral.'

'Do you know anything else? The gentleman's occupation perhaps?'

Charlotte stares. 'He searched Papa's study after the wake. I thought he'd gone, but I found him at the desk. He inveigled an invitation, then abused it. I don't trust him.'

Murray ignores the discomfort of not being able to speak directly. She is astute, he thinks, but all he says is, 'How curious.'

'I assumed he was a gentleman,' Charlotte adds. 'I'm unaware he has any occupation.'

'He cannot be a gentleman exactly,' Murray admits. 'I understand he is in somebody's employ, though in what capacity I've yet to ascertain.'

They are at checkmate. Neither of them can admit to knowing more without revealing one secret or another. Tell me about Helensburgh House, Charlotte wills silently. She will not go first. She does not wish to feel like an open book, read and discarded while Murray's pages remain uncut.

Some seconds pass. Murray checks his pocket watch. 'I must take my leave,' he says.

'Yes.' Charlotte narrows her eyes. If their positions were reversed, she is sure she would tell him, if she truly considered him a friend. But the idea that the affairs of old Urquhart might require discretion seems hugely optimistic. She is lost for what to do next. The house at Greenock is empty, she does not know where Blanche Nicholl has gone and she has no idea how to divest herself of the paintings. 'I've some reading to do,' she says and climbs into the carriage.

Murray watches as the horse trots westwards, but his eye is drawn to the south, towards the river. He pulls his gaze away; his father has made it clear, the account is closed and he is not to go there.

Chapter Nineteen

At St Enoch's Square, after dark on the eighth of the month, a satisfied lethargy has fallen over the studio that is unaccustomed for a
Wednesday evening. The air feels heavy like the aftermath of a party
the star guest has left, and indeed Grace Sutherland was photographed here today and now has gone. The cosmetics tray is set with
the grape salve and crumbled wood ash with which Miss Sutherland
allowed Jeremiah to paint her face, the ash to her eyebrows and her
lips in a cupid's bow. A dark red negligée, the colour of port, ribbons
for Miss Sutherland's hair, a pair of delicate slippers and matching
stockings with garters are bundled into a bag now to go back to the
theatre. Jeremiah sits back and yawns. It is only after six of the clock
but he did not sleep the night before. He and Mr Lennox played
cards till late and then played other, more diverting games till even
later. There was no point in sleeping. 'That went well,' he says.

Ellory glances at the print room. 'I think so.' She feels as if she has
swindled somebody. It was too easy: Grace, like Jane, was an excellent model.

Jane returns from fetching the sign they put on the door downstairs. 'Private sitting. Come back tomorrow.' She stows it in a
drawer. It will be dark soon enough and Ellory intends to work late
making the negatives so she can make prints from them when the
sun comes up. However, they know already that the pictures are

scandalous. From the moment Ellory watched the actress climbing down from her carriage, she knew they would be.

Miss Sutherland arrived outfitted in burnt-orange silk with a glamorous trail of feathers. She took the stairs elegant as a cat about to catch a mouse. Once she had changed, they all had to wait as she spent a good deal of time considering her image in the mirror. 'These are my shoulders,' she said, her still eyes inspecting her perfect pale flesh, a long pearl necklace draped across her creamy clavicles. 'These are my ankles,' she turned her gaze downwards. Then she held a joyous, silent laugh just as she had in Ellory's office, but this time watching herself in the mirror. She shifted and did so again at a slightly different angle. Mr Hill's female models were never so studied but none were near as beautiful. There is a self-possession to Grace Sutherland which is wild in its ambition. She is a living mannequin; perfect and contained. A goddess of skulduggery.

The image they all prefer is one where Jeremiah draped a white feather boa across Grace's body, creating the line of a Japanese print. Jane stepped into the frame, an accustomed model herself now, and made to undress the lady as if she were Miss Sutherland's maid. Jeremiah brought her a white apron and cap while Ellory set the camera on the edge of the table. There was something intimate in the moment: Grace reflected in the mirror and Jane standing next to her, fixing her buttons.

When the image was captured, Jane helped the actress change back into her wide orange overskirts.

'That was a clever pose. If you ever want a place at the theatre, call to me,' the actress offered. She peered at the girl. It was the first time she'd noticed anybody else all day. 'There's something about you, isn't there?' she said without expecting a reply.

Afterwards, Miss Sutherland disappeared downstairs as soon as she was dressed, leaving a dissipating trail of bergamot wafted by the feathers. Now the three of them sit at the table as if the air has been sucked out of the room. Jane is about to enquire if she should fetch something from the tavern for supper when there is a knock at the door.

Ellory jumps. Jane gets to her feet and opens it. In the hallway Charlotte Nicholl hovers. She peers across the threshold. Ellory's face betrays her surprise at the unannounced visit and her discomfort too. In this moment the studio feels like the scene of a crime.

'It's an inconvenient time,' Charlotte says apologetically. 'I ought to have sent a note.' She shifts her skirt, turning to go back down.

'No,' Ellory objects. 'Please. Come in.'

A glimmer of a smile passes across Charlotte's lips. She decided to come to the studio only a quarter of an hour before. Since the poisoned letter, she has had no callers. She thought that was what she wanted, but now the most she has to keep her busy is to go over the menus for the week with Mrs Cullen and stew in her situation. She visited a gallery in town but could not bring herself to broach the subject of her father's paintings. So instead she has spent the afternoon sitting at his desk feeling lost, the list of items before her like an impossible conundrum on a chessboard, all moves leading to checkmate, no matter what she does. She had a vision of Venus and Cleopatra and Circe – all the women locked in the cupboard. Goddesses. Princesses. Queens. Each with a life of her own. 'I must break out,' she muttered under her breath. So here she is.

Jeremiah picks up the bag of Miss Sutherland's properties to take his leave and motions at the set. 'I'll have the rest lifted by cart tomorrow.' Jane sees him to the door and then fusses round the studio, lighting the lamps. The smell of burning tallow emanates as Ellory offers her visitor refreshment, and then, realising that they have not eaten all day, sends the girl for bread, cheese and small beer from Sloans. The last shilling or so for now. Her purse will not be empty much longer. 'It's only a simple meal,' she says apologetically.

Charlotte waves off the comment. 'Small beer,' she repeats. She has never tasted it. Then she raises her eyes. The moon is a translucent ghost in the last of the blue sky beyond the glass ceiling, like a kind of promise. It feels magical. She's glad she left the dark study and wonders why houses have windows that always look outwards rather than up. 'The moon is almost full,' she says, motioning above. 'Have you taken photographs today?'

Ellory nods.

'The portrait of a lady?' Charlotte hazards.

'What makes you think that?' Ellory's skin tightens. Can Miss Nicholl see her soul?

Charlotte motions towards the mirror. 'I don't imagine a gentlemen would pose thus.'

Ellory relaxes a little. 'The subject was an actress,' she confesses cautiously.

'Did she sit as a character from a play?'

Ellory shakes her head. She's glad Charlotte has come, but if she knew the impropriety of Grace Sutherland's poses, she certainly would not stay. The photographs have felt like an exciting experiment until now, when a lady's eye might uncover them.

'I suppose such images would be useful in the theatre foyer,' Charlotte observes lightly and Ellory does not contradict her. 'Excuse me,' she says, getting to her feet. 'I must go down to the lavatory.'

As the door closes, Charlotte soaks in the excitement of being left alone in the studio. For a moment she fantasises the place is hers and she is earning her living as a kind of artist. She feels a sting of freedom. She is not the type, of course. As a child her governess taught her to draw, but the images were always stilted. 'You're better with words,' the woman said and encouraged Charlotte to write poetry. She has not written anything more than mere correspondence in a while, nor has she set herself to embroidery, the other skill her governess deemed a particular talent. She has not made anything, in fact, bar playing Liszt on the pianoforte; a celebration of somebody else's talent, not making something of her own.

She gets up and inspects the cameras, realising the smaller is the result of the innovation Ellory told her about. She dare not touch it. Then she moves on, peering through the open door of the print room and the office. On Ellory's desk there is a leather album, which

Charlotte imagines must be a new portfolio. Ellory will have more images now than the pictures of Edinburgh Castle and the urchins on the grass. Curious, Charlotte opens the cover and peers at the first image of Jane, dressed as a housemaid with a white apron rather than her leather one. She lifts the book into the studio where the light is better and turns the page. There is Jane again but this time getting dressed in a lady's bodice with two petticoats, inspecting herself in the mirror as she pulls on a stocking. Charlotte puts the album on the table. Her blood runs cold. The studio no longer feels like somewhere she could be free. She pieces together all her memories of Ellory, the betrayal hurting like a fresh bruise of the same sort that bloomed when she discovered the secret cupboard. There was no sign of this, she thinks, and sinks onto a plain pine chair. Is every apple rotten at its core? Clutching her courage, she opens the album again and turns the page. There is Jane in another pose, still half dressed and not in her own clothes. The compositions are perfect, she thinks, and then jumps as Ellory returns, the horror of being discovered written clearly on her face.

'Please,' Ellory starts, her face flushing as she rushes forwards. This is the worst thing that might have happened. 'Do not think badly of me.'

'Badly?' Charlotte repeats the word as if trying it for size.

Ellory snatches the album, crying now. She passes her gloved hand across her cheek to dry it. 'Please,' she repeats. Both women feel as if they are tumbling. But for different reasons.

'I can't believe it,' Charlotte gets out. 'Why would you ever—?'

'We were trying something new.' Ellory's voice is panicked. She has pulled Jane into her circle of wickedness and now she is overcome by regret, drowning in a dark pool and all for a few guineas.

'How could you?' Charlotte snaps. It seems there is nobody upon whom she can rely. She draws herself up, stalks out of the studio and down the stairs.

With her cheeks burning, Ellory shoves the album into the drawer of the desk and locks it for good measure. Her mind races at what

Miss Nicholl might do. She cannot tell what. And that is not the worst of it. Tonight she must make Miss Sutherland's negatives so she can print them in the morning. Jessie's voice chimes in her ear like a doomsday bell. She is unworthy – of course she is. She is her mother's daughter and no better than her sister. The lowest of the low. The truth about her will travel up and down the town like a musical scale. The thought turns her insides to stone. And with the regret there is a twist of anger because she knows her work is good. She is making money from it where those without her eye have failed. How do you make progress without trying new things? How do you make enough money without selling pictures at a premium that only a certain kind of gentleman, it seems, will pay?

When Jane appears, Ellory pulls herself together.

'I bought enough for three, miss,' Jane says, laying the basket on the table.

'Miss Nicholl was called away,' Ellory replies as steadily as she can manage. 'I'll go to the darkroom now.' She no longer feels like eating.

Jane looks up, like a puppy called to heel. 'Can I help?' she offers. 'I'll be quiet.' The girl is always keen.

Ellory needs to pause. She holds up her hand as if holding back the tide. 'Give me a minute,' she says, then disappears into the cocoon of the print room and lights the amber lamp. She glances at the jar of jam, but cannot face a spoonful. Then she steadies her hands quite deliberately. I must not think of shame, she decides. I must be determined that I'm lucky to be here and making things work. I must deliver all these pictures as quickly as I can.

Chapter Twenty

The next morning, white crocuses appear across the lawn in the park at Blythswood Square as if nature has sprinkled flakes of salt across the grass. The previous day, Murray Urquhart dispatched a note to Reverend Patterson inviting him to the Urquharts' Bath Street offices. Today when the reverend arrives, his frame shrouded in a heavy woollen winter coat which reaches almost to his ankles, he removes his hat and hands it to the clerk, agitated and fingering his collar as he is shown in. 'We've grave matters to discuss, Mr Urquhart,' he announces.

'It's a fine day, Reverend.' Murray motions towards the chair.

As he sits down Patterson grimaces. 'We must accept each season,' he declares with fatalism. 'The winter is as much of the Lord as the summer sun.'

Murray sighs. It feels like Patterson has embarked on a sermon already. 'I asked you here because Charlotte Nicholl received this.' He lays the note on the desk. The reverend draws a pair of spectacles from his inside pocket and reads slowly, sucking the flavour of each word as if it is a sour boiled sweetie. Eventually he lowers the page. 'In my view, Miss Nicholl requires occupation,' he says. 'Ladies are always required in the running of the Garrick Temperance Hotel on Stockwell Street. It's a charitable endeavour. She might like to address herself to something of that nature rather than the unsuitable activities that have prompted this missive.'

Murray clears his throat. 'The note is unacceptable. It was clearly sent by one of your flock, Reverend.'

Patterson's expression does not flicker. 'Mr Douglass's campaign is unacceptable. The note is regrettable. But Miss Nicholl has put herself in the way of this harm.'

'Because she attended a lecture?'

Patterson's mouth twitches. It is not a smile exactly. 'She accompanied you, as I understand it. At night. And returned in your carriage to Blythswood Square where she's been living entirely alone since her father's demise.'

'What are you insinuating?' Murray asks as calmly as he can. Is there a single soul in the whole of Glasgow, he thinks, who does not wish to pair him and Charlotte? It is as if people cannot help themselves.

'I'm not insinuating anything. I'm saying it's downright inappropriate,' the minister rejoins.

'Had the lecture been about needlework you would not find it so,' Murray snaps. 'Is intellectual curiosity and open debate no longer welcome in our dissenters' kirk?'

Patterson's eyes glaze as if he is looking straight into Murray's soul. 'You know you've done wrong,' he thunders.

Murray lifts the paper. 'This person has done wrong, Reverend. Miss Nicholl and I are people of conscience. Do you have any idea who penned the letter?'

The minister shakes his head. 'Miss Nicholl's independence is the problem, Murray. Several members of the congregation have mentioned the girl needs to be protected. Do you think her father would have taken her to a radical meeting? Douglass is an extremist.'

'She wanted to go. It's not illegal or immoral, sir, to listen to a point of view.'

'You're her guardian now, are you?' Patterson taunts him. 'You certainly take a good deal of interest in the lassie's affairs.'

'I'm her solicitor,' Murray objects.

'Aye. Her solicitor accompanying her out in the middle of the night. You can make it respectable if you want. Do you style yourself Charlotte Nicholl's husband?'

'I've known Miss Nicholl lifelong,' Murray says, straining to keep his temper. 'The lady shows no interest in matrimony with me or anybody else. She's not the type.'

'The lass is nigh on 25. No one will want her soon enough. It's not too late for her to be welcomed back into the fold, but she has to change. She cannot be seen out gallivanting accompanied by a single gentleman, and you know it.'

Murray pauses. He is being led off the point. Yet he is driven to defend his friend.

'She's done nothing wrong, Reverend. Lately, in fact, she's developed a great deal of confidence.' Patterson lets this worrying remark pass but the young solicitor pushes ahead. 'It's hard enough that she's alone, sir. Her father having died so recently, and new responsibilities heaped on as a result, without spite being piled on top because she attended a lecture. You can tell your congregants if they wish to vent their spleen, they might write to me. Like Miss Nicholl, I believe Mr Douglass has the right of it. Whether this letter is inappropriate or regrettable, it must not happen again.'

Patterson sits back in the chair. The situation, he sees, is worse than that gossiped of in fancy drawing rooms over the New Glasgow Bridge of an afternoon. There, at least, they assume Murray knows he is wrong. 'I won't pursue the person who penned this letter. It's a sacred duty to rebuke sinners, and you and Miss Nicholl have sinned.' He gestures towards the note. 'Douglass's campaign is divisive. Freedom of speech is one thing but what you're doing is disloyal. I can't support dissent of that kind.'

'But you'll support this spiteful bullying? One might have hoped for more compassion. Jesus himself might have expected it,' Murray counters.

'Charlotte Nicholl is a godless wretch,' Patterson rejoins. 'The girl had to be forced even to wear black to mourn her father. Poor

Mrs Grieg is distraught. Charlotte banned the old woman from her house, a lifelong friend of the family. She's out of control.'

'That's ridiculous!' Murray exclaims, deciding he has no choice now but to take a stand. 'I regret to inform you that Miss Nicholl and I have agreed that if the money is not returned, we'll leave the Free Kirk. Your stance today will accelerate that decision. You cannot abandon a congregant like this, sir, and still expect their loyalty.'

Time stops. Patterson lets out a puff of air that feels as if it is his last breath. He glares at Murray. 'And what has your father to say?'

'I'm my own man,' Murray replies firmly. 'Though I'll not lie, I intend to make the case that my father should leave along with me. I'm afraid you have lost both Miss Nicholl and me as it stands.'

'You'll regret this in business, boy.' Patterson makes the threat as if he is enjoying it, a smirk playing around his thin lips.

Murray remains steady. 'Perhaps you will too. You've lost a wealthy congregant. But then your lack of action in her defence would have lost her anyway.'

The reverend's eyes narrow as he measures Murray's response. 'You place your souls in peril,' he warns.

'My soul is mine to do with as I wish. And Charlotte's is hers. Good afternoon, sir.' Murray cuts off the reverend and holds out his hand. Enough is enough.

Patterson considers then shakes. As he leaves, Murray hears him muttering all the way down the stairs, 'Scunnersome quine.'

From the window, he watches the minister step onto Bath Street. Patterson does not raise his hand. Tomorrow he will report what has transpired to the elders and recommend that if they are quick enough, they might cast out Charlotte Nicholl and Murray Urquhart before they officially leave of their own accord. The renegades' fate might at least have the benefit of discouraging others from taking this ridiculous stand on behalf of a Black man who is only trying to stir up trouble. It is a shame about the money Miss Nicholl might have provided, but of all the things wrong with Reverend Patterson, he cannot be bought.

Inside, Murray clears his desk.

'I'm off to Blythswood Square,' he tells the clerk with a prick of conscience that he has quit the Kirk on Charlotte's behalf on the basis of his own temper and half a conversation they have had. He feels he is only representing her to part of his ability because he cannot tell her the whole truth. In the past when a gentleman has had a private clause in his will there has always been enough money to execute it properly and enough family left to provide comfort to each other. Charlotte is in the invidious position of being quite alone and not well enough provided for, and has now lost her minister, though, Murray thinks, perhaps not having to deal with Patterson is a gain. Still, she is more and more isolated.

Outside, he takes the hill at a pace and cuts through the garden. At the door, Mrs Cullen takes his coat and hat and shows him up to the drawing room where Charlotte, sitting tidily on the blue sofa wearing a plain peach gown with her hair pinned in place, perfectly contained as always, has taken up a long-abandoned piece of embroidery.

'Hello,' he greets her, and she tells the housekeeper to send in tea.

'Are you all right?' she asks. There is a fire in his eyes which she recognises from when they were children and some lads from Grahamstown threw stones on account of his spine.

'I quit the Kirk,' he says.

'I don't blame you.'

'I'm afraid I told Patterson you'd quit too.' Murray pulls the letter from his pocket and lays it on the side table. 'He wouldn't condemn it,' he adds. 'The spite.'

'It's not only the letter, is it?' she says with a sigh. 'I'm sure people have been reproaching me behind my back since the funeral. For not wearing mourning. For living alone.'

Murray worries that he has put her in this terrible position. 'They'd probably have you back, Charlotte. But you'd have to condemn Mr Douglass's argument and placate Mrs Grieg. I'm sure we could find you a companion. Somebody you'd like. You might write to Patterson if you wish and blame it on me. He's not as much like John Knox as he thinks he is. For my part, however, I've burnt my bridges. I will go.'

Charlotte considers. Going back is the easier option but it does not feel clean. 'The Kirk must send back the money. It's the price of blood,' she says, quoting Mr Douglass.

'I reminded him of your father's generous bequest, but it did not bring him round.'

Charlotte's eyes light like starbursts. She has spent hours at her desk trying to figure out what to do but the books will not balance, not in the long term. And then there's the business of her misjudgement of Ellory. 'It's all money, isn't it?' she bursts out. 'Mrs Grieg and that stupid clock. The Kirk and its filthy lucre. They wouldn't accept donations from people who had enslaved white men, women and children. It's venal. Everything is.' She casts her eyes in the direction of the cupboard downstairs. It seems there is nothing she can trust.

'I don't disagree,' Murray says. 'Mrs Grieg means well but she's wrong.'

Charlotte thinks that meaning well is not enough. She has been surrounded all her life by people from the Kirk, folk who sought her society because she was James Nicholl's daughter. Without him everything has fallen apart. The world is entirely unreasonable and she feels lost within it. She flings down the embroidery in temper.

Murray is taken aback. He assumes she must be more religious than he thought. 'Are you afraid?' he asks. 'Without Patterson, I mean?'

Charlotte considers telling him that she knows about Helensburgh House and has discovered her father's trove of naked women and worse. But she cannot bring herself to. The thought of having to say the words out loud to Murray makes her blood run cold. What even are the correct words for these things? she wonders. 'Fear is inevitable when you take a leap of faith,' she says, more to herself than to him. Then, recovering her equilibrium: 'I read that somewhere. The thing is, Murray, everything has gone wrong.'

Murray senses she is talking about something else. His mind races through what could possibly have gone wrong for her beyond the note, the gossip and the money.

'Everything?'

'My father's estate,' she says vaguely.

'Ah, the money. Well, I'm working on that,' he says.

Charlotte, though, knows what James Nicholl did with his money. He squandered it. 'There's nobody. Nothing,' she adds. 'I don't know what I'm going to do.'

Murray is straitened. He has put Charlotte in this position and it's a vulnerable one. He pulls back, guilty that he cannot level with her, nor can he blindly say that everything will be all right financially. He has had every warehouse Nicholl ever used checked over, but has found nothing. He suddenly judges himself selfish. Charlotte has been his friend as long as he can remember. He feels his shoulders stiffen. She's right, he thinks, she is cruelly constrained, and if he can't find what Mr Lennox is looking for, then she'll spend the rest of her life scrimping to get by. 'There's a way out,' he says slowly. 'I didn't know you felt so . . . overwhelmed.'

Charlotte sniffs. She wonders if he is about to tell her about Helensburgh House.

Murray continues. 'You shouldn't be alone, if you don't wish it. We've always been friends, have we not? We shoulder things together.'

She nods.

'And you miss your father's companionship?'

Charlotte smiles. 'Yes. In a way.'

'He's left you in a difficult position. Financially, I mean.'

'That was unexpected,' she admits.

He holds her eye steadily. This is my duty, he thinks. 'We could marry, Charlotte,' he offers. 'If you like.'

There is a moment of absolute silence as they both reel at what he's said. Murray takes a breath with some difficulty. Charlotte feels her cheeks burning and looks away.

'It would solve your problems or at least some of them,' he rushes to add. He hopes she realises that he is making the offer for the sake of her honour.

Charlotte looks horrified. 'No,' she bursts out.

He ignores this and continues speaking. 'It's my temper that's isolated you – today in any case. People expect us to marry. Patterson and my father and the Griegs. More than only them I should think.'

'And you have suddenly decided to do what Reverend Patterson and your father wish?' Charlotte snaps. 'It doesn't sound like you.'

He lets out a laugh. She is wrong, he thinks. He usually follows his father's advice. He is doing so now in more ways than she knows. 'Papa knows we've been friends since we were children. He said you wouldn't . . . *distract* me,' he adds limply. 'And you are, as you pointed out, alone and living on a modest income. One I might easily augment. I want to help, Charlotte.'

Charlotte leans towards him as if sharing a confidence. She is every inch the woman Ellory Mann photographed the week before.

'You do not want this any more than I do,' she says steadily. 'Stop it.'

Murray feels as if he has been slapped. He knows his argument is unconvincing. Still, he feels it somehow shouldn't be. He is about to reply when Mrs Cullen comes in with the tea tray. They wait awkwardly for the housekeeper to leave. As the door clicks behind her, Charlotte continues. 'Do you think it's truly my life's work simply not to distract you? Is that the best I can hope for?'

Murray looks sheepish.

'I hope my refusal doesn't offend you. You're my only friend, Murray, and you were trying to be kind, I think. But tying us to each other wouldn't be kind. Not in the long run, would it?'

Murray regards her. Most women would be broken by the Kirk abandoning them. Most being left in inadequate funds would run headlong into any marriage. Not Charlotte Nicholl. Her integrity pulls him up. He stares at the painting above the mantel. She looks much younger, surrounded by white roses. Behind, propped in a plain silver frame on the pianoforte, Ellory's calotype image provides a contrast. Only a few days ago Murray thought his childhood friend was more like the woman in the first picture than the second. He is unsure whether she has changed or if he simply did not know her well enough. He feels in this moment that he hardly knows himself. 'You're not alone,' he adds. 'I don't want you to feel that way.'

'Thank you,' she says. 'But we're not a true match.'

He nods in agreement then smiles cautiously. Charlotte smiles back.

'For my part,' she continues, 'I regret not having any family. But I'm not the romantic sort . . . it is not in me,' she motions. 'And it is in you, I guess. Which is why we make better friends than lovers. Will you tell me about your time in London?' She lowers her voice to a whisper. 'Mrs Grieg says you sowed your wild oats.'

The young solicitor coughs. 'Charlotte!'

She regards him frankly. 'As you're my ally, I feel you owe me the truth about the world. We'll never have a connection of that sort together, but I admit, I'm curious.' She waits, hoping he will tell her. The images of Jane in Ellory's portfolio are inexplicable, she thinks, but perhaps understanding why people seem to need such connections will illuminate the issue. Her father saw something in it.

The solicitor sighs. People assume he debauched himself in London. Perhaps by the standards of the Free Kirk he did. He certainly owes Charlotte something after making such an ass of himself. 'I met a great many people. I attended balls and pleasure gardens and exhibitions and lectures. But I was there to study. That was the main thing.'

Charlotte ignores this attempt to divert her. 'Pleasure gardens?'

'We don't have them here because of the weather.'

'What goes on in such a place?'

'Drinking, music and juggling mostly.'

'And women?'

Murray smiles. 'I'm not a rake, if that's what you are asking. You know that, surely.'

'Did you fall in love?'

'Not quite.' His tone is tight.

Charlotte knows he does not want to tell her, but she persists. 'Why did you return?'

Murray regards her with candour. 'Because Glasgow is my home.'

'Your father's house, you mean?'

'No. Glasgow,' Murray repeats. 'I want to build this city.'

'That sounds very grand.'

He gives a lopsided shrug. 'I've invested in dredging the river. It's a kind of patriotism, I suppose. It's important to see the world, but in the end I realised that whatever I saw, I wanted to bring it back. That's my real interest.'

'You'll be opening a pleasure garden at Garnethill before we know it,' she says. 'When you said you had *not quite* fallen in love, though, what did you mean?'

He shifts. He has, after all, just offered his hand. 'Most gentlemen seek a mirror, but I prefer a view. A window,' he admits.

'And you almost fell in love with such a lady?' she asks, thinking she is neither a mirror nor a window. She worries momentarily that she might be a wall.

'The lady was a doorway,' Murray says. 'Which is to say she was wealthy and educated but had few opinions. I realised that was not my desire,' he presses. 'If marriage is a partnership I want someone who can truly partner me, not simply do what I say or wish for what I wish. What about you?'

'You will think me mad.'

'Just because you don't wish to marry me doesn't make you insane,' he counters wryly.

'Everyone gets so excited about marriage. I can't even imagine it.'

His eyes are drawn to the calotype once more. 'I wonder what Miss Mann would make of me,' he says wistfully, 'were she to take my image.'

Charlotte ponders, with a sudden stab of clarity, whether this is the most frank thing he has said. Is it not the function of art to illuminate life? The attraction people feel for each other is a tide that pulls them unbidden, an undercurrent that seems impossible to resist. Though she has no interest in dipping in her toe, that does not mean that swimming itself is bad. If Ellory is making a living from her photographs, it must be because people want to pay for such images. The tree provides women hope. The calotype of the castle perhaps pride or awe. Do the other images, the ones in her father's cupboard, inspire devotion or loyalty along with their baser function? And here is Murray wanting to be seen in a particular way, by a particular person. If some consider marriage holy, perhaps that is why. Though it is, she thinks, not for her. 'Maybe I'll be an old spinster in a house a good deal less fine than this one. Perhaps I'll get used to being alone and come to like it,' she says.

'That's not you,' he replies, but it's true: he finds it difficult to imagine Charlotte married. He watches as she takes the poison letter from the side table and deposits it into the fire. 'We'll have to find somewhere else to worship,' she says.

Afterwards he does not want to return to his office. Instead he has a horse saddled to ride into town. The river helps him think. The Thames was the same. As he passes St Enoch's Square he looks up. High above, Miss Mann's glass box has papers in it, in the sun. Beyond the buildings, a mere block to the south, the rigging shifts with the swell of the Clyde, as the moored vessels sway. Out of sight, laughter floats round the corner from Jamaica Street and mingles with the calls of street vendors as far as Anderston in one direction and the Saltmarket in the other. A crowd of barefoot children plays with a ball on the other side of the square. He scents the smell of woodsmoke and burning coal. The braziers on the dockside. He feels guilty not telling Charlotte what he knows but he is professionally obliged to keep her father's secrets. Poor girl. He will do the best he can for her. He casts his eyes upwards, wondering if he can spot the familiar bun of red hair, and thinks, Thank goodness Miss Nicholl said 'no'.

Chapter Twenty-One

McLaren's Hotel

The next morning, a squall is tipping out of the sky. Lennox is snoring with his mouth open but the shards of water battering the window wake Jeremiah. Then there is a knock at the door. He gets up and pulls the older man's silk dressing robe about him as he comes to, yawning as he opens up. The bellboy says nothing, only solemnly hands over a tea tray (one cup, Jeremiah notes, though they know he is here) and two missives from London. Jeremiah turns over the letters as he pours the tea and drinks it in one, tracing the crests on the wax seals with his finger. Then he refills the cup and takes it through. Lennox grunts and sits up, eyeing Jeremiah in his robe. 'Take that off,' he says.

Jeremiah does as he is told, and Lennox sips, steady-eyed, still watching the younger man, now naked, the blue snake wound round his arm.

'I'm going out,' Jeremiah announces, reaching for his drawers. 'I've a job to do.'

Lennox's tone is gruff. He expects to be Jeremiah's first priority. 'When will I get my album?'

Jeremiah pulls on a knitted semmit, ruffling his hair. 'It was almost done yesterday. They start work early at St Enoch's Square. I'm sure she'll come when it's ready.'

Lennox pours a shot of brandy into his cup from a silver hip flask on the side table. Then he opens the less interesting-looking missive. It is from the man who valued James Nicholl's collection and says simply: *To answer your enquiry, I visited Mr Nicholl at his home at Blythswood Square, sir. The paintings and artefacts were laid out in his study.* Lennox sighs and puts down the teacup. None of the items his master has bought are in the study any longer. He rifled it himself.

'Everything all right?' Jeremiah asks.

'Yes, yes,' Lennox is brusque. 'Business,' he dismisses the news. 'I'll need that album anyway. It'll buy time.'

Jeremiah pulls on his breeches. He was accosted the evening before on his way back to McLaren's by the chap with the patent shoes from the cockfight. 'I want another picture of my little maid,' he said, tarrying on the flagstones outside the theatre. Jeremiah told him that wasn't possible. 'I've no more pictures of her, sir, and none coming.' The man grabbed his arm. 'Why not? Is the girl too occupied on St Enoch's Square?' Then the fellow smirked as the concern lit in Jeremiah's eyes. 'I've tracked her down,' he boasted, 'but I'd prefer you to act in the matter.' He pulled a card out of his waistcoat. *George Gibson. 10 Nelson Street.* 'Bring me a calotype. I'll pay half a sovereign like before. And another half sovereign for a proper introduction.'

Jeremiah pulled his arm back. 'The lady isn't willing, Mr Gibson.'

Gibson snorted. 'Lady!' he repeated as if this was a grand jest.

'Not willing,' Jeremiah said again and walked away, but the exchange still concerns him. He cannot stop thinking about it, though he must get to the theatre. He fingers the card in his pocket. He should visit Mr Gibson to make the point more forcefully as soon as he can.

Lennox heaves himself out of bed to the writing desk. He scribbles a note to Urquhart on a piece of headed paper, saying his enquiry has borne no fruit. The items are clearly no longer at Blythswood Square. 'Send up the boy,' he says over his shoulder as Jeremiah leaves. 'I must have this delivered.'

*

At the studio, Ellory fits the last of Mr Lennox's prints into the tan leather album and surveys her work. It would do Mr Hogarth proud, she thinks; Mr Hill too, come to that. Then she berates herself for the sin of pride. Her lack of church attendance does not mute the Reverend Reid's voice in her head. Jessie's too if she's honest. The evening before, seeing Miss Nicholl with the album, her heart almost stopped. She spent the night tossing and turning over what the lady might do. In fitful sleep she dreamed of being sucked into the telescope on Calton Hill and falling through the lens, down the steep slope to the slums. And yet she can't help feeling there is value in what she has made. She intends to wrap the pictures in brown paper and top the parcel with an invoice for the balance of payment, but for now she does not want to cover it. Together she, Jane and Jeremiah have created a story that feels real – a strange emotion mixed with her shame.

She cannot sign the photographs as Mr Hill does, but it feels wrong not to own them. She stares at the bottle of India ink on the table and remembers a mason's mark at Rock House, an uneven triangle carved into the stone beside one of the windows. 'They were illiterate men,' Jessie said with a sniff. 'But they made their sign.' Now Ellory lifts a quill and draws two interlocking squares that make an eight-pointed star, like prints lying on top of each other that together transform into something new. Satisfied with her design, she lifts a knife and heats the blade on the stove, then she brands the inside of the portfolio at the back, small, with the tip of the blade. Eight lines one after the other and the star appears. The air smokes with singed leather. She blows on it, satisfied that she has claimed the images. This will be her sign. She can wrap the book now.

Leaving Jane to look after the prints on the sill, she says she will be out for a while as she dons her brown coat and bonnet over her forest-green day dress. 'If he pays directly we'll have pork chops tonight,' Ellory promises and takes the stairs, the album under her arm. It is as well to get rid of it sharp.

Wellington Street is not far but she stows the parcel inside her coat for the rain today is dense enough to soak the paper. Ellory has come to know Glasgow quickly. Edinburgh, which is to say, the New Town, is a mass of interlocking crescents, terraces and lanes, but this city is comprised of a plain grid much easier to navigate and near St Enoch's Square the long streets are punctuated by shipping offices running away from the Clyde and warehouses parallel to it. Beneath her feet the detritus borne from farms and manufactories outside the city make the flagstones slippery. These are the streets her mother knew, she thinks, feeling a connection across time as she turns the corner, passing a rag-and-bone man, his cart piled high. Ahead, she enters the double doors to McLaren's Hotel. The hallway smells of beeswax polish and candle wax. At the reception desk she asks for Mr Lennox and is sent up to the suite. Lennox is at his desk, a glass of port at his elbow now, smoking and reading a periodical.

'I've brought it,' she says, offering him the parcel.

'Jeremiah sent you,' Lennox notes and she does not contradict him as he burns the string efficiently with the tip of his cheroot and pulls aside the brown paper. He stands up to flick through the images, assessing each carefully. Plain Jane admiring herself in her mistress's mirror, her ankles on show. Trying on a lady's clothes, caught in the act by the camera in a velvet chair. Plain Jane in her undergarments, jauntily admiring her own image. Plain Jane buttoning her boots and checking the time for she must get back to her duties. Ellory suppresses a smile, for the serious consideration Lennox is giving the photographs is flattering. Alexander Hill looks at David Octavius's compositions the same when they arrive at his gallery.

'This is good,' Lennox pronounces. He reads the invoice as carefully as he perused the images. Then he goes to his leather bag and removes a purse of coin, counting the balance of payment. Ellory cannot quite believe it is so easy. Sometimes Mr Hill has to wait months for payment. But then, Mr Hill's images are never indecent.

'Here,' Lennox says, handing over the money as she receipts the invoice.

'You'll not make images the same for any other?' he asks, though it is not a question.

'No, sir.' She curtsies and means it. Charlotte has given her a fright and she has learned what there is to learn from the process. She leaves, both hands clutching her reticule as if she has got away with something. She will make for the butcher directly and stop for a sprig of rosemary to season their supper. After Miss Sutherland has paid she intends to treat them to a bottle of claret. She wants to mark each success with a celebration. Jam today.

Outside she starts to walk up the muddy hill. She is about to turn for the butcher when a carriage halts sharply on the roadway, the horse giving a sudden whinny. The window is opened and Charlotte Nicholl peers out, her face framed by a plain straw bonnet with blue edging. 'Miss Mann,' she calls, opening the door. Ellory's gaze falls to the tips of her shiny tan boots, anticipating the humiliation of a dressing-down in public. She glances at the turning but it is past the carriage. She is trapped. It feels a little like drowning, but before she is fully submerged, she realises that Charlotte Nicholl does not look angry. Quite the reverse. In fact, Charlotte is hovering nervously on the kerb now, her buttoned black boots balanced on the edge. She clears her throat. 'I'd like to speak to you,' she says, indicating the carriage. 'I realise I was unfair.'

'The album's gone,' Ellory replies in a snap. 'I won't make another.'

Charlotte pauses. After Murray had left the day before, she had spent a long time considering their conversation. It seemed to her then that there had been too much judging by everybody of her situation. And of Murray's too. She had stared a long time at Ellory's calotype of her and concluded that Miss Mann has an excellent eye. Like the picture of her in the spencer, the images of Jane had been framed beautifully. The tone of Miss Mann's raunchy prints ought to have been the invitation to start a conversation, she realised, with the only person she knows who might not judge her for the contents of her father's cupboard. In fact, the only person she knows experienced in such matters, for Ellory is an artist.

As Charlotte settled to sleep very late, it came to her that she had done nothing but judge and, for that matter, condemn her father out of hand. The pictures shocked her, of course, but she does not wish to be like Mrs Grieg and the others. It is too easy to lose people that way. She is alone for many reasons but one of them is that she has decided to be so. She has pushed people away. Mostly, this has been for the best, she thinks. But Ellory felt like a friend. Someone to admire. Besides, her pictures leave a good deal more to the imagination than the contents of her father's secret cupboard. When Charlotte woke, she realised that she had been her own worst enemy. Just because I do not wish to . . . She paused her own discourse for she still could not quite find the words for the act of love. Just because I do not wish *carnal* knowledge – yes, that is it – does not make every picture of female flesh a bad thing. Finding the album was an opening, if only she had not been such a dunce. A 'door', as Murray would have it. And Ellory Mann a friend, if only she would let her be so. The writings were another matter, of course, and some of the more graphic . . . again, words failed her, but Charlotte had come to a decision. She had changed.

Now she hovers on the kerb. 'I'm sorry,' she apologises. 'I was a fool to react as I did. It was the shock, I think. I intended to write you a note. The thing is, I need help. I don't know how to . . .' Her voice trails.

'What is it?' Ellory cocks her head. The last thing she had expected Miss Nicholl to do was apologise.

Charlotte glances back at the carriage. 'If you can forgive me . . .' she starts, lowering her voice. 'Nobody must know. Some pictures have come into my possession.'

'Do you mean pictures like . . .?' Ellory cannot say it either, even in a whisper.

A porter in one of the buildings further down the hill is hovering on the doorstep, watching. Charlotte glances at him. 'Oh no. Much worse,' she confides quietly. 'I wonder would you come with me?'

Ellory considers only a second before nodding her agreement. 'But where?'

Charlotte motions her to the carriage and they climb inside. 'Home,' she instructs the coachman. Settling into her seat she says, 'I was on my way to your studio, you see. I'm so glad to have spotted you on the road.'

The carriage enters Blythswood Square from Blythswood Street. The garden feels unexpected after the long climb, the herbaceous border blooming beyond the railings. The women are admitted into the house by Mrs Cullen. Ellory notes the hallway smells faintly of vinegar. The mirrors must have been cleaned today, she thinks, as the housekeeper takes their coats and hats and opens the study door. Charlotte sits in her father's chair, her purple skirt billowing as she does so, as if it is giving a sigh of relief. 'Tea?' she offers.

'I'm fine, thank you,' Ellory says. 'Perhaps later.'

Mrs Cullen disappears and Glasgow's most-talked-about heiress slumps in her seat. 'Thank you for coming,' she says. 'I need an ally.'

'Life is to learn,' Ellory rejoins. She had the phrase from a university professor who visited Rock House once. 'I'm sorry,' she says, 'about what you found on my desk. It was a commission. An experiment in innovation.'

'Life is to learn,' Charlotte repeats, waving away the apology. 'I shouldn't have been poking among your things.' She pauses, considering all the things she has learned of late. 'We shall put that behind us, shall we? I would prefer it.'

Ellory nods.

'Now you're here, you must swear,' Charlotte says. 'Do you mind?'

'Swear what?'

'To keep my secret. The reason I brought you.' Charlotte's stomach shifts. Showing Ellory exposes both of them. She needs Miss Mann's competence but she wants her assurance too.

215

Ellory looks round the room with its well-made furniture. 'You know my secret,' she says. 'Is that not bond enough?'

Charlotte takes this in. 'I've a great deal to lose,' she gets out.

'Because you're a lady,' Ellory elucidates.

Charlotte blushes. 'I'm coming to realise it's a cage. Everyone simply expects me to marry. And to marry, a woman must be spotless, it seems.'

Ellory sits down. Working-class women have more freedom in that, albeit coupled with less financial power. She's curious. It's a schoolgirl pact but she'll make it. 'All right,' she says.

'You must say the words,' Charlotte insists.

'I swear.'

The purple taffeta rustles as Charlotte crosses the room, her footsteps strangely loud. The fire is alight in the grate, the morning's ash heavy on the embers. 'My father died here,' she says as she locks the door. 'It's strange to think it was less than a month ago.'

'It must have been a shock.'

Charlotte pauses. Things have changed a great deal since then. 'He wasn't the man I believed him to be.'

'The mistress you told me about, you mean?'

Charlotte nods curtly. 'More than that. Several days after the funeral, I discovered what I'm going to show you. I thought it out of character at first, but the truth is I'm learning who he really was.'

Ellory feels suddenly nervous. 'Can't Mr Urquhart help?'

Charlotte stiffens. 'My father's will enjoins secrecy. Murray and his father are bound by the terms of it. I'm fond of Murray but I can't fully trust him.' She looks down. 'But it is not only for that reason. It's the disgrace, Miss Mann. I haven't been able to bring myself – I've been frozen.'

The hillock of ash tumbles into the grate – a kind of revelation.

'I can tidy the fire,' Ellory offers and then stops herself. She is not in service any longer. The habit is hard to break.

'I'll call the maid after.' Now Charlotte has started, she does not wish to stop. Sharing the burden is a kind of relief. She lights a candle in one of the brass sticks on the mantle and crosses to the drinks tray where she clicks the latch and removes the key. 'My father had this made,' she says, opening the door. 'A secret cupboard behind the bookshelves. It must've been installed when the house was built. Papa oversaw the design. He must always have had secrets, you see. Now they are mine.'

Ellory peers into the darkness. The hairs on the back of her neck prickle. Charlotte enters. She cannot say any more. How on earth would she put it? Instead she motions Ellory to follow. Inside the photographer looks round. 'It's full in here,' she says.

Charlotte flicks through the first stack of paintings. 'It's all the same subject,' she says, motioning into the darkness with the candle so that the contents of the cupboard surge. 'Are you shocked?'

Ellory finds that she is not shocked. She is, in fact, interested.

'It makes him a monster,' Charlotte pronounces, thinking of Miss Shelley's creation, sitting upstairs on her bookshelf, bound in red Morocco. 'The shame of it. Not the paintings so much, but the rest.'

'I don't believe that,' Ellory replies, flicking through the first stack of canvases. 'The composition of the Whore of Babylon is lovely.'

Charlotte looks confused.

'The woman with the flowers. Here. I've found, in making my own images, there is a lot to learn from such painterly compositions,' Ellory admits.

'Would Mr Hill paint such a woman?' Charlotte asks.

'The fact he wouldn't is not a bad thing,' Ellory replies. 'Mostly Mr Hill paints grand views. These are classical figures. They might hang in a gallery. Any artist would be proud to make them,' she adds. She suddenly feels proud of her own pictures. It is an odd cocktail. She made them for the money, of course, but there is more to it. Now she takes the candlestick and walks into the darkness. 'May I?'

Charlotte decides to let Ellory discover for herself the greater depravity on the inner shelves. As her friend opens the box with the netsuke and leafs through the old engravings, Charlotte watches her face. The paintings may be classical, but these are not. Ellory catches her friend's eye. 'Oh my,' she says, the realisation dropping like a stone into water. 'What are the books about?'

'The same but in words. Mr Burns,' Charlotte says. 'I had no idea . . . They say he was a rake of course, but the phrases he uses, Ellory . . . the things he says.'

Ellory does not open the pages. 'I've heard Mr Burns was a terror. He left a cluster of bastards in Edinburgh. They're old men now.'

'He sounds violent when he writes of the act of love.' Charlotte's cheeks flush. 'And then "O my Luve's like a red, red rose" and "A Man's a Man for a' that". How could he?'

'The further in, the worse it gets,' Ellory says, referring to the cupboard although she might as well mean Mr Burns's collected works. Mr Hill and Mr Adamson, like most Scottish gentlemen, revere Burns's poetry. This casts a different light on their interest and a softer light on her own. 'I wonder where your father got all this. It's the volume that's shocking, don't you think?'

Charlotte has not thought in these terms. It interests her that Ellory's view is not moral but, in fact, professional. Just what she needs.

'Do you have a favourite?' Ellory asks.

Charlotte's head moves to catch a view of the Cleopatra as she considers the brushwork. The Boudica with her sword raised. 'Perhaps the Whore of Babylon, as you say. She's beautifully painted,' she admits. 'Or there's a small one of Circe. Or maybe Joan of Arc.'

Then, from the study there is a sharp knock on the door. 'Quickly,' Charlotte squeals and the women burst back into the room like water leaking under pressure. Ellory slams the cupboard and blows out the candle. Charlotte checks around before turning the key in the door. 'Ah, Mrs Cullen,' she says airily. 'We were engaged in reading aloud. The fire requires attending. Would you send Franny?'

Mrs Cullen casts a surly glance at Ellory, but she leaves.

The women sink onto the chairs closest to the fire. Ellory is distracted now, considering Miss Sutherland in the manner of a

French engraving. It crosses her mind that what's acceptable in one medium lies beyond the bounds in another. The contents of the cupboard are a step beyond her own work, but not so very far. Still, because photographs look real, the nudity in these paintings shown in a calotype would be little short of depraved. She feels better about the pictures of Jane and the image of Miss Sutherland lounging on her chaise, for apart from anything else, she realises now she is part of a tradition. Charlotte arches an eyebrow. 'What do you think?'

'I don't know,' Ellory replies. 'I'm taking it in. You want me to be practical, I assume?'

'I have to get rid of it. I've no idea what my father was thinking.'

'Gentlemen who collect art generally display it. For the pleasure of seeing the pictures.'

Charlotte snorts. 'He could hardly have done that.'

'He might have hung some of the paintings,' Ellory ventures. 'The female form, and the male form, for that matter, is taught in schools of art. These pictures can't be viewed to advantage in a cupboard.'

'He couldn't hang them all. The sheer quantity. And his place in the Kirk would have forbidden it. Doesn't it disgust you?'

Ellory shakes her head. 'You've seen the pictures I've made,' she says. 'The shock here is in the quantity, it's true. And some of the more *graphic* items. The images you discovered on my desk will titillate, I'm sure,' she admits. 'However, my guess is that not everything in the cupboard was made with that same purpose. Perhaps that's the difference.' She thinks she would like to make an image that celebrated a woman's story. A naked goddess to be revered not sullied. Grace Sutherland's calotypes come close. 'If your father kept a mistress, as you suppose, why didn't he house these paintings with her?' she asks.

Charlotte shifts. It is a fair point. Having somebody to discuss it with is a boon. 'I don't know,' she says.

Ellory continues. 'I understand why he wouldn't place the carvings about. And some of the prints. Can you imagine Mrs Grieg's demeanour?' Ellory pulls a shocked face, as if she is an elderly lady peering over her spectacles. 'We must save a young lady such as yourself from this infestation of flesh,' she mimics the doctor's wife.

Charlotte laughs. Miss Mann's friendship is becoming a pleasure. She's glad she stopped the carriage.

At the door, Franny appears silently and tips the ash in the grate into a bucket, piling wood on top of the embers. 'Thank you,' Charlotte says, as she opens a silver box on the desk and lifts a cigar. 'I've never smoked.' She picks a spill from the mantle. 'Shall we?'

'I always liked the smell when I came down in the morning. Reverend Reid smoked cigars in the evening,' Ellory says.

Charlotte efficiently clips the ends of two cigars. She lights the spill and transfers it to the tobacco, handing one to her friend. They both inhale. Charlotte wheezes as Franny leaves, closing the door behind her. 'You can see why I need your expertise. I can't leave the collection here.' She gestures towards the wall. 'It's a bruise on the fruit. I may have to move house.'

Ellory takes a deep draw. 'You might move?'

'To somewhere smaller. I'm alone, you see, and the truth is, I have need of money. I'm not as well provided for as everybody assumes.'

Ellory does not comment on this but the look on her face makes her surprise plain. 'Money,' she says almost wistfully, and Charlotte realises, for the first time perhaps, that Ellory has to make her living. That while she herself has capital, Ellory has only her talent.

'At first I thought to destroy the paintings,' she admits. 'But you're right – they have artistic merit. And besides, if I lit a fire in the back yard, people would be bound to see. And the marble items would not burn and one should not destroy books, of course, even if they're—'

'Oh no, you mustn't!' Ellory cuts in. 'They are fine things, Charlotte, whatever you may think of them. I know somebody who'll be able to help. To sell them, I mean,' she offers, breathing out a cloud of fragrant tobacco.

'I hoped you might,' Charlotte says gratefully. 'The thing is, I could never display them in a gallery. If anybody found out they were mine – the minister, the congregation . . .' She knows this is not logical. She has quit the Kirk, but still she hopes one day to join another or perhaps be welcomed into a respectable home.

'I didn't mean a gallery,' Ellory says. She sees Alexander Hill before her eyes, Mr Hill's brother, straight-backed and cold-eyed against the red walls of his Princes Street premises. Once Mrs Robertson submitted a painting that caused a sensation, for the female figures were judged too close together. Mr Alexander Hill and Mr Thomas Hill visited David Octavius at Rock House and, after long discussion, Alexander returned the picture to Mrs Robertson, who was working at the Royal Court in St Petersburg, with a curt note which contained a great many words in Greek. Later they heard the picture had sold in London for a small fortune. Ellory continues, dispelling the image. 'What I meant was, I know somebody who could act as your broker. For a fee.'

'A gentleman?'

'Not exactly,' Ellory admits. 'His name is Jeremiah Catto. You'd have to pay for his discretion. I suspect he'd be good at this though. You saw him at the studio the other evening.'

Charlotte places her cigar in a marble ashtray. She stands in front of the fire. What Ellory is suggesting is to trust somebody else. She had hoped Miss Mann would be able to help without involving any others but that, she sees now, was foolish. 'He's discreet, this friend of yours?'

Ellory nods. 'I'll send him as soon as I can,' she promises. Then she gets up. She must get back. Jane will be hungry.

'I'm tremendously relieved. Thank you.' Charlotte also gets to her feet. 'I worried I was going to have to marry Murray Urquhart after all,' she declares lightly.

Ellory freezes. It surprises her that she feels a sudden wave of anger, which she only just manages to subdue. 'You're to marry Mr Urquhart?' Her heart is sinking.

'Oh no,' Charlotte lets out. 'It's only that he asked yesterday. He felt sorry for me is all. My position has been tenuous and his father encouraged him. The whole thing was confused.'

221

Ellory's jaw tightens. She knows her feelings are unreasonable. Mr Urquhart is a gentleman, well above her station. He has not called in several days. This, she thinks, must be why. 'Goodbye,' she says and sets off, her mind racing. She feels a fool. The gentleman was kind to her is all. Of course he will want to marry somebody of his own class. She must be wary. Her feelings are running beyond her reach. As she rounds the corner, she thinks she might still catch the butcher if she keeps up a good pace.

Charlotte is oblivious to the feelings of confusion she has prompted and returns to the study and lifts the cigar once more. The taste is not unpleasant. She can see why gentlemen like it, she only wishes it didn't make her cough. Mrs Cullen has left her father's copies of the *Glasgow Herald* on the desk, three in all – one each week since he died. Papa always said the *Herald* was a passable newspaper if you didn't mind reading between the lines. Charlotte stares blankly at the advertisements for wild-cherry balsam and an auction of goods on Pitt Street. Then she turns the page, her eye only momentarily resting on the story of a public meeting in Lanark where Mr Douglass has spoken. The paper says that next the Black lobby will expect British citizens to forgo American sugar and cotton. *An impossibility*, it says. Charlotte shrugs. She can do without sugar and cotton if need be, she decides, and continues leafing towards the notices, where she reads her father's obituary twice before placing the paper on the fire.

Chapter Twenty-Two

The same evening

Murray Urquhart is aware of his father quietly clocking every minute of his day. The young Mr Urquhart only occasionally attends the cockpit or drinks in alehouses along the Broomielaw near the Old Glasgow Bridge. As a child he remembers his father's clients living in this part of the city, where fishermen still haul salmon out of the river to sell on the Saltmarket. These days the last of the wealthy have moved across the Clyde or else further west, and the houses seem old-fashioned, occupied by shopkeepers and the like. The clientele at the bars comprises a mixture of nostalgic older gentlemen and dockers who live in the tenements beyond the Mercat Cross, and sometimes a lawyer or two, like Murray, for the court is further up the High Street near the university. It is here he pretends he is going after dinner this evening, for he does not want to face his father's ire over his real intention to visit Miss Ellory Mann.

Old Mr Urquhart does not object for he knows that keeping up contacts to the east of Glasgow plays well when one of the Urquharts' clients requires to go to court. Besides, Murray is in no measure dissolute, albeit he enjoys a drink now and then. 'I want to speak to you. Soon,' the old man says, forbiddingly. 'This business with the Kirk,' he adds.

And Murray promises that he will stay in the following night.

'I need only ten minutes,' his father adds like a rumble of thunder.

It strikes Murray that this, then, is serious. When discussing fine legal points, he has known his father to drone on for half an hour about nothing. He considers loitering but is still drawn out of the door. 'Tomorrow,' he promises. Instinctively over the last few days he has found himself going past St Enoch's Square too often, though his father's instruction has kept him from going in. Then when he proposed to Charlotte, her clarity inspired him. He has been thinking of it ever since and knows that now he must be brave for he has realised Miss Mann is his view. His window. He thinks of the way she negotiated the rent that first afternoon. Buying the camera. Taking her images. He admires her confidence. He likes her creativity. She is a woman who can take on Glasgow with him. And a beauty too. He need only trust his feelings enough to act on them.

Darkness has just fallen when he tethers his mare outside St Enoch's church and gives a barefoot boy tuppence to mind it. 'Fetch her some water,' he says, 'and there'll be another tuppence when I return.' Then, excitement mounting, he takes the stairs.

The studio is lit by lamplight. The air smells of fried chops and rosemary. A loaf of bread and a curl of butter are still on the table. Ellory greets him, her tawny colouring alight in the glow. 'Mr Urquhart,' she says. 'I've not seen you in some days.'

'Business,' he lets out and her green eyes fall on him as if examining the word. She waits though she is not sure what for. Why would he tell her about his marriage plans? For a second she worries that he has found out Charlotte Nicholl's secret? Or worse, hers. But he shows no sign of either. 'Have you been well, Miss Mann?' he asks, suddenly formal.

Ellory motions him to sit at the table. 'Yes,' she admits. 'Business is brisk. Thank you for the custom.' She cannot admit, after all, the business upon which she has mostly been engaged. 'Might I offer you a small beer?'

They are awkward together, like two strange birds negotiating a drinking spot at a pond. Jane pours Murray a cup and clears the dishes, loading two empty jugs into a basket and disappearing out of the door, to return them to the tavern on Argyle Street. 'Have you been selling the smaller pictures?' Murray enquires, his mouth dry with nervousness. 'A stroke of genius, if I might say,' he adds, taking a sip of the beer.

'I only had the lens because the gentleman at the observatory threw it in.'

'Have you have taken many portraits with it?'

'I built a new camera. Today we had a queue,' she admits. 'I made small images of the tree for a shilling.'

'And they're selling?' He feels like a fool, making such small talk when there is something much larger and more important to say.

'Tolerably well, thank you.' Ellory is modest. Four images is more than Mr Hill has ever sold on the same day. She stops and regards Murray. Is this what he really came about? She has missed him, but if he is expecting her to divulge her feelings, she will not do so. Gentlemen, she knows, find it easy to take advantage of women and then blame them for it. 'They are for a different kind of client,' she says, keeping to business. 'Working women can afford them, you see.' He catches her eye, for the tree was the point of their first contention – the moment he realised she was different from every-one he had ever met.

Then he declares, 'Capital!' loudly, like an overenthusiastic rake who has won a foolish bet.

She stares at him. 'And what business has kept you occupied, sir?' she asks, wondering if he is trying to string her along with his interest.

'I've been attending my clients. Miss Nicholl, of course, among others.'

'Of course,' she echoes him. 'And is Miss Nicholl hale?'

'Charlotte is not unlike Queen Victoria, as I judge it,' he says, bluff again. 'Do you recall when Her Majesty first came to the throne, she was derided? Too young a lass. Too green, they said. But she tamed the court. Charlotte is like that.'

'She'll be all right then?' Ellory checks. 'Like Queen Victoria?'

'Oh yes.'

'I imagine she will marry soon.'

Murray stops. 'She's not the type,' he says, sounding genuine for the first time. 'It is not in her.'

'Some fortune-hunter will ask her, I'm sure,' Ellory bites her lip. She does not wish to be mean. 'A gentleman,' she adds.

Murray changes the subject. He has no intentions towards Charlotte. It is Ellory who makes his heart race. 'Do you miss Edinburgh, Miss Mann?' he asks.

Ellory looks away. 'Not at all, though it's a beautiful city.'

'People tend to like one or the other. Glasgow or Edinburgh, I mean,' he continues.

'My mother was from Glasgow.'

'You said that when I fetched you from the station. She would be proud of your accomplishments, I'm sure.' He wants to scream. This is all so polite that it feels inconsequential. He came here like a medieval knight on a quest and here they are, talking as if they have been introduced during the course of a genteel 'at home'.

Ellory's cheeks burn. She senses his discomfort and it feels as if he is needling her. Perhaps he is getting his own back for her jibe about Charlotte. She cannot bear not talking directly. 'I know you proposed to Miss Nicholl,' she snaps.

'That was nothing,' Murray lets out.

'You are easy with your affections, sir.'

'No, no,' Murray insists, bumbling on. 'I was inauthentic, I admit it. Charlotte is not somebody one might ever feel passion for. Not like you, Miss Mann. That is the thing.'

Ellory's temper flares. This feels like an insult. Does he assume that women like her are made for passion alone, but that Charlotte

226

is someone who will be an angel in his house? Gentlemen like that revere ladies and use women in the lower orders ill.

'I want to help you,' Murray adds, and Ellory snorts. It is as if he thinks she owes him more than payment of his invoice for what he has done. 'I understand what you are here for,' she almost spits. 'I want to be plain that though you're a gentleman, I'm not that kind of woman. I thank you for your help, of course. You've been most kind.'

Murray's gaze hardens. His forehead wrinkles. 'How could you know what I have come for?'

'Women of my station are easily tossed on the tide,' she retorts.

Murray understands. 'You think I want to dishonour you?' He lets out a laugh like a gun firing, though he has arrived here alone at night. He can see how it looks but it's not as if he can make a social call to her in the normal way. Still, it stings. 'You think I'd take advantage,' he rages, 'because you have pretty hair and pretty eyes? That I would propose marriage to Charlotte because she is a lady?'

She cuts him off. 'Well, did you not?'

He stumbles over the words. 'Not because of that. I offered her my hand as a friend. It was a matter of honour. She's in an invidious situation.'

'And then you came here, to see if you might have your way with me. Because I do not come from a fine house on Blythswood Square.' Her eyes bore into his skin.

Murray is horrified. He respects minds. He always has. He likes Ellory's dignity, her innovation and her talent. He has met a hundred daughters of Glasgow's millionaires and knows he would choose this woman over any of them. Other fellows pursue girls for their looks and their fortune. He could never. He goes quite pink with shock. 'You're determined to think the worst of me.'

'It's not fitting for you to be here. At night,' she says.

He rises and admits, 'You're right.'

Her eyes widen. She is shocked that he has said he is in the wrong. 'I'm sorry,' he apologises.

Suddenly she feels panicked at the idea of him leaving. 'It's only that I've seen the worst happen,' she lets out. 'A woman abandoned. Someone I knew.'

He takes this in. 'I'm sorry,' he says again and then, 'it's plain that I'm drawn to you. I've known since I was young I'd settle with a Glasgow lass.'

'Settle?'

'It was disrespectful of me to come at night. I see that now. But my daytime is taken and so is yours. This is not some drawing room where afternoon calls can be made.'

'If I were a lady—' she starts.

'I don't give a damn about that,' he cuts in. 'Can't you see?'

'If I were a lady,' she repeats, determined to finish, 'you would not look at me so . . . You would not . . .' She cannot quite get there.

Murray makes an awkward little bow. 'Please believe that my intentions are honourable. I find you . . . *attractive*, Miss Mann. I've admired you since the moment we met.' It is hopeless. The more he says, the worse it feels. 'I'm sorry,' he repeats. He must raise the question of marrying Ellory with his father before he can go any further. He thought to sound her out is all. To see if she feels what he does. And, he thinks, perhaps now he considers it, she does feel it too. 'How do I look at you, Miss Mann?'

'I beg your pardon.'

'You intimated that I look at you in a certain way.'

Ellory blushes. 'Like a man swimming across a river,' she says haltingly.

'And how do you look at me? I wondered this afternoon how you might pose me for one of your calotypes.'

She stares at him for what feels like a long time and he thinks he will melt. Then she draws herself up. 'I've always liked you, Mr Urquhart.' They both hover, confused. 'So you do not hope to marry Miss Nicholl?' she gets out.

'No,' he says. Murray's eyes fall to Ellory's gloved hand. He touches the fingers gently. Her heart feels it will stop beating. 'I've made you angry. I'll go,' he offers, and before she can say anything he disappears out of the door and she is left there, in the studio, listening to his steps receding down the stairs, simultaneously bemused that she does not want him to leave, yet she is also afraid of what might have happened had he not gone.

Chapter Twenty-Three

On Saturday, 11 April, just after noon, Ellory delivers Miss Sutherland's prints to the theatre. She follows a huge arrangement of red roses in a gaudy vase being trundled up the corridor on a low trolley towards Grace's dressing room. The door is guarded by the coachman, Owen, for the fellow at the main entrance is hardly as impenetrable as required for a honeypot of Miss Sutherland's calibre. He waves Ellory through and it is like walking into a dream. The kind of place a princess might dress, all gilded mirrors, ostrich feathers and so full of flowers already that it smells of lilac, lilies and roses. Grace lounges on a velvet chaise with a box of *pâte de fruits* on a marble-topped table beside her. She pops a lemon jelly festooned with candied violet into her mouth. 'Ah, Miss Mann,' she says as if she has been looking for Ellory all morning, like a lost button. 'There you are.'

Unhurried, she has her grey-haired maid hold two lamps aloft so she can inspect the prints in the proper light. 'Higher, Betty,' she instructs and Ellory worries that the old girl will tumble. 'You've never made anything like this before?' she checks. Mr Hill once photographed a gentleman nude. It was to be like a Greek statue. Ellory and Jessie were sent out for the afternoon and Mr Adamson made the print himself. Ellory cannot remember if Mr Hill sold the piece in the end. Nobody seemed ashamed of it anyway.

'No, never,' she says. Grace smiles, satisfied.

She slips the images back into the leather portfolio Ellory arrived with. 'Good,' she says and unlocks a drawer in her dressing table, removing a pouch of coins. Carefully she counts the agreed fee. 'I'm trusting your discretion, Miss Mann.' She motions Ellory forward and leans in to whisper, 'You will not do this for any other actress. Do you understand? Especially any actress who might work in the other theatre.' She holds her gaze steady.

Betty looks shocked. Miss Sutherland will not allow anybody to mention the old Grahamstown theatre where classical opera and Shakespeare plays are performed rather than the more ramshackle variety shows and earthy comedies preferred in this auditorium. She is surprised her mistress has done so. Ellory makes the promise and takes the cash. 'And you will sell it to an admirer?' she asks.

'I think so,' Grace says, as if she might have laid out all that money purely for her own pleasure. 'I have a chap or two in mind to bid upon it.' She laughs at Ellory's expression. 'You think that kind of thing is beneath you?' she snorts. 'Gentlemen and their desires? Don't you know it's the stuff of the world? I'm a fine lady on account of doing what's beneath me. Sometimes, you know, if you're lucky in your gentlemen, it can be the most tremendous fun. I'm surprised you haven't partaken, Miss Mann. It's not as if you've a position to think of.'

Ellory shakes her head. 'But might you not fall . . .?' She cannot put a name to it. The worst thing that can happen.

'Might I not fall what?' Grace's eyes widen. 'Oh, Miss Mann. Do not tell me you're an accomplished artist and a woman of science and do not know the little medicine that might prevent the thing all women fear.' She mimes a pregnant stomach emanating from her tiny, corseted waist.

'Medicine?'

'They are clatty bastards every one,' Grace continues. 'But pennyroyal tea with aloe and rue syrup will see you right. Not too strong,' she adds, eyeing Betty. 'I had that once, didn't I, Betty? And was on my back a full week and earning not a penny from it.'

Betty looks mournful, the mixture being too strong clearly her fault.

'I knew that if it happened one might get help, though it's dangerous,' Ellory says slowly.

'You don't want to leave it till after, for heaven's sake. That involves more dreadful men and a good deal of blood.' Grace stops. She might be a queen of sorts but she can still feel the ground beneath her feet. Ellory looks genuinely upset. 'Are you all right, Miss Mann?'

Ellory opens her mouth. The shame is almost overwhelming. Worse than any of the pictures. 'It's only I knew somebody once . . . a woman who died.'

'The work of one of those butchers?'

'After having a child. She wasn't married and everyone blamed her. The man deserted her, you see, and she would not tell her family his name. She died a fortnight after the birth.'

Grace Sutherland touches the photographer lightly on the shoulder. 'I'm sorry,' she says. 'Too many good women do not survive. What became of the child?'

Ellory finds she cannot look the actress in the eye. 'He was sent away. The family insisted on that. He'd be six years old now.'

Grace stares, her eyes blank as a camera obscura. 'You recall the age of your friend's child?'

Ellory's heart races. She does not know what to say. Grace does not push her. 'I'm sorry for your trouble, Miss Mann,' she says. 'Thank you for your help. I'm going to make a pretty penny for my work in front of your lens.'

'Yes.' Ellory pockets the coins.

'We shall have an auction,' Grace adds smugly.

Outside Ellory walks back to the studio along the Clyde, the shame curling in her belly so sharply she thinks she might be sick. She has always tried to be good. Not a lady exactly, but still. She has chosen her clothes carefully, minded her manners and yet she can see acceptance is more complicated than a simple set of rules. Some secrets, she thinks, do not get lighter with time. She had lost her temper with Murray Urquhart the night before. Now she wonders if she should have. Miss Sutherland, no doubt, would have handled it differently.

Inside, Jeremiah sits at the table with Jane. 'Did she like the prints?' he asks.

Ellory pulls herself back to business. 'She paid the invoice directly. She's going to auction them,' she says.

'Oh she'll do that all right. Poor bastards. She's quite admirable, you know. We could all learn from Miss Sutherland.'

'What do I owe you?' Ellory asks.

Jeremiah shrugs. 'She paid me already.'

'Good,' Ellory says and sinks into a chair, suddenly remembering Charlotte. She berates herself for being selfish. For getting side-tracked like some kind of child. 'There's another thing I meant to put your way, Jeremiah,' she says. 'My friend Miss Nicholl has some works of art she wishes to sell.'

Chapter Twenty-Four

On Monday morning, Jeremiah breezes past the man on the ebony desk and out of McLaren's door. Walking up the hill, he ponders how this could possibly have happened. He has always been the one in charge. It is his demands that are generally met. But here he is, less than a week after meeting Lennox, and he already does not want to leave the blighter, even for a couple of hours in which he has the prospect of earning a generous fee. It is perplexing.

He loiters on the corner of Blythswood Square, the Nicholl mansion in his sights. Two fat wood pigeons coo beyond the grass. At home he would have snared them but here he can buy whatever he wants for dinner. Life is better than ever before. Jeremiah knows he'd best not show his feelings, but in truth, it is hopeless. Lennox is so composed in his company that he wonders if the old man cares for him at all. Then his belly turns, for he knows he has had this effect on several gentlemen and felt not a jot for any of them. Lennox will leave when his business is done, and then what?

Crossing the square, he decides to ring the bell on the upper house rather than present himself at the kitchen. He is not a servant in this matter, he is a broker. He's the one who will save this young lady from getting her hands dirty. 'She wants rid of the collection,' Ellory explained. 'But nobody must know.' Jeremiah's importance to Miss Nicholl's good name does not prevent the housekeeper from eyeing him warily and peering along the pavement when she answers the bell, as if she expects the disapprobation of the neighbours. 'Mr Catto for Miss Nicholl,' he says, and she takes his hat and coat though the woman does not have the opportunity to announce him before Charlotte Nicholl appears.

'Ah, Mr Catto,' she says as if she expected him this very moment. 'About the dressmaking,' she adds. 'Mrs Cullen, I will speak to Mr Catto in the study.'

This is an odd atmosphere, he thinks. The house does not feel as if it is anybody's home. He does not know Miss Nicholl, but he understands her breezy attempt to get rid of the housekeeper. 'Are you well, miss?' he asks when Charlotte closes the study door. She pauses, reminded of Mrs Grieg talking about a woman she suspected of *lightness*, which is to say, she was a thief. She knows immediately that Jeremiah is light the same way but with words. After Ellory's note said she'd send him, Charlotte did not sleep for worrying about how to dispose of the paintings. 'Mrs Cullen is to believe we are contracting the business of a new coat,' she says.

Jeremiah finds himself, for once, unsure what he ought to reply. He tries not to laugh. Miss Nicholl is as proper as a governess on her first day in the schoolroom. 'Might I say how excellent I thought Miss Mann's calotype of you,' he gets out.

'Thank you.'

The two of them hover awkwardly until Jeremiah breaks the silence. 'Miss Mann told me of the items you wish to dispose of,' he says, keeping his voice low. 'Could you give me some idea of them? The detail, I mean?'

Charlotte's eyes flick towards the drinks tray and Jeremiah wonders optimistically if she might offer him a dram. 'They're shocking,' she whispers back. 'I must get rid of it all without anybody knowing. Sell them. Or destroy them.'

'I see,' Jeremiah says. He does not want to destroy anything for there will not be much money in that. 'Ellory told me the nature of the paintings,' he confides, 'but I wondered exactly how many and the sizes. It's terrible that the size is important, but it's relevant to the price. If I might see them?'

Charlotte lays her hand on the mantel. 'Can I trust you, Mr Catto?' she asks, her eyes on the door. 'Truly?'

He nods.

'They're here,' she admits in a whisper. 'In this room.'

Jeremiah's forehead wrinkles. He looks round. This woman is highly dramatic. He is surrounded by actors, singers and dancers all the time and Miss Nicholl at this moment could top any of them for affectation. 'Please, madam, if you want my help, I must set eyes on what you wish me to sell. It cannot be a riddle.'

Charlotte knows he is not being unreasonable, but she feels uncomfortable about going into the cupboard with a man. 'All right,' she says. 'I'll let you in and return later to release you. How long will you need? Half an hour?'

Jeremiah gives a little shrug. 'Half an hour,' he repeats, thinking Ellory ought to have warned him that the lady is much stranger than she appeared in the calotype.

Charlotte locks the study door. She lights a candle and holds it up like a sentinel as she flicks the lever on the side table to remove the key and swiftly opens the bookcase. Jeremiah grins. It is like a fairy tale from *One Thousand and One Nights* and Charlotte an unexpected Scheherazade. Open sesame.

'Hurry,' she says. 'Take the candle.'

Walking into the cupboard, the hairs on the back of his neck rise. The warm light of the flame casts only a small way into the long darkness. He turns to ask a question but the door closes, cocooning him in a pool of yellow like a yolk encased in a shell. It takes a few seconds to absorb it: the stack of paintings against the wall, the curve of the woman's hip and her ghostly white skin. He stares, appreciating the painter's technique. Then he gets to work, flicking the frame forward to peruse the next image and the next. He counts a dozen large paintings in fancy frames, each as accomplished as the last. There is no doubt this is the work of master painters, he thinks, as he notes the details of the hands, the trees and the fruits, because for him the women are of no more interest than anything else depicted. The collection is of the best quality, that is the nub. He will be able to sell these pieces easily, he thinks with a sting of excitement. They are worth a great deal of money.

He works through a pile of smaller oils further in. Then the French prints and the books. He cannot help laughing. A low chortle at first. If a calotype of Jane showing her ankle is worth half a sovereign, these are worth several sovereigns each. It is like treasure in a tomb, piled high in the dark. He stops to read a few poems and slips a gold coin embossed with a pair of lips into his pocket. Further in still, he is less distracted by the quality and finds himself marvelling at the dedication required to curate such a collection. By the time he opens the box of netsuke, he has calculated that he will be able to retire on the proceeds of the sale. He will take 25 per cent, he thinks, for his discretion, for that is what the lady is most concerned with. That much is plain.

At the end of the cupboard he comes to the statues. With the concentration of a hungry man opening a box of chocolate creams, he runs his fingers over each naked woman and naked man. Then he steps back to consider the collection as a whole. His time inside the cupboard has been so diverting that he has no idea how much of his allotted half hour is left. His pewter pocket watch is useless for he cannot recall the time he came in. He pushes the door, but it does not move. Then he stands, listening carefully, but the cupboard is built of stone and so well lined that no sound can penetrate it. He puts his shoulder to the wood, but the bookcase does not shift.

Jeremiah's hands become clammy. The first picture of the naked woman crowds him and he gasps for breath as he runs his hand around the door frame, looking for a catch, but finding only a smooth architrave. Sinking backwards he thinks he must remain calm. Charlotte will return. Perhaps it has only been ten minutes. Perhaps more. But she will come for him. He crouches against the far wall and closes his eyes, leaning his forehead on the cool Carrara-marble thigh of a Venus figure. He tries not to dwell on the fact he is trapped and instead considers how he would like Charlotte to find him when she opens the door. Reading nonchalantly, he decides, and reaches for a book but just then the candle starts to smoke and the light gutters. 'Miss Nicholl,' he calls tentatively as the candle dies. 'Shit!' he says into the darkness and lays his palms on the floor, absorbing its coolness.

He sits a long time or no time at all. In the silence there is no way to tell, but his thighs feel stiff and he wishes he had a cushion. He recites poetry in Gaelic quietly. An ancient widow's lament last given voice by the fireside on the croft. Here in the dark, it is difficult to believe that Glasgow lies beyond the bookcase rather than the black houses of his childhood. The enveloping darkness of a moonless night 400 miles north. The power of the sea. He thinks of Lennox. A vision of the older man drinking whisky by elegant firelight, set against the hotel room's red damask curtains. Now Lennox is Jeremiah's lighthouse, his church spire, he thinks. It is suddenly sprung, but it is the truth. They must be together.

When a loud click cuts the silence, Jeremiah squints into the light. Charlotte peers inside. 'Oh, Mr Catto, I'm sorry,' she says. 'Did the candle go out?'

Jeremiah gets to his feet and glances backwards at the contents of the cupboard. 'What time is it?' he manages.

'One of the clock. Lunchtime. Are you hungry?'

He shakes his head. Emerging feels like a rebirth and he is disturbed that in the darkness his mind returned to the discomforts of Banff first of all.

'Will you take the commission?' Charlotte asks. 'Will you act for me in the matter?'

Jeremiah feels breathless. It is a huge amount of money. He isn't sure he can pull it off. 'Twenty-five per cent,' he says.

Charlotte does not even blink. 'You must be discreet,' she says. 'I can't see how we will remove the items without anybody knowing.'

Jeremiah feels suddenly that he could run for miles. Or dance, perhaps. Some kind of celebration. Still, the job will be challenging. The truth is he has no idea how he will sell the collection. It is beyond the scope of his visits to the cockpit and the bare knuckle. He thinks of a gentleman's club he heard of once, in Edinburgh. The Royal something or other. He does not know where it is. He wonders if he should have asked for a third of the money, but the nub is that he has to sell the thing, for a quarter of nothing is nothing, and so is a third. He is sobered by a glimpse of his own reflection in the window. Glad of his well-made sky-blue waistcoat and smartly cut woollen jacket, he regains his customary flair. He will do it somehow. 'Have no worry, Miss Nicholl,' he says. 'You've been perfectly clear.'

When he glances back into the cupboard, something at the far end catches his attention.

'I made a list,' Charlotte says. 'The number of items and so forth.'

'Do you have another candle?'

She fetches one from the box as if she is his assistant. Jeremiah lights it off the fire. He dives back inside and moves some of the statues as if he is pushing through a crowd. 'What's this?' he asks. It is a rhetorical question, Charlotte thinks, as she peers towards the end of the cupboard. It is obvious that it is a small door. She feels her stomach shift. How did she not notice it? 'Give me the key,' he says and smiles as he turns the new lock. On the other side there is another door, this time inside the Howarths' house, also locked. Miss Nicholl's key does not work on this one. The men made a pact, Charlotte realises. A way out for both of them.

'That might be useful,' Jeremiah says. 'Who has the other key, do you think?'

'Let me consider what might be done,' Charlotte muses.

Silent, they close the cupboard and unlock the study door. Mrs Cullen is summoned with Jeremiah's hat and coat. 'Good day, miss.' He gives a little bow and adds for the housekeeper's benefit. 'I'll return for a fitting soon.'

Chapter Twenty-Five

As the Urquharts leave their office that evening, the hallway is illuminated by the light of the moon through the long back window. Willie Duff is long retired to one of the public houses on Sauchiehall Street. Murray locks the door and his father checks it. Then they progress up the hill in silence, Murray's strange silhouette in the shadows between the gas lamps, and old Mr Urquhart leaning on his silver-topped ebony cane. 'We'll discuss our business at home,' he says. Murray has his own business to raise. He cannot woo Ellory in secret as he'd hoped, so he must declare his feelings to his father. He knows he will have a fight on his hands.

They are almost at their own front door when a dark carriage grinds to a creaky halt and Dr Grieg leans out. 'Urquhart!' he calls. 'You need to control your boy! This business with the Black lad is a disgrace.'

Mr Urquhart pauses before turning his head. 'Dr Grieg,' he says calmly, 'Good evening.'

Mrs Grieg appears framed by the carriage's tiny window, pushing her husband out of the way, her white hair piled in a mass of ringlets, a strange mixture of mutton and lamb. 'Murray Urquhart,' she spits, 'I hope Charlotte provides you a decent pocketbook for your infamy. Your soul must be as deformed as your body!'

Murray swallows but the words hovering on his lips do not disappear. 'If you tolerate the Free Kirk's position, it follows you value money over morality, Mrs Grieg,' he says. 'And you will be damned.'

'See how he talked to me!' Mrs Grieg appeals to her husband and then to the old solicitor. 'Are you a turncoat too, Mr Urquhart? Does disloyalty run in the family?'

Mr Urquhart will not have that. 'That's a libel, Mrs Grieg. Are you sure you wish to utter it?'

The doctor huckles his wife backwards. 'You should consider your position, Albany,' he says.

Mr Urquhart raises an eyebrow. Nobody has used his first name in years. Dr Grieg bangs on the roof and the coach disappears down the hill like a leaf borne in a squall. The night air feels suddenly heavy. Inside, the Urquharts remove their coats. Old Mr Urquhart points up the stairs with his cane.

'It's a matter of principle, Father,' Murray starts as soon as the drawing-room door is closed. He had hoped to start with his intentions towards Ellory but events have overtaken that.

Mr Urquhart raises a hand. 'We will not fash about the Griegs,' he says flatly. 'They had substantial slave holdings.' The words drip off his lips like the poison Murray knows them to be. 'I organised the disposal of it all. I shall remind the good doctor of that when I next see him.' He sits and motions Murray into the chair opposite. 'You can see, however, that we must turn our attention to this. This afternoon I had the clerk compile everything he could find about your Mr Douglass.' Murray has the good sense to stay quiet. 'The fellow has the right of the matter, of course,' Albany Urquhart pronounces. And then adds, 'Though they'll not return the money.'

'It's a matter of principle,' Murray objects.

'We must be on the right side of that,' his father pronounces.

'So you'll quit the Kirk?'

'Och no,' the old man says categorically. 'You've quit the Kirk. I'll make the case without leaving. That way, however it falls out, we have one of us on the right side,' he says, pouring himself a whisky.

Murray sighs. He knows his father is wrong but also that his father is right. Still, he will agree to this plan for it allows him to take what he sees as the right side. Mr Urquhart grinds on like an ancient harbinger. 'Firms will close over this. Business will be withdrawn. A cross is one of the easiest targets of all. That's what my father used to say. However, if we play our hand right we'll keep our clients and gain new ones. I've often thought the MacDonalds of Govan would make us some excellent business. They spend several hundred a year on legal work. I'll sow some seeds. The younger MacDonalds are principled sorts.' He downs his whisky. 'I'm hungry,' he announces. 'Perhaps we can discuss the business of James Nicholl's collection over dinner. He has secreted it like a magician.'

'There's something else, Father,' Murray says.

Albany Urquhart looks curious, or at least, as curious as he ever does.

'I know for a while you've hoped I'll take a wife. I've made my decision.'

The corners of Albany's mouth twitch. It is the closest he might come to betraying his surprise. 'Good, my boy,' he says almost enthusiastically. 'But I take it from your demeanour, it's not Charlotte Nicholl?'

Murray shakes his head. 'You'll object, I know.'

'Well, who is it?'

'The lady photographer. Ellory Mann.'

'McPhee's charity case?' Albany cannot believe it.

'She's talented and hard working,' Murray presses, trying to explain without resorting to declaring his feelings which he knows hold no sway with his father.

Albany makes a sound like a locomotive creaking before it moves. Then another like gravel shifting in the tide. He is laughing, Murray realises. 'Where do you think such a match will take you?' he gets out.

Murray regards his father, wide-eyed. 'I don't even know if she'll have me,' he says.

The old man continues to chortle. 'It'd be grand if you were both half mad, you for wanting such a match and she for not being willing. Don't be ridiculous.'

Murray narrows his eyes. 'Have you never wanted anything, Father? Anything other than what society expected you to want? Something personal?'

Albany looks as if the boy is talking in tongues. All he has ever desired is peace to do his work. 'Could you not just take your pleasure of her, boy? If that's what you're after.'

'That's not what I want!' Murray bursts out, thinking his father is making the same assumption Ellory did the night before. 'She's beautiful, that much is true, but it's her talent, her forthright way, that I admire. She's a pioneer – exactly what this city needs.'

Albany cannot help himself. 'They are all as Eve in Eden, boy. What Glasgow needs is more investment in the dredging of the Clyde. A woman with money in her purse . . .'

'Is that why you married my mother?' Murray snaps.

'Of course,' Albany replies smoothly. 'She came from a good family, though I must say I have placed you to do better. I was only starting my career.'

'Mother was miserable,' Murray shouts. 'Do you not know that?'

Albany eyes the whisky decanter for several seconds before he replies. 'There was no reason for her to be so,' he says. 'Your mother made herself miserable.'

Murray feels like punching something. 'It was her situation. She was trapped. You and she had nothing in common.'

'We had you,' Albany objects.

'It takes more than that to make a family,' Murray lashes out, finding his father's ability to remain level most irritating.

'You need to calm down,' old Mr Urquhart pronounces.

'I don't wish to cross you, Father, but this is my will. You must trust my judgement. I'll marry her if she'll have me.'

Albany arches his fingers in front of his face exactly as he does when considering the finer points of a leasehold. 'We know nothing about her,' he declares.

'I know enough,' Murray rejoins. 'I do everything asked of me, Father. But I want this.'

'Have I ever led you astray?'

Murray shakes his head. He wants to say it is too early to tell. That he suspects that it would be better if he were more frank with Charlotte about her father's affairs, but that is a fight for another day.

'Tell me what you know about this woman.' Albany waits for his son to elucidate, which, after a pause in which Murray tells himself this is progress, he does.

'Miss Mann assisted David Octavius Hill in Edinburgh,' he says. 'McPhee was sufficiently impressed to back her. She has set up her business from scratch and made startling innovations in only a month. All of which is perfectly admirable.'

'And her family?'

Murray shrugs. 'She was orphaned young.'

Albany raises an eyebrow as if to proclaim this somehow suspicious. 'Is that it? We look into a minor investment more carefully than you have looked into this lady's past,' he points out. 'How would it be if I charged you with doing so? Go to Edinburgh. Speak to Hill. Find out what you can. Then we'll see.'

'You want me to sneak behind Ellory's back?' Murray demands, outraged.

'Yes,' says Albany frankly. 'I certainly do. As soon as you can. My guess is you'll find her wanting.'

Murray gets up. He looks out of the window onto Bath Street. He knows that if he does not go to Edinburgh, the old man will like as not send a clerk on the same business. Besides, he cannot conceive of what he could find that would put him off the idea of marrying Ellory. He knows already that she does not come from money.

'All right,' he says. 'I'll go the day after tomorrow.'

Chapter Twenty-Six

That same evening Jane loiters behind the house on Ingram Street waiting for Cormac, to snatch a few minutes. Tonight, it does not take long for him to do so and he can hardly believe that his sister has been of service to the famous Grace Sutherland. 'Lummy,' he says, for that is how the first footman, who is from Essex, declaims his surprise.

Jane eyes her brother dubiously. 'Och, folk are just folk,' she retorts.

This evening Cormac cannot tarry long and after he heads back inside, Jane makes for the Gallowgate, for the stew at the Saracen's Head is worth the walk and she has a shilling in her pocket, given by Miss Mann, who is generous when she is in funds. Along Ingram Street she lingers, listening to quartets through long-windowed drawing rooms and the piano being played while carriages with restless horses wait for their masters and mistresses. Further along, the sound changes to the rammy of fiddles playing in basements that reek of beer and tallow as the door opens on drunken singing that is more like shouting 'Bridekirk's Hunting'. The last day or two there has been more warmth on the air even at night.

At the Saracen's Head Jane pays for the stew and a tin filled with milk. By the time she comes out, the sky has darkened and she walks back along the Clyde to pick up a jar of cockles at one of the boat sheds. As she turns up Dixon Street, she lifts her skirt for there is water pooled behind the church, a pothole that fills in the rain. Across from the door to the studio a gentleman in patent galoshes is waiting. The fellow who winked. He looks up. 'There you are,' he says. 'I'd recognise that ankle anywhere.'

Uneasy, Jane does not meet his eye. 'Excuse me, sir,' she says. 'I must get inside.' In the darkness his galoshes catch a sliver of light from the gas lamp on Argyle Street as he moves to block her path. He smells stale of drink. 'That's no way to greet an ardent admirer,' he objects and removes a small bunch of spring flowers from behind his back. 'I brought you these.' He thrusts them towards her. Her mind races. There is nobody around. She tries to sidestep but he blocks her again. 'I'm the fellow who bought your picture,' he insists. 'I want to make your acquaintance is all.'

'I'm sorry, sir, but I'm expected,' she lies. The man mumbles something about his money being as good as anyone's. 'I don't want to quarrel. The reverse, in fact,' he says and touches her arm.

'I've no interest, sir,' she says firmly.

'Don't be silly,' he retorts and puts his arm round her, but Jane slaps him hard and he reels in shock as she turns on her heel and disappears inside.

The Ramsays are a large family and Jane was brought up with brothers, not only Cormac but three more. The boys spent their childhood in a tumble, play-fighting about the floor, wrestling in the close and rolling down the grassy slope beyond the main road. Jane held her ground when she was growing up and, as a result, has no qualms about lashing out against a fellow if he steps over the mark. When the gentleman tries to pull her off the bottom step, her reaction is immediate. The moment he touches her she kicks hard, holding the stew aloft. He folds over and she trots up the first run of stairs. 'You're a feisty piece,' he mutters. His blood is up now and he is determined as he overtakes her. 'I only want to talk,' he insists, pushing her against the wally wall.

Jane catches a waft of stale whisky as she stamps hard on his foot.

'Excuse me,' she repeats. The jar of cockles cracks in her pocket and the juice seeps down her skirt, filling the hallway with its salty tang. She'd feel nauseous if she wasn't so panicked.

'Stop,' the gentleman says, clamping his fingers round her wrist so hard she knows she will bruise. She can feel the flesh becoming tender as if she is a strawberry melting in a jelly pan.

'Get off me!' she shouts, trying to shake free.

'You don't mean that. Saucy hure. How would you like ten pounds a year, eh?'

He tries to kiss her and Jane bites him hard, realising by the taste on her tongue that she has drawn blood. 'Get off me!' she repeats, kicking again.

But he's in her way, flabbergasted, standing on the stair, a trickle of blood down his chin, leaning against the banister. 'Help!' Jane shouts upwards, but the caretaker is in his crib with a quarter bottle by this time and Miss Mann won't hear her in the studio, three floors up. She's in the office, Jane thinks, on the other side of the building. The safest way out is the street, she calculates, so she shoves past him and bolts downstairs. On the threshold, she drops the tin of milk onto the flagstones. The flowers he brought lie trampled as she takes off, holding the pot of stew to her chest. A couple of cockles slip from her pocket and roll down her skirt.

The gentleman chases her. 'Where are you going?' he shouts. But Jane has heard a hundred stories from other girls, and has no intention of having a tale to tell of her own. Glancing back, she sees he has folded over again. She must have kicked him very hard. She keeps going, round one corner and another until without aiming for anything other than getting away, she is at the stage door.

She launches into the theatre. 'Lass?' the doorman says. 'Are you all right?'

'Jeremiah!' she calls as if it is a kind of password. She bounces off the buff wall without slowing down as she turns the corner. Two dancers in costume appear at the door to Jeremiah's wardrobe. 'Are you all right, wean?' one says.

She coughs. Then she lets out his name again. 'Jeremiah.'

'Yes, mo ghràdh,' Jeremiah emerges from within. 'What have you got there?'

Jane promptly hands him the stew. She has no idea why she held onto it. 'A gentleman was waiting outside the studio. He was most insistent,' she stammers. 'The one who bought the picture.'

Jeremiah's expression hardens. He knows what it is to be pursued. 'Are you all right?'

'I bit his lip,' she says, wiping her arm across her mouth. 'I drew blood.'

'Good,' Jeremiah says and puts his arm around her to draw her inside. One of the dancers follows as he fetches a blue glass pot from the shelf. 'It's arnica. It'll save you from bruising. Do you need a doctor?'

Jane shakes her head. She sits on the wooden bench and rubs the cream into her wrist.

Jeremiah pours a whisky and passes it over. 'For the shock. That bastard.' He feels guilty. He has been taken up with everybody else's business but Jane's. 'I'm sorry,' he says. 'I have the man's card. I meant to warn him off.'

'What is the gentleman's name?' Jane asks.

Jeremiah searches in his jacket pocket. 'George Gibson. 10 Nelson Street,' he reads. 'You can leave it to me now.'

'You?' the dancer lets out in disbelief.

Jeremiah squares up. 'Aye. Me.'

The woman laughs. 'You're a powder puff, Jemmy. Men like that require muscle. I'll fetch Owen from Miss Sutherland's door. She's on stage now.' And the woman disappears. When she returns she has clearly briefed the footman.

'I'm sorry for your trouble, miss,' Owen says. 'If Miss Sutherland releases me, I'll gladly talk to the gent.'

'I'll come with you,' Jeremiah insists.

'It's better I go on my own,' Owen pronounces. Jeremiah passes him the card. 'What do you want, miss?' he asks Jane.

She stares at the coachman. 'Want?'

'Miss Sutherland usually gets a payment,' he says.

'I never want see him again. He was waiting for me, where I live.'

Owen shifts from foot to foot. 'I can see to that all right. But my experience is that gentlemen expect to pay.'

'They all have to pay,' the dancer chimes. 'This one time—' She stops abruptly at Owen's stony gaze.

'But you'll get rid of him?' Jane checks.

'Yes, miss. I've done it before.'

Jeremiah kneels in front of her. She's brave, he thinks. 'I'll see you back to the studio,' he says. 'Though he'll rue the day. You'll have given the cad a bruise. A scar too, I imagine.'

Jane manages a smile. 'I did,' she gets out with some satisfaction.

'Are you all right then? You're sure?'

She nods. 'I don't think I'll go abroad at night so much,' she adds. 'And I don't think I shall like to pose for Miss Mann again. I've been thinking my real place is behind the lens, not in front of it.'

Chapter Twenty-Seven

Bright and early, on Blythswood Square the next morning, Charlotte hovers at the window like a gossip with nothing better to do. The Howarths are regular in their routine. Christopher Howarth leaves for the rivet manufactory in Govan sharp on ten of the clock, Mondays, Tuesdays and Thursdays, which means he will go today – Tuesday. As soon as the Howarths' carriage is brought round, she jumps to her feet and picks up a blue silk Hanway by the door, crossing the pavement, dangling the garden key in her free hand. Mr Howarth tips his hat, which is a pleasing shade of dark-green felt. 'Miss Nicholl,' he says. 'Good morning.'

Charlotte approaches him, using the open Hanway to block the coachman from seeing her and staring at Mr Howarth with a queer expression so he knows what she is about to say is a lie. 'Please,' she says, 'I can't get my key to turn.'

Mr Howarth hesitates. He understands. 'Let me help,' he says. They cross the street and he opens the gate. 'Is something wrong, Miss Nicholl?'

Charlotte's eyes flick further into the garden and Mr Howarth offers his arm. They promenade towards the blossom tree which is shedding its petals in a perfect circle on the grass beneath its trunk. When Charlotte was a child, she believed the pink circle belonged to the fairies. She tries to speak but finds it difficult, her earlier purposefulness failing her now she has to actually say the words.

'I understand you have an ideological problem, Miss Nicholl,' he starts the conversation.

'Ideological?'

'An issue with the Free Kirk?'

Charlotte curses silently. The Griegs must have told everybody on the square. 'That's not why I wanted to speak to you, Mr Howarth,' she says. 'My problem is more . . . *architectural*.'

'Is something wrong with the roof?'

Charlotte hesitates. Why is it so difficult to raise this? she berates herself, when the man must know the cupboard is there. 'I hope you'll be able to help me with a void in the wall of my father's study,' she manages.

She feels Howarth's arm tense through the sleeve of his lined woollen coat. 'What do you mean?' he asks crisply.

'There's a door at the far end of the void, sir.'

Howarth's lips purse. 'I believe there are two doors, Miss Nicholl,' he says, pointing out the impenetrability of his wife's day room.

Charlotte continues. 'My father kept certain items in the void. I need to remove them and I don't want anybody to see.'

Mr Howarth assesses this statement and decides he must admit what he knows. 'Your father's paintings, you mean?'

Charlotte feels her cheeks burn. Her hand drops to her side and she steps backwards. 'You know?'

He nods curtly.

'Do you have a collection the same?'

'Good heavens, no.' Mr Howarth looks shocked.

'You planned the rooms together though? When the houses were built?'

Howarth's expression mutates. Now he looks remorseful. 'The builder had worked in the New Town in Edinburgh. Your father said he had learned from his mistakes and would make our terrace perfect. How did you find the room?'

Charlotte feels a sting of annoyance. She suspects he is wondering what would happen should he die unexpectedly. Howarth is a younger man than her father, but not that much younger. 'Trial and error,' she says mysteriously.

'Your father offered to let me invest,' he says. 'In his collection, I mean.'

'Did you?'

'I have my own interests,' Howarth says flatly.

She dreads to think. Still, this is interesting. A viewpoint into James Nicholl's world. What happened in the slivers of time they were not together. 'He considered the collection an investment then?'

Howarth smiles pleasantly. 'Gentlemen face the problem of where to put their money. The colonies provide profitable opportunities but . . .'

'My father objected to indentured labour when the enslaved were freed?'

'Exactly. And conditions in many places are no better than in America.'

'He sold his railway shares.'

'Long before the crash. He advised me to sell mine, which thank god, I did.'

'So he viewed this collection as a money-making scheme?'

'He said he liked the investment because it harmed nobody,' Mr Howarth states.

Charlotte feels she has been harmed by the endless procession of mostly female flesh but does not say so. Sensing Mr Howarth might have been privy to more than one of her father's secrets, she sees an opportunity to cast light on another mystery. 'I also understand my father kept a mistress, Mr Howarth,' she ventures, the words leaving her lips almost involuntarily. She has nobody else to ask. 'At Helensburgh House?' she adds.

Howarth's eyes harden. 'He said nothing of that to me.'

Charlotte searches her neighbour's face for any suggestion that this is Mr Howarth's reply because he has a mistress of his own, but she finds none.

'I love my wife, Miss Nicholl,' he adds. 'You can't understand, of course, because you're a young lady. But one becomes attached in a certain way that renders any other attachment unthinkable. It is, I believe, how your father felt about your mother. Not all men are the same, but your father and I had that in common.'

Charlotte goes pale at the thought of marital congress.

Howarth apologises. 'I've gone too far,' he says and offers her his arm once more.

Charlotte waves him off. It crosses her mind that if the occupant of Helensburgh House isn't her father's mistress, then who on earth is it? But she has more important fish to fry. 'I need your help, sir,' she gets out. 'I need to get rid of everything he hid. Do you see?'

'Perhaps a gallery might be able to help?'

'No,' Charlotte almost squeals. 'The nature of my father's collection renders a public sale . . . impossible. I've a fellow who will act as a private broker. But we need to get the items out of the house. I'm sure you're aware that I'm under rather more scrutiny than might be normal. Because Papa died. Because I'm on my own and this business with the Free Kirk, a stand of which I'm sure my father would approve.'

Howarth takes a moment to consider. 'Are you asking if I'd allow you to take it out through my house?'

Charlotte nods.

'Past my private things? The staff? Mrs Howarth?'

'I thought to wrap the items,' Charlotte says. She knows it is a weak response. 'Please, Mr Howarth. For my father's sake. It's impossible you see.' She hates to beg. Slowly he shakes his head and Charlotte panics. 'Can you imagine your daughter being left to dispose of your collection? It's a terrible burden. I'm sure Papa would never have wanted it. It exposes me terribly, and he always sought to protect my position.'

Howarth considers the anguish writ clearly in her expression. The most gentlemanly course of action is unclear, but he considered Nicholl a friend. And Charlotte is on her own. At length he says, 'We're to go to my wife's cousin on Arran, at the end of next week.'

Charlotte's face lights. 'The whole family?'

'I suppose I might give the staff a day off and be delayed overnight about my own business,' he says. 'Two of the maids and the valet will go ahead. The coachman too of course, with the rest of the family.' He casts his eyes towards his carriage, the horses waiting patiently past the gate.

'We could take Father's things through the back and hide a cart in the stables while it was being loaded,' Charlotte ventures. 'Nobody would know.'

Howarth is absolutely still. She cannot tell what he is thinking. 'I might send the butler to see the wine merchant at Leith on my behalf,' he posits. 'That would be useful.'

Charlotte feels a flood of relief. 'Thank you,' she says enthusiastically. It's all she can do to stop herself jumping up and down.

Mr Howarth puts up his hand. 'I shall think on how to dispose of the rest of them. The housekeeper and so forth. There's a great deal that must be organised before anything can go ahead. I shall check which day Mrs Howarth intends to make the expedition. My own things cannot be disturbed, you understand. They're extremely valuable.'

Charlotte puts aside her joy. Her brow furrows. 'Mr Howarth,' she asks, 'what are your things?'

'I'll put dustsheets over them. They must not be knocked.'

'Of course,' she says. He is not going to tell her and she will not push him in the matter. Not now he is her saviour.

'Leave the staff to me.' He consults his pocket watch. 'I must go to Govan. I'll send a note.' Charlotte recalls her father receiving missives from Christopher Howarth late at night. 'Your key will work? The gate?' He checks as if he did not know it was a ruse.

She watches as he strides back up the path, then she rests the Hanway on her shoulder. The rain is intermittent. She can hear the brisk trot of Mr Howarth's carriage setting off. Matters are in hand. It occurs to her that if her father thought the pieces as good an investment as Mr Howarth says, she might even make some

money and that will solve another of the problems he left behind –
the matter of how Charlotte is to pay her way for the rest of her
life. She realises she might do anything now if she can only manage
the removal. She could leave Blythswood Square with her head
held high, away from the many prying eyes of her neighbours. In
fact, if it takes her fancy she can leave the city entirely. She sets off
down the path, considering further that Mr Howarth made a good
point about the problems gentlemen face in their business. She
knows the Quakers have strong views on the matter and thinks she
might put some of the proceeds of the sale into a chocolate manufactory like the Frys in Bristol. Or something wholesome like the
manufacture of soap perhaps. It occurs to her that her father was
right: she cannot see how anybody might be harmed by his collection, though most people of her acquaintance would be offended.

Suddenly she feels immensely optimistic that the whole thing will
be off her hands. As soon as next week, perhaps. She wants to jump
in puddles, exactly as she was discouraged from doing when she was
a child. She is curtailed in this activity, however, when the gate on
the other side opens with a familiar creak. Mrs Grieg enters with two
other old women, congregants of Reverend Patterson whom
Charlotte has known all her life. None of them casts her more than
the briefest glance in their dowdy capes and old-fashioned hats, as
they start down the petal-strewn pathway. When Charlotte raises her
hand, all three swivel, linking arms to stroll pointedly in the opposite direction. Past the railings, towards Douglas Street, she notices
the drawing-room curtains shift on one house, and a man quite
plainly eyeing her from the ground-floor window of another.
Straitened, she turns homewards at a ladylike pace, to the sanctuary
of her own front door.

When she lets herself in, Mrs Cullen is in the study refilling the
decanter from a pottery jug of whisky and muttering under her
breath. Charlotte hears the word 'Amen' as she slips behind the
desk. There is a tray of tea freshly set out and she pours a cup into
the orange-and-blue Spode laid ready. Her hands are shaking.

Mrs Cullen stands back. Behind her, the drinks trolley feels like an accusation.

'Couldn't one of the maids fill the decanter?' Charlotte asks lightly.

'Your father always had Mr Boots see to it. I don't like to tempt the girls.' She does not catch Charlotte's eye.

'Can our girls be tempted?' Charlotte ponders. Beyond the window Mrs Grieg and her companions have made a full circuit of the park. Charlotte turns her back on the window and realises there is something about the way Mrs Cullen sidestepped the wing-backed chair by the fire. Something about how she has not looked at the drama section, where her gaze would naturally fall. It causes her to recall her father's bequest to the housekeeper. She plucks up her courage. 'You don't want the girls finding the hidden key. Is that it?'

Mrs Cullen looks younger than her 50 years, suddenly alert as a wise well-fed rabbit listening for a fox. 'Miss,' she says.

'You know of the hidden door?' Charlotte asks directly.

The old woman relents. 'Mr Boots helped your father when he required it. Boots confided in me.' Mrs Cullen is a tomb for secrets, Charlotte thinks. Boots knew that. So did her father. This is the most words she can remember the housekeeper ever stringing together.

Charlotte smiles. The bequests make a good deal more sense now. Plenty of folk leave their staff money, but her father was generous. She will sound out the old woman, she decides, for accommodating a wealthy man in such a matter is different from accommodating a young lady the same, her father being a stalwart of the Kirk and she now being isolated in society. 'I'm going to confide in you too, Mrs Cullen. You've heard I'm leaving the Free Kirk?'

Mrs Cullen nods.

'I know there's been a deal of gossip. But that does not mean that my morality has changed. It is the Kirk that has fallen in my perception. I didn't know the source of its money before. Do the staff mind, do you think?'

Mrs Cullen shakes her head.

'Do you mind?'

'No, miss. I believe you have the right of it,' she ventures.

'Good. You know of the cupboard, so I'll be plain. I'll not have these items in my house. I'm having everything removed. I need the staff sent away for a day. I'll let you know when it's to be managed. I'd like you to attend me, however, if you don't mind, and you might take two days free afterwards, in lieu.'

Mrs Cullen pauses. The glance she directs at her mistress is shrewd. 'That man was not a tailor,' she says.

'He is a tailor,' Charlotte admits. 'A good one. But you're right. That's not why he was here. Will you help me, as Mr Boots helped my father? I shall reward your loyalty.'

Mrs Cullen bobs a curtsy. 'Yes, miss,' she says. 'I'm always at your disposal.'

'Thank you.' Charlotte casts her gaze through the uneven glass. The world is watching, not that it would meet her gaze were she to defiantly stare it out. 'Would you draw the curtain on your way out?' she says. 'I'm not keen today on the view.'

Chapter Twenty-Eight

Murray quits the silent house that evening after dinner, past ten of the clock, and walks the dark streets down the hill. It is not that he means to end up at St Enoch's Square, though it is Ellory that is in his thoughts. He intends simply to loiter for he wants to know that she is near. He is set for Edinburgh the next day, and while he feels optimistic, he is also uncomfortable that Ellory does not know his intentions. He cannot call now, however. If eight of the clock was too late, past ten is positively scandalous.

As he crosses Argyle Street the studio's long skylight is dark and the clock face on St Enoch's almost at eleven. Two spoons on the totem tree clang as if urging him on. Then he sees her: a flash of white, her face turned upwards behind the glass, staring, as he judges it, at the moon, tipped just into waning now. She is a sign of life, and before he knows it, he has picked up a pebble and hurled it upwards. It clatters against the window and she starts, looking down. Then she fiddles with the casement and leans out, her hair in a long ginger plait over her shoulder.

'What are you doing here?' she hisses.

Murray feels foolish. 'I'm not coming up,' he says. 'It's not fitting.'

Ellory stares. She is afraid that she's glad to see him. But she is. The night air smells of iodine and woodsmoke and somewhere far off a gull cries out. A night-soil cart clops along Argyle Street. They both shift, uncomfortable to be seen by the driver who gees up his horse, clicking his tongue. 'Is everything all right?' Ellory calls down.

Murray laughs. So much is not all right. Not being all right is the way of the world. His father. James Nicholl. They are like statues he admired in childhood ready now to topple.

'I told my father,' he says.

Ellory blinks. 'Told him what?'

'About you,' Murray says simply. 'I cannot say it here.'

She looks over her shoulder. She thinks of Grace Sutherland. 'Jane is asleep,' she says. 'But you can come to the door.'

Murray is up the stairs at a lick, already at the threshold as Ellory opens up and steps backwards. She is wearing a nightgown with a wine-coloured knitted shawl cast about her shoulders and long cotton gloves. It seems so silent Murray can hear his own heartbeat. There is a chill on the air. The stove is lit but the glass ceiling leaches heat into the cold spring sky. Behind Ellory, beyond the window, the clock face of St Enoch's looms, paler than the moon.

'I'm sorry,' he says, for he knows how strange this is. 'It was not my intention to come up.'

'You said.' She smiles. He always looks so handsome, she thinks. Then she steels herself for she must be careful. Seeming is not being, she remembers Reverend Reid saying. But she's glad to see Murray nonetheless, after the other evening. She was afraid she might never see him again. 'What did your father say?' she asks.

Murray does not want to talk about that. It's his business and he'll see to it. Now he's here, he wants to clarify Ellory's feelings. His father does not matter a damn if she has no interest. 'Miss Mann, might I ask something?'

She nods.

'Do you care for me? I know I'm not the kind of man most women seek.'

Ellory's eyes widen. She does not want to care about him, but she does. 'I feel what you feel,' she says and looks down. 'I panicked is all.'

There is a moment of absolute silence. Then Murray asks, 'My deformity does not disgust you? Please, be honest.' He has to say it, the echo of a hundred girlish giggles prompts him.

'Your twisted shoulder has always seemed strong to me,' Ellory does not demur. 'From the moment I saw you, I thought you were a green bough on a hardy tree. The shape of you.'

Murray is surprised to feel himself blush. 'My father hopes I'll choose someone with a dowry who'll keep a house and raise my children, but I don't respect that,' he says. 'I want a virago. I've always known the woman I marry must have an occupation. It's a modern notion but I believe it a happy one.'

Now as well as his own heartbeat he is aware of hers. Further in, the place smells of scrubbed pine and milk warmed in a copper pan. 'Marry,' Ellory repeats. She has never been in love nor anywhere near but now all she wants is to melt into him. She puts her hand on the door frame to steady herself.

'What you've achieved is extraordinary,' Murray says. 'It's a testament to your hard work and your talent.'

Suddenly Ellory is overcome by shame. He has no idea of the images she has been capturing. Jane posed in fancy undergarments. Grace Sutherland lounging in lace. If he did he certainly would not be talking about marriage. 'I couldn't possibly . . .' she starts. 'It would dishonour you. I'm the last thing you deserve.'

Murray cuts in to reassure her. 'I'm sure my father will come round. He must. There's a strong connection between you and me. You said you feel it too. The old man cleaves to the notion of marriage as a kind of business proposition. It works for some folk, of course, but I believe we will be friends and lovers and more, Miss Mann, if you will have me.'

Ellory panics. If he knew, she thinks, he would never. 'You should go,' she snaps. 'This is not fitting.'

But Murray does not go. He puts up his hand as if calming a flighty kitten. 'I'll not force you, but forgive me, I've seen a great deal in my offices. Whatever you are thinking is the worst, I doubt it.

Sometimes I think there's scarce a family in the city that doesn't have a secret. There's nobody awake but you and I,' he says. 'Is there something you'd like to tell me?'

Ellory wishes the floorboards would part. She looks at him straight and swallows. So few people are capable of frankness. If only it were one thing. 'Come in,' she says stoutly. 'I had better show you.' One thing, she thinks, will get rid of him. He need not know the rest. Murray stands by the table as she goes into her office, returning with a small sheaf of papers; a single image of Jane that was too dark and two prints of Grace Sutherland that smudged. Murray considers them. He laughs. 'That's your maid,' he says. 'And the actress . . . what's her name?'

'Grace Sutherland. We sold the pictures of Jane to a gentleman. There was more coin in it than I expected. The picture of Miss Sutherland belongs to her. She'll sell it to one of her admirers, by auction she said.'

Murray laughs again. She wonders if it is because he is shocked. 'I'm sure.' He gives a smile.

Ellory tears the image of Jane in two. 'I'm unworthy of your attention, sir. A grand lady at Mr Hill's studio once said that people find their level. She meant in the New Town. The dross was left in the Old, and that's where I come from. I don't understand why Mr McPhee gave me the money. I didn't deserve it. Look what I'm like. I can't bring myself to truly regret it because I'm interested in form. In shape. But I know I am too low.' She looks genuinely regretful and cannot continue.

Murray lays his hand on the pictures. 'Ellory, I don't believe life is so simple that God rewards the deserving and there's no more to it. I also don't believe that people have the right to judge others the way Reverend Patterson does. Even a beautiful, talented woman such as yourself.'

Ellory shakes her head. She cannot bear it. 'You don't understand,' she cuts in. 'I'm ugly. You haven't seen me.' There are no words. Instead she peels back her gloves. Murray is rendered silent.

He stares at her stained skin in the low light. 'What happened?' he asks. But her face only twists in humiliation. 'Please, tell me,' he begs. 'You can't say you're ugly. Not to me.' When she still gives no reply he determines to show her. He removes his jacket and the patterned waistcoat beneath it. By the time he takes off his collar, Ellory's mouth drops. He opens his shirt revealing the hunch of his back. 'Look,' he says. 'You say you're interested in shape – my shape is that of a monster.'

'No,' she objects louder than she means to. Then she does as he asks and simply looks. He's like a mountain, she thinks. Nothing will shift him. 'People who look ordinary seem so frail,' she gets out and lays her stained hand on his back. Murray feels he will weep. He steps away. Ellory mumbles an apology but he stops her. 'I don't need anyone else to hide from,' he gets out. 'And I don't want you to hide from me.'

Across the studio the mirror reflects their image. The line of his body a sculpture. Her hands ungloved. The light and the shade of their skin taking unexpected turns. 'We're odd creatures,' he says. This image of them together will haunt him like a dream he can never fully understand. Ellory shrugs but does not take her eyes off the glass. They are a better match than she thought.

At length, he pulls his shirt back on. Then he takes her blackened hand and kisses it. Ellory is out of her depth. It is so unexpected.

They remain still, regarding each other. Then Murray taps the torn scraps of paper that were once an image of Jane. 'The gentleman who commissioned this will say nothing?'

Ellory shakes her head. 'He's not the sort.'

'Good.' Murray lays his waistcoat and jacket over his arm, strangely formal. He has never shown himself to a woman like this. There were two in London but always in the dark. Both mistakes. This connection has been worth waiting for.

'If you would like your lawyer's advice, perhaps more trees and sailors and fewer petticoats,' he says. 'If that is all right with you.'

'It is.'

265

'I must go.'

As he turns to leave the studio she panics. She knows she must tell him everything, though it makes what he's suggesting impossible. The pictures are not the worst of it. Nor her skin. 'My family—' she gets out.

Murray puts his fingers to his lips.

'Listen! My sister was a good person but we're cursed. That's what my cousin says.'

'It'll be fine,' he says with a wink. This sounds like an odd family squabble. 'We'll have time to tell each other everything later,' he says.

'People will talk,' Ellory bursts out.

Murray cannot help laughing. 'My guess is people will scarcely be able to draw breath for the talking,' he says. 'What's between us is a compulsion, Ellory. Honestly, I had to tell you. I had to come. Do you not feel its power?'

She nods. She cannot deny it.

'In that case, I don't care what they say,' he says. 'I'll manage matters. My father will come round. I'm a lawyer and I'll make our case. If you'll have me, that is the only thing that matters.'

She bites her lip but she cannot get out the worst thing. Instead she lets herself enjoy the feeling of being Murray Urquhart's intended, even if it is impossible. He kisses her hand once more. 'Goodnight,' she says.

As Murray closes the door, he pauses at the head of the stairs and allows himself a smile so bright it could light up the hallway. There is much to manage but he has it in hand. Below, the caretaker emerges from the dunny and eyes Murray pulling on his jacket.

'Goodnight, Mr Urquhart,' the man says with a knowing wink. 'Visiting the lady photographer, aye?'

'Goodnight,' Murray says firmly and continues out into the chilly night air.

Chapter Twenty-Nine

The same evening

While Glasgow mostly sleeps, Grace Sutherland entertains late. She does not finish at the theatre till ten, after all, and glories in lighting her rooms as bright as the star she wants to be. Tonight she dines on a slab of veal that could feed a family for a week and a bottle of claret to wash it down. Then she turns her attention to the three missives sitting on a salver on her desk, each branded with a different seal. These are the bids for her calotype. She is about to set herself to opening them, when Betty knocks. 'Miss Sutherland, Mr McIntyre is at the door,' she says, casting her eyes upwards, for Miss Sutherland's gentlemen are considered trying by her staff. They make a joke of it.

Donald McIntyre submitted one of the three envelopes with which Grace is toying. His is of thick cream paper branded with his family crest – a hand clasped around a sword in green wax. Grace lifts it between elegant fingers and consults the elaborate cloisonné clock on the mantel. It is almost midnight. 'I can't imagine what he wants,' she says, her gaze shifting to her reflection in the mirror. 'Send him up.'

Donald is almost 50 years of age and married to his second cousin. He is a large bear of a fellow with a tightly trimmed beard and tonight is wearing rather flamboyant evening dress, with a purple satin tie, his cloak lined in a matching shade. He has taken drink, she notes, immediately apparent as he bursts into her chamber. 'Grace!' he hails her. 'I've been thinking.'

Thinking, Grace notes drily, is not Donald McIntyre's strong point, however she does not say this out loud. 'What have you been thinking?' she asks coyly instead.

'About that image of you.'

'Indeed?'

'Is it only the one? I mean, are there more, Grace?' He flings himself into a chair beside the fire.

Grace pours him a whisky, the way she knows he prefers, with only a little water to open the flavour. 'There are more,' she coos. 'Not the same, mind. Different.'

He grunts as if to say that he knew it. 'I don't mind being extorted,' he says, taking a sip, 'but I'd like to be comprehensively extorted, if that's what it comes to.'

Grace perches prettily on the opposite chair, far enough away that he cannot lay his hands on her. 'I don't know what you mean,' she says. 'If you wish to withdraw your bid, I can return it.' She removes the McIntyre envelope from her décolletage, feeling satisfied that Donald lets out an involuntary gasp as she does so.

He does not snatch the paper, however. 'I merely seek to clarify, not to withdraw,' he says.

Grace sighs. 'Clarify what?'

'That you're selling one image, but that you have more.'

'Yes.'

'How many are there?'

Grace chose three of Ellory's prints. She decides to admit this. 'Three,' she says.

'And you intend to auction the others?'

'In time. Of course.'

'I want to up my bid. I want to buy the lot. To take you off the market, picturewise, do you see?' Donald says, looking pleased with himself.

Grace gets up and takes a turn around her chair. She leans over the back of it. 'Oh, Donald,' she says with great seriousness, 'that would cost a lot of money. I have three bids for the first one alone. The other gentlemen would be terribly disappointed.'

'Show me the envelopes,' Donald says.

Grace does not want him to make some mad grand gesture and throw the papers on the fire. This foray is promising but she will not toss her options aside without knowing what is to her best advantage. She goes to the table and lifts all three sealed envelopes and fans herself with them. 'These?' she says. 'You want to see these?'

'You haven't opened them?'

'Not yet.'

Donald grins. 'Very well. I propose a wager.'

He is revoltingly pleased with himself, she thinks, though she has to admit she is intrigued. 'Go on.'

'I'll pay you a sum for possession of all three prints and an undertaking that you will make no more, unless they are for me.'

Grace looks perplexed. '*Never* make more?'

'Aha,' Donald says, passing his eyes over Grace's curves. 'It will be a tempting figure.'

'It will have to be,' she counters.

'You must take it or leave it. But if you take it you must do so blind. You cannot open those envelopes. Not mine. Not any of them.' He puts out his hand. 'Do we have a deal?'

Grace's jaw hardens. She does not like being backed into a corner. 'You know that I'm not a possession, Mr McIntyre. I cannot be bought.'

McIntyre puts his hands in the air, his brown eyes twinkling. 'I know that, Grace. To my detriment.'

'And you would not share the images or reproduce them?'

McIntyre gives a curt nod to confirm. 'They're only for me.'

'Interesting,' Grace says. He is leaning forward now and she wonders if he might tumble onto the Persian carpet if he goes much further. 'There's only one thing left to discuss then.'

'What's that?' He passes a well-manicured hand across his beard.

Grace laughs. 'The figure,' she says lightly as if it hardly matters and then, 'the money,' more earnestly emphasised.

McIntyre raises a finger. 'Ah yes.' He reaches into his jacket pocket and brings out a paper. 'The amount, my dear, is up to you,' he says and hands it over.

Grace casts her eyes over the spidery scrawl and realises it is a contract laid out in the terms he has just spoken of. She squints. Unlike her parents, she can read but it takes her time. 'I see,' she says, as if he is being foolish. 'Do you expect me to sign this thing now?'

Donald raises an eyebrow. He clearly does. 'Simply fill in the figure. Then you shall sign and I shall sign,' he says. 'That's how it's done.'

Grace glances at her desk. She plucks a quill from the drawer and dips it into a pot of vibrant blue ink. 'You are a taskmaster!'

'That,' he says with a hint of humour, 'is what you like most about me, I imagine.'

Grace considers. He is giving her carte blanche, quite her favourite thing. She makes a show of thinking and writes down that she wants 1,000 guineas. She hands back the paper defiantly. Donald squints at it and then removes a monocle from his waistcoat pocket to check he is reading correctly. 'Ma behookie,' he says and starts to laugh. 'Aye. All right then.' He takes the quill from her and signs the contract, handing it back to Grace who decides, grudgingly, to do the same. 'Well,' he says, eyeing her, 'we're settled then.'

Grace holds out her hand for him to kiss, which he does and then lays his palm on her waist. 'Well,' he repeats.

'You bought pictures, Mr McIntyre,' she reminds him. 'Not my person.'

'I know. I'd like to see them,' he says.

'Of course.' She steps away and fetches the portfolio case.

'It's a grand sum for three wee prints,' he points out.

'And no more for anybody but you,' Grace reminds him, her tone seductive. 'That's the value of it, don't you think?'

Donald opens the leather folder and considers the images one by one. 'Good heavens,' he says, returning to his favourite, the picture of Grace scantily clad and laughing, the one he had seen before, which he had hoped to buy for 100 guineas – for that is what he wrote in the sealed paper until he thought the better of it. 'I'll think on this till I'm an old man,' he remarks. Grace smiles prettily and does not say that as far as she is concerned he is an old man already. 'Will you send a banker's draft?' she checks, wondering if she should have asked for more.

Donald nods.

'And will you stay for something to eat? I can have Cook send up a tansy pudding.'

Donald lifts his drink. 'Aye,' he says and then adds cheekily, 'that'll sweeten the deal.'

Downstairs the news spreads like wildfire, for Betty, who was listening at the door, blabs immediately to Owen and Cook and the two other maids. 'A thousand guineas!' Cook declares, adding, 'There are no flies on the mistress. You've got to admire her, really.'

Chapter Thirty

In the morning, Murray wakes, replaying the conversation he had with Ellory the night before. He feels troubled rather than ecstatic, for he realises Ellory was trying to tell him something and he was so keen to cement the matter of his own feelings that he did not let her speak. He stares at the ceiling of his bedroom, fringed in laurel plaster cornicing, and listens to the birdsong in the half-light beyond the dark velvet curtains. The lady clearly has reservations, but she did not reject him. She called him a strong branch, he remembers with a sting of desire. He has waited what feels like a long time to find this woman. And suddenly here she is; his chance at having a family. The two of them together and perhaps more than that in time. He only has to manage it. She agreed to refrain from taking unsuitable pictures, he thinks. And nobody but he needs to know about her skin. But, he now understands, there is something else. Something about her family. It sounded like a feud. Her cousin called her cursed. But, he tells himself, families fall out all the time.

The firm of Urquhart & Son prides itself on turning up information. Normally they set a clerk to that kind of business, or in extreme cases Mungo McVey, a solid warehouse foreman they keep on a generous retainer for the purpose of dealing with blackmailers, kidnappers, out-of-hand mistresses and the like. But this is Murray's own affair and he's glad his father gave him the opportunity to see to it himself. He will find out what Ellory was trying to tell him, which is for the best given that his father will uncover whatever is on her mind, when he sets a clerk to double-check, which he most assuredly will. He dresses swiftly, taking less care than usual to match his waistcoat to his jacket. Downstairs, the housemaid bobs a curtsy. He picks up a bread roll from the dresser and slathers butter over it carelessly. 'I'm out for the day,' he instructs cheerfully and disappears out of the door.

The train ride to Edinburgh is fascinating, so much more convenient than the coach, and he steps onto Princes Street not much later than the hour he habitually arrives at his office. At the station entrance he turns east, asking directions to the studio of David Octavius Hill. The weather is better than in Glasgow. By the look of the ground here, no rain has fallen for days. This part of town is practically rural, he thinks, turning off Waterloo Place onto a twisting road paved with whinstone flake in the lee of Calton Hill. The studio is not what he expected – a rough stone dwelling that looks as if it is harled with cinder toffee. Beyond, a Carver chair lies abandoned incongruously in the middle of the lawn. Ahead, the sun casts an elongated shadow that distends his top hat, as if it belongs to a fashionable dandy from a ridiculous cartoon. He walks up the path and raps on the door, which is opened by Jessie Mann wearing her customary severe black day dress with long gloves.

'Can I help you, sir?'

'Is this the photography studio?' Murray asks.

'Yes.'

'I'd like to speak to the photographer.'

Jessie's lips purse. 'Neither Mr Adamson nor Mr Hill is here.'

Murray shifts. 'I can wait,' he announces but she does not move.

'Perhaps you should make an appointment. I don't know if the gentlemen plan to work today.'

'Are you the housekeeper?' Murray asks, noting the woman's gloves.

Jessie holds her ground. 'I'm the gentlemen's primary assistant,' she says crisply, despite the fact that no junior assistant has been taken on to replace Ellory.

'Your name?'

'Jessie Mann.'

A grin spreads across Murray's face like butter melting in a pan. He would not have guessed it. This woman's appearance is a stark contrast to Ellory's rosy countenance. 'You're related to Miss Ellory Mann, the photographer on St Enoch's Square?' he asks warmly.

Beneath Jessie's wide skirts her knees almost buckle. 'Ellory's my cousin.' Her voice is lower now as if the words are a guilty confession.

Murray takes in her discomfort. 'Your cousin is most talented, miss,' he says to reassure her. Jessie steps backwards and Murray enters. The new maid of all works is not in today. They are alone in the house and Jessie does not close the door. He removes his hat, but she does not offer to take it. Together they go into the parlour.

'What has she done?' Jessie snaps.

Murray notes that Miss Mann's first words are not about whether her cousin is well or to echo his compliment of Ellory's skill. Perhaps this is the cousin with whom Ellory has had the feud and if so, he can use the woman's bad feeling to find out more. 'I've come to make enquiries,' he says. 'I'm here to check Miss Mann's credentials.'

Jessie can hardly look at him. 'Oh god,' she breathes.

'Do I sense you're not comfortable to recommend your own cousin, Miss Mann?'

Jessie looks as if she might burst into tears. 'I shouldn't have let her go,' she says. 'My brother berated me after. But she was fired up with this odd story about starting a studio. I knew it made no sense. She went off with not a minute's notice and I haven't heard from her since. Mr Hill was most upset. I knew she'd cause trouble. I secured her the position. But blood will out.'

Murray is trained to get the most out of people, but Miss Jessie Mann is one of the most eager witnesses he has ever broached.

He restrains himself from defending Ellory and encourages her to continue. 'Blood, Miss Mann?'

'On her side of the family,' Jessie adds hastily, as if she shares nothing with Ellory of blood or bone. Murray thinks she is almost comic in her insistence that she has done nothing wrong. 'Her mother. Her sister. All the McHale women,' Jessie gets out, rat-a-tat, 'red-haired, doxy quines. As I understand it, she hasn't taken the child with her.'

Murray's heartbeat feels suddenly syncopated. Jessie does not seem so comic now. 'The child?' he repeats.

Jessie snaps shut like a clam sensing the presence of a hungry seagull. Murray forces a smile. To get more he must appear sympathetic. 'Miss Mann,' he says gravely, 'we all have family problems. I can see you're an upright person. I'm sure you understand, I came because I suspected Miss Mann was not, shall we say . . . as upright as you are. Perhaps I ought, after all, to speak to the gentlemen photographers. I'm sure I can find them about the town. They'll be able to enlighten me about this child.' He lets this sink in.

It does not take longer than three seconds. Jessie cannot bear the thought of this fine gentleman washing her family's dirty linen in front of Mr Hill and Mr Adamson. Even the mention of Ellory's name causes her brother to pace the front room of his house in Morningside and drink more than a sufficiency of port. She wants to stop this conversation and there is only one way to do it. She must deal with this man herself.

'The child is a bastard, of course,' she spits. 'We placed him with a wifie in a cottage on the old Gayfield Estate. Ellory pays his board and his schooling. That's why I was surprised that she had collected enough money to start her foolish venture. She had little opportunity to save.' This, Murray notes, is said with a strange kind of satisfaction. Jessie continues with a hand on her heart. 'It was a condition of Ellory's employment that she didn't associate with the boy. My family felt it was best for everyone.'

Murray blanches as the revelation sinks in. Miss Ellory Mann has a bastard. No wonder she fled 50 miles west. He feels like telling

Jessie to shut up, but at the same time he is compelled to hear more. Ellory does not seem innocent, exactly, but she never struck him as the kind of woman to have this kind of secret. He feels betrayed. His father was right. 'What is the child's name?' he asks.

'Robert McHale Mann,' Jessie says, as if to clarify the matter, for bastards take their mother's surname.

'Thank you,' Murray says coolly. 'We're most interested to know this.'

Jessie looks horrified. 'We? But, sir, please, you must not tell anybody.' A tear slips down her cheek. 'My brother is a solicitor. We can't have . . .'

Murray latches onto her distress. He could walk away now and part of him wants to, but another part wants more information, as if he is picking at a wound. 'Miss Mann agreed to put the boy into the care of another woman?' he checks. He thought Ellory had more integrity. He thinks of her pictures. The clarity with which she sees her subjects. And then he considers the subjects she has chosen, or at least some of them. Of course she isn't an innocent. He just couldn't see it.

Jessie's world, meanwhile, is tumbling too. Everything she has taken pains to conceal is coming out. 'You'll not speak of it, will you, sir?' she pushes Murray. It is this insistence that finally lights his temper.

'While I appreciate your frankness, miss, I'll speak of it to whomever I need to,' he says.

Jessie gasps. Her greatest fear has always been that Ellory would unmask the Manns' disgrace, and yet it is she that has done the job. It is unthinkable that having helped this gentleman, he will not consider her wishes. 'If Mr Hill or Mr Adamson were to hear . . . My job . . .' She struggles to get out a coherent sentence. 'I can't see how to bear it.'

It gets worse, he realises, every time this woman speaks. 'You mean Mr Hill and Mr Adamson took you on – took on your cousin – without knowing of this?'

Jessie lets out a sob. Her side of the family has known the Hills and the Adamsons since they were all children in Fife, but Mr Hill and Mr Adamson do not know the truth about Ellory and her sister. Ellory's surname was her reference and neither Jessie nor her brother disabused them of the notion that all the Manns were good eggs. Now Jessie's cheeks burn at the thought of Mr Hill and Mr Adamson finding out. The shame of having put their sitters in the way of the Manns' disgrace, so many ministers of the Kirk among them. They will hold her responsible. They will hold Alexander responsible. Jessie's hands begin to shake. 'I want to help, sir,' she gets out, 'but please don't tell anyone.'

Murray wonders momentarily what to do. If his enquiries were on behalf of a client, he would certainly want to see the boy. 'The Gayfield Estate,' he checks. 'Is that what you said?'

'It's nearby, sir,' Jessie motions in the direction of the open front door. 'To the north.'

'I'll seek it out.' Murray makes to leave but Jessie cannot have that.

'I'll fetch my bonnet,' she says. 'I'll go with you.'

'There's no need,' he snaps but Miss Mann is insistent.

They set off northwards down the lane and onto Leith Street, beyond which Broughton Loan is buzzing with activity. Flower girls cry their wares along Albany Street. Two men unload an upright piano into one of the houses from a horse and cart. As they cross the thoroughfare at Forth Street, maids are queuing in a gossipy file, sent to buy onions from a French fellow with a barrow from the market garden on the fringes of Hillside. Murray's mind is racing. He feels a degree of both anger and regret. Why didn't Ellory tell him this? But he knows she tried. He runs over her words the night before and curses himself for not letting her speak. She said something even before that, he recalls, about a woman being abandoned. Did she mean herself? He tries not to picture another man laying his hands on her, taking advantage, but he cannot entirely banish the image. No wonder she refused him so stridently at first.

They are within sight of the tollbooth when Jessie motions to turn right. The Gayfield Estate lies east of the loan, though like the old Rocheid lands across the Water of Leith, it is diminished now, portions feued off to build houses and establish gardens. As the land levels before running down to the water, there is some rough ground and a run of old cottages. Outside, thin chickens peck the earth and a ramshackle hut contains three pigs, one of which has a scatter of piglets squirming to the suckle. Jessie gestures up the path that leads to one of the cottages. It is peppered with smashed pantiles that have slid off the roof. Murray raps with his cane and a plump old woman appears at the ill-fitting door, wiping her hands on a greying apron.

'Sir?' she greets him, mystified to see a person of such quality on her doorstep. Then she notices Jessie. 'Ah, Miss Mann,' she says. 'Is this Robbie's father?'

Murray laughs. He does not know if he is more angry or shocked.

'This gentleman has come to see the boy,' Jessie says regretfully.

Inside, Robert McHale Mann is one of three boys sitting in front of the hearth building a tower from a collection of dolomite chips collected from the detritus outside. The boy looks something like his mother, Murray notes, rosy-cheeked, with auburn hair and a smattering of freckles. The red hair of the McHales. Doxy quines, Jessie said. The other two children have sandy brown mops and sallow skin. Twins perhaps – and no relation.

'Robbie,' the old woman calls, 'this gentleman has come with your cousin.'

Jessie blanches. She does not recognise the connection. Robbie, however, grins. 'Hello,' he says and puts out his hand. The child is forthright, Urquhart thinks. He has dignity despite his surroundings and seems quite charming. He is Ellory's. Of course he is charming, Murray berates himself – he feels on the cusp of not caring about this and yet how could she not have told him? His mind is racing.

'My name is Murray Urquhart,' he says and shakes the boy's hand.

'I like your cravat,' Robbie says.

'Don't be rude,' the old woman tells him off. 'I'm sorry, sir,' she apologises. 'He's not used to meeting gentlemen.'

'He's a good boy, though? Bright?' Murray checks. An innocent, like all children.

'He goes to the dame school. Second top of the class,' the woman confirms.

Murray smiles. 'Good,' he says. 'Well . . .'

He hovers a moment for he is not sure what to do. Then he takes his leave.

Outside he does not stride up the path but instead stands outside the cottage, Jessie bobbing next to him as if she is a buoy in open water. 'Will you keep it secret, sir?' she asks.

'I must think,' Murray snaps. But he is not thinking, he realises. He is feeling, and what he is feeling is new. From inside the cottage he hears the tower tumble and the boys laughing. 'Hush,' the old woman shouts and they quiet down. Murray feels calm as he applies all his reason to the situation. The boy is just a normal lad but with Ellory's eyes. A bright child. In other circumstances he might have real prospects. Murray had pictured himself with Ellory as the Urquhart family, the beginning of a new branch. Now he imagines them together with a child from the off. A straight-backed boy. Only a few hours ago he judged his love a certainty. Is he really such a prig that he would change his mind over something that may be a blessing? A new Urquhart family, ready-made. His father will have to know, of course, but it might be managed in the wider sphere. Ellory after all might be a widow. If she was taken advantage of, abandoned as she said, might he forgive her for this? Even welcome it?

Robbie appears at the door to the cottage. Jessie cannot contain herself. 'Go away,' she snaps.

'Robbie could live with his mother,' Murray says, out of the blue.

The child looks taken aback. His eyes fill with tears and the old woman who has looked after him these last six years appears in the doorway and glares.

'I expect what Mr Urquhart is wondering,' Jessie cuts in, 'is why you do not live with your Aunt Ellory. You remember her, do you, boy?'

Robbie pulls back from the edge of a crying fit.

'Thank goodness,' the old woman says. 'I was worried . . . as if a ghost had risen.'

Murray eyes Jessie. Then he looks at the boy again. He pulls Jessie to the side. 'Ellory's sister is the boy's mother?' he whispers. 'Is that it?'

'I thought it was clear,' Jessie snaps. 'I wouldn't have allowed Ellory the position at Rock House if she had a child out of wedlock herself. This boy is her sister's disgrace, for which she bears the responsibility.'

'Her sister?'

'Nora. She died just after he was born.'

'And the boy's father?'

'No one knows. She was in service. A laundress,' Jessie sniffs disapprovingly. 'We tried but she wouldn't tell us.'

Murray's cheeks blaze. He feels a stab of shame that he thought the worst of the woman he loves. Then a rush of fury on Ellory's behalf that the Manns have made a deal of smoke from this little fire. They have tarred her for doing the right thing, paying for the boy's upkeep. This makes his decision for him. Murray, at heart, is a family man. People trip themselves up easily on the way to what they want, his father always says. He decides that he will not turn his back on his own happiness out of a misguided need to conform. Ellory has in fact looked after Robbie, so a belief in family is something they have in common. He can make this work by bringing her secret mostly into the open. This child, orphaned and in the family, can live with them respectably.

'Come along, Robbie,' he says as if it is an announcement. 'You're coming with me. We shall to the railway station.'

Jessie coughs. At least the gentleman no longer wants to speak to her employers. 'To Glasgow? Are you saying you'll look after him?' she says weakly.

Murray's eyes narrow. 'To Glasgow and Miss Mann will look after him,' he says. 'She's to be married. Have you ever been on a train, boy?'

Jessie's jaw is slack. Murray ignores her.

From the doorway the twins regard their playmate, their faces writ plainly with jealousy. 'I've never seen a train, sir,' Robbie says. He falls in obediently and Jessie takes her place behind him. 'Will you say goodbye?' Murray asks the child and Robbie gives a little wave.

'Be good,' the old woman admonishes her charge.

'Yes, ma'am,' he says gravely.

Jessie cannot see the coin that Mr Urquhart gives to the old woman but the wifie curtsies to him and Jessie resents that he has been generous. The auld quine has had enough Mann money over the years, she thinks, though she paid not a penny of it.

The three of them make an odd caravan walking back up the hill to the railway station where Murray buys two tickets and takes his leave of Jessie, who awkwardly pats Robert on the head for she feels she ought to do something. Inside the first-class carriage, the boy sits straight. 'Don't be afraid,' Murray says. 'You mustn't lean out, all right?'

As the train pulls away Jessie stands on the platform. When it disappears into the tunnel, she checks the time by the station clock: only two of the afternoon. Slowly she pulls herself together and thanks the Lord that the crisis has been averted, perhaps even for the better. She can hardly believe her luck. The boy is no longer less than a mile from Rock House. She wonders briefly who Ellory is marrying. She should have asked but there was so much else going on.

As she climbs the slope that leads out of the station and turns towards Rock House, she imagines her cousin's studio as a grubby place, disorganised and downmarket from Mr Hill and Mr Adamson and their cohort of well-shoed Edinburgh clients. Ellory's new husband will be some rough type, Jessie thinks. A butcher, perhaps.

Yes, that would be fitting. Still, this evening when she gets home, she might tell her sister about today, if not her brother. Then, she thinks charitably, she might include the child in her prayers. Nora's boy. Robert. Gone out of their lives at last.

Chapter Thirty-One

The train from Edinburgh is not busy this afternoon. In a first-class carriage, Robbie Mann cannot contain his excitement and has to sit on his hands. They are heading to a city the child has never visited to an aunt he hardly knows. Murray is surprised that it feels entirely natural to travel with the child. 'Is there anything you would like to ask?' he offers.

'Please, sir, how does it go so fast?'

'It's a steam engine,' Murray replies. 'They burn coal under water till it boils and the steam drives a set of pistons attached to the wheels. It's a Scottish invention,' he adds. 'James Watt, an engineer born in Greenock, not far from Glasgow, where we're going.'

Robbie stares at him, clearly in awe of somebody having this knowledge at his fingertips. Then he grins. 'Thank you, sir.'

As they pull into Haymarket Station, Murray points out the water tower at the far end. He is so engaged by the child he does not notice Reverend Patterson getting onto the train, but the minister spots him through the window and makes straight for Murray's carriage. 'Mr Urquhart. Who's this young fellow?' he asks, taking a seat.

Murray notices a musty smell, like a rowan tree in bloom. He does not want to introduce Robbie to Reverend Patterson, but he has little choice. 'Robert, please shake hands with this gentleman.'

Robbie obliges. Patterson's eyes narrow as if he is trying to match the boy's appearance to one of his parishioners. 'What's your full name?' he barks at the child.

'Robert McHale Mann, sir,' Robbie trots out obediently.

Patterson gives a look of satisfaction. 'Mann,' he says. 'The lady photographer? Ah yes, I've heard tell of the woman. Undercutting gentlemen photographers, I believe. Miss Mann is a client of yours, Mr Urquhart,' he adds, putting the emphasis on the word 'miss'. 'You're always solicitous to your female clients.'

'Robert is Miss Mann's nephew,' Murray explains.

Patterson looks faintly disappointed. The carriage falls to silence as the train pulls out and the men eye each other surreptitiously. 'I was in town to speak to a committee of Kirk ministers,' Patterson volunteers.

'About Mr Douglass?'

'How did you know?'

'Mr Douglass's campaign is the main issue facing the Kirk at present. I'm not alone in taking a stand. It doesn't surprise me you're holding meetings. You stand to lose your congregation, sir.'

Patterson stares out of the window. 'We're not minded to give in to bullying,' he says.

Murray does not want to have an out-and-out argument in front of the child, who is gawping at the flash of fields as the train speeds past the city limits at Roseburn. Murray has heard however that the Kirk's campaign against Mr Douglass is no longer restricted to picketing meetings. Threatening letters have been sent to inns that accommodate him, to meeting halls that host his talks and even to printers who make his fly-posters. Patterson was made for such activities, Murray thinks. It is not the Kirk that is being bullied.

'You're visiting your aunt, Master Mann?' Patterson turns to the child. Murray places a hand protectively on the boy's shoulder. 'Has it been a long time since you saw her?'

'She doesn't come; only sends the money,' the boy replies.

'Your parents are dead then?'

'Yes, sir.'

Murray cannot bear it. 'For heaven's sake,' he says. 'Miss Mann is without blame. Her sister died and the child had to be cared for.'

'Miss Mann's sister, you say?' Patterson's jaw is taught. Murray curses himself for handing the minister this information. It takes only a second for him to reason the meaning of the surname. Scandal, after all, is meat and drink to the man. 'So this is a bastard you're ferrying about?' he snorts. 'This is where your liberal lectures have taken you, to the door of the very devil. Running errands on behalf of illegitimate orphans for the sister of a dead hure.'

Robbie's gaze falls from the window to his feet. 'It does Miss Mann credit that she has always supported her nephew. I'm honoured to help care for the boy,' Murray says stoutly.

'Your firm cares for many of the town's waifs and strays, as I understand it. Anyone with money that has a problem,' Patterson snarls, 'on either side of the bedsheet.'

'I'll not discuss my clients' business, sir,' Murray retorts. He takes Robbie's hand and they move carriage.

At Queen Street Murray does not tarry. Robbie and he walk up the platform and Murray hails a hansom. The boy falls asleep on the short journey to St Enoch's Square, his hand on his empty stomach, for since a potato farl and a cup of milk at midday, nobody has thought to feed him. Usually there would be pottage by now and a slice of bread. At St Enoch's Square Murray pays the driver and lifts the boy onto his shoulder. At the top of the stairs he pauses a second before knocking.

Jane admits him. Ellory is at the table eating a slice of pie. Her face changes as Murray lays the boy carefully onto the comfortable chair used by her sitters. The child sighs but does not wake.

'I wanted to tell you—' she starts, a wave of nausea crashing over her as she starts to babble an explanation.

Urquhart puts up a hand to stop her. He reaches into his pocket and gives Jane a bob. 'Fetch some bread and milk, please, Jane.'

'There's bread on the side, sir,' Jane says, eyeing the child.

'Milk then.'

The girl looks at Ellory who nods her agreement, then she disappears out of the door, knowing that she must not come back for a while, when she will hopefully discover what the arrival of this child is about.

Outside the long windows the sun is setting and the moon is beginning to rise. Murray momentarily takes in the sight of Ellory. Her dress is printed with sprigs of sage. Wisdom, he thinks. Her hair is held in a careless bun, a few ginger wisps escaped. She looks fresh despite a day about her business. He feels the rush of her presence and the grounding between them of the child sleeping in the chair, though she is agitated. 'I met your cousin,' he says.

Ellory's heart sinks. This feels like some dreadful prophecy coming true. 'I tried to tell you—' she starts again. 'But I couldn't bear the disgrace.'

'It's your sister's disgrace as I understand it,' he says.

Ellory swallows. It has been a long time since she talked about Nora. Jessie would never allow it. The memory still stings. 'She wouldn't say who dishonoured her,' she starts. 'I didn't push, but Jessie's brother was relentless. Nora had a job in the laundry, like our mother. It's a common enough tale. She was alive, you know. That isn't how most people put it, of course. They called her a hure. Why did you fetch the boy? Was he not being cared for?'

'Not as he should be,' Murray admits. 'They sent him to the dame school but he's a bright child. He needs better tuition and, of course, all children need a family.'

'I intended to send for him once I was set up,' Ellory says. She feels humiliated, a tree uprooted in a storm, the ground disappeared under her.

'I should have talked to you about it,' Murray admits. 'Before, I mean, but it seems I'm decisive once I know what I want.'

She does not pick him up correctly. 'I'll not hold you to your promise, Murray. What you said last night.'

Murray shakes his head. It is the slightest of movements. 'You judge me the sort of fellow who changes his opinion according to what suits him? I can't say that I didn't feel anger and I'm not sure what else. But I meant what I said. I love you, Ellory Mann.'

'But you've found out the worst.' She covers her face with her hands. Suddenly it is all she can do to breathe. 'There have been whispers all my life about Nora and me. She bore this child out of wedlock and I'm making money in a way that would shame my family.'

'People can be shallow. Jealous.'

'Why would anybody be jealous of me?'

Murray wants to touch her but he holds back. 'I've always been on the outside of things,' he admits. 'I'm Murray Urquhart the cripple. People will gossip about anything unusual but I've come to realise that's telling of them, not of me. Not of you either. Or your late sister. I want a family, Ellory. You and I and the wee lad can be that. It's a start. There's a new day school on Elmbank Street – the Glasgow Academy. I'll vouch for Robbie.'

Ellory starts to cry. 'You're so kind,' she gets out. 'I don't deserve it.'

Murray hands her his handkerchief. He waits. 'I think I'm going to become a Quaker now I've quit the Free Kirk,' he says. 'They're witnesses. I don't have the hang of it yet.' He takes her hand. 'I found Robbie because I went to investigate your past. My father thought it would uncover something to stop us being together. But it's only made me want this more.' He draws on her palm with his finger. She follows the movement. He is writing. Four letters in she realises the words are 'Marry me'.

She cannot help but smile. It's like the sun coming out. 'This is madness,' she says.

'I can offer you protection,' Murray insists earnestly. 'We're stronger the two of us and the boy. I'll never forsake you, Ellory Mann.'

'They'll say I bewitched you,' she says.

'They used to say I was cursed. I only care if you will join me. That's what matters.'

'But your father will not bless such a union.'

Murray pulls back. Albany Urquhart has helped 100 families negotiate the skeletons in their closets. 'My father is nothing if not practical. He'll come round. Healing rifts is his stock-in-trade. That and burying evidence. It's simple; he wants me to marry and I've made my choice, if you'll have me, that is.'

His seriousness shakes her. 'What about my work?'

'I wouldn't dream of arresting your vocation,' he replies solemnly. 'I love that you've made this place.'

'And my nephew? You're sure?'

'I think we should adopt the boy. We'll look like an older married couple than we are. That we found each other sooner. I wish we had.'

It does not seem real. Her excitement mounting, she searches for a way to ground herself. Her eyes dart to the shelves near the stove.

'Are you all right?'

'I'm afraid,' she says. Anyone she has ever believed in has let her down. He's a gentleman, she keeps thinking over and over. It cannot be possible.

'I thought you were hungry,' he grins.

'I crave a little sweetness is all.' She gets up and fetches the jam and a spoon. Murray laughs as she slips a scoop of raspberry onto her tongue and offers him the jar.

'I've not done this since I was a child,' he says.

She does not tell him she does it often. She does not wish to feel foolish.

'You've not answered my question,' he says, jammy-lipped. 'Is it my appearance that's holding you back? You must be true now, Ellory.'

She shakes her head. He seems beautiful to her. His brown hair, slightly too long, and brown eyes. She thought he was warm the moment she saw him at the railway station. 'I've nothing to give you,' she says. 'That's the thing.'

Murray stares at the boy in the chair and then back. 'You're the heart of me,' he says simply. 'Don't you feel it?'

She knows what happened to her mother and father but she wonders if instead of falling, they might have risen, if it had not been for the Manns. It seems so random. Nora died for love. Robbie was abandoned for it. And yet, she feels hopeful. This is raw and strong and beautiful. 'How do Quakers marry?' she asks.

Murray laughs with relief. 'Is that a yes?'

'Yes,' she declares and when he kisses her there is an overwhelming rush of berries, the sweetness of summer yet to come. 'Will you take down your hair?' he whispers. 'I want to see it.'

She pulls out the pins and he watches her red tresses tumble. She is, he thinks, the most beautiful woman. She has the most dignity of anybody he knows. He pauses before he kisses her again and Ellory feels as if she is flying. Did it happen to Nora the same? This heat? This flicker inside, jolting them together?

'You've nothing to worry about,' Murray assures her. 'Not from me.'

In the chair the boy stirs, interrupting them. 'Aunt Ellory,' he says, rubbing his eyes.

She crouches next to him. 'Hello,' she says.

'Where am I?'

'My studio. Where I make calotypes? Do you remember what I do?'

'In the orange house?'

'Not any more,' she says.

'I'm hungry,' Robbie announces.

Ellory fetches the jar of jam and bread from the shelf. 'My assistant will return with milk,' she tells him. 'Would you like a jelly piece?'

As the child eats, Murray says goodbye. 'I'll organise everything,' he promises.

Downstairs he decides to walk back to Bath Street though it feels more like flying. The moon hangs so low this evening, it's skirting

291

the roofs. As he heads up the hill, he sees Reverend Patterson ahead in company with another man in black, taking one of the side alleys onto Hope Street. He wonders if they are making for the cockpit or the bordello above it. It is all what you know, one secret or another, but nothing can dampen the young solicitor's mood tonight. He has something to fight for now. At home he hovers in the doorway, the light in the drawing room above still lit for Albany Urquhart is reading. Up the hill, Murray can see the corner of Blythswood Street. He feels guilty about Charlotte and the things he has not told her. Family is everything, he thinks. Once you find it. And then with a sting of excitement he heads inside and as good as dances up the stairs to speak to his father.

Chapter Thirty-Two

Saturday, 18 April 1846

Mr Frederick Douglass is unperturbed by the Free Kirk's counter-campaign. The storm around him is gaining the force of a hurricane, which Douglass considers necessary to shake the world loose. He is becoming quite the celebrity. Scotland's periodicals print details about Douglass's life, the suffering he has endured. He does not like the countryside, they say. The creaking of trees makes him jumpy, for the sound reminds him of escaped slaves being lynched. Such details capture the imagination and several ladies, not appraised of the fact Mr Douglass is married, send love tokens to his lectures. When the great man climbs Salisbury Crags in Edinburgh with two respectable lady Quakers and attempts to carve 'SEND BACK THE MONEY' into the vertiginous dolerite rock overlooking the Old Town, he lights a touchpaper. Douglass's companions are said to be the renowned Misses Whigham, and though they are not successful in etching the slogan onto the landscape, an artist's impression is drawn of the intention and the newspapers sell out.

The Quakers for all their seriousness are good at publicity, it seems, and in due course arrangements are made to take Douglass's image. The sitting is organised by a lady in Glasgow – a Miss Smeal who has heard of a new photographer working from a studio on St Enoch's Square who has a camera obscura that makes affordable prints. A note is sent. Ellory accepts the commission. *He will come to your studio on Saturday, Miss Mann. We must be discreet,* Miss Smeal adds by postscript. Ellory is certainly used to exercising her discretion. This time it will be in a good cause, she thinks. But her efforts are to little avail for Miss Smeal's maid, Lizzy, hears of the matter and tells her sister, Ina, who adheres to the tenets of the Free Kirk so strictly she would put Mrs Grieg to shame. At night the girl slips across her master's hallway smooth as a ferret and down the servants' stair to deliver the news to those with an interest, and the matter is out. On Saturday morning when Ellory peers out the window at St Enoch's clock, a crowd is gathered below.

'What's that?' she asks, the shouts snaking upwards like an indistinct echo. She squints, spotting one of Charlotte Nicholl's neighbours touting a placard.

Indeed, Mrs Grieg and her ladies have been key to organising the protest. They have spent hours painting placards and fly-posters in the Griegs' drawing room. From above, Ellory, Jane and Jeremiah crowd the little window as the minister of St Enoch's tries to reason with the protesters, but there is little point in that, and he quickly decides to herd the sheep to safety instead. Downstairs, the caretaker has closed the front door, so Mr Douglass, due in a mere five minutes, will have to ring for entry if he can fight his way through at all. Jane retreats to the stove where Robbie, now settled with his aunt, is building a tower of wooden blocks. Jeremiah consults his pocket watch. 'This is a rum do,' he says.

Ellory sighs. She has been reading a collection of Miss Whigham's pamphlets borrowed from Charlotte the day before. Mr Douglass's cause inspires her. 'Do you think he'll still come?' she asks nervously and as if by reply there is rap on the door. They all look at each other. 'Go on,' Ellory instructs Jane.

The maid opens up. 'Sir,' she says and lets Frederick Douglass inside. He is dressed in a navy frock coat over a matching thick velvet waistcoat. His snowy cravat is tied with precision and held by a yellow gold pin, topped with a sphere, like a tiny sun.

'Mr Douglass,' Ellory greets him. 'However did you get through?'

'By the back door,' Douglass says with a smile. His voice is smooth as taffy and quite unperturbed. 'They're angry because I'm right,' he adds. 'I'm not afraid of them.'

'Come in. Please,' Ellory says. 'It's kind of you to sit.'

'Miss Smeal says you have made an innovation, Miss Mann. A smaller image. Cheaper too. She thinks the production of it will support the campaign.'

Ellory likes that he gets straight to business. 'The pictures cost a shilling,' she says, pointing out the small camera. 'Though I thought we might take an image of a larger size too. If you're happy to go ahead?'

Masked by the table, Jeremiah kicks her ankle. He cannot imagine why Ellory would ask such a question. Mr Douglass is here, isn't he? 'Miss Mann is the best photographer in Glasgow,' he cuts in. 'She's modest is all.'

Ellory blushes and gets to the nub. 'Tell me, Mr Douglass, how would you like to appear?'

Douglass smiles. He is not fond of airs and graces and he takes to this lady immediately. 'Like any man,' he says bluntly. 'To be seen as I am. Miss Smeal suggested the picture might celebrate my manumission, which I hope for soon. She thought people would like to have copies. Symbols are important.'

Jeremiah cocks his head. 'You're moving then from one state to another? Slavery to freedom,' he surmises.

Douglass's face assumes a serious expression. 'I'm escaped. In America I remain owned in law. I hope to be free soon enough.'

Jeremiah pauses. From outside the sound of the crowd chanting continues to float upwards. 'Perhaps we ought to leave the studio,' Jeremiah suggests. 'Wouldn't it be grand to encapsulate the change you're making in the picture, sir? To give the portrait more meaning?'

Ellory understands what Jeremiah is thinking of straight away. 'To the bridge? For Mr Douglass is making a crossing. That's a clever idea. But what if they see us?'

Jeremiah stares. 'If Mr Douglass is prepared to take the risk, I think we should too.'

Douglass's expression hardens. 'I escaped from Baltimore to Philadelphia pursued by violent men who wanted to send me back to my owner. For money of course. I'll not be put off by a crowd of old ladies.'

They are decided. 'Bring the dark box,' Ellory directs Jane, 'and papers for both cameras.' The girl takes off. 'I'll carry the small camera. Jeremiah, you take the large one. Come along, Robbie,' she encourages the child. 'You can help.'

As they emerge into the back alley, they look like a party embarking on a picnic, carrying the various boxes and little Robbie bouncing a ball. The lane comes out far enough away from the square that the protesters have no notion they are gone. They move swiftly in the direction of the New Glasgow Bridge beyond Jamaica Street. 'In my previous position I photographed several ministers of the Free Kirk,' Ellory remarks. 'Ironic, isn't it?'

At the bridge, she sets up both cameras quickly. Douglass peers over the side and then turns, standing with the bank behind him, the water flowing beneath the pale stone arches that span the Clyde and the terrace at Carlton Place beyond. The air feels fresh, the warmth of approaching summer on the breeze and the light as clear as a slap in the face. Ellory decides not to include the moored ships as Jeremiah places Mr Douglass, dapper in his frock coat, his hair parted to one side beneath his top hat. He puts a walking stick from the properties cupboard into Douglass's gloved hand. 'There,' he says, glancing at Ellory, who understands immediately that the stick will guide the eye in the final picture. She considers how Mr Hill composes his titled sitters, posed in front of their grand mansions, and decides she will do the same with Douglass and the terrace behind. It will place him squarely in Glasgow, here on the bridge, in the centre of town. The water is casting pure light today. Ellory is learning to use it to show her sitters as they wish to be seen.

'You must stand still,' Jeremiah tells Douglass.

'Whatever else might I do?'

'It's not easy,' Jeremiah adds, 'to hold a stare without tension.'

He steps back like Robbie does when he has built a tower of bricks and is waiting to see if it will tumble. Then, satisfied Douglass is in place, he scoops up the child. 'Look,' he says as Jane hands Ellory the first paper. 'Your aunt is at work.'

She makes the large image first, counting the seconds, her gaze fixed on Douglass. After, just as Ellory used to at Rock House, Jane removes the exposure to the dark box. They work quickly, as a team. Two large images: the first as Jeremiah posed Douglass; the second from lower, as if he is a statue. As Ellory and Jane switch boxes, a carriage rumbles slowly across the bridge. From inside a man and woman glare. 'You're a disgrace!' the man shouts knocking on the glass. 'That money is in the service of God!' Everybody ignores him as the horses clip-clop onwards, though Jeremiah keeps an eye to the north in case the fellow informs the crowd they have sneaked away. Ellory gathers herself. 'Perhaps a second pose,' she suggests. 'Something different.'

Robbie is placed back on the setts and Jeremiah moves Mr Douglass so he is standing straight onto the bridge, the river twisting behind, ships moored along its banks. When he is done, Ellory takes three small images, changing the papers as rapid as it gets. Then the sun disappears behind a cloud and the light diffuses. 'Just in time,' she says.

'When might I see these?' Douglass asks, handing back the cane.

'A couple of days. I'll deliver the prints to Miss Smeal,' Ellory promises. 'Was it the same, sir, when your image was taken in America?'

Douglass considers. 'They made more fuss,' he says with his eye on Jeremiah. 'You're most efficient, miss. If you're done, I'll go back across the other bridge. It will be more . . . peaceful.' He tips his hat and wishes them a good day.

'You should sell the small prints to his supporters at one shilling and tuppence,' Jeremiah says as they watch Douglass depart. 'Then you can donate the tuppence to Mr Douglass's cause.' Ellory considers this. She is not sure how much money that might raise. If Miss Smeal buys a print and Miss Nicholl, it is at least fourpence, she supposes.

'I'll think on it,' she says, lifting the dark box which now feels more precious than the camera. She will ask Murray what he thinks when he next calls. 'Come along.' She takes Robbie's hand. And they proceed without incident along the lane and back upstairs.

'I'd best be off,' Jeremiah says, once the equipment is safely stowed. He downs what is left of the small beer they meant to serve Mr Douglass. Then he disappears downstairs and out the back door. Robbie returns to his building blocks in front of the grate. Jane follows Ellory into the print room. They must make the most of the light until the sun sets. If they go hard they might finish the printing today. It is one of the clock now and the protesters sound as if they are tailing off. The clock is ticking.

'Right,' Ellory says and brings down the silver iodide from the shelf. They start with the large papers. As the images emerge they peer into the tray.

'Queer to see him so pale,' Jane says as Ellory tips the negative over. The salted silver will take an hour to develop in the glass box on the sill.

'This one is for the Royal Society's summer exhibition in Edinburgh,' she mutters, a kind of promise to herself. A stand.

'An exhibition, miss?'

'I doubt they'll show it.' Ellory shrugs. 'A female photographer's work. And Mr Douglass is a controversial figure.' She does not add that Mr Hill is on the Hanging Committee and is so thick with the Free Kirk that anything that might support sending back the money will not see the light of the Royal Society's day. 'I'll try, at least,' she resolves. She pictures a cardboard box containing prints stamped with her name being delivered to the grand hallway at the Society's rooms in Edinburgh. This is exactly what she had hoped for from her new venture, and now she is here.

*

As Jeremiah rounds the corner onto Argyle Street he passes Mrs Grieg climbing into her carriage, holding a placard that says 'THIS IS HERESY' in capital letters. 'You're the lad who visited Miss Charlotte Nicholl the other day,' she hails him. 'I saw you going in.'

Jeremiah doffs his cap. 'Aye, ma'am,' he says. 'I'm her tailor.'

Mrs Grieg squints. Charlotte has been using the selfsame seamstress for years. 'There's something going on in that house,' she says balefully. 'Her father will be birling in his grave, poor man.'

Jeremiah stands back as the coachman closes the door. Mrs Grieg leans out.

'You were protesting, madam?' Jeremiah bates her.

'It's evil nonsense,' the old woman spits. 'The American slaves regained their liberty long ago. It's done with.'

'Mr Douglass's campaign, you mean?' Jeremiah says. 'I'm surprised to hear you say that. I thought everybody supported his cause. It's in the papers, you know.'

Mrs Grieg looks as if she might have a conniption. She knocks on the box icily and the coachman drives on. Jeremiah chortles. The old woman is like a character from a penny dreadful, though not as popular, he thinks as he heads for James Morrison's, where they sell pies at the counter. He must keep his strength up. His plans to remove Charlotte's collection are not yet complete.

Chapter Thirty-Three

The following Monday, Albany Urquhart sits at his desk with a cup of coffee and a balloon of brandy. The old lawyer never eats until noon. Behind him the window has been opened two inches and the sound of carriages up and down Bath Street is like breaking waves, punctuated by the shouts of costermongers engaged in their morning rounds and the high-pitched flirtation of kitchen maids sent up to the pavement to buy Ayrshire tatties and spring leeks and fresh butter from Renfrew.

Old Mr Urquhart has always thought Murray would marry but hoped his son would mirror his own experience and choose a rich and distant spouse. Murray's feelings for a woman who comes from nowhere and has no people nor any kind of dowry baffle him.

The Urquharts rarely engage in anything as open as a fight, but he and Murray have been spatting the last two days. The boy is determined, he'll give him that. 'This woman comes from nowhere,' Albany found himself repeating. But Murray is not minded to care, it seems.

'It's not where she comes from, Pa, it is who she is,' he insisted, listing several accomplishments that Albany does not associate with ladies, such as the setting up of photographic studios and having an excellent artistic eye. The boy keeps saying he wants to make a family of his own. Albany has never seen his son in such a state and woke this morning to the realisation that he must meet the woman at least. Murray's parting shot the night before was to shout that he did not like lying to Charlotte Nicholl either. 'It's the wrong thing, Pa,' he raised his voice. 'She deserves to know. It's her family.' Albany, older and wiser (or so he believes) can cite a multitude of cases where people found out the truth about their families and never recovered. But he did not say so as Murray stormed out of the room. Neither of the Urquharts got much sleep last night.

Now the clerk knocks on the office door and announces Dr Grieg is waiting. Urquhart & Son has executed the doctor's business for decades but Albany has to entertain that his old friend might have come to remove his custom. He recalls the fire in Grieg's eyes as he shouted through his carriage window the other evening. He raises his hand to beckon the doctor in. 'Good morning, Forbes.'

'Good morning, Albany.'

It feels like stalemate already.

'How can I help?' Albany tries.

Dr Grieg's eyebrows ripple. It is a tiny movement; a sign of distress. 'It's about James Nicholl,' he says. 'The thing is that I invested money . . .' the doctor cannot quite get out the words, 'in one of James's ventures.'

Urquhart motions towards a chair. 'Please, sit down. Would you like brandy?'

'Brandy in the morning. Whisky after noon,' the doctor says. It was this sage medical advice that had resulted in Urquhart's choice of breakfast tipple many years ago. Murray does not adhere to his father's customary liquid breakfast. Perhaps, Albany muses, that is the problem with the lad.

'You've seen my constitution right over the years,' the lawyer says. He pours two brandies and hands one to the doctor. 'Now tell me, what venture and how much did you invest?'

Grieg's eyebrows shift again, this time more dramatically, like wee grey mice. 'It's a matter of 160 sovereigns.'

'Investment in . . .?'

Grieg sips nervously. 'I have a certain predilection, Albany. I'm not proud of myself.' The doctor looks, on the one hand, as if he might burst into tears, Urquhart thinks. But on the other, he also appears unaccountably eager. 'It's Jezebel,' he manages to get out. 'The hure from the bible.'

Urquhart tries not to smile. He has had years of practice. 'You mean a painting of Jezebel?'

'Naked,' Grieg admits. 'Nicholl said the harlot could double my money in a year. Mrs Grieg has no idea. I used cash from her endowment. James said it would be back to me by now. I can't cover it much longer.'

This is the closest Urquhart has come to finding Lennox's hoard. By his estimation, knowing what the entirety has sold for, Nicholl would have more than doubled his friend's investment and been in a position to keep a cut for himself. 'Do you know where James kept the painting?' he asks, as if casually.

Grieg shakes his head. 'It was close, he said. I always thought the basement of his house.'

Urquhart sighs. 'I know of the matter,' he admits. 'The item is included in the manifest of James's estate. We've been searching for it in fact, though I didn't know you had an interest.'

This emboldens the doctor. 'Nicholl's estate owes me money. I can't bring it up with Charlotte,' he says huffily. 'Especially not now she has fallen out with my wife. But it must be settled.'

Urquhart arches his fingers. From long experience, the doctor knows this means he should listen to what Albany is about to say.

'The estate only owes you the money if you can prove your claim,' he says. 'Do you have a contract?'

Grieg bangs his fist on the desk. 'In a matter of this nature? Of course not. James was utterly reliable.'

'James is dead,' Urquhart says flatly. 'If we find the painting, I'll honour the debt. But I'll not pay you out of hand from Charlotte's funds. She has no idea, as you say. Nor should she. Have you no notion where he kept the painting?'

Grieg shakes his head. 'He showed it to me in his study, propped on the mantle. One night after dinner. I couldn't believe my eyes.'

'Think,' Urquhart urges him. 'Did he say nothing else about it?'

Grieg concentrates. 'It's by a French painter.'

Urquhart licks his lips, a sign of his annoyance. 'And he kept it close, you say?'

'He said he'd look after her for me and I could come to see her whenever I wanted.'

'And did you?'

Grieg nods, patently ashamed.

'And when you did, it was always in the study?'

'At night. After the ladies had retired. I'd send a note before dinner and he'd reply by return.'

Urquhart lets slip the ghost of a smile. The image of Grieg rushing across Blythswood Square to ogle a naked hure paints an amusing picture. Better than the painting that is missing – in his estimation anyway.

'Leave it with me,' Urquhart sighs. 'It's interesting what you say about it being kept close.'

Grieg downs the rest of his brandy and gets to his feet.

'Forbes,' Urquhart adds, 'I know you have strong views on this matter with the Kirk . . .'

Doctor Grieg makes a humphing noise. Urquhart continues. 'Perhaps it's best for people in glasshouses not to throw stones. Charlotte Nicholl shouldn't be made a pariah. My son neither. You've known them both since they were children.'

Grieg takes this in. It is not exactly a threat. 'I'll leave the matter of the money with you,' he says. 'But my wife is most put out about the way Charlotte has behaved.'

Urquhart tries to shrug but he is not supple enough. He has enough on Forbes Grieg to sink him. 'Well,' he says, 'I only wanted to mention it.'

Once the doctor is gone Albany downs the last of his brandy. 'Where did you hide it, James?' he mutters under his breath as he pens a missive to call off Big Mungo McVey from searching ware-houses on the river, which is what Urquhart had put him to out of sheer desperation. He pulls on his greatcoat. Outside he decides to walk, for his carriage might be spotted. It is a fine enough morning and down the hill he sweeps into McLaren's Hotel and asks for Lennox. A boy shows him to the second floor. When he knocks at the door, a young man answers in a state of sartorial disarray quite at odds with the hour, for it is almost midday. His waistcoat is open and his sleeves rolled. He smells faintly of cedar-wood soap.

'I'm looking for Mr Lennox,' Urquhart announces.

'He's gone to the dock,' the young man says. At Urquhart's hesita-tion, he adds, 'Would you like to wait?'

Inside, the room is plush, if untidy. An apple lies half-eaten on the mantle and the dregs of a bottle of wine. 'I'm Mr Urquhart,' the lawyer announces.

'Jeremiah Catto,' Jeremiah puts out his hand.

'Forgive me, are you a relation of Mr Lennox?' Urquhart tries.

Jeremiah thinks on his feet. 'His private secretary.' Urquhart takes in Jeremiah's appearance. 'We were up late. Working,' Jeremiah says by way of explanation as he buttons his waistcoat and puts on his jacket which had been hurled onto one of the chairs in the throes of passion. He brushes up both well and quickly, he knows from long experience.

'Has your master found the paintings?' Urquhart enquires.

Jeremiah controls his features. This is interesting. He clears his throat.

'It's all right to talk of it.' The old lawyer lays out his credentials. 'I'm contracted to find the damn things. Lennox came to me, in fact, to do so.'

Jeremiah's brain is working like an abacus. He has been trying to find a suitable buyer, seeking the location of the gentleman's club in Edinburgh he had heard of, but all he has turned up is that it is somewhere near St Giles. He has also been considering buying a

ticket to the opera and finding a mark among the boxes at the interval. He has a good deal of practice in spotting both the richest and
the most deviant persons in any room. And then this gentleman just
walks in and declares that Lennox is after some missing paintings.
Jeremiah must ascertain more detail immediately, he thinks, for if
they're the same lost paintings, wouldn't it be marvellous?

'It's such a mystery,' he says. 'One would think the content would
make them easier to track down, eh?' His eyes twinkle as he waits to
see what Mr Urquhart will do. If he acknowledges the nature of the
collection, then it must be the same one. How many lost collections
can there be in Glasgow of such dubious content?

Albany thinks this is a strange fellow, but then Lennox lives in
London. 'Despite what your master found when he went poking
about, I suspect the collection may be hidden in the Nicholls' house
on Blythswood Square after all. Or close to it.'

Jeremiah has a flashback to being trapped in Charlotte's cupboard.
Then he feels the sting of success. Lennox has been seeking what he
wants to dispone. It is perfect. 'Really?' he manages.

Urquhart continues. 'James Nicholl had access to the paintings
on short notice,' he explains. 'He kept them nearby. Tell Mr Lennox
we are getting closer.'

'I will, sir,' Jeremiah promises.

Urquhart looks round the room. Lennox intrigues him. 'What's
your master's business at the dock?' he enquires, deciding to tarry.

'He's meeting the captain of *The Rodney*,' Jeremiah says. Lennox
had said so as he left.

Mr Urquhart's eyelid flickers. It is an unaccustomed movement.
'That's a naval vessel,' the old solicitor says. 'Ninety-one guns.'

Jeremiah takes in this information. He had no idea. 'He had
papers to collect,' he ventures.

'And he didn't send you?'

Jeremiah gives a little shrug. 'He doesn't always dispatch me about
his business, sir. Mr Lennox is most particular. Perhaps he's making
arrangements to transport the paintings once your job is complete.'

Urquhart considers this fanciful. It is unlikely the Royal Navy is at Mr Lennox's disposal. Still, Lennox has not said a word, not one, about who he works for and the exact nature of his employment. 'You must be looking forward to going home, Mr Catto,' he says.

Jeremiah pictures himself in front of the newly renovated Buckingham Palace, which is the only building in London he is familiar with. He saw an engraving of it once in a magazine though he never dreamed he might see it in person. 'I'll give Mr Lennox your message,' he promises airily. Then he crosses the room and opens the door. Urquhart departs, and once he is gone Jeremiah flings himself onto the sofa. This is a rare stroke of luck. Miss Nicholl's cupboard is why Lennox is in Glasgow. I've found my buyer, he thinks. I'm practically living with him. It is too perfect. He will not have to endure the opera, after all.

Chapter Thirty-Four

Before Lennox returns to his suite, Jeremiah receives a missive from Charlotte Nicholl. She has secured the help of both her neighbour and her housekeeper and, she says, the collection might be removed by the rear of the property next door through a coach house on the mews. She is making arrangements to excuse her staff. They must manage it after dark, she underlines. Not too late. The neighbour has set the date that suits him: Friday.

At the table Jeremiah dips Lennox's pen in brown ink and lists what he needs. Boxes and canvas and two carts, as well as at least two porters. All these are available at the theatre and might be purloined at a price. The set movers are like donkeys and accustomed to working all hours. He considers how long it might take. Charlotte wishes the removal in darkness, but everything has to be packed properly. Nothing can be damaged. He pens a note suggesting that Friday night will be fine. Then he realises he is hungry and rings for mutton pie and a jug of beer. It is brought up just as Lennox arrives.

'How did you get on at *The Rodney*?' Jeremiah asks.

Lennox removes his hat and gloves and watches the bellboy lay the tray on the table. 'I'll require a bottle of Rhenish,' he says. 'And cheese. None of this muck.'

'Yes, sir,' the boy says and disappears out the door.

'You're fancy!' Jeremiah teases as he bites into the pie.

'Don't you have work to go to?' Lennox retorts and musses Jeremiah's hair before taking possession of his seat, halfway between the window and the fire. He lights a cigar.

'It might be that I'm at work now,' Jeremiah posits cheekily. 'And this is my office.'

Lennox regards him. He did not expect a shakedown, at least not yet. Jeremiah's body is taut as a statue. Beautiful men always require payment. 'You're so symmetrical,' the older man says wistfully. 'Get up. Turn round.' Jeremiah does so with his pie in his hand. Lennox then catches sight of himself in the mirror, the antithesis of symmetrical, his face thick-skinned and lopsided, his body burly and old.

Jeremiah follows Lennox's gaze and understands. 'Fuck symmetry,' he laughs, full-throated. 'Fuck it.' And he kisses Lennox full on the lips for the first time, despite everything else they have done. The older man's mouth is fleshy and he tastes of whisky. Toasting a deal on the deck of *The Rodney* perhaps. For a moment the two of them move as if reaching deep inside each other. Then Jeremiah pulls back. Lennox pauses. 'You'll miss me then when I go?'

'You should know I will.' Jeremiah returns to the table and pours a glass of beer. 'I've been thinking I'd like to see London. You've had a few weeks of my town, perhaps I should see yours.'

'You have no manners. You ought to wait for an invitation,' Lennox says.

'Invite me then.'

'In London my time is not my own. I serve my master more directly.'

'Yes, yes,' Jeremiah says dismissively. 'I'll make my own sport. I'll find a job. There are theatres, are there not? Photographers? I wouldn't wish to sit with you all day. We don't do so here.'

'I can't judge you for wanting to quit this godforsaken place,' Lennox says.

'Godforsaken place?' Jeremiah gestures round the lush hotel room. 'Glasgow is the second city of Empire. What do you mean?'

Lennox sighs. 'You're too forward,' he says. 'Asking for an invitation.'

'Too forward, am I?' Jeremiah's gaze falls to the buttons on the older man's cashmere breeches. 'Too forward,' he repeats. 'Don't you want to take me home? Do you think I'll be dissatisfied there? Or are you ashamed and think I'm not worthy of the capital?'

Lennox hesitates. He has not allowed himself to think of having Jeremiah with him longer than the duration of his trip. It is not that he doesn't want it, but rather that there are complications. Jeremiah does not yet know who his master is and that always causes what Lennox's mother used to refer to as 'a skatoosh'. He imagines however that Jeremiah would like London. 'Drury Lane is lined with playhouses where you might find work,' he concedes. 'And as for photographers, there are a scramble.'

'In that case, I'll not moon about waiting for your attention, will I?' Jeremiah quips.

'Will you not?' Lennox looks directly into Jeremiah's eyes. There has been, he realises, a change in the balance. 'What's happened?'

Jeremiah realises he must get to the nub. 'I've come into knowledge of a certain collection which may interest you.'

Lennox shifts as if the velvet pillow beneath him is not comfortable. He is all ears. Jeremiah continues. 'I understand you're looking for some paintings. Some carvings. Statues and the like.'

'Where did you hear that?'

'A friend,' Jeremiah lies blithely, for what else can he say? 'The items were hidden, as I understand it. They were in the keeping of a gentleman who is no longer with us. That's why you came to Glasgow, isn't it?'

'Where is the collection?' Lennox asks, straight.

'You wish to buy it then?'

Lennox shakes his head. 'It's already sold, Jemmy. The gentleman did the deal before he died.' This is not entirely true as the transaction was not completed, but Lennox is not going to get into negotiations over something his client effectively owns. Especially not with Jeremiah. 'There is, however, a fee in locating the collection, if it's the one I'm looking for,' he adds.

Jeremiah smiles. It is unlikely there are two stashes of paintings of naked ladies, prints of couples engaged in coitus, marble goddesses unclothed and orgies carved out of ivory – the similar property of two recently deceased gentlemen. Glasgow is not so large nor, sadly, so degenerate. The Dear Green Place. God's own city. Jeremiah finishes the pie and licks his fingers. 'A fee?'

'A generous fee,' Lennox assures him.

'How generous?'

'You can procure it, then?'

'For this generous fee plus the carriage, I can accomplish that.'

'Discreetly?'

Jeremiah decides he will pack the items himself. The porters will not know what they are moving. 'Aye,' he says. 'Where would you like it sent?'

Lennox does not take long to consider. '*The Rodney*,' he says. 'When can you deliver?'

Jeremiah feels a twinge of sadness that when he dispatches the collection, he delivers the reason Lennox will leave. The old man seems keen on going and has not said he would like Jeremiah to come with him. 'Who is your employer?' he asks, his instincts excellent as ever.

Lennox's gaze becomes especially inscrutable. 'You know I can't divulge that.'

It was worth a try. Jeremiah shrugs. 'The removal must be done at night,' he says, getting to business. 'There are arrangements to be made but I might manage it at the end of this week. Though you still have not told me my fee.' He cuts to the heart of the matter.

'Fifty sovereigns?' Lennox hazards.

It is a fortune, but Jeremiah laughs dismissively. 'You're wasting my time. I can't be bought so cheap. The collection has value far more than that and I'm your only way to it. I'd thought to be more of a broker working on commission. How much is it worth? In total?'

There is a sharp rap at the door and the boy arrives with Lennox's wine and cheese. The men are armies standing down while the tray is left. Lennox gets up and pours himself a glass, before taking a draw on his cigar. It does not surprise him that Jeremiah is no fool. 'You know I'll not tell you the value. You must tell me, what did you have in mind?'

'Considerably more than 50,' Jeremiah says. He has honed his negotiation skills over the years on gentlemen who do not want their wives to know about their night-time activities. Albeit this will be more money than he has ever extracted before, and this time for a legitimate service. 'We must consider the discretion required,' he delivers a long-accustomed line. 'The cost of the removal. The person selling it offered me 25 per cent of the value,' he adds.

'Who do you think is selling it, Jeremiah?' Lennox's gaze is sharp as the point on a well-kept foil. When Jeremiah does not answer Lennox continues. 'You thought to charge at both ends, did you? That will not happen. It is sold already. Who do you wish to work for here?'

Jeremiah cannot say who owns the collection for in doing so he will make himself redundant. Lennox might walk up to Blythswood Square and treat with Miss Nicholl himself. He will remake the deal, he decides. 'All right,' he says. 'We might change to a fee basis if you like, but we will name it in guineas.'

'Twenty-five per cent,' Lennox chortles. 'I shall not permit that. Nor tell you the value either. But, all right – ask me what you want as a fee. A flat fee, mind. A generous one. In guineas. And when we agree it, I shall undertake that it will come to you.'

Jeremiah eyes him. He was ambitious with Miss Nicholl perhaps. 'Shall we say 500 guineas then? And 50 guineas up front?'

Lennox lets out a puff of air but he does not say no. It is not an entirely unreasonable fee when it comes to it. The deal is worth thousands. 'I have a manifest of the items,' he says.

Jeremiah's stomach turns over. Five hundred guineas is enough to retire upon. He realises that 25 per cent of the sale must be a higher figure, but he understands the difference between ambition and greed. His arrangement with Charlotte never seemed quite real. 'We're agreed then,' he says. 'It'll take a few days to organise. The porters to engage and so forth.'

'A few days?'

'Aye. I expect to manage the removal this Friday night. Everything must be properly packed, you see.'

'How do I know you have access to the goods?' Lennox asks.

Jeremiah reaches into his jacket pocket and pulls out the gold coin with the lips. 'Is this on your manifest?'

Lennox's eyes harden. 'It is. Why do you have it?'

Jeremiah just stares. Lennox's expression speaks volumes. 'Don't fret.' Jeremiah puts the coin into the old man's hand. He treats life as a game and is disquieted by Lennox's earnestness, though, he thinks, perhaps the old man is holding back because he does not trust him. Men like Lennox are tumbled for money every day. Jeremiah knows because he has done it often enough. He needs to earn the old man's trust now. 'I knew I might have to prove myself,' he says. 'But I have everything you're looking for, or at least I know where to get it. Aphrodite and Cleopatra and some naughty editions of Mr Burns. It's all safe and sound. I'll deliver everything.'

Lennox closes his fingers over the coin. 'Very well,' he says and goes to his travelling case. He pulls out the manifest and a purse of sovereigns. 'I will deduct the value of anything missing from your fee,' he says, laying the paper on the table and pushing the purse across the surface with the efficiency of a dealer at a French casino. 'Do we have a deal?'

Briefly Jeremiah peruses the manifest. It is comprehensive. 'I'll bring you everything that's there,' he counters. 'That's the deal and you must trust me on it. I've no intention of stealing anything.'

Lennox's jaw tightens and Jeremiah softens by return. 'You're changing me, sir. Making me an honest man,' he admits. It's true. He feels it. He cannot see that he will ever grow bored of Mr Lennox. His previous liaisons with gentlemen now seem too simple. 'I'm sure other fellows you have felt for have treated you falsely, but I will not.' Jeremiah offers his hand and Lennox shakes it, then kisses him.

Chapter Thirty-Five

Friday morning, early

There is a great deal to be managed at Blythswood Square and none of the servants can know of it. There are seven staff living in besides Mrs Cullen, and Miss Nicholl has contrived to send them all away from first thing Friday until Saturday morning. She furnishes them an extra shilling each. Franny will return to Ayrshire with Cook, who will go to her mother, a woman of 80, living in a tithe cottage at Beith. The rest of the staff will be scattered about Glasgow, excepting the coachman who is given leave to take the bay and ride to his sister in Cumnock. As they go, the footman is heard to mumble, 'A shilling will not last long,' but the maids at least are glad of it. They are told Miss Nicholl must sort through her father's things and wishes to be alone. It is not entirely a lie.

Mrs Cullen sets an ashet of ham sandwiches in the dining room with a plate of cheese and enough Burgundy to last a week. 'And a jug of fresh milk that won't spoil till tomorrow,' she adds. Charlotte notes that Mrs Cullen cannot cook. But it is fine. They will picnic. She closes the lower shutters in the study, the morning sunshine streaming through the panes above as if extra light and warmth have been corralled up the way. Charlotte thinks how different things are now the Griegs and Reverend Patterson no longer call. She smiles at

Mrs Cullen. It feels magical to be alone. 'We shall begin,' she says, efficiently opening the door of the hidden room and propping it with a log from the basket. Mrs Cullen pushes the study furniture against the wall and carefully the women ferry out the items, one by one, propping the paintings against the bookcases, laying the smaller carvings on the desk and piling books onto the chairs.

At eight of the clock they breakfast on sandwiches washed down with milk. A nursery meal as Charlotte has it. 'I remember you in the nursery, miss,' Mrs Cullen says. The conversation however is interrupted by someone at the door. Charlotte peers on tiptoe through the half-shuttered glass.

'Jeremiah Catto,' she announces with relief as she brushes the crumbs from her fingers. 'I'll go.' It's thrilling to see to things herself. There is something empowering about it. As she opens the door, it comes to her that she could do anything: play hopscotch in the hall-way, dance like a Highlander round the dining room, venture below stairs to rummage in the pantry or climb to the top of the house and peer into the maids' rooms and onto the roof to where they smoke on the slates. Today she is bringing out her father's pictures as if she has no shame. Until now, it has weighed heavily.

Behind Jeremiah, a cart is loaded with empty wooden crates, bolsters of canvas and a box of tools. Ellory Mann jumps down. 'Good morning,' she says as the driver tethers the horse. A boy sits on the back, his legs dangling. Jeremiah checks his companions cannot see into the study, then instructs them to unload. 'Quickly,' he says. 'Into the hallway.' They jump to it, used to quick changes on stage. Charlotte keeps her eye on the street through the sidelights. Across the square two carriages trundle past. She imagines the occupants notice the cart but consider it like any other delivery. People work all hours.

Once everything is in the hallway, Jeremiah sends the boys away. Ellory closes the front door and opens the study. 'You've started,' she says, inspecting the stacks.

'I'm in the habit of seeing to my own business now,' says Charlotte. 'Like you.'

Jeremiah peruses the items. 'The canvas is to cover the paintings and there are boxes for the books. I'll frame the statues with wood and cover them too,' he says.

Charlotte's fingers flutter. It has felt like fun, but now Jeremiah is here and the plan must be executed, a curl of shame opens in her stomach. 'Nobody will see?' she checks.

'Not till it's unpacked again. The lads will return at sunset to load it,' Jeremiah confirms.

'And the purchaser?'

'A collector as keen on his anonymity as you are on yours. He'd already treated with your father. The money will arrive at your solicitors as an outstanding transaction on your father's estate.'

Charlotte finds an edge of the chair to perch upon. 'I see,' she says, thinking Murray Urquhart must know her father was selling the collection then. His monologue about curating art comes into sharp focus.

'The man has been searching for the collection,' Jeremiah continues.

'Mr Lennox.' Charlotte pieces it together.

Jeremiah stares. 'You know Lennox?'

'He tried to hoodwink me. He searched the study but found nothing. Will the solicitor pay your cut?' she asks.

'The buyer. I will not cost you a penny now, Miss Nicholl,' he says stoutly.

Charlotte's eyes land on Ellory. 'I don't expect any money.' Ellory raises her hands. 'I'm here out of friendship, Charlotte.'

Charlotte smiles. 'Thank you. Both of you,' she says.

'We must get on.' Jeremiah removes his jacket and ties a tan leather apron round his waist. Then he lays the tools in an orderly line on the desk: a hammer, two boxes of nails, a knife to cut the canvas and a ball of twine. 'You might stack the books and prints into boxes,' he suggests. 'I'll nail the lids once you're done. The small carvings can be stowed in the packing cases and protected with straw.' Charlotte looks over her shoulder as if he is speaking to somebody else. Jeremiah laughs. 'It'll be quicker if you help,' he says.

They set to it. Once the books are cleared and the ornaments packed, Mrs Cullen starts helping Jeremiah, handing him nails and cutting the cloth to the right sizes as he tacks the canvas in place, as tidy as hemming a gown. Charlotte offers Ellory a drink. 'We've Burgundy or milk,' she says as they cross the hall.

Ellory chooses milk. 'I have a deal of news,' she admits, 'now we have a moment.'

Charlotte sits in front of the window with the light behind her. 'You look well. Is it your grape salve?'

Ellory squints across the table. The sunshine forms a halo round her friend. It is like speaking to an angel. 'I know I can trust you with my secrets,' she says.

'You've more than one?'

Ellory takes a breath before she confides her news. 'I'm to be married to Murray Urquhart. I know he asked you, but now he has asked me and I said yes.'

Charlotte's face lights. 'He only asked me out of pity. Ellory, this is wonderful news. But what of your work? Your studio?'

'I shall keep it,' Ellory says. 'Murray likes what I do.'

Charlotte's brow peaks. It is an unusual arrangement. She can tell there's more.

Ellory sips her milk. Her stomach flutters. 'I have another confidence. My nephew, my sister's boy, has come to live with me,' she admits. 'My sister is dead. Mr Urquhart and I plan to adopt him after the wedding. To be a family.'

Charlotte's face lights. Murray has been busy. 'Mrs Urquhart,' she tries the name. The last time she used it was to address Murray's mother, a lady, she recalls, who was quietly unhappy. But then, no wonder.

Ellory covers her eyes. 'Mrs Urquhart,' she repeats.

'What's the boy's name?'

'Robert. Robbie. Jane, my maid, is looking after him. I'm not as accustomed to children as she is. She has brothers and sisters at home.'

Ellory hesitates. 'Are you shocked, Charlotte? He is illegitimate, you see. My sister never married.'

Charlotte adopts an inscrutable expression, casting her eyes in the direction of the study. 'You know what we're doing today,' she says flatly. 'I'm done with respectability.'

Ellory admits the point. 'Then will you be my maid of honour? Will you stand with me at the wedding?'

Charlotte has never been asked before. She has attended several wedding breakfasts; frothy affairs. Not being the marrying sort, she considered the excitement staged. Now she pictures Murray and Ellory together she can see the rightness of it. Two unconventional people creating something new. 'Family,' she whispers. This may be the closest she'll come now. 'Don't you have cousins in Edinburgh?'

Ellory dissembles. 'They're not on my side.'

'I'd be honoured to attend you.'

Ellory has the sudden memory of feeling like this as a girl, with Nora. Of standing together. 'Thank you,' she says. 'Murray considers you the closest he has to a sister.'

Charlotte considers this. 'Me too,' she realises. 'We were both only children, I suppose.'

Jeremiah is still packing when the women return. He scarcely stops hammering long enough to eat three sandwiches set on the desk beside him. In the afternoon Charlotte and Ellory stack the paintings by the inner door. Mrs Cullen sees to the boxes and then sets off to check the Howarth house. Mrs Howarth and her daughters left last night for Arran, but the remaining staff will not be excused until later in the afternoon. Charlotte watches the housekeeper out of the window, climbing the kitchen stairs and disappearing into the basement next door. She has felt watched by her neighbours but now she realises a great many things can go on in a house with nobody being the least aware. The eyes at the window simply make you monitor yourself, she thinks. An ingenious system.

As she turns back into the room, Charlotte puts up her hand as Jeremiah reaches for a small painting with a gilded frame. 'I wish to keep that,' she points at the fleshy nude.

Jeremiah props the image with his foot.

'It'll be a memento,' she says. 'It's Ariadne in love with Theseus. I've been thinking I ought to keep one picture to remind me. Something small.'

'Lennox has bought the whole collection,' Jeremiah says.

Charlotte squints at Ariadne. Her eyes shift to a naked, furious Medusa. She definitely does not want to hold onto that one.

'Lennox has a manifest. If you wish to keep that you must write me a note or I will be held responsible,' Jeremiah explains.

Charlotte picks up the painting. 'All right,' she says and puts it in the hallway. She will take it up to her dressing room later. Then she scribbles a few lines at the desk.

By six they are ready. Twilight descends on the gardens, the pigeons cooing. Jeremiah checks his pocket watch. He likes the gloaming; it marks the onset of his day for he is a night owl, not a lark. The cart will arrive soon. Another three hours at most, then everything can be delivered to *The Rodney*. Outside, on the square, he lights his pipe. This moment's respite will sustain him better than sandwiches. The gaslights are flaming but he tarries out of their reach, on the other side of the street, contemplating the splendour of the Nicholl mansion. One day, he decides, he will live in such a place. He is about to knock out his pipe on the railings when Mrs Grieg rounds the corner, her black satin cape glossy as a raven's wing. She is carrying a basket as if to make a delivery and squints into the darkness as she gets closer. 'You!' she says. 'What are you doing here?'

'A fitting.' Jeremiah knows this is unconvincing.

'In the evening?' The doctor's wife peers at him. She sniffs. 'You smell like a navvy.' Her eyes cast to the house, the lamps lit in the study, their light sneaking round the shutters' edge. A single candle in the dining room. Every other window is dark. 'Something's not right,' she says.

He makes to object, but the old lady crosses the road smartly and rings the bell. Thus summoned, Charlotte appears at the door. 'Mrs Grieg,' she says, tight-lipped.

'What're you up to now, Charlotte Nicholl?'

'I'm clearing my father's things. Not that it's anything to do with you.'

'With your tailor?' Mrs Grieg glances at Jeremiah. 'You think folk are fools.'

Charlotte feels a sting of fury. 'You old busybody! What do you want?'

Mrs Grieg's anger overspills. She pushes past the girl and into the hall. The door to the study is closed. The hallway is the same as it always was, except for the painting, sitting on the chiffonier. Ariadne. She picks it up. 'Your father would be ashamed,' she spits.

Charlotte only just manages to hold back from saying her father was, as far as she can tell, not nearly ashamed enough.

Summoned by the women's raised voices, Ellory appears and Mrs Grieg swings round. 'I can see this household's gone downhill. You're the woman who took a calotype of that dreadful man.' She is unable to manage the courtesy of naming Mr Douglass. 'I might have known.'

'Ellory's most talented,' Charlotte says.

'Nobody will publish your image,' Mrs Grieg retorts smugly. 'We'll see to that.'

'You've not noticed you're on the losing side, Mrs Grieg.' Charlotte remains calm. 'More people support Mr Douglass than are agin him.'

Charlotte is about to once more eject her father's old friend from her house when Dr Grieg appears in the doorway. 'Good Lord,' he says. 'I'm following you to the MacKenzies, my dear. I thought you were going ahead with the medicine.'

Mrs Grieg lifts the Ariadne. 'Look, Forbes!' she says. 'The depravity of it!'

The doctor's face spasms at the sight of the image. His eyes widen in terror. 'I'd never condone such a thing!' he exclaims. Charlotte thinks this is an odd thing to say as nobody has asked him to.

Mrs Grieg's colour is up. 'You mark my words, Reverend Patterson shall hear of this!'

'God made man in his likeness,' Charlotte says smoothly, taking back the painting. 'And woman too.'

Mrs Grieg looks set to implode. 'That's hure's talk!' she snaps. 'You shame us all!'

'Get out of my house!' Charlotte retorts.

Dr Grieg transmutes suddenly into a surprising voice of reason. 'Come, my dear.'

Mrs Grieg eyes her husband. 'That man outside is not a tailor,' she says. 'We don't back down in Glasgow!'

'Come, now. You're exercising yourself.' The doctor casts his eyes towards the study and suddenly Charlotte understands. It is the men. Do they all know, she wonders? Have they been laughing at her, so proper and buttoned up, while they did whatever they wanted, with only the thinnest of veneers? Her father, Mr Howarth, Dr Grieg and the Urquharts? She will never trust any of them again. 'Out!' she repeats and Dr Grieg tries to huckle his wife onto the street, but she resists, and in the skirmish they push through the study door and knock over one of the wrapped paintings which topples against a boxed statue that in turn flips open to reveal a naked woman kissing another naked woman. Mrs Grieg squeals. 'Is that—?'

'It's a classical statue,' Charlotte says with nary a waver.

Dr Grieg meanwhile considers the wrapped painting that revealed the figures. It is the correct size and the frame juts in the right places. He pulls at the canvas which comes away to reveal his Jezebel.

His wife understands the look of desire on his face. 'Forbes,' she says, narrowing her eyes. The doctor stands suddenly upright. He looks at the piles of paintings and boxes, realising the extent of what James Nicholl achieved. And he only ever saw one image. He grabs Charlotte's arm and drags her to the foot of the stairs away from his wife. 'James took my money. Urquhart thought it lost,' he hisses. 'That painting is mine.'

Charlotte regards the doctor candidly. 'Nothing's lost, sir. My father sold his collection before he died. You have no right here.'

'I gave him 160 sovereigns,' the doctor objects. 'I've not slept since he died.'

On the threshold of the study, Mrs Grieg looks like a black balloon about to burst. She glares at her husband, then bundles the basket over her arm and stalks out of the door. The doctor stares after her. 'Oh god,' he says. 'Did she hear me?'

Charlotte shrugs. 'You must contract your business through Mr Urquhart, sir,' she says, adding, 'You had better go after your wife.' The doctor stands frozen in some confusion and a little fear as he takes in what he has done. Then he scuttles away.

After that, speed becomes of the essence. Mrs Cullen runs to Mr Howarth to open the connecting door and they work, all hands together, to ferry everything to the other house. The carts arrive, the horses kept in harness in the Howarths' mews. The boxes and covered paintings are stacked in the Howarths' hallway now, the boys about to take it out the back to secure it on the cart with tarpaulin, when, at a distance, they hear the bell at Charlotte Nicholl's front door. Everyone stands straight. Mrs Cullen makes the sign of the cross, then stands wide-eyed, as if she cannot believe what she has just done. Charlotte takes her hand. 'We'll go,' she says. 'It's probably the Griegs again.' Ellory follows them, closing the double doors and the bookcase behind. She and Charlotte pull the study chairs into place while Mrs Cullen answers the bell. Ellory's heart is racing.

Charlotte, however, finds she is made of sterner stuff. 'The Griegs will not succeed in bullying me,' she says. 'I've had enough.'

But the Griegs have not come back. Charlotte has just lit the lamp when the housekeeper shows in Reverend Patterson, followed by two other men Charlotte recognises as elders of the Kirk. She thinks that they have the air of dogs on a dank day. 'Charlotte Nicholl!' Patterson thunders. 'What have you done?'

'Reverend.' Charlotte hides her hands behind her back for they are suddenly shaking. Her heart however remains stout. 'What do you mean?'

Patterson looks round. 'The doctor's wife said there was depravity here.' She thinks he sounds hopeful. 'We've come for your own good, girl.'

'My own good?' Charlotte's hands stop shaking as her temper flares. 'I'm no longer part of your congregation, sir,' she reminds him.

Patterson ignores this. 'A woman living alone runs against all decency. Against the law,' he rants. 'This house might as well be a brothel!'

'Do you see something awry in my house?' Charlotte asks calmly.

Patterson momentarily stiffens. Mrs Grieg promised chaos. A regular Sodom and Gomorrah, but it's surprisingly ordered in Mr Nicholl's old study. 'Mrs Grieg saw,' he objects.

'Mrs Grieg is an old lady with a vivid imagination.' Charlotte gets up as if she is scolding a child in the nursery. 'She saw a painting of my father's, of Ariadne. The lady is wearing very little, I admit. She was from Minos, you see.' The two men standing behind Patterson display disapproving expressions. 'Why don't I show you?' Charlotte says and brushes past them into the hall.

She lifts Ariadne from the chiffonier.

'There!' Patterson splutters but they all know the painting, at 18 inches square, is not enough to damn anybody. 'And your staff is sent away.' The minister scrapes for evidence. 'There was a man. A tailor. Most irregular.'

'Mrs Cullen was here,' Charlotte continues. Mrs Cullen nods to confirm it. 'And my friend Miss Mann.' Ellory gives a shallow curtsy. 'And yes, a tailor,' Charlotte admits. 'We spent the day clearing my father's wardrobe. The man said he might buy Papa's old clothes. I feared to be upset with the staff about. I'm still bereaved, you see. I thought to donate the money to the poor,' she adds, 'now I'm a Quaker, and I'm sure you're aware that Quakers are most practical.

It seemed wrong to keep Papa's old things when they might be of use to somebody.' She does not smile at her dry little joke.

One of the gentlemen peers round Patterson. 'A Quaker?' he says disapprovingly. 'That's an odd choice, Miss Nicholl.'

'Disagreement is allowed between churches, sir,' Charlotte dismisses him. 'I'm not the only one to quit, as I'm sure you know. I'm sorry Mrs Grieg disquieted you. She thought the boxes of Father's clothes contained more paintings perhaps.'

'Poor old thing,' Ellory cuts in. 'She did seem distressed.'

'She's not here, is she?' Charlotte adds, as if this denotes Mrs Grieg might know she was wrong, which the old lady has certainly never done, not in all her life.

'I knew your father well,' the gentleman behind Reverend Patterson says. 'I cannae see he'd own a piece such as this Ariadne.'

Charlotte manages not to laugh. 'It surprised me too,' she says lightly. 'We found it in his dressing room. Perhaps,' she adds, her confidence growing, 'you ought to ask Dr Grieg about my father's state of mind. But if there's hysteria anywhere, gentlemen, it's not in this house.'

The men stand like strange black herons marooned on a stretch of river.

'Well,' says Charlotte, 'as I'm no longer your congregant, Reverend, I think it's fitting you should go.' The men shift and Mrs Cullen opens the door.

'Goodnight,' Charlotte calls cheerily as she dispatches the elders onto the square. 'You know your way to the Griegs, don't you?'

Patterson glowers but they walk away from the Nicholl house and the Howarths'. That is the main thing.

'Charlotte, you amaze me,' Ellory lets out as if the words are a sigh.

Charlotte laughs. 'I've had enough Glasgow nonsense,' she says. 'All these overbearing men.' The women hover by the sidelights and wait till the elders are gone, then they open the cupboard and sneak through. At the rear, the goods are secured and covered with tarpaulin in the mews. Jeremiah and his stage-shifters sit on the cart, as silent as if there's a performance on stage and they must not disturb it.

'You should've seen Miss Nicholl,' Ellory says, low. 'She was magnificent. Do you think you can get away?'

It comes to Jeremiah that some folk don't consider the back entrances nor the byways between the main roads. 'We'll stay clear of Douglas Street and Bath Street,' he says. 'I reckon we'll make it easiest down the back of Sauchiehall. If we take it casual, like.'

Charlotte, Ellory and Mrs Cullen watch as the vehicles recede slowly down the lane. It starts to drizzle. The lamps on the road reflect light off the damp paving stones. In the houses, windows glow like marzipan squares as people dress for dinner and servants ready the tables. The air is scented with roasting meat. The women make their way back through the Howarths' house. 'Thank you,' Charlotte says to Mr Howarth, who locks his door behind them.

On their final sneak through, Charlotte peeks under the covers of Mr Howarth's collection. She is greeted by a gruesome array, which she thinks were the jewelled body parts of saints. Valentine's heart and Catherine's hand, both labelled. Mrs Howarth, being Episcopalian and having an aversion to unnecessary ornamentation, would not approve. But that, Charlotte decides, is Mr Howarth's business. She knows she will never be able to change the privilege men enjoy to possess their secrets.

*

At the dining table Charlotte and Ellory drink Burgundy and eat cheese. 'I feel free,' Charlotte admits. Certainly something of her father is gone now, as if he was hanging in the air these last weeks and a window has been opened. I've nothing to keep in that damned cupboard, she thinks, and is grateful for that. Then they laugh, going over the ins and outs of the day, Dr Grieg and Reverend Patterson. Charlotte offers Ellory a dress for her wedding but Ellory says she'll be wed as herself.

'That's the beauty of it,' she says. A sense of gratitude washes over her that she is here, with her friend. That her future husband knows everything about her. It is almost magical what acceptance can do – that and a little money.

'I have come to a realisation,' she admits. 'I want to print images of people who inspire others. People who change things.' What she means is not the stuffy ministers in Mr Hill's portfolio. What she means is that she can do without Jane's ankles and Miss Sutherland's sauce. It is a dream of course, but that is the point.

'That's a wonderful idea,' Charlotte says.

As they finish their meal, the doorbell rings again. 'Who now?' says Ellory.

Charlotte sneaks to the window and announces, 'Murray Urquhart. This will provide some sport, don't you think?'

Ellory tidies herself demurely and Charlotte takes a swig of Burgundy. 'You'll follow my lead?' she prompts as Mrs Cullen shows him in.

Murray has abandoned his dinner after his father received a note from Dr Grieg that Albany handed silently to his son. The missive scanned like it was written by a madman. The doctor described a scene of devastation at the Nicholl house: naked ladies kissing each other. He claimed Charlotte had stolen his Jezebel and said his wife had called for Reverend Patterson. *MY INVESTMENT MUST BE PROTECTED, URQUHART,* he had scrawled in capitals at the end and underlined it in a way that was reminiscent, Murray thought, of the underlined words in the spiteful note Charlotte had received a few days before. 'You go,' old Mr Urquhart said.

'Is everything all right?' Murray asks now, taking off his hat, damp from running up the street in the rain, thinking it an emergency. 'Grieg said something about Patterson.'

'I believe I'm to congratulate you on your nuptials,' Charlotte replies lightly.

Murray grins. 'It does my heart good to see you ladies together.' He looks round. 'Where is the rest of your staff?' His eyes fall to the plate of cheese and what is left of the sandwiches.

'Half-day,' Charlotte explains. 'Mrs Cullen is looking after us single-handed. Will you join the table?'

'Dr Grieg said there were women about the house. That the minister had been called for.'

Charlotte cocks her head. She is enjoying this now. The fact she is not supposed to speak of anything distasteful for once is working in her favour. 'I can't imagine what you mean,' she says. 'Do you think the doctor's all right? He and Mrs Grieg appear almost deranged in their dotage. It's the matter of Frederick Douglass's campaign, I expect, playing on the old folks' mind. Send back the money,' she adds.

'But Grieg said his wife had sent for Patterson.' Murray ignores her chorus and does not add that Dr Grieg said a good deal more.

Charlotte looks round. 'I'm sure the reverend has more to do than trouble ladies at their dinner. I'm not one of his congregants any longer, thanks to you.'

'But the doctor said . . .' Murray continues, insistent.

'What?'

Murray catches Ellory's eye but she does not betray her friend. 'Charlotte will be my maid of honour,' she says cheerfully. 'Isn't that grand, my dear?'

Murray casts his eyes over the dining room. Through the open door he can see across the hall and into the study. Everything appears as it should be. He searches for the words to ask directly about James Nicholl's collection, but the woman he loves is sitting at the table patiently and Charlotte has her head to one side, examining him. He simply cannot. 'Well, if there's no commotion . . .' he gets out. It certainly does not seem as if a commotion might emerge.

'Miss Mann, I fear for your fiancé's well-being.' Charlotte announces with an intriguing smile.

Ellory's grin is more open. 'Will you not stay, Mr Urquhart?' she offers.

Murray senses he is being set up. He's not a complete fool. 'Cook has baked a fish,' he says. 'I should go back.'

'Good,' Charlotte says. Then, with immaculate timing, 'I believe there's a payment due. From those shares. If you don't mind my bringing up business in the evening. Now you're here.'

'Shares?' Murray repeats.

'Father's shares. The ones that went missing,' she says as if he is a forgetful old codger. 'I think Papa owed Dr Grieg 160 sovereigns from the transaction. It's over my head, Murray. Perhaps that's what the old man was upset about.'

'Perhaps,' Murray says slowly, sensing a way out. They both know, he thinks. And yet they seem quite calm. 'I'll see to it, shall I?' he suggests.

'Don't let us keep you.' Charlotte is loving this. It feels good to get ahead of the men.

'I bid you goodnight then,' Murray says, and the women wait until the door closes before allowing themselves to giggle. He can hear them from the pavement and their merriment makes him smile. They are quite extraordinary, he thinks, and is glad there is no reason to go into the details. The money from the shares, he decides, yes, that is what we shall call it from now on.

*

At the dock, Jeremiah's boys unload straight onto *The Rodney* with the sailors' help. Lennox stands under a candle lamp hoisted by the gangplank in the rain and watches every piece going aboard. Jeremiah hands him the note about Ariadne and Lennox sighs. 'Sellers' regret,' he says. 'It sometimes happens.'

'I'm sorry if it causes you trouble.' Jeremiah means it. 'Everything else on the list is there.'

'I'll take stock,' Lennox tells him. 'Once I'm satisfied, the balance of payment will be made in your name at this bank.' He hands over a card. Jeremiah reads it twice. Child & Co., on Fleet Street.

'This address is in London,' he says flatly.

'Aye,' Lennox confirms. 'You said you'd like to come. We raise anchor on the midnight tide three days hence, on Monday, if you wish it.'

Jeremiah catches the older man's free hand and squeezes.

As he walks back down Carrick Street alone, he listens to the sound of his shoes on the setts. When he left the croft, his feet were soft on the earth, unknown to paved streets until he got to Dundee. Now his whole world is built upon and he is leaving with 450 guineas in a private bank and 47 more in his pocket, for he paid the others in cash, one shiny gold coin each. He flicks a coin between his fingers in the low light and decides he will buy a parting gift for Jane. He will pick something up on his way to the theatre, for it is not yet nine and the curtain has not fallen. The scene-shifters are returning the cart and will come behind. Four hundred and fifty gold coins. He can hardly believe he pulled it off.

Chapter Thirty-Six

The day after the removal, Ellory Mann sets the completed small calotype of Mr Douglass in the glass box at the studio door with a notice explaining the shilling and tuppence charge. Quaker ladies, dressed solemnly, queue down the stairs all afternoon and by evening Ellory has earned more than a pound in her strongbox and two whole shillings towards Mr Douglass's campaign. Half a dozen copies of St Enoch's tree have sold as well and the orders dispatched by delivery boy. Coming from nowhere, she cannot believe she has earned so much in her first month and learned so much too. She does not entirely trust her success. Still, it has kindled a fire in her belly and the money, coupled with Charlotte's steely constitution the day before, has given her the confidence to write to Miss Whigham in Edinburgh asking to take the lady's picture. Murray sends notes daily now, delivered by a boy who runs from Bath Street to St Enoch's Square and back again for tuppence a journey. This morning's reads: *I hope to introduce you to my father soon*, and Ellory knows this may prove the sticking point in their engagement, for the elder Mr Urquhart clearly remains opposed to the match though Murray is engaged on bringing him round.

Once the studio is closed for the evening, she cuts east, past the vinegary tang of a sandy-haired soused-herring boy calling his wares, and heads for the theatre. She wants to pay Jeremiah for his assistance with Mr Douglass and tell him about the success of his idea with the extra pennies towards the cause. 'Good evening,' she calls to the porter as she passes down the buff corridor. Laughter emanates from the dressing rooms. A boy crouches at the foot of the wall downing a peck of mussels. A man tunes his violin. As she passes the wings, she can hear the low thrum of the audience. It is almost eight of the clock. In his room, Jeremiah stands admiring a pink costume festooned with sequins, fitted to a curvaceous sack-cloth dummy. 'Hello,' he greets Ellory. 'I've sewed blue among the pink. When it catches the light it'll lift the colour.'

'That's a clever idea. The tuppence extra has gone well,' she says.

Sometimes money comes easy, he thinks, like luck.

'What do I owe you?' she adds. 'For your help with Mr Douglass?' He waves her off. An extra shilling or two does not matter now. He smooths the sequins and gives a satisfied sigh. 'Would you like a keek at the audience?' he offers. 'Since you're here?'

He leads her down the corridor to the edge of the red velvet curtain. Beyond, the auditorium is lit by gaslight's amber glow. Past the footlights lies a scene from a picture book, redolent of luxury, gold plasterwork round the boxes like a fancy plant mounted on a trellis. Beyond, the grand circle stretches, ladies fanning themselves like tropical birds. Gentlemen removing their capes and top hats, bowing and kissing gloved hands. The buzz of voices. In the stalls, working men sip beer from pottery tankards. 'I can slip you in if you'd like,' Jeremiah offers. 'There's always room up the back.'

Ellory is about to answer that it's a long time for her to be away, when she spots a familiar outline at the top of the dress circle. Murray Urquhart in evening dress is making his way to a box. His hunched shoulder is distinctive. Beside him a flash of white, like a shooting star. A lady. Ellory squints. 'Oh,' she says, her heart skipping and then slowing. The woman's skin is pale as ice and her blonde hair is piled in a complicated design. She is wearing a cream gown with no sleeves, her arms like slips of light above pale gloves emerging from an oyster satin cape. Her lips are so glossy, Ellory is sure they are painted.

332

Inside the box, Murray pulls out the lady's seat and Ellory thinks she is almost Charlotte's negative. Most people would never see it, but Ellory is used to examining images in reverse, the pale dark, and the dark pale. There is no dark about this lady. People cannot help but notice her brightness. In the stalls and circle the audience stares, a murmur passing through the crowd. Murray gazes stonily ahead but the lady gives an odd smile as if she likes the attention. 'Do you know who that is?' Ellory asks Jeremiah.

Jeremiah peers through the crack. 'Bean taibhse geal,' he whispers in awe. And adds in English, 'I think she's a ghost.'

Ellory snorts. 'Tosh,' she says fondly. 'A spirit indeed.' Though it hurts that Murray is here with another woman. One so unmarked in every way. *What is he doing?* she wonders with a stab of jealousy. Then she hears herself ask, 'Might I stay here? I don't want to be seen.'

'I can put you where the flats come down.'

He leads her past huge ropes hoisted on hooks, holding up the scenery. At the rear, the two lads nod, recognising her from yesterday. Ellory settles on a stool. 'It's a belter of a show,' Jeremiah says. 'You'll like the singers.' But she has placed herself to keep an eye on Murray. He is sitting at a distance from the woman now though they are talking. Jessie would judge him faithless straight off, and the truth is, Ellory cannot pretend that she is sure of him. That's the trouble with giving a gentleman your heart. They hold the power.

The show starts. The dancers are as light as Jeremiah promised. The tricks as astounding. Slapstick, three dwarfs build a wall of satin bricks which they climb with tiny ladders, their perfectly timed banter making the audience laugh on cue. The singers are moving. But Ellory trains her eye on the audience, the light from the stage enough to keep Murray in view. She tells herself she should go back to the studio and that watching him secretly like a peeping Tom is wrong, but she cannot tear herself away.

After the interval, Grace sings. Dancers crowd the wings. The conductor stands straighter as he leads the little orchestra. It is more than singing, Ellory thinks, as Grace takes over the room, first with a cheery number that has the front rows joining in. 'Gang oan yersel,' a man shouts over the applause. A gentleman throws a white flower onto the stage from the circle. Above, the white lady is rapt but Murray's face betrays patience, not delight. Grace's performance continues with a saucy song almost drowned by the excitement of gentlemen catcalling. After this, a rousing anthem. The auditorium is in uproar. Several people in the stalls cry into their handkerchiefs. The clapping continues as the curtain comes down. Then up again. Nobody is leaving, not least Miss Sutherland, who after dissembling sings an unaccompanied song by Robert Burns.

It is after ten of the clock when her performance is finally done. Ellory realises Jane will be wondering where she has got to. In the box, the pale lady dons her oyster cape, as radiant as an angel, and Murray follows her out. A carriage will be waiting, no doubt. Ellory gets up. There is no question that she is going to follow them. There will be cabs for hire and she has an abundance of coin. Outside, the woman is easy to spot, her cape catching the lamplight like a beacon. Feeling dowdy in her workaday brown dress, Ellory pushes into a cab and tells the driver to follow. Urquhart's coach takes a familiar route along Argyle Street and up Wellington, pulling to a halt at McLaren's. Ellory watches the couple go into the hotel, her palms clammy. What is he up to? Her stomach sinks at the thought of what he may have come to an hotel for, but she pays the driver and slips through the front door. Inside, Murray and the angel enter the residents' lounge and meet an old gentleman who springs rather sprightly to his feet. The fellow in reception recognises Ellory.

'Mr Lennox is out,' he says. 'He commonly does not return until late.'

'I'll wait,' Ellory replies. 'I'd like a scalded port.'

The man gestures towards a chair. This affords her a restricted view of the lounge. Behind, two waiters scurry to set a table for the Urquhart party. They lay a thick, white cloth and a silver candelabra. Glassware. Cutlery. A small crystal vase of daffodils and glossy laurel leaves. A late supper.

'Your father wouldn't have wanted you to travel. Think of your condition,' the old man says fussily. 'Your skin.'

The angel laughs. 'My father is dead, Mr Urquhart, and I've been contained long enough. I wish to see the world. I hope my house at Greenock pleases someone soon.'

Mr Urquhart? Murray's father, Ellory surmises. They do not look alike. *I hope to introduce you to my father soon*, she recalls; something he clearly has not had to wait for with this lady. Her stomach shifts at the possibility that he is playing her false. Then: 'When will you return, Miss Nicholl?' Murray enquires.

Ellory peers around the edge of her seat. Miss Nicholl?

The waiter pours champagne into saucers and the angel seems transfixed by the movement of the bubbles. 'I've no idea,' she says. 'Perhaps I'll settle in France. The money can be managed from anywhere, can it not?'

'Your father made excellent investments,' the older Mr Urquhart says as if he is about to start a lecture. 'There'll be a large payment soon from a pending transaction.'

'I plan to spend it all,' the pale lady cuts in. 'He gave me little enough attention when he was alive. The bequest will be some compensation.'

'That's unfair, madam,' the old man objects. 'Your father was much taken up in business and wanted you to reside in the sea air, as was the advice of the best medical minds.'

The woman does not accept this. 'I believe my father was ashamed of my condition. That's why he never visited.'

Ellory squints. She overlays the image of Charlotte's face onto the pale lady and finds an almost perfect match once more. The angel is more ethereal. Charlotte looks healthier with her pink cheeks and mousy hair. But essentially they are a pair. The woman raises her glass. 'To the world,' she says. 'I have bought two parasols and a pair of green spectacles for the sun.'

Both Urquharts lift their drinks. 'Sláinte,' they say in unison. 'Chin-chin.'

'You've visited France, haven't you?' the woman asks Murray.

'Paris is a beautiful city. Fountains and squares,' he replies.

She leans forward. 'And the opera?'

'Indeed. And an excellent ballet. The Tuileries Garden is beautiful. Though the people are the best of it,' he admits. 'The fashions.'

The pale lady's eyes shine. 'I want to see Versailles. I've read about the Revolution, of course, and the Bonapartes.'

'You must take a companion, Miss Nicholl,' old Mr Urquhart says.

'Someone boring enough to keep me inside when I might promenade the boulevards with my coachman for protection?' she declares.

Murray objects. 'I'm sure we could find you someone lively.'

The woman shrugs. It is clear she is little interested in the lawyers' opinions.

'You have to be careful. You're an heiress now,' the older man says.

'I've been careful too long, sir,' the angel rejoins. 'A gentleman in my position might do exactly as he pleases.'

A waiter arrives with Ellory's scalded port. She sips as her mind races. She isn't jealous any longer, but outraged on behalf of her friend. This, she supposes, is a relation of Charlotte's. A sister or a half-sister, or a stepsister or somesuch. Can that possibly be? Beyond the open doorway, kidney soup is served from a silver tureen. The scent snakes towards her, rich and appetising. In the lounge, Murray excuses himself. Ellory considers only a moment before she follows, cornering him on the way to the water closet.

'Murray!' she hisses, as he rounds the corner.

'Ellory!' His face lights, then his brow furrows. 'What are you doing here?'

Shamefaced, Ellory regards the thick red carpet beneath her feet. 'I saw you in the theatre,' she admits. 'With the lady. I followed you.'

Murray glances in the direction of his table. 'That lady is a client,' he says.

Ellory raises her eyes 'That lady is a relation of Charlotte Nicholl.'

Murray pauses. His eyes dart but he cannot deny it. 'How did you know?'

Ellory decides not to admit eavesdropping. 'They look so alike.'

'It's her sister,' Murray admits. 'Blanche.'

'But Charlotte has no family.'

Murray now has the air of one of the clowns onstage, juggling. 'Their father did not wish them to know,' he starts. 'Dr Grieg advised that Miss Blanche – who is, as you can see, somewhat frail – was not expected to survive. As an infant, I mean.'

'But she has survived. The lady doesn't look frail to me,' Ellory says.

'No.'

'So neither sister knows about the other?'

Murray shakes his head. 'That's how Mr Nicholl enjoined it to be. In his will. It was his decision.'

Ellory thinks of how it would be if she had never known Nora. She cannot imagine it. 'How could you?' she berates him. 'Oh, Murray.'

'You must not tell Charlotte,' he cuts in.

Ellory casts him a look that makes it clear that is not a possibility. 'You have to tell her,' she says. 'You must tell them both. This is an outrage.'

'But Mr Nicholl specifically instructed—'

'Mr Nicholl is dead,' Ellory snaps. 'This lady is the occupant of Helensburgh House, isn't she?'

Murray splutters. 'How on earth do you know that?'

'You judge Charlotte a fool, but she read her father's will,' Ellory says, hoping that she isn't betraying her friend too much. 'She thought her father had a mistress, Murray. What kind of a person are you, to keep these ladies apart?'

'I've felt uncomfortable about it,' Murray admits.

'Uncomfortable!' Ellory's eyes blaze. '*Your* discomfort! They are each other's only family! You must tell them now, or I will do it.'

337

Murray shifts. 'My father,' he objects and then holds up a hand as Ellory is about to cut in. He takes a moment to consider. 'You're right,' he admits, as realisation dawns. 'Absolutely right.' Then, 'Do you think Charlotte will forgive me?'

Ellory shrugs. 'I've no idea. It's a serious business.'

He reaches for her hand, holding her fingers in his palm. 'You're better than I am,' he says. 'I suppose . . . I just didn't think of it the way you did.' She will always call him to account, he realises. She will always open his eyes.

'Did you never want a brother or sister?'

Murray has honestly never thought of it. As the penny drops, his stomach turns at having to admit what he's done. Not only to Charlotte but to her sister too.

'Come with me,' he says simply. 'You should meet Miss Blanche, and my father.'

He offers Ellory his arm. In the dining room Mr Urquhart gets up. 'Ellory, this is my father, Mr Albany Urquhart,' Murray says. 'Father, this is Miss Ellory Mann, who I told you about.'

Mr Urquhart's face freezes. 'Good heavens,' he says. 'How inappropriate.'

'Miss Nicholl,' Murray continues seamlessly, 'this is my fiancée, Miss Mann.'

Blanche Nicholl claps her hands. 'Oh, what fun,' she bursts out.

Ellory curtsies but her eyes return to Murray. Shifting uncomfortably, they sit down. Mr Urquhart looks most disquieted. Then Murray leans in. 'Miss Nicholl,' he says, 'my father will not approve of what I'm about to tell you, but I have realised that I must do the right thing. You're my client now, not your father, do you see?'

'Yes,' Blanche says. 'He's dead.'

Albany Urquhart narrows his eyes. 'Murray,' he warns.

Murray meets his father's gaze with a previously unknown degree of firmness. 'They must know, Father.'

'Know what?' Blanche asks lightly.

'There's no gentle way to tell you,' Murray admits. 'You have a sister, Miss Nicholl.'

Blanche's cheeks flush with colour, the palest peach. 'A sister,' the lady repeats as if it is a word she has not heard before.

'James Nicholl's other daughter,' Ellory confirms.

Albany Urquhart clutches his cane. 'I do not approve of this,' he says, but Blanche waves him off.

'I'm sorry. It must be a shock.' Ellory addresses the other woman directly. 'Murray was bound not to speak of it, but Charlotte – your sister, that is – read your father's will. She's been searching for Helensburgh House ever since. She discovered she shared her father's estate with its occupant, you see. You.'

'The estate? Shared?' the pale woman repeats. 'And her name is Charlotte?'

Murray nods. 'Where is this lady?' Blanche asks.

'She lives on Blythswood Square, here in Glasgow,' Murray says.

The pale woman gasps as if the address provokes a memory. Her eyes fill with tears. They are the lightest blue fringed with pink and look as if they might melt. 'You said my father's house was closed and the hotel would provide better accommodation.'

Murray nods. 'I apologise,' he says. 'It was wrong of me. Your father's will enjoins secrecy, but it was unkind. Miss Mann berated me for keeping you in the dark – rightly, I believe. It was she who insisted I tell you the truth.'

Albany Urquhart eyes Ellory with fresh venom.

'You must not blame Ellory,' Murray insists, turning to his father. 'This is the right thing. Truly. The Misses Nicholl have no other family, Father.'

The pale woman cocks her head, and turns away from the older Mr Urquhart. Then she says, 'You must take me to my sister. At once.'

*

Supper abandoned, they decide Murray should go ahead to Blythswood Square to tell Charlotte, and that Blanche, accompanied by Ellory, will follow.

'I do not condone this,' Albany repeats. 'I'll not come with you.' Nobody points out that he has not been asked to do so. As they get up from the table, the old man pulls Murray aside. 'James Nicholl is not our only client with such instructions in his will,' he hisses.

'I know,' Murray whispers back. 'But neither of these women is illegitimate. Let's take it on a case-by-case basis, shall we?'

'We'll lose the account,' Albany insists.

Murray cannot deny this is a possibility. The Nicholl sisters might never forgive him. More important, he may lose Charlotte as a friend. He sees now that he has been faithless. 'We must do the right thing,' he repeats.

'Well, it must not get out,' Albany snaps, dry as ever.

Murray decides he can argue the toss over this later. He takes his leave. 'Give me ten minutes,' he says to the ladies and has a horse brought round. On Blythswood Square the light from Charlotte's drawing room leaks onto the paving stones from around the edges of the thick blue curtains as he tethers the mare outside. Mrs Cullen answers the door and sees him into the drawing room where Charlotte sits alone, reading a novel by Susan Ferrier. She puts the book down unwillingly for she has got to a section that is most diverting. 'Murray,' she says. 'Is everything all right?'

He shakes his head. 'You may not forgive me, but I've something to tell you. Your father did not want you to know it.'

Charlotte folds her hands in her lap. 'Is it the paintings?'

He shakes his head once more. 'I understand you've heard of Helensburgh House.'

She smiles. She has been waiting for this admission. 'I wanted to ask,' she gets out in a rush. 'I'm glad you've decided to talk of it.'

He feels that he might be sick right there on the pale blue carpet.

'I'm not the protected young lady you think I am,' Charlotte continues. 'I know my father wasn't a paragon. Far from it. Please. Go on.'

He finds he cannot come further into the room. 'You think James Nicholl had a mistress?'

'I'm resigned to it,' she says cheerfully. 'I just want to know.'

'It's worse, Charlotte,' he admits. 'And better. I didn't know till after James died. My father explained and I should have told you straight away. You have a sister. Your parents had another child.'

Charlotte cannot move. She knows she is sitting on the sofa in front of the fire, but it feels as if she is tumbling. 'A sister,' she repeats. 'But how?'

'Her name is Blanche. They called her that because of her condition. Dr Grieg believed she would not survive infancy.' Murray looks sheepish.

'Blanche,' Charlotte repeats. 'My sister.'

'You don't remember then? It doesn't surprise me. You can only have been an infant yourself.'

'And she's ill?'

Murray shakes his head. 'She's not ill. She's only pale, as far as I can reckon it. Grieg expected she would be an invalid lifelong, but as I understand it she rides out daily. I just spent the evening with her. She's two-and-twenty years old and as hale as you or I.'

Charlotte finds she is crying. She is about to ask where her sister is, when there is a strangled shriek from below and it feels she is floating as she pushes past Murray into the hall. Over the banister she can see Mrs Cullen at the door.

'Miss Blanche?' the housekeeper says. 'Is it you?'

The pale lady's face does not betray her feelings as she steps inside, Ellory behind her. 'How do you know my name?' she asks.

Mrs Cullen falters. 'I was here when you were born, miss. Upstairs in this house.'

Blanche looks up and sees her sister. 'You're Charlotte,' she announces. 'I'm Blanche.'

Charlotte has never run in her life but she takes the stairs in an instant. On the flagstones, side by side, the women regard each other like a print and its negative. For a moment they simply stare.

Then they fall together. 'They separated us,' Blanche lets out, the understanding dropping.

The sisters pull back, their fingers intertwined. It is the first time Murray has ever seen Charlotte touch somebody voluntarily. 'I have a sister,' she says. 'I'm not alone.'

Chapter Thirty-Seven

The first night at Blythswood Square, Blanche sends for her maid and directs her things unpacked into Mr Nicholl's old suite. Then, late, the women quiz Mrs Cullen about their mother. 'She died a fortnight after you were born, Miss Blanche,' the housekeeper confirms. 'Two children so close together. Some women aren't strong enough.'

'What was her name?' Blanche asks.

Charlotte is shaken that her sister does not know. 'Margaret. Maggie,' she says. 'She liked riding, as you do, I believe.'

'But not you?' Blanche surmises.

Charlotte admires the satin and crêpe snowstorm in the wardrobe and thinks it fitting that her sister inhabits her father's room for she has proved unable to. We shall be a kind of team, she thinks.

'Did we reside in the same nursery?' Blanche turns once more to Mrs Cullen.

'Yes, miss. For three weeks.'

'Then I was sent to Greenock?'

'For the air on the Clyde Firth.'

'And when I survived? By the time I was 10 or 12 or older? My father did not think to bring me home?' Mrs Cullen does not reply. Blanche continues. 'I knew he resided here in Glasgow, not 30 miles off. I ran away to find him when I was 14. After they caught me, he wrote to berate my efforts. I was expected to be sickly. But I'm not sickly,' she says. 'I didn't care for Father after I received his letter. It will be strange to know him now through this house. Through your memories.'

Charlotte turns to the housekeeper. 'Why did he not bring my sister home, Mrs Cullen?' she presses.

Mrs Cullen looks nervously from one woman to the other. 'Your mother was dead, miss. Nobody mentioned it, not within my hearing. He did what the doctor said.' The housekeeper pauses.

'Go on,' Charlotte encourages her. 'Whatever it is will not be the worst thing we have heard this evening.'

Mrs Cullen fixes her gaze on Mr Nicholl's fine Carrara-marble mantle. 'It was for your marriage prospects, miss, as I understand it. People not to know there was a problem in the family.'

Charlotte's jaw sets. She squeezes her sister's hand. 'A problem indeed,' she says. 'I'm sorry for the insult, Blanche. Papa tried to make me the perfect lady. The Kirk and Mrs Grieg and so many governesses, as if I was a masterpiece to be painted without a flaw.' She stops dead. 'I know I can't make up for what he did, but I swear, now we'll declare we're sisters.'

Mrs Cullen notes that when the women laugh, they make the same sound, musical as a duet.

There is no sleeping the first night. Into the small hours, the Nicholl sisters gossip like schoolgirls, sipping hot milk in the drawing room. They agree their father restricted both their lives: Blanche by his neglect and Charlotte by his attention. Charlotte tells her sister about their father's secret collection and how she divested herself of it. Blanche hoots with laughter and they inspect the Ariadne. Then Blanche shares stories of her foxing her governesses. It is becoming clear they are both daredevils in different ways. They cannot help being drawn back again and again to ponder James Nicholl's motives, but quickly Blanche simply declares him a liar.

'I think that's his whole story. He didn't want to be seen as he was, vulnerabilities and all. So I was a secret and so were you, in a way.

He was a clever fraud,' she says, thinking of the investments. 'That was to our benefit at least. He was a conformist in everything. It's why he banished me; it's why he sent you to church and surrounded you with those awful people. He didn't give a fig for either of us, as we truly are. But his tactic hasn't worked. The truth is, he did not tame me. I don't care for convention.'

Charlotte considers this. 'Nor do I,' she says. 'Less and less.'

'You were his masterpiece.' Blanche stares at the painting of her sister among the roses. 'I was his shame.'

'I'll not forgive him that,' Charlotte vows. 'For keeping me in ignorance. Perhaps about the paintings, but never for what he did to you. You were truly alone.'

'But you loved him,' Blanche confirms.

'I thought so, but in truth I didn't know him. If he had shown himself, perhaps I would have, but it's hard to admire dishonesty.'

They are a handsome pair. Charlotte in her reds, blues and pinks, with a fondness for taffeta, her hair in a perfect tidy bun, and Blanche in white, oyster and cream with blonde tresses piled in a complicated chignon, her jackets edged in snowy ermine, as well-finished as any young lady sent to Switzerland. Their upbringings were different, yet had a certain congruity. On that first evening they discover that they were given the same allowance and received similar gifts on their birthdays: books and handkerchiefs and bonnets alike. Gold, pearl and garnet brooches bought from the same jeweller on the Argyll Arcade. Perfume from the apothecary on the High Street when they were 18 – lily of the valley. They were taught from identical schoolbooks. Two governesses who tutored Charlotte also spent time at Helensburgh House teaching Blanche, without mentioning the sisters to each other. 'A grand deception,' Charlotte declares. 'He managed it all.'

On Sunday morning, the women do not attend Sunday service for where would they go? After a sleepless night, Blanche rides along the torrent of the Kelvin, relishing the horsemanship required to negotiate the uneven ground by the river. Charlotte waits at the breakfast table, the eggs cooling on her potato cake. When Blanche returns, her clothes are streaked with mud. Charlotte springs from her seat. 'Are you hurt?' she asks. Blanche laughs and declares it was only a tumble. 'It's dangerous along the river,' Charlotte points out, and Blanche insists that is what she likes about it.

They pass the day dozing, reading and talking before they retire early. Charlotte kisses her sister's cheek as she turns to her rooms. Blanche sips cocoa in her father's bed. 'I'm home,' she says, putting the empty cup on the nightstand, the last words on her lips before she falls sound asleep.

The following day, the sisters visit the Necropolis. There is, by chance, a burial taking place, Reverend Patterson at its head. The Griegs, old Mr Urquhart and others in the Free congregation ring the newly dug grave while two old men Charlotte vaguely recognises throw flowers onto the coffin. As the Nicholls pass, the Griegs shift, turning their backs. Later Mrs Grieg will mention to as many people as she can that neither of the girls is attired in mourning dress. 'Cream at the graveside. And pink,' she will tut. 'Poor James. He's only dead past a month.'

Charlotte notices the old couple are not standing as close together as usual. But that is none of her business. She has some-one of her own to stand next to now. It seems impossible that the day before each woman believed herself an only child. 'Is that Mother?' Blanche asks, indicating the gravestone next to James Nicholl's plot.

Charlotte nods. 'I've commissioned a similar stone for Father with his name and the dates.'

'We should be on it too,' Blanche says. 'The two of us.' She claps her hands and her white kid gloves make a dull echo.

Charlotte cannot see what such a stone could possibly say. 'He wasn't the father we thought he was,' she gets out.

Blanche walks round the grave. Her smile is brighter than the marmalade sunrise they witnessed a few hours before. 'I know,' she says, composing out loud.

James Nicholl 1780–1846
Husband to Margaret
Father to Charlotte and Blanche.
He bequeathed his daughters choice.

'We should say that. I'm sure he'd hate it,' she adds delightedly. 'Everything out in the open.'

'I wish we'd had our childhoods together,' Charlotte muses.

Blanche is silent a moment. 'She would not have done it to us,' she says, eyeing their mother's gravestone. 'I'm sure of that. But we've found each other now and must live as we please.' She gestures grandly. 'Our lives must be better than something that's merely made from decisions that were foisted upon us.'

Charlotte is warmed by the sentiment. She would have been different, she thinks, had Blanche been brought up in the same house. Braver perhaps. Less sad. She cannot consider what might have happened had their mother lived, but she knows the fact she died has made her daughters' loss greater.

Clouds gather overhead and a shadow creeps across the ground and up the gravestones. Charlotte turns back towards the other burial. 'Has everybody secrets the same, do you think?' She gestures at the stones around them.

Blanche shrugs. 'It's time to go,' she says.

As they set off, Charlotte swears she catches a whiff of roses that brings to mind Maggie Nicholl. Perhaps their mother has been looking after them, after all. She pulls her cloak round her shoulders with a wave of gratitude that she is an heiress and a sister and a benefactor rather than a cautionary tale. She knows it might have transpired differently.

At the gate Albany Urquhart is waiting for his carriage, the funeral at an end. 'I'm glad to see you visiting your father, ladies. Most fitting.' He gives a stiff, little bow.

'I wish to write my will, Mr Urquhart,' Charlotte directs. 'I wonder if you might tell Murray I've decided I'm leaving everything to my sister. You're to be owned now, Blanche,' she says.

'We belong to each other,' Blanche replies. 'I'll do the same.'

A smile almost raises the corners of Albany Urquhart's mouth but the muscles are not sufficiently practised. 'You still wish my son to represent you, Miss Nicholl? And you too, Miss Blanche?' he checks.

'He's going to have to make a proper apology,' Charlotte says earnestly. 'But yes. He's set to marry my friend, Miss Ellory Mann, you see.'

Blanche thinks – but does not say – she is sure all men would have behaved the same, so what would be the point of changing the notary.

Albany's nod is no less stiff than his bow. He ushers the Nicholls to their carriage and once they are seated he leans in and whispers, 'I'll write to you of it, but your father's estate has been credited in the sum of something over 40,000 guineas. Of course,' he adds, 'my fee must be deducted, but you young ladies are in high funds. Miss Blanche, is it still your instruction to take Helensburgh House to the market?'

'It is, Mr Urquhart,' Blanche says. 'Please get rid of the place. As sharp as you can.'

'Right you are,' Urquhart says and closes the door. He watches as the carriage drives off. It is not lost on him that James Nicholl hid his pale-skinned daughter less efficiently than his damn paintings. Still, it has been a good year for the Nicholl account, well worth the time Murray devoted to the women, who of late have proved more demanding than all the firm's other clients put together. Now, he thinks, they will occupy each other. The secret is out and they do not appear to hold the keeping of it against him.

'Home?' says Blanche smugly, as the carriage rumbles westwards.

'Where else?' Charlotte replies.

They relish the intimacy of this and at Blythswood Square settle in front of the fire in the study, not the drawing room. The money is another worry laid to rest. They can do whatever they want. 'So that woman is to marry our solicitor?' Blanche checks. 'The lady who made him tell us the truth?'

'I'm to be her maid of honour. You shall have to come too of course.'

'I'd like to. Whatever shall we wear?'

Charlotte decides she will have a simple dress, nothing fancy.

'You're an awful blue stocking,' Blanche declares.

'That's me.' Charlotte accepts the slight. She adds, 'It's a Quaker marriage. It'll be a quiet affair.'

Blanche raises her eyes and her sister smiles indulgently. The younger Nicholl would demand dancing and drinking and gentlemen in tight breeches, her sister thinks. And everything covered in lace. Blanche gets up and goes to the window. The house is fine, but her ambitions extend beyond Glasgow. 'Charlotte, after the wedding, do you have plans?'

The question hangs. Charlotte will be the family general, she thinks, making all their practical plans. Blanche is a seer, a high priestess. The one who will guide them.

'I had a thought, you see,' Blanche continues. 'Before I knew you. I hope you'll come too.'

'Come where?' Charlotte retakes her seat.

Blanche gestures dramatically. 'Elsewhere. London. Then France or Italy. As gentlemen do. It's always been my ambition. Say you'll join me. Please. There's a good deal of money now. We might travel in style.'

Charlotte considers. Not everyone is lucky enough to escape what people say of them. She would never consider such a thing were she alone. But she is not alone any longer. 'We must take our Ariadne,' she says decisively. 'I'll have a case made.'

Chapter Thirty-Eight

Robbie is asleep, an afternoon nap in the bed he shares with Jane, who has taken charge of the boy. Since he arrived, her chores have come to include walking him to and from his new school, where Murray Urquhart secured the boy a place the week before. It has opened a new part of the city to her, past Garnethill at Charing Cross, and not much further to Woodside where by the road she met a girl who told a tale of an old soldier who went into the woods to pick hazelnuts a few autumns before and tumbled down an old mine-shaft, where he languished for three days and nights before being rescued.

The first day the boy was bullied, but he is a resilient soul and the second day announced he had made a friend. Jane also helps with his homework. She swears she's learning as much as he is: Latin declensions and long division, beyond the scope of her meagre education. Now she sits at the window, sipping a glass of milk and watching people on the street – the hurly-burly of Glasgow.

She spots Jeremiah disappearing into the door beneath her gaze and counts the 20 seconds it takes to climb the stairs, before she opens up. He is dressed especially well today in a yellow waistcoat and a red cravat; quite the dandy. 'You're alone?' he checks.

'Robbie's sleeping.'

Jeremiah pulls out a chair and climbs onto the table, placing his feet on the seat as if he is perching on the edge of possibility. 'I've come to say goodbye,' he announces.

Jane blinks. 'Och, Jemmy, don't say that. You're the only person I know in Glasgow,' she objects.

Jeremiah makes light of this. 'Nonsense!' he says. 'You know plenty folk about the doors. What about your brother?'

Jane shudders as if her brother has walked over her grave, though it is the thought of waiting at the back of Ingram Street in the dark that has moved her. Jeremiah is no fool. 'It's still with you, then?'

Jane nods. She received a dozen sovereigns from Grace Sutherland's coachman, paid privately in the office. Owen pushed the coins across the desk in two piles of six. 'I did my best,' he said and apologised, though Mr George Gibson did not do so. 'He'll not come back. I hope you're feeling better, miss.' Jane clinked the coins into a jar beneath the floorboard under her bed. A dozen sovereigns is a good price for something she did not want to sell. Miss Sutherland might get more, but for the virtue of an ordinary lass, it is more than fair. Jane isn't sure she will ever be able to spend the coin for it stands to good sense that there is a curse on it. 'Where are you off to?' she asks.

Jeremiah smiles. 'London,' he says proudly. 'You shouldn't let a fellow as low as George Gibson put you off, Jane,' he adds. 'You have talent. Next time you pose you'll become something so far beyond what you really are that the connection can't be made. I see you dressed as a dancer from the corps de ballet. I see you as a fairy queen. The prints might make a deal of profit.'

Jane shakes her head. 'Thank you, but I'll learn the print room,' she says steadily. 'It's a real profession. Not just standing about.' Then she lets out a sob. 'I don't want you to go.' She'll miss him. The smell of him: tobacco and tailor's chalk.

'Don't be silly. You'll fall in love. You'll marry and when that happens you'll be illuminated. You'll be . . .' Jeremiah searches for the word, 'enabled. That's how it'll be.'

Jane pulls a dun rag from her sleeve and blows her nose. 'That's why you're leaving? You've fallen in love?'

'With a gentleman,' Jeremiah admits. 'And he's fallen in love with me. It's the most unthinkable thing.'

Jane stops dead.

'You knew, of course,' he says. 'Of me and my gentlemen?'

She shakes her head. 'But you're a man yourself.'

'I am,' he laughs. 'You're the only person I seem able to say it to. I've not told anybody else that I'm going. That I am . . . what I am. Others may assume it, but I can say to you that I love him. That I'm leaving.'

Jane reaches for his hand. 'I didn't know.'

Jeremiah brings out a box from his pocket. It has been spoiling the line of his coat all afternoon. 'I brought you a present,' he says.

Jane opens it. Inside lie a matching pair of hat pins with pearl heads and a folding knife with an ebony-and-brass handle. 'For protection,' Jeremiah explains.

Jane opens the knife. The blade is serrated and ends in a savage-looking tip. Behind it a leather holster sits in the box. She smiles. The bruises on her wrist are faded but last night she was on an errand as the sun set and her heart pounded as she raced back to the studio before the light could fade. Carrying protection will give her confidence. It's the perfect gift.

'It goes around your ankle,' he says. 'Or your thigh, if you prefer.'

She smiles and illuminates the studio just as she illuminated the photographs. 'Thank you.'

'You'll have to practise pulling the pins out fast. You must jab as hard as you can.'

She picks up the hat pins and threads them through her hair, securing the ends in the ribbon that binds it.

'You'd have taken his eye if you'd had them before. I'll write to you. From London.'

'When are you off?'

Jeremiah's eyes sparkle. 'Tonight. There's a tide past midnight. The journey will take three days. Quicker than by carriage,' he adds knowledgably. That afternoon, at McLaren's, Lennox instructed the housekeeper to pack his things and arranged to settle his account in cash. Two brass-bound, ox-blood leather trunks were brought up. Jeremiah liked the quality of them. 'We're to reside at St James's. I don't know where that is,' he admits, bashfully. Then, he adds, 'You'll be all right, won't you?'

Jane picks up the knife and presses the catch so the blade springs open. She takes up a stance and jabs with determination. Jeremiah regards her. He is an excellent dressmaker, of course, but he has done as well as he has by being a better confidant. 'I'll miss you,' Jane says, 'but I'll be fine, aye.'

He takes a seat by the screen, the plush velvet one used by Miss Mann's sitters. 'So, you're a nursemaid now?'

'I like the wee man,' she admits.

He regards her. 'But that's not your vocation.'

She shakes her head. 'I'm to stay here. By myself. When Miss Mann marries she and Robbie will move in with Mr Urquhart.'

'And you're not going with them?'

'I had the choice, but I'm not a nursemaid. I'll be like Miss Mann was at Rock House before.' He can see she is delighted by this notion.

'What will you do exactly?'

Jane's eyes burn bright. 'I like Miss Mann's pictures. She plans to take more. She wants the ladies climbing club.' Here the girl raises her eyes as if this is ridiculous. 'And Miss Eliza Whigham. And one of the surgeons has commissioned her to take pictures of his clients who are mad. And she has been raving about capturing images at night. Of the stars. The moon.'

'Is it possible?'

'Not yet. Mr Naysmith has conducted experiments. She bought his book. We will figure it out together, perhaps.'

'So you will help?'

'I will,' Jane says confidently. Then she leans in. 'When Miss Mann lived at Rock House, she made her own calotypes,' she confides.

'You intend to do the same,' Jeremiah surmises. 'But what will you make photographs of?'

Jane is too shy to say she would like to picture the women at the steamie and the girl who plays a fiddle for ha'pennies at the gate to Glasgow Green. That she has befriended two of the dancers from the theatre. Now she thinks on it, Jeremiah himself would make a rare image. 'Would you sit?' she asks. 'You can be my first.'

Jeremiah regards himself in the mirror. The light will fail soon. 'Now?' he asks, and Jane runs for the camera.

He decides with a smirk he will not take up Grace Sutherland's pose or Jane's either, though as she readies the paper he avails himself of the grape salve. There is only one square of light bright enough this late in the afternoon and Jeremiah steps into it as if he is stepping on stage. Jane regards him. She pulls his jacket down a quarter of an inch. 'Hold there,' she says and opens the lens. As she counts, Robbie wakes in the other room and comes in, rubbing his eyes. 'I'm hungry.'

'Twelve seconds,' she tells him, and the strangeness of this accuracy renders him silent. He sits on the floor. When Jane closes the aperture, she says, 'This is our secret, Robbie,' and disappears into the darkroom.

Jeremiah casts round. 'What would you like to eat?' he asks and the boy motions towards the jar of blood-red jam. Jeremiah pours milk and hands Robbie a spoon. 'She won't be long,' he promises. 'Let's watch the sunset.' They go to the window where the first stripes of ginger are stroked on the horizon. 'You're happy here, aren't you?' Jeremiah asks.

'Aye,' Robbie says. 'Glasgow is grand.'

*

Jeremiah does not say goodbye to anybody at the theatre or send word to his mother. When the curtain comes down, he collects his things, but it is not strange to see him with a suitcase, and nobody remarks upon it as he leaves. As he rounds the corner onto Argyle Street he takes out his cigar case and lights a smoke, striking a match down the doorway of a shabby haberdasher's and illuminating a display of satin ribbons tied neatly around a pole, the colours of the rainbow. Then he walks steadily down to *The Rodney*, where Lennox is already aboard. 'My man,' Lennox introduces him to the captain, and Jeremiah does not feel sullied by the lie. It is a naval vessel and sailors get lashed if they are caught. He can be Mr Lennox's valet for a few days. The old man could use one. His buttons are awry, and his collars are shocking.

They stand on deck for the departure and Jeremiah watches the tallow lights of the tenements and the candles of Glasgow's fine terraces slide past in the darkness as they sail down the Clyde. The pinprick glow of street lamps spreads across the city like a scatter of stars. To the east, the black blocks of the Bridewell and the slums of Rottenrow. Once the lights have gone past, there is only the slap of the boat cutting through the water under the low moon.

'I think I'll like London,' Jeremiah whispers as he and Lennox go down to the cabin, holding a candle lamp ahead.

'It's a powder keg, Jemmy,' Lennox replies. 'But let's see what you make of it.'

Chapter Thirty-Nine

The day of the wedding is May day. 'Worth waiting for,' Jane says when her mistress tells her. 'It's surely a lucky morning to be wed, the first of the month.' That said, it starts like any other. A man arrives and buys a copy of the wishing tree for his wife. 'She's in the family way again,' he says as he hands over his shilling. 'This will mean the world.'

Ellory puts the coin into the strongbox. 'I'll to the other room to get dressed,' she tells Jane. 'You'd best clean the lamps.'

Inside, she takes her time. The scent of soapy water emanates into the studio as she washes. She has not bought a new dress for the wedding, but she aired her grass-green Sunday frock and spent almost an hour the evening before polishing her boots. Now she puts it all on and pins up her red tresses prettily for a good 20 minutes in the mirror. The flower girl from Exchange Place delivers a jasmine posy tied with yellow velvet ribbon and extra flowers to pin on. Jane helps her.

'You look like a lady, miss,' she says, standing back to regard Ellory across the wide boards.

Ellory shakes her head. 'I can't see I'll ever be that,' she says.

Jane does not contradict her mistress. By quarter to twelve the women are waiting outside, Ellory swaying from foot to foot, clasping her gloved hands nervously. 'You look fine, miss,' Jane says. Murray has sent a hansom cab.

It is to be a private wedding with no showy touches, not even wedding rings, for that is not the Quaker tradition. At North Portland Street, the seats are set in a circle. It occurs to some of the guests that Blanche Nicholl looks more like a bride in her cream silk gown than the woman getting married. Charlotte squeezes her sister's arm as they take their seats, though when she spots Ellory arrive she sneaks to the hallway. 'Let me go,' she tells Murray.

Ellory waves Jane into the meeting room. Murray peers through the open door but Charlotte lifts a finger to berate him and he turns away. 'Congratulations!' she declares to her friend. 'You look lovely.'

Ellory grins. 'It's only a few weeks since I came to Glasgow,' she says for she can hardly believe it. How far she has come.

'A few weeks,' Charlotte echoes. 'We've become firm friends in the shortest time. You gifted me a sister, Ellory. I'll never be able to thank you enough.'

Ellory peers into the meeting room.

'I'm your bridesmaid, though one of the ladies told me that Quakers do not hold with such things. You're to go in with Murray, just as you will leave – together. That's the way.'

Ellory likes the rightness of this.

'I'll fetch him,' Charlotte offers. 'Shall I?'

Inside, Murray is stationed next to his father. Albany had to be reminded the wedding was today, or at least pretended that was the case. He has not come round. The night before over dinner he remarked, 'The thing is, Murray, there is no easy way in law out of a bad match, once the marriage is enacted.'

'I'm not seeking a way out, Father. I'm lucky she will have me,' Murray replied.

Albany only just refrained from snorting outright at this, but Murray meant it. As they had driven away from Blythswood Square the night Charlotte and Blanche had found out about each other, Ellory's green gaze had remained on Murray as the carriage jerked down the hill and he had realised how terrified he was that he might lose her for his misjudgement. 'I'm glad they've found each other,' he hazarded.

'No thanks to you,' she replied steadily.

'Today marks a change, I can promise you that,' he said.

Ellory had accepted this but went further as the carriage bounced along. 'I don't want anything unsaid, not any longer. Between your secrets and mine there's been much to fall foul of. Let's both be in the right from now on,' she proposed. 'Everything in the open.'

This morning Murray fetched his father from the office, where the old man headed at nine, deliberately ignoring what was about to happen, instead musing that the Royal Navy did not generally ship paintings and that Lennox's master must be a duke at least. Well, well, he thought, surveying his account book, a fellow from Glasgow, or near it, in service of such a personage is quite impressive. Now the old solicitor is seated among the assembled crowd grudgingly, for though he can see how happy his son is, he is pessimistic about marriage in general and marriage to lasses with no dowry in particular. Jane would normally sit at the back of any congregation, but there is no notion of such a thing here, so she chooses the seat furthest away and Urquhart notices this and thinks at least the wee maid knows her place.

Everyone waits, settled in silence, as Charlotte whispers in Murray's ear, 'Your bride is waiting.' He gets up and goes to the hallway. The light is warm through the uneven glass fanlight over the door. Ellory Mann and Murray Urquhart regard each other. 'You look beautiful,' he says.

'You too.'

They smile. Ellory takes his arm, feeling a twinge inside as she touches him. Murray has notions of being a better man, she knows, but she hopes to be a freer woman for this match and likes that they will both be improved by it.

Inside, it is simple. He makes his oath and she makes hers, then those assembled are given time to speak. Accustomed to such matters, Miss Smeal, the Quaker lady who commissioned Ellory's portrait of Mr Douglass, rises first and declares she is glad the couple have found each other. Another lady says she admires Miss Mann's

talent and hopes she will be happy. Prompted, then, Albany gets up
and gruffly welcomes the new Mrs Urquhart to his family. Charlotte
follows the old man and says that the marriage of Ellory and Murray
delights her; the coupling of a new friend and an old one. 'We have
cake and champagne at our house on Blythswood Square,' she adds.
'You're all invited.'

The party removes west then. In their carriage, Murray slips his
arm round his new wife's waist. They make a handsome couple.
'I've a surprise for you,' he says, and the journey passes quickly,
for they kiss all the way. At Blythswood Square they are the first
to arrive. In the hallway three large portmanteaux and several
leather travelling bags are stacked by the door. 'Is Blanche leaving?' Ellory asks.

'Both of them are,' Murray tells her and leads her upstairs to the blue
drawing room, where a large, iced cake is set upon a plinth by
the window. Mrs Cullen directs the footman to open the champagne.

'Do you like it here?' Murray asks.

'Miss Nicholl has always made me feel at home,' Ellory replies.

'It's a beautiful room, don't you think? The blue.' Murray seems
eager.

'It's Charlotte's colour,' Ellory agrees.

Downstairs they hear the others arriving. Jane is taken down to
the kitchen and given a luncheon plate. She makes friends with the
other maids by sharing it. Blanche chats to Miss Smeal as they climb
the stairs. 'You must cut your cake, Mrs Urquhart,' she announces as
she bursts into the room. 'Do Quakers eat cake?'

Miss Smeal takes this question in her stride. 'As much as we can,'
she retorts.

Blanche glances at the clock on the mantle, showing just past one
now. 'I'm starving,' she admits, and Mrs Cullen sighs inwardly. Miss
Blanche demands hot chocolate in the middle of the night and sandwiches late in the afternoon. Yesterday Cook declared that the new
mistress believes herself to be Marie Antoinette. The staff are quietly
glad the Nicholls are going away for a year, they say, maybe more.

Cook has outdone herself with the cake, flavoured with vanilla and lemon and moistened with butter cream and raspberry jam, which Murray had told Charlotte was his new wife's favourite. The party continues merrily until two of the clock, when both Nicholl sisters rise. 'We're off!' Charlotte declares and kisses Ellory's cheek.

Ellory gets up and catches her new husband's hand. 'Let's go downstairs and wave them away,' she says.

Miss Smeal departs. Albany Urquhart kisses Charlotte and Blanche's hands, then turns to his new daughter-in-law. 'My dear,' he says as he stiffly pecks her on the cheek before making his way along the pavement. She knows he does not approve but, she tells herself, perhaps that will come in time. Respect needs to be earned. At the kerb, the Nicholls' coach is loaded. Charlotte and Blanche fuss over their hats and coats.

'You like it here, don't you?' Murray checks again.

'You asked me that already,' she chides.

'I hope you do. Because we're staying.'

'Staying?'

'I have let the place, staff and all, from the Nicholls,' Murray replies. 'We can't live in Bath Street with my father.'

Ellory reels. 'Here?' she says looking round. The hallway alone is larger than Rock House. The cornices are like sculptures.

'Here,' he replies, delighted by her surprise. 'There's a room for Robbie at the back. We shall install a bookcase for his school things. I've taken on a girl to look after him. It'll be more convenient for the Academy here. And us too.'

'But—'

'Mrs Cullen has been briefed. She's to run the place. You won't have to do anything.'

'Here?' Ellory repeats. 'In this house?'

'Yes.'

Her face lights. Her smile widens into a grin. 'It's lovely!' Ahead, the Nicholls crowd the threshold as if they are the ones off on honeymoon.

'What's your itinerary?' Ellory asks, sad and excited at once.

'London and Paris and Rome. I don't know.' Charlotte flings her arms round the bride, newly affectionate now she has her sister's hand to hold. In the street the Howarth girls are leaving for an engagement. Mrs Howarth waves and Mary whispers something to her sister. Then they giggle.

'Don't mind the Howarths,' Charlotte says. 'They're good neighbours when it comes to it.'

'Goodbye, dear Ellory.' Blanche kisses her on the cheek. Then she pulls her close and whispers, 'The secret cupboard will make an excellent darkroom, don't you think?' and trips down the steps.

*

Upstairs in the drawing room, Ellory sits by the fire. She thinks it would make a pretty picture if she could capture the colour of her green dress and the yellow ribbon. She titles it 'The Lady's New Drawing Room' and wonders momentarily if she is supposed to read aloud or take up cross-stitch between the ice-blue walls. What would Reverend Reid think of her in this fine house? Or Jessie? She knows she will never truly grow accustomed to it. She will never forget that she shared a bedroom with her maid and scrabbled to find a few pennies for dinner. She must write to Mr McPhee, she thinks, and thank him. Perhaps the next time she visits Edinburgh, she will call. She cannot believe now that she hesitated in taking her chance all those weeks ago. What might she have missed?

Murray hands her a glass of champagne. 'You belong here as much as anyone,' he says, sensing her thoughts. 'We're settled now.'

Ellory takes a soothing sip. She will capture the moon here, quite literally, for she has several ideas about how to take photographs of the night sky. She only requires the leisure to try them. The craters and hills are a promised land accessible here from the vantage point of the roof. She'll take the jam when it's offered. But that is for later. Her eyes light and she reaches for Murray's hand. 'Show me where we sleep,' she says. 'I want to see it.'

Epilogue

Travelling is more tiresome than the Nicholl ladies anticipated but arriving is more thrilling. They have been in London ten days and are promenading down the green ribbon of the Mall, arm in arm in the summer sunshine, when Charlotte spots Mr Jeremiah Catto, riding past the trees in a smart red coat and black top hat. 'My god,' she says. 'I can't believe it,' and waves at him like an excited schoolgirl.

Jeremiah peers. He jumps from his horse and leads it by the rein. A thin mist rises, the scent of scythed grass on the morning air. 'Miss Nicholl,' he greets Charlotte with an extravagant bow.

'My sister, Blanche.' Charlotte makes the introduction and Jeremiah kisses the lady's hand.

'What are you doing in London?' Charlotte asks.

'What am I not doing?' Jeremiah replies flirtatiously.

He loves Lennox's tall brick house on Jermyn Street, full of mahogany furniture, thick woollen rugs and dark oil paintings of venerable old men. Lennox's manservant, Buckley, is old and pale and lives in the basement. 'Buckley will fetch you oysters and see to the claret,' Lennox said when they first arrived. Ever since, Jeremiah has been like a kitten exploring new territory, the house the centre of his world. Soho, eastwards, is his most exciting discovery, full of cutlers and tailors and chop houses. Actors and writers and malcontents. He falls into conversations in taverns and asks after work at the stage doors. At Westminster he found a rat pit and won a wager. He rides every day now on the Mall with Buckingham Palace at the end like a fancy cake. Jeremiah has heard a chap can, with luck, fumble in the bushes come nightfall with members of the Queen's own guard. He does not avail himself of this experience, the rain being off-putting and Lennox, despite long absences, generally being present at night.

Jeremiah waits for him, reading pamphlets of all kinds, poetry and politics, both very rude. He has written to Jane, telling her about the canopied shops stretching west along Regent Street with their long colonnades. And a commission he has, to make a dress for a gentleman. *Can you believe it? It's for a show in Covent Garden in a private house. I've had six guineas and the use of a workroom.* Every time he passes a lady adorned with feathers, he thinks that Grace Sutherland would kill to see this city. After a week, he writes to her care of the theatre and suggests a visit. A holiday in Belgravia. There is so much money here he can smell it.

The Nicholl girls chatter about the rooms they have taken on Oxford Street and make polite conversation about an outing to the picture gallery in Dulwich.

'I presume our old pictures, Mr Catto, are safely housed?' Charlotte enquires. 'We got the payment.'

Jeremiah swivels his head towards Buckingham Palace and back again. 'Mr Lennox's master is happy with the collection.' He leans in to share a confidence. 'The gentleman has had the goddesses hung in his bathroom,' he whispers. 'He's spoken to an architect about extending his library. Something locked. For the books.' He extends a finger towards the palace, this time without looking at it. Blanche, in particular, is thrilled.

Charlotte takes in a sharp breath at this heavy-handed hint. 'No! But—Albert?' she declares. 'What about Her Majesty!'

Jeremiah winks.

Blanche giggles. 'Good heavens,' she says. 'And what are you doing in London, Mr Catto? Apart from amassing the most tremendous gossip.'

Three days earlier, Lennox had presented Jeremiah with an introduction to the photographer Henry Fox Talbot, but when Jeremiah visited the gentleman at his club, they did not hit it off. Fox Talbot, an erstwhile Member of Parliament and conservative of mind if not of party, was clearly bemused by this unconventional if well-connected young man. The Fox was not interested in talking about how to make photographs better in anything other than technical terms, which is to say timings and chemical solutions. He as good as yawned when Jeremiah mused on which subjects might have most impact in a gallery, or if it would be possible to add colour to a sepia print by means of watercolours and a fine brush. Jeremiah left after half an hour and decided on the way back to St James's to take a different path. He is resolved to learn about art with a view to becoming a broker. It suits his nature and fits with his other activities, the creation of clothing for the stage and other performances.

'A little of this and a little of that, ladies,' he says brightly now. 'I'm working with different artists, performers and photographers. I wonder if you might like to have an image taken? The two of you together?'

The sisters lock eyes. 'Oh let's,' Blanche gushes. 'Mr Catto, we would love that!'

Charlotte smiles at the rightness of it. Mr Douglass, after all, said photographs were a vast power. The sisters will make a perfect picture. If only she were back in Glasgow she'd bury that in her father's grave. *Look at us. We found each other.* She decides she will write to her friend, Mrs Murray Urquhart, and include a copy of the image for she is bound to be interested.

'Tomorrow?' she offers.

Jeremiah thinks he must go straight to Covent Garden and engage a photographer. He has heard of a chap with a studio who took on an assistant who was dismissed from the apothecary's on Swallow Street for just the kind of bad behaviour Jeremiah appreciates. The studio is said to have but one client, an earl who commissions calotypes of his dogs. Room there, he thinks, to extend the fellow's repertoire. He will ask for a quarter of the fee. If he jumps to it, he has time to organise a set for the Nicholl sisters; something individual that will reflect their unusual looks, Miss Blanche's paleness will stand out in front of a dark swathe of velvet and, he ponders, he will pose Miss Nicholl next to her sister, in front of a lighter cloth. He takes the Nicholls' address and says he will call the next day at 11 of the clock, then he sets off to play with dark and light.

Charlotte and Blanche turn in the direction of Oxford Street. They like the anonymity of this city. And the fashions. Brightly coloured Hanways and mutton sleeves. Ladies outfitted in a profusion of lace and velvet capes with long hoods. As different as Glasgow is from Greenock, Blanche pointed out the day after they arrived. They are in no rush to continue their travels, though Paris is certainly enticing. It will be next.

'It was plucky of you to agree to a picture,' Blanche says. She is the one who craves new experiences, early morning rides and trips to the opera.

'You forget I've had my photograph taken before,' Charlotte objects. 'It might easily be considered that you are the more adventurous of us,' she licks her lips, 'but we shall see, Blanche. We shall see.'

Acknowledgements

This book was a breech birth, a difficult baby, and one which would not have made it were it not for the many who generously gave me their time.

Thanks are due to the historians who helped me find sources in the lives of real women for my fictional characters. Elizabeth Ewan at the University of Guelph, Kevin Hall engaged on his doctorate at the University of Edinburgh, and Ruth Mazo Kerras at my Alma Mater, Trinity College, Dublin. Kate Lister (whose social media presence as @whoresofyore is ever an inspiration) and Cordelia Beattie. Thanks are also due to those who engage with history in different ways to prompt us to think about the diversity of where we come from. Academic history, I hope, is evolving to more readily recognise that we do not only come from male, white, heteronormative, able English speakers. Among the band of inspirational folk who talk to me endlessly about this kind of thing: Claire Mitchell KC and Zoe Venditozzi (always full of fabulous ideas!), a huge and heartfelt thanks for all things witchy and for their brilliant campaign to bring more justice to the world of women's history – their Accused Witches of Scotland stand is an important contribution to our country's social history and how we relate to it. It has informed this book in empowering me to look more widely at where we come from. Life tries to bully the powerless and forget them. We must stand.

To Grainne Rice of the Scottish National Portrait Gallery, for listening to my Victorian photographic chit-chat and being supportive right from the start – a huge thank you. Curators and archivists are always the *best* and Grainne put me in touch with several experts at the galleries where I investigated all things photographic and what was considered erotic and what was not. Anne M. Lyden generously shared her fascinating stories about Scottish photography during the period and facilitated my access to the archive when it opened after the Covid crisis. I so enjoyed the time we spent together viewing Adamson and Hill's original negatives and prints. Thank you, Anne. Also, at the National Galleries of Scotland, Louise Pearson was hugely helpful as she steered me patiently in all the interesting directions! I sat on my sunny doorstep on the phone to Frances Fowle who gave me erotic painting tips from the era, the inside track on Victorian art dealers and made me laugh a lot. Thank you, Frances.

Caroline Douglas patiently explained to me how to make a calotype print. I had met Caroline a couple of years before when we both spoke about women's history at an event at the National Portrait Gallery on Queen Street in Edinburgh. Her project remains an inspiration. We both had a difficult year and it was lovely to have a reason to catch up. Professor Richard Thomson at the University of Edinburgh talked to me about the history of art during the period, particularly his expertise in French painters, and kindly tipped me in the direction of the saucy lithographic prints of the 1790s which feature in Mr Nicholl's collection.

Ashley Douglas kindly helped me with my Scots – all errors are mine – but Ashley and her wife Eilidh are always generous in their support and I'm ever interested in what they have to say! Lastly, Paul F. Burton, who is an archivist for the Society of Friends in Glasgow was very helpful (and prompt – thank you so much) in providing information about the Quaker Meeting House in Glasgow during the 1840s.

On Twitter I drew a good deal of inspiration from the historical fashion accounts of @astitchintime13, @wikihistorian, @madamegilflirt and @katestrasdin, who provided outfits aplenty to fire my imagination when the museums were closed and I could not browse the fashion halls in real life. Thank you for brightening my lockdown fashion obsession. A shoutout also to @Yourwullie and Niall Murphy for smarts relating to Glasgow's disarming Victorian architecture: you helped me to create the streets that my characters inhabited. Our built environment defines our opportunities, so finding glass-topped buildings that were artists' studios and seedy alleyways for Jeremiah to loiter in was important to make the story real, as much as understanding the move fashionable Glasgow made from the mansions round Carlton Terrace and Abbotsford Place on the south side of the river to the area around Blythswood Square and beyond to the west. That Partick was considered a distant village where residents of the city went on holiday still makes me smile.

Thanks also to Ali Bacon for her novel about David Octavius Hill, *In the Blink of an Eye*, which I read avidly. Ali's Jessie Mann, Hill and Adamson are different from mine, but I so enjoyed them. Thanks also to Dom Miller-Graham, the chairperson of Our Story Scotland. Dom helped me make sure that Jeremiah read like a real gay man. I am acutely aware that middle-aged straight ladies do not always know. Dom's help and support is valuable always, but thanks to him for snooping around queer Victorian Glasgow for me with an eye to the detail. Thanks also to fashion guru Barbara Kosalinski, for her chat around boudoir wear for Grace Sutherland. And all the love to Lesley Riddoch, who let me stay at her gorgeous Tayside cottage when I had to get my head down and just edit. You saved my novel-ish bacon, Lesley, and are always an inspiration.

I'd like to thank everyone at Hodder, who made my publishing experience so fulfilling. Lily Cooper, my editor, who is always upbeat and interested in my weird historical fascinations (while talking me down from showcasing the most bizarre of them). Lily stepped into her editorial position halfway through my writing *The Fair Botanists*. She didn't have to like what I was up to and we didn't have to get on, but she did and we do! We didn't get to meet in person for ages because she had to go into isolation just at the moment she was due to get on the train to the Edinburgh International Book Festival in 2021. I mean, it was a good plan, but it didn't come off. Eventually we had dinner in London when things opened up. Anyway, her landing the editorial role was a happy accident and I'm so glad she went on to commission this story from me and want to say that working with her is a delight though she makes me edit *very hard*. OMG! A shoutout too to Sorcha Rose and Gale Winskill, who also helped with the editing of this book – all eyes welcome.

Thanks also to Steven Cooper who has put in all the hours publicising the book and is an advocate I feel I can trust 100 per cent in guiding as many people as possible to my stories. Time spent with Steven feels serene, no matter how many bookshop signings we try to lever into an afternoon. I value his cool eye, his expertise, his ambition and enthusiasm. The team at Hodder have my back in 100 ways: cover-design geniuses, layout designers and the editors who fixed my terrible spelling. Thank you. Thank you. Thank you.

My agent, Jenny Brown, keeps me right always. Without her I would not be writing what I'm writing, or publishing nearly as many books. Always there with a cappuccino, sound advice, advocacy when things get tricky and a glass of champagne when things go well. Thank you, Jenny. A huge vote of thanks also to the booksellers who have championed my work – windows and tables and personal recommendations mean the world. I will never get bored of my books being on your shelves and also the great recommendations you give me, cos I'm a reader as much as a writer. I treasure the time when I can read (cos my imagination can only hold one story at once). Anyway, all ye in the bookshops help and make sure I read some good ones! Also, I'd like to thank the readers who have been prepared to embark with me on what Lily once called 'history in technicolour'. It's a hypervivid leap of the imagination to enter that time machine (aka a historical novel) and truly a workout for the brain to go back to where we've come from. I know there are easier books to read but hopefully not many that are more amusing. I love being taken away by a story and if I can do that for you, then I am honestly happy. Thank you for making the effort.

Almost last, an apology to Ian Rankin and James Oswald, who are proponents of the one-viewpoint-per-chapter rule. This, as you will realise if you have read this far, is not my kind of rule *at all*. It's just no good for gossip.

And at the end, thanks always to my family – what a year we had when I was writing this. 2021 into 2022 was tricky! We were ill, we were tired, we were bereaved, we were despondent and it was difficult to keep going. Early in 2022 I spent some time in hospital and then had to embark on the Mother of All the Edits. Reader, my darling family sent encouraging texts, made tea and served ice cream instead of meals without judging me. They are the *best*. To Al and Molly and our wee canine superstars – Dotty the Dachshund and Miss Kim Chi the Staffy (cos barks, licks and snuggles matter too) – I could not choose a more brilliant team. Thanks in the millions.

Sensitivity Statement and Reading List

I am hugely grateful to Dr James Dawkins for providing a thought-provoking report on the sections of this novel which feature Frederick Douglass. Today, the term 'slave' is increasingly construed as offensive by the descendants of enslaved African people since it suggests that slavery was the natural state of their ancestors (which is to say, that they were born slaves). The term 'enslaved' is considered more appropriate since it highlights the fact that African people were forcibly placed and maintained in the condition of slavery by another cohort of individuals (primarily white people). The growing use of the word 'enslaved' is part of the broader effort to encourage individuals of white-European heritage, who have largely benefited from slavery, to acknowledge their responsibility for this dehumanising form of commerce. I have used 'enslaved' where possible in this book, but given that this awareness was not present in 1840s Glasgow, I have also used the words 'slave' and 'slavery', particularly in speech, where it would be the authentic way of referring to an enslaved person at the time. Similarly, at the Quaker Meeting House, when Charlotte sees a 'Chinese men and three women of mixed race' today we would say 'of Chinese heritage' and 'multiracial'. However, these concepts would not have been true to the era.

Enslaved people endured a myriad of horrors, being placed on an auction block, purchased, sold, used as collateral for recouping debts, beaten, terrorised, intimidated, subjected to hereditary enslavement, which meant every generation of their families (alive and unborn) would be bound to eternal toil. An enslaved person was legally defined as subhuman, constitutionally classified as three-fifths of a person, had no protection under the law, was denied the fruits of their labour, their children were owned by their master, they faced punishment for reading, writing and becoming numerate, had a European name and European values forced upon them, whereas their African culture, traditions and language were outlawed. In the novel, Charlotte doesn't enumerate all this when she talks about Mr Douglass's enslavement, but for the avoidance of doubt, I have listed these crimes here.

Frederick Douglass did not only campaign against enslavement, but also for the rights of women. Again Charlotte only refers to this in the book when she praises him, but I want to be clear here that the conditions imposed upon white women in Europe are not equal to the conditions endured by Black people who were enslaved. However, I think it is fair to say that many women in this country were drawn to the campaign because they themselves felt the need for emancipation of various kinds and also endured being held as a form of property, albeit in an entirely different way. In his sensitivity report Dr Dawkins provided the following reading list, which I am including here in case readers want to investigate further.

Frederick Douglass

Douglass, Frederick, *Narrative of the Life of Frederick Douglass, An American Slave, Written by Himself* (Rochester: The North Star Office, 1848).

Douglass, Frederick, *My Bondage and My Freedom: Part 1 – Life as a Slave. Part II – Life as a Freeman* (New York and Auburn: Miller, Orton & Mulligan, 1855).

Douglass, Frederick, *Life and Times of Frederick Douglass, Written by Himself: His Early Life as a Slave, His Escape from Bondage, and His Complete History to the Present Time, With An Introduction by Mr. George L. Ruffin, of Boston* (Hartford, Conn: Park Publishing, 1882).

Saunders-Hastings, Emma, '"Send Back the Bloodstained Money": Frederick Douglass on Tainted Gifts', *American Political Science Review*, Vol. 115, No. 3 (2021), 729–41.

Women and Property

Erickson, Amy Louise, *Women and Property in Early Modern England* (London and New York: Routledge, 1993).

Women and Anti-slavery (Britain and America)

Midgley, Clare, *Women Against Slavery: The British Campaigns, 1780–1870* (London and New York: Routledge, 1992).

Clapp, Elizabeth J. and Roy Jeffrey, Julie (eds), *Women, Dissent and Anti-Slavery in Britain and America, 1790–1865* (Oxford and New York: Oxford University Press, 2011).

Fagan Yellin, Jean and Van Horne, John C. (eds), *The Abolitionist Sisterhood: Women's Political Culture in Antebellum America* (Ithaca: Cornell University Press, 1994).

Terminology

Nottingham Museums, *A Glossary of Terminology for Understanding Transatlantic Slavery and 'Race': Key Stages 2 to 4, Teachers' Resource* (Nottingham: University of Nottingham and Nottingham City Council, 2021). Available at: 3a.-Slavery-and-Racial-Terminology-Glossary-Omitted-Terms.pdf (nottinghammuseums.org.uk)

Historical Note

Writing this book shortly after *The Fair Botanists* was difficult. Every single review of the Edinburgh novel mentioned the vivid details I'd used of the city's Georgian past. Besides which, *The Fair Botanists* is set in my hometown. Yet here I was, 50 miles to the west, writing about a city I knew only half as well. One which treated its history differently in every way – from the built environment that it decimated over generations, leaving little or nothing of the Georgian town let alone anything of the medieval; to the modern-day incarnation of Glasgow's politics, the roots of which can be seen as distorted through a fairground mirror, and at root the story of a city founded on the Church, unlike Edinburgh, which has its civic roots in the aristocracy and defence of the realm. Glasgow remains to this day a fascinating conundrum of conflicting influences, still more aware of religion than the capital and more cutting-edge – a place built by the people who lived there rather than invested in by an elite whose primary concern was their country estates. As a village originally, springing up round the cathedral with its surrounding seminaries and nunneries, there has been over time a lot to rebel against, which is why I think perhaps Glasgow is more fun. But it is also a hotbed of sectarian racism – a direct product of the city's history which is hinted at in Charlotte Nicholl's wariness of all things Roman Catholic, a view she has been educated to, like so many west-coast Scottish Protestants before and after her.

The life of women was also different in this period only 20 years later than *The Fair Botanists* but a world away. The Victorian era (even as early in Victoria's reign as this) was already invested in the 'angel in the house' notion of women being sacred homemakers and little more. Although some (mostly upper-class women) managed to break free of this notion (particularly through travel), the idea of the fawning, silent, compliant wife was more prevalent than ever before, with admissions to mental hospitals rising and Lock Hospitals and Magdalene Houses setting up across the country. Far too many women incarcerated in these institutions were kept on the flimsiest of pretexts. Many were admitted simply because men who found their womenfolk inconvenient got their way. The angel in the house made women more vulnerable to bad actors and more reliant on the support of male allies in particular. In *The Fair Botanists*, there are selfish characters, but little actual malevolence. The world of 1840s Glasgow felt darker. Though in the book women find the support they require, in real life much worse happened to scores of their sisters, but that is another novel to write, not this one, which is a different tale to *The Fair Botanists* simply because of the difference between Glasgow and Edinburgh and the changes in society over the 24 years between the stories.

The real-life sources and inspirations for this novel came from a variety of places, partly from my own life and experience. As I wrote *The Secrets of Blythswood Square* I planned a house move from Edinburgh to Glasgow and, as a result, was particularly curious about the contrasts between Scotland's capital and its largest city, and where in history these came from. The book also tapped into my personal interests and experience. In 2016, I cofounded a perfume company, REEK, with my daughter, which was designed as a protest against a cosmetics industry that sells customers a sanitised version of themselves, including photoshopped women's bodies. Through REEK my understanding of photography, as a means to both seduce and communicate, blossomed. We didn't Photoshop! Instead we open-cast our models, used natural light for all images and strained the norms within the existing frame of a misogynist cosmetics industry. In *The Secrets of Blythswood Square*, we see the beginning of that 'female gaze', something that I experienced viscerally through REEK, both working with models (and giving them a voice in creating their image) and in being photographed myself. This took me back to my twenties when, making extra cash, I took a job nude-modelling for a friend's evening drawing class, to my fifties (still nude-modelling for a book about toplessness shot by Erica von Stein in Glasgow in 2018). Women are so bound by their bodies – far more than men – that even seeing them with a kind eye feels a radical act. Ellory has that eye.

In 2021, as I started to write the novel, the archive remained closed at the tail end of the Covid crisis and I had to find resources online, including a Victorian statistical analysis of Glasgow which claimed the city was no rainier than Edinburgh (this led me to question everything else in the document) and the 1854 publication *Rambles Round Glasgow* by Hugh MacDonald, the narrative voice of which merged in my mind with the slightly florid style in which Dr Grieg speaks. I played with some of Glasgow's later Victorian history, including imagining a precursor of the Hielanman's Umbrella (the bridge over Argyle Street that leads to Central Station) in the Hielanman's Hanway – a lip jutting over the road rather than the bridge that was not yet built.

As things began to open up, I was lucky enough to be given access to the archive at the National Galleries of Scotland with the help of Grainne Rice, who introduced me to the generous experts mentioned in the thanks above. Through Anne Lyden I discovered a female photographer in Glasgow, May Borthwick, who appears in the records in 1849 and into the 1850s, and who incensed the male fraternity (mostly based on Buchanan Street or, if more adventurous, at Woodside) by undercutting prices. May charged only four shillings for a daguerreotype image (still out of the reach of most working-class people). We do not have any of May's images in our national collection – or at least we do not know if any of the images in the collection were shot by her – but having already imagined Ellory, I was excited to see that in real history sassy women were setting up studios in the city, though they did not, it seems, sign their work.

The 1840s and 1850s were an exciting time in Scotland. Photographers in England were hampered by Mr Talbot's patent on the photographic process, but this did not apply under Scottish law, and a new creative industry blossomed as a result. Photographs were hugely exciting – most people had never seen a real-life image of themselves. While Adamson and Hill were working at Rock House, the Edinburgh Calotype Club (where in the novel, the gentleman on his way up to the observatory has attended a single lecture after which he considers himself expert) was set up in 1843 to inform amateur photographers (all gentlemen) and disseminate their work. This is the real-life background to the novel – Adamson and Hill's studio was made possible by it, alongside several other professional and amateur photographers who launched their careers in the period. Rock House never had Scotland's trademark marmalade-coloured harling but I think it should have – it would have looked great – so I added it for my own architectural pleasure. Today Hill's old studio is an Airbnb. My view is that it probably ought to be a museum.

Adamson was an almost-silent partner in this arrangement and most likely the technical brain behind what he and Hill achieved as Scotland's most innovative and interesting photographers of the 1840s. Much of what I say about them in the novel is true. Hill was a widower with a daughter, Charlotte, to bring up. As well as creating a huge number of photographs and many paintings, he also taught art at George Watson's College. As the duo's front man, Hill was a sociable fellow – famously always the last to leave a party – and full of energy for his photographic projects which never made the money he hoped they would. The team at Rock House, including Jessie Mann in real life, were a kind of 'Fife Mafia' who had known each other for many years before moving to Edinburgh. Several of Hill and Adamson's more famous subjects were also from Fife – Professor Sir Douglas Maclagan, the Surgeon General of Scotland, among them. The men chose calotypes over daguerreotypes because they were cheaper to produce, but also because of the more atmospheric nature of the prints and the shorter sitting time they require. Although daguerreotypes have higher definition, they are also more delicate. Hill and Adamson hoped to sell albums of images and set up the first volume production of calotype prints – astonishingly, thousands and thousands of images. Nobody is quite sure how they managed to do this: a huge achievement given the quality of the prints they routinely produced. While Hill, as a painter, posed his models in a painterly style (they were always given something to do with their hands!), he also pushed the boundaries by photographing some of his models at ease. His most used female model was Elizabeth Rigby, as referred to by Ellory, who went on to become Lady Eastlake. Eastlake was an advocate for Hill and Adamson's work. In the book I have downplayed Hill's talent though – he pioneered the use of contrast, understanding it well because of his painting skills, and using stray top hats and open umbrellas to demonstrate depth in his images.

Hill however never took an image of Frederick Douglass, which seems crazy! He photographed other abolitionists (all white men), but Douglass was in Scotland for months at this time (and in close proximity to Rock House more than once). It's likely that Douglass's campaign to shame the Free Kirk into returning the money it had received from those who profited from the enslavement of others meant that Hill deemed him an unfitting subject. Given the amount of time and energy Hill had put into photographing Free Kirk ministers and painting the Dissolution of the Church of Scotland, that certainly makes sense. The argument was heated and it would have been difficult not to take sides. As a result, though Hill never photographed a Black subject, he did take an image of Peter Jones, a multiracial man of Welsh and Native American heritage, on 4 August 1845. Hill's photograph of Douglass, had he taken it, would, most likely, have been the most enduring image of his photographic career. The story is, I suppose, a kind of warning to creatives – take your chances for heaven's sake! For the record, the Free Kirk did not return the money and Douglass's campaign was ultimately unsuccessful.

I deliberately put some of Ellory's methods and ideas ahead of their time. So, for example, the photographs she agrees to take of the inmates of an insane asylum were in fact taken later in the 1850s by Hugh Welsh Diamond. These days, these images are considered ethically questionable. Likewise, her fascination with making images of the moon and stars did not in fact come to fruition until almost a decade later. The female gaze is always ahead as far as I'm concerned, and with so many completely unattributed and mostly undated photographs in the archive, it's not too great a leap to believe that these photographs may have been taken slightly earlier than we know. I had in mind the great Agnès Varda, who said, 'The first feminist gesture is to say: "OK, they're looking at me. But I'm looking at them." The act of deciding to look, of deciding that the world is not defined by how people see me, but how I see them', which is a milestone. This remained at the forefront of my thinking as I developed Ellory's career and Jane Ramsay's capacity to model. Ellory's signature – the eight-sided star, comprised of two overlapping squares, known as the Star of Lakshmi – was inspired by the signature of Glasgow artist Hannah Frank, the youngest Glasgow Girl, who signed her early work as Al Aaraaf, the star between heaven and hell (from Edgar Allan Poe's poem of the same name).

So, to the character development. One of my main interests in writing historical fiction is finding a time machine to go back to where we come from. I long to inhabit the lives of our foremothers and understand their lives – a different dimension from understanding the men who came before us, who are far better recorded in conventional historical sources. In this book, both main female characters were born of their own history. Ellory Mann and her trauma, exacerbated by poverty and on top of that the shame of her sister's secret as a single mother, which led to her death, was the experience of thousands of our foremothers, to the point that it was not in the least unusual. Years ago I had a long conversation with brilliant historical novelist Elaine Thomson about how many working-class women killed their babies, unable to bear the stigma that went with unwanted pregnancy. It is a difficult statistic to track in an era before DNA. Elaine said she wanted to write a book about it, and I hope one day that she does. Anyway, this is the secret I chose for Ellory as ballast to her burgeoning photographic talent and business nous. She is a survivor who comes to terms with the reality of her life and family (helped by Murray Urquhart to do so).

Charlotte's character sprang from my fascination with the Disruption of the Church of Scotland in the 1840s, which I first came across through David Octavius Hill's photographs and his painting of the ministers who left the established Church. The Scottish National Portrait Gallery's exhibition of this work in 2017 fired me up, though I had already seen many of Hill and Adamson's prints over the years. For Glasgow in particular, as a city founded on religious activity, the Disruption of the Church of Scotland was key. The Free Kirk's influence remains more prevalent in the west to this day. Reading the history always enrages me – both the religious world and the photographic world are presented as almost exclusively the province of upper- and middle-class white men. Although there are glimpses into more diversity here and there, much of the power and money was tied up in this way – plus ça change. As I realised how embedded David Octavius Hill was in the art world – for example, as Secretary of the Royal Society and with a brother, Alexander Hill, who ran one of Edinburgh's key private galleries sited at 67 Princes Street – I began to wonder how much bearing his talent, as opposed to simply his connections, had on his success. Charlotte is mired in this world and finds herself quite alone in it, until she meets Ellory. Later, in Blanche, she finds her sister shadow – a key who can help her unlock her world. Blanche is extraordinary: almost anybody who didn't look 'normal' in the Georgian and Victorian eras was hidden away, and yet she escapes, though only because of James Nicholl's death. James might have been a fraud and a liar, and also I suppose, a control freak when it comes to his daughters' lives, but he was also fair-minded enough to leave them unencumbered funds and the means to raise more (assuming he might have expected his girls to uncover his guilty secret and capitalise upon it, given that he died unexpectedly early). It is those funds that truly liberate the women. Glasgow was home to many wealthy Victorian heiresses, most of them widows rather than daughters. My favourite in real life is Isabella Elder, who gifted a lasting legacy to the community in Govan – Elder Park. They are an extraordinary genre of women who are remembered because they named buildings and landscapes after themselves! There's a lesson there, of course.

Moving on, Frederick Douglass's visit to Ireland in 1845 and Scotland in 1846 had already caught my eye. Douglass was 28 when he came to Scotland and was, under American law, still enslaved, though he had escaped his master in 1838. Part of the reason he'd decided to come to Europe was his fear that in America he might be returned against his will to the person who legally owned him. Typing these words makes me shudder. During his visit to Europe, however, his manumission was bought by two Quaker women, the Richardsons, for £150, the sale being completed in December 1846, after which he returned to the US a free man. Douglass went on to become an icon and, among his many achievements, was the most photographed American of the 19th century. The first photograph of him was taken in 1841 at the age of 23, so he'd already sat to the camera by the time he came to Glasgow. For him the act of being photographed was political – it asserted his right to exist as a free person. This ethos is similar to that of minority groups today, including body positivity activists who seek to normalise difference the same way. As I started to write the book in the summer of 2021,

Isaac Julien's multiscreen installation and photographic exhibition about Douglass was staged at the Gallery of Modern Art in Edinburgh. Already interested, I felt viscerally attached to Douglass after only a couple of hours among Julien's evocative work. I must say thank you to Julien and to the curators at the gallery who championed his work. Douglass's life was extraordinary and we get to see only a slice of it in *The Secrets of Blythswood Square*.

In particular, Douglass is key to challenging Charlotte's sense of herself. Charlotte has a lot of advantages – her generous inheritance not the least of them, alongside her classical education, though she is still at a disadvantage simply because she is a woman. As a woman she needs a man at her side (not a husband in this case, but an ally) and Murray steps in to help. Charlotte's greatest challenge, however, is the same issue that faces many, if not most, people today – to outgrow the bounds of her upbringing and interpret the world on her own terms. Douglass holds a mirror to that. His presence makes her do it. When she takes up his cause, she is asserting her right to freedom as much as his. The Free Kirk's opposition to her, and to the photograph Ellory takes, mirrors real history where the Kirk staged demonstrations during Douglass's visit to try to stop him speaking about the handing back the money the Church had been founded upon. The Kirk also attempted to stop Douglass finding accommodation in Scotland in a precursor of the *No Blacks, No Jews, No Irish* policies of landlords across Britain in the decades to come. Ellory encourages her friend in her transformation and Blanche seals it. It was important to me that Charlotte discovered some family to take her part – I didn't want to leave her always alone. Many of her foibles come from her inherently atypical mind. She's definitely on the spectrum.

I am a pedant so here I am driven to confess that the slogan on Salisbury Crags was first suggested by campaigner George Thompson, and Douglass and his two lady friends took it up in May of 1846. In the book it is placed some weeks earlier. Also, the campaign's popular contemporary anthem, which is mentioned but not included in full in the book, runs:

Send back the money! Send it back!
'Tis dark polluted gold
'Twas wrung from human flesh and bones,
By agonies untold:
There's not a mite in all the sum
But what is stained with blood;
There's not a mite in all the sum
But what is cursed of God.

Moving on to the real women whose histories I used. Eliza Whigham was already known to me because I featured her in my remapping of Scotland according to women's history, *Where are the Women?* (Historic Environment Scotland, 2019). Also included in that book was Hill's long-suffering assistant, Jessie Mann. Originally I had considered the Ellory character just being Jessie Mann, but as I researched Mann more, I realised that Jessie was a conformist at heart and seemed like a woman who knew (and was happy in) her place. This would never do for my story and I felt uncomfortable about writing her a 'new character', so Ellory was born. However, it was Jessie in real life who reputedly wore gloves to cover the scars left on her skin by photographic chemicals and Jessie who prepared the plates at Adamson and Hill's studio at Rock House. Her support was vital to both their work, making calotypes is a time-sensitive and technical process. The preparation involved, the taking of the image, the complexities of making a negative and subsequently making prints requires great skill, and the sharpness of Adamson and Hill's images owes a great deal to Jessie's talent. In real life Adamson lived at Rock House until he died in 1848 (as well as working there with David Octavius Hill). I took a liberty in moving him out and letting Ellory move in – though in real life, he often did remove back to Fife during the darker months of the year. I should also say that Adamson developed many of his own calotypes, making his own improvements to the process originally developed by Henry Fox Talbot (the Fox). However, today there is increasing interest in the role of Jessie Mann, and rightly so.

I have written before about my interest in creating working-class characters that exist outwith the terms of their employment. It is a bugbear of mine that in so many stories ordinary people just don't matter. So, Ellory Man as well as Plain Jane, Jeremiah Catto and Grace Sutherland were opportunities to look at working-class notoriety (Jeremiah) and celebrity (Jane and Grace), and explore the diversity of working-class life in early Victorian Scotland. Social mobility was rarer than we think in the era, but it was possible for people to pull themselves out of poverty by both luck and determination. The Scotland of the 1840s was a place where there were large population movements and at least three commonly spoken languages. I've gone gently on the Scots and Gaelic in the book, but it always blows me away that there were areas in Scotland's cities where many people spoke three languages fluently. That these linguistically talented folk were mostly poverty-stricken remains a heartbreak. Our culture lost a great resource in not helping them to extend their talents within this period. The current revival of both Scots and Gaelic delights me. So I scattered Scots words in particular through the speech of my protagonists and I'd like to just say for the record that our history did not happen in English. Not even half of it.

Jeremiah, as a gay man in the 1840s, was not only a minor criminal in civil law but an outcast according to the Church. However, gay subculture was also joyous (I am drawn, of course, to the many photographs of gay couples that were shot during the Victorian period). Academic historians find it difficult to recognise queer culture in history because it was, for obvious reasons, hidden and many academics want written evidence that does not require reading between the lines. Still, the extent to which obvious associations are ignored astounds me. 'They were close friends' appears again and again because that's how people living at the bounds of sexual convention often referred to themselves, but it does not take much to look beyond that, especially where written evidence does exist, albeit sometimes cloudily. Gay poetry of the era, for example, is routinely interpreted with a 'just friends' gloss. Novelists, however, have a different brief. We have a duty to engage imaginatively in order to understand a period emotionally. I wanted to create Jeremiah as a sassy Victorian reflection of some of the wonderful gay men in my life. So many facets of Victorian culture were queer. It just was! Jeremiah was a joy to write and quite himself the minute he appeared on the page, to the extent that my editor once asked me if I was in love with him. (For the record, the answer is *no* – Murray is far more my type.) In any case, in *The Fair Botanists* there was so much else happening that I didn't get to foray into the queer underworld, which was my only frustration in writing the book. However, I swore that in *The Secrets of Blythswood Square*, I'd venture just a wee way into the gay side and here we are. Welcome, Jeremiah.

I keep venturing to the fringes of the royal court though I am a republican through and through! Mr Lennox, as a fixer for the Crown, is an ugly, rambunctious, effective operator, dedicated, dangerous and privileged. I would not like to come up against him. I liked the fact he felt ominous when he arrived in my imagination and at first I wondered if he had murdered somebody. I cannot say for sure that he hadn't, but that wasn't his story in this book. And then I got the idea that he would dominate Jeremiah and that Jeremiah would like it. I hope my gay characters ring true in the reading – they bring a glimpse into a 19th-century world of sneaking and peeking and having sex in the dark and I enjoyed writing it. Glasgow Green was an infamous gay pick-up haunt – most parks in big cities were, as Jeremiah will no doubt discover of St James's Park in London. Illicit sex in St James's was still a thing in the 1940s, when Winston Churchill declared he was proud to be British when he was told that 'our people' were having outdoor sex there in the freezing winter weather, whatever their preferences. However, Lennox likes comfort and has a very nice hotel room so I did not send him or Jeremiah to Glasgow Green. (Jeremiah prefers gentlemen. He is not after a bit of rough.)

Lastly, in today's world, saturated in photographic images, it has been a pleasure to look back at the beginning of the medium. From its genesis it has been an important advance and studying it cast a light for me on the images we need to shoot to represent our world – our bad, our good and, most importantly, our change. I like the photographs of David Octavius Hill, but I wish he'd shown us more and different. Scotland in the 1840s and 1850s definitely had such images to shoot. We come from a rainbow of places in our rainy country and I miss the female eye, the Black eye, the working-class eye and the queer eye most especially. We have treasures, of course, but we had more and they are lost now, the sight of them only available in imagination. I wish Ellory Mann had been real! This is the true work of this novel – creating sight of images that show where we come from, what formed us culturally and socially; the things we will never see from our past hanging like ghosts in the air over a Glasgow that doesn't exist any more; buildings only of pale stone not yet red; a working-class culture that is yet to be altered by mass Irish immigration; and a world where women have fewer rights than men. Though honestly, in that regard, we are still too quick to judge women and too slow to support them.

Sara Sheridan, Edinburgh, 2022

If you loved *The Secrets of Blythswood Square*, discover
Sara's critically acclaimed novel *The Fair Botanists*

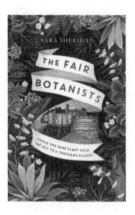

'Compelling, fascinating . . . A cracking good read'
Val McDermid

'An evocative, enjoyable portrait of 1820s Edinburgh'
Sunday Times

1822. When newly widowed Elizabeth arrives in Edinburgh to
live with her late husband's aunt Clementina, she's determined
to put her unhappy past in London behind her. As she settles
into her new home, she becomes fascinated by the beautiful
Botanic Garden which borders the grand house and offers her
services as an artist to record the impending bloom of the Agave
Americana – an event that only occurs once every few decades.

In this pursuit, she meets Belle Brodie, a vivacious young
woman with a passion for botany and the lucrative, dark art
of perfume creation. Belle is determined to keep both her real
identity and the reason for her interest, the Garden, secret
from her new friend. But as Elizabeth and Belle are about to
discover, secrets don't last long in this Enlightenment city . . .